Also by Alice Munro

Friend of My Youth

Friend of My Youth

STORIES BY

Alice Munro

Alfred A. Knopf   New York   1990

THIS IS A BORZOI BOOK
PUBLISHED BY ALFRED A. KNOPF, INC.

Copyright © 1990 by Alice Munro

The stories in this work were originally published in the following:
The Atlantic: "Hold Me Fast, Don't Let Me Pass,"
"Pictures of the Ice."
The New Yorker: "Friend of My Youth," "Meneseteung,"
"Oh, What Avails," "Oranges and Apples," "Goodness and Mercy,"
"Differently," "Five Points," "Wigtime."

Library of Congress Cataloging-in-Publication Data
Munro, Alice.
Friend of my youth : stories / by Alice Munro. — 1st ed.
p. cm.
ISBN 0-394-58442-2
I. Title.
PR9199.3.M8F7 1990
813'.54—dc20   89-43295 CIP

Manufactured in the United States of America
Published March 23, 1990
Second Printing, April 1990

To the memory of my mother

Contents

.

Friend of My Youth

Friend of My Youth

WITH THANKS TO R.J.T.

I used to dream about my mother, and though the details in the dream varied, the surprise in it was always the same. The dream stopped, I suppose because it was too transparent in its hopefulness, too easy in its forgiveness.

In the dream I would be the age I really was, living the life I was really living, and I would discover that my mother was still alive. (The fact is, she died when I was in my early twenties and she in her early fifties.) Sometimes I would find myself in our old kitchen, where my mother would be rolling out piecrust on the table, or washing the dishes in the battered cream-colored dishpan with the red rim. But other times I would run into her on the street, in places where I would never have expected to see her. She might be walking through a handsome hotel lobby, or lining up in an airport. She would be looking quite well—not exactly youthful, not entirely untouched by the paralyzing disease that held her in its grip for a decade or more before her death, but so much better than I remembered that I would be astonished. Oh, I just have this little tremor in my arm, she would say, and a little stiffness up this side of my face. It is a nuisance but I get around.

I recovered then what in waking life I had lost—my mother's liveliness of face and voice before her throat muscles stiffened and a woeful, impersonal mask fastened itself over her features. How could I have forgotten this, I would think in the dream—the casual humor she had, not ironic but merry, the lightness and impatience and confidence? I would say that I was sorry I hadn't been to see her in such a long time—meaning not that I felt guilty but that I was sorry I had kept a bugbear in my mind, instead of this reality—and the strangest, kindest thing of all to me was her matter-of-fact reply.

Oh, well, she said, better late than never. I was sure I'd see you someday.

When my mother was a young woman with a soft, mischievous face and shiny, opaque silk stockings on her plump legs (I have seen a photograph of her, with her pupils), she went to teach at a one-room school, called Grieves School, in the Ottawa Valley. The school was on a corner of the farm that belonged to the Grieves family—a very good farm for that country. Well-drained fields with none of the Precambrian rock shouldering through the soil, a little willow-edged river running alongside, a sugar bush, log barns, and a large, unornamented house whose wooden walls had never been painted but had been left to weather. And when wood weathers in the Ottawa Valley, my mother said, I do not know why this is, but it never turns gray, it turns black. There must be something in the air, she said. She often spoke of the Ottawa Valley, which was her home—she had grown up about twenty miles away from Grieves School—in a dogmatic, mystified way, emphasizing things about it that distinguished it from any other place on earth. Houses turn black, maple syrup has a taste no maple syrup produced elsewhere can equal, bears amble within sight of farmhouses. Of course I was disappointed when I finally got to see this place. It was not a valley at all, if by that you mean a cleft between hills; it was a mixture of flat fields and low rocks and heavy bush and little lakes—a scrambled, disarranged sort of country with no easy harmony about it, not yielding readily to any description.

The log barns and unpainted house, common enough on poor farms, were not in the Grieveses' case a sign of poverty but of policy. They had the money but they did not spend it. That was what people told my mother. The Grieveses worked hard and they were far from ignorant, but they were very backward. They didn't have a car or electricity or a telephone or a tractor. Some people thought this was because they were Cameronians— they were the only people in the school district who were of that religion—but in fact their church (which they themselves always called the Reformed Presbyterian) did not forbid engines or electricity or any inventions of that sort, just card playing, dancing, movies, and, on Sundays, any activity at all that was not religious or unavoidable.

My mother could not say who the Cameronians were or why they were called that. Some freak religion from Scotland, she said from the perch of her obedient and lighthearted Anglicanism. The teacher always boarded with the Grieveses, and my mother was a little daunted at the thought of going to live in that black board house with its paralytic Sundays and coal-oil lamps and primitive notions. But she was engaged by that time, she wanted to work on her trousseau instead of running around the country having a good time, and she figured she could get home one Sunday out of three. (On Sundays at the Grieveses' house, you could light a fire for heat but not for cooking, you could not even boil the kettle to make tea, and you were not supposed to write a letter or swat a fly. But it turned out that my mother was exempt from these rules. "No, no," said Flora Grieves, laughing at her. "That doesn't mean you. You must just go on as you're used to doing." And after a while my mother had made friends with Flora to such an extent that she wasn't even going home on the Sundays when she'd planned to.)

Flora and Ellie Grieves were the two sisters left of the family. Ellie was married, to a man called Robert Deal, who lived there and worked the farm but had not changed its name to Deal's in anyone's mind. By the way people spoke, my mother expected the Grieves sisters and Robert Deal to be middle-aged at least, but Ellie, the younger sister, was only about thirty, and Flora seven or eight years older. Robert Deal might be in between.

The house was divided in an unexpected way. The married couple didn't live with Flora. At the time of their marriage, she had given them the parlor and the dining room, the front bedrooms and staircase, the winter kitchen. There was no need to decide about the bathroom, because there wasn't one. Flora had the summer kitchen, with its open rafters and uncovered brick walls, the old pantry made into a narrow dining room and sitting room, and the two back bedrooms, one of which was my mother's. The teacher was housed with Flora, in the poorer part of the house. But my mother didn't mind. She immediately preferred Flora, and Flora's cheerfulness, to the silence and sickroom atmosphere of the front rooms. In Flora's domain it was not even true that all amusements were forbidden. She had a crokinole board—she taught my mother how to play.

The division had been made, of course, in the expectation that Robert and Ellie would have a family, and that they would need the room. This hadn't happened. They had been married for more than a dozen years and there had not been a live child. Time and again Ellie had been pregnant, but two babies had been stillborn, and the rest she had miscarried. During my mother's first year, Ellie seemed to be staying in bed more and more of the time, and my mother thought that she must be pregnant again, but there was no mention of it. Such people would not mention it. You could not tell from the look of Ellie, when she got up and walked around, because she showed a stretched and ruined though slack-chested shape. She carried a sickbed odor, and she fretted in a childish way about everything. Flora took care of her and did all the work. She washed the clothes and tidied up the rooms and cooked the meals served in both sides of

the house, as well as helping Robert with the milking and sep-
arating. She was up before daylight and never seemed to tire.
During the first spring my mother was there, a great housecleaning was embarked upon, during which Flora climbed the ladders
herself and carried down the storm windows, washed and stacked
them away, carried all the furniture out of one room after another so that she could scrub the woodwork and varnish the
floors. She washed every dish and glass that was sitting in the
cupboards supposedly clean already. She scalded every pot and
spoon. Such need and energy possessed her that she could hardly
sleep—my mother would wake up to the sound of stovepipes
being taken down, or the broom, draped in a dish towel, whack-
ing at the smoky cobwebs. Through the washed uncurtained
windows came a torrent of unmerciful light. The cleanliness was
devastating. My mother slept now on sheets that had been
bleached and starched and that gave her a rash. Sick Ellie com-
plained daily of the smell of varnish and cleansing powders.
Flora's hands were raw. But her disposition remained topnotch.
Her kerchief and apron and Robert's baggy overalls that she
donned for the climbing jobs gave her the air of a comedian—
sportive, unpredictable.

My mother called her a whirling dervish.

"You're a regular whirling dervish, Flora," she said, and
Flora halted. She wanted to know what was meant. My mother
went ahead and explained, though she was a little afraid lest
piety should be offended. (Not piety exactly—you could not call
it that. Religious strictness.) Of course it wasn't. There was not
a trace of nastiness or smug vigilance in Flora's observance of her
religion. She had no fear of heathens—she had always lived in
the midst of them. She liked the idea of being a dervish, and
went to tell her sister.

"Do you know what the teacher says I am?"

Flora and Ellie were both dark-haired, dark-eyed women,
tall and narrow-shouldered and long-legged. Ellie was a wreck, of
course, but Flora was still superbly straight and graceful. She

could look like a queen, my mother said—even riding into town in that cart they had. For church they used a buggy or a cutter, but when they went to town they often had to transport sacks of wool—they kept a few sheep—or of produce, to sell, and they had to bring provisions home. The trip of a few miles was not made often. Robert rode in front, to drive the horse—Flora could drive a horse perfectly well, but it must always be the man who drove. Flora would be standing behind holding on to the sacks. She rode to town and back standing up, keeping an easy balance, wearing her black hat. Almost ridiculous but not quite. A gypsy queen, my mother thought she looked like, with her black hair and her skin that always looked slightly tanned, and her lithe and bold serenity. Of course she lacked the gold bangles and the bright clothes. My mother envied her her slenderness, and her cheekbones.

Returning in the fall for her second year, my mother learned what was the matter with Ellie.

"My sister has a growth," Flora said. Nobody then spoke of cancer.

My mother had heard that before. People suspected it. My mother knew many people in the district by that time. She had made particular friends with a young woman who worked in the post office; this woman was going to be one of my mother's bridesmaids. The story of Flora and Ellie and Robert had been told—or all that people knew of it—in various versions. My mother did not feel that she was listening to gossip, because she was always on the alert for any disparaging remarks about Flora— she would not put up with that. But indeed nobody offered any. Everybody said that Flora had behaved like a saint. Even when she went to extremes, as in dividing up the house—that was like a saint.

Robert came to work at Grieveses' some months before the girls' father died. They knew him already, from church. (Oh, that church, my mother said, having attended it once, out of curiosity—that drear building miles on the other side of town, no organ or piano and plain glass in the windows and a doddery old minister with his hours-long sermon, a man hitting a tuning fork for the singing.) Robert had come out from Scotland and was on his way west. He had stopped with relatives or people he knew, members of the scanty congregation. To earn some money, probably, he came to Grieveses'. Soon he and Flora were engaged. They could not go to dances or to card parties like other couples, but they went for long walks. The chaperone—unofficially—was Ellie. Ellie was then a wild tease, a long-haired, impudent, childish girl full of lolloping energy. She would run up hills and smite the mullein stalks with a stick, shouting and prancing and pretending to be a warrior on horseback. That, or the horse itself. This when she was fifteen, sixteen years old. Nobody but Flora could control her, and generally Flora just laughed at her, being too used to her to wonder if she was quite right in the head. They were wonderfully fond of each other. Ellie, with her long skinny body, her long pale face, was like a copy of Flora—the kind of copy you often see in families, in which because of some carelessness or exaggeration of features or coloring, the handsomeness of one person passes into the plainness—or almost plainness—of the other. But Ellie had no jealousy about this. She loved to comb out Flora's hair and pin it up. They had great times, washing each other's hair. Ellie would press her face into Flora's throat, like a colt nuzzling its mother. So when Robert laid claim to Flora, or Flora to him—nobody knew how it was— Ellie had to be included. She didn't show any spite toward Robert, but she pursued and waylaid them on their walks; she sprung on them out of the bushes or sneaked up behind them so softly that she could blow on their necks. People saw her do it. And they heard of her jokes. She had always been terrible for jokes and sometimes it had got her into trouble with her father, but Flora had protected her. Now she put thistles in Robert's bed. She set his place at the table with the knife and fork the wrong way around. She switched the milk pails to give him the old one with the hole in it. For Flora's sake, maybe, Robert humored her.

The father had made Flora and Robert set the wedding day a year ahead, and after he died they did not move it any closer. Robert went on living in the house. Nobody knew how to speak to Flora about this being scandalous, or looking scandalous. Flora would just ask why. Instead of putting the wedding ahead, she put it back—from next spring to early fall, so that there should be a full year between it and her father's death. A year from wedding to funeral—that seemed proper to her. She trusted fully in Robert's patience and in her own purity.

So she might. But in the winter a commotion started. There was Ellie, vomiting, weeping, running off and hiding in the haymow, howling when they found her and pulled her out, jumping to the barn floor, running around in circles, rolling in the snow. Ellie was deranged. Flora had to call the doctor. She told him that her sister's periods had stopped—could the backup of blood be driving her wild? Robert had had to catch her and tie her up, and together he and Flora had put her to bed. She would not take food, just whipped her head from side to side, howling. It looked as if she would die speechless. But somehow the truth came out. Not from the doctor, who could not get close enough to examine her, with all her thrashing about. Probably, Robert confessed. Flora finally got wind of the truth, through all her high-mindedness. Now there had to be a wedding, though not the one that had been planned.

No cake, no new clothes, no wedding trip, no congratulations. Just a shameful hurry-up visit to the manse. Some people, seeing the names in the paper, thought the editor must have got the sisters mixed up. They thought it must be Flora. A hurry-up wedding for Flora! But no—it was Flora who pressed Robert's suit—it must have been—and got Ellie out of bed and washed her and made her presentable. It would have been Flora who picked one geranium from the window plant and pinned it to her sister's dress. And Ellie hadn't torn it out. Ellie was meek now, no longer flailing or crying. She let Flora fix her up, she let herself be married, she was never wild from that day on.

Flora had the house divided. She herself helped Robert build the necessary partitions. The baby was carried full term—nobody even pretended that it was early—but it was born dead after a long, tearing labor. Perhaps Ellie had damaged it when she jumped from the barn beam and rolled in the snow and beat on herself. Even if she hadn't done that, people would have expected something to go wrong, with that child or maybe one that came later. God dealt out punishment for hurry-up marriages—not just Presbyterians but almost everybody else believed that. God rewarded lust with dead babies, idiots, harelips and withered limbs and clubfeet.

In this case the punishment continued. Ellie had one miscarriage after another, then another stillbirth and more miscarriages. She was constantly pregnant, and the pregnancies were full of vomiting fits that lasted for days, headaches, cramps, dizzy spells. The miscarriages were as agonizing as full-term births. Ellie could not do her own work. She walked around holding on to chairs. Her numb silence passed off, and she became a complainer. If anybody came to visit, she would talk about the peculiarities of her headaches or describe her latest fainting fit, or even—in front of men, in front of unmarried girls or children—go into bloody detail about what Flora called her "disappointments." When people changed the subject or dragged the children away, she turned sullen. She demanded new medicine, reviled the doctor, nagged Flora. She accused Flora of washing the dishes with a great clang and clatter, out of spite, of pulling her—Ellie's—hair when she combed it out, of stingily substituting water-and-molasses for her real medicine. No matter what she said, Flora soothed her. Everybody who came into the house had some story of that kind to tell. Flora said, "Where's my little girl, then? Where's my Ellie? This isn't my Ellie, this is some crosspatch got in here in place of her!"

In the winter evenings after she came in from helping Robert with the barn chores, Flora would wash and change her clothes and go next door to read Ellie to sleep. My mother might invite herself along, taking whatever sewing she was doing, on some item of her trousseau. Ellie's bed was set up in the big dining room, where there was a gas lamp over the table. My mother sat on one side of the table, sewing, and Flora sat on the other side, reading aloud. Sometimes Ellie said, "I can't hear you." Or if Flora paused for a little rest Ellie said, "I'm not asleep yet."

What did Flora read? Stories about Scottish life—not classics. Stories about urchins and comic grandmothers. The only title my mother could remember was *Wee Macgregor*. She could not follow the stories very well, or laugh when Flora laughed and Ellie gave a whimper, because so much was in Scots dialect or read with that thick accent. She was surprised that Flora could do it—it wasn't the way Flora ordinarily talked, at all.

(But wouldn't it be the way Robert talked? Perhaps that is why my mother never reports anything that Robert said, never has him contributing to the scene. He must have been there, he must have been sitting there in the room. They would only heat the main room of the house. I see him black-haired, heavy-shouldered, with the strength of a plow horse, and the same kind of sombre, shackled beauty.)

Then Flora would say, "That's all of that for tonight." She would pick up another book, an old book written by some preacher of their faith. There was in it such stuff as my mother had never heard. What stuff? She couldn't say. All the stuff that was in their monstrous old religion. That put Ellie to sleep, or made her pretend she was asleep, after a couple of pages.

All that configuration of the elect and the damned, my mother must have meant—all the arguments about the illusion and necessity of free will. Doom and slippery redemption. The torturing, defeating, but for some minds irresistible pileup of interlocking and contradictory notions. My mother could resist it. Her faith was easy, her spirits at that time robust. Ideas were not what she was curious about, ever.

But what sort of thing was that, she asked (silently), to read to a dying woman? This was the nearest she got to criticizing Flora.

The answer—that it was the only thing, if you believed it—never seemed to have occurred to her.

By spring a nurse had arrived. That was the way things were done then. People died at home, and a nurse came in to manage it. The nurse's name was Audrey Atkinson. She was a stout woman with corsets as stiff as barrel hoops, marcelled hair the color of brass candlesticks, a mouth shaped by lipstick beyond its own stingy outlines. She drove a car into the yard—her own car, a dark-green coupé, shiny and smart. News of Audrey Atkinson and her car spread quickly. Questions were asked. Where did she get the money? Had some rich fool altered his will on her behalf? Had she exercised influence? Or simply helped herself to a stash of bills under the mattress? How was she to be trusted?

Hers was the first car ever to sit in the Grieveses' yard overnight.

Audrey Atkinson said that she had never been called out to tend a case in so primitive a house. It was beyond her, she said, how people could live in such a way.

"It's not that they're poor, even," she said to my mother. "It isn't, is it? That I could understand. Or it's not even their religion. So what is it? They do not care!"

She tried at first to cozy up to my mother, as if they would be natural allies in this benighted place. She spoke as if they were around the same age—both stylish, intelligent women who liked a good time and had modern ideas. She offered to teach my mother to drive the car. She offered her cigarettes. My mother was more tempted by the idea of learning to drive than she was by the cigarettes. But she said no, she would wait for her husband to teach her. Audrey Atkinson raised her pinkish-orange eyebrows at my mother behind Flora's back, and my mother was furious. She disliked the nurse far more than Flora did.

"I knew what she was like and Flora didn't," my mother said. She meant that she caught a whiff of a cheap life, maybe even of drinking establishments and unsavory men, of hard bargains, which Flora was too unworldly to notice.

Flora started into the great housecleaning again. She had the curtains spread out on stretchers, she beat the rugs on the line, she leapt up on the stepladder to attack the dust on the molding. But she was impeded all the time by Nurse Atkinson's complaining.

"I wondered if we could have a little less of the running and clattering?" said Nurse Atkinson with offensive politeness. "I only ask for my patient's sake." She always spoke of Ellie as "my patient" and pretended that she was the only one to protect her and compel respect. But she was not so respectful of Ellie herself. "Allee-oop," she would say, dragging the poor creature up on her pillows. And she told Ellie she was not going to stand for fretting and whimpering. "You don't do yourself any good that way," she said. "And you certainly don't make me come any quicker. What you just as well might do is learn to control yourself." She exclaimed at Ellie's bedsores in a scolding way, as if they were a further disgrace of the house. She demanded lotions, ointments, expensive soap—most of them, no doubt, to protect her own skin, which she claimed suffered from the hard water. (How could it be hard, my mother asked her—sticking up for the household when nobody else would—how could it be hard when it came straight from the rain barrel?)

Nurse Atkinson wanted cream, too—she said that they should hold some back, not sell it all to the creamery. She wanted to make nourishing soups and puddings for her patient. She did make puddings, and jellies, from packaged mixes such as had never before entered this house. My mother was convinced that she ate them all herself.

Flora still read to Ellie, but now it was only short bits from the Bible. When she finished and stood up, Ellie tried to cling to her. Ellie wept, sometimes she made ridiculous complaints. She said there was a horned cow outside, trying to get into the room and kill her.

"They often get some kind of idea like that," Nurse Atkinson said. "You mustn't give in to her or she won't let you go day or night. That's what they're like, they only think about themselves. Now, when I'm here alone with her, she behaves herself quite nice. I don't have any trouble at all. But after you been in here I have trouble all over again because she sees you and she gets upset. You don't want to make my job harder for me, do you? I mean, you brought me here to take charge, didn't you?"

"Ellie, now, Ellie dear, I must go," said Flora, and to the nurse she said, "I understand. I do understand that you have to be in charge and I admire you, I admire you for your work. In your work you have to have so much patience and kindness."

My mother wondered at this—was Flora really so blinded, or did she hope by this undeserved praise to exhort Nurse Atkinson to the patience and kindness that she didn't have? Nurse Atkinson was too thick-skinned and self-approving for any trick like that to work.

"It is a hard job, all right, and not many can do it," she said. "It's not like those nurses in the hospital, where they got everything laid out for them." She had no time for more conversation—she was trying to bring in "Make-Believe Ballroom" on her battery radio.

My mother was busy with the final exams and the June exercises at the school. She was getting ready for her wedding in July. Friends came in cars and whisked her off to the dressmaker's, to parties, to choose the invitations and order the cake. The lilacs came out, the evenings lengthened, the birds were back and nesting, my mother bloomed in everybody's attention, about to set out on the deliciously solemn adventure of marriage. Her dress was to be appliquéd with silk roses, her veil held by a cap of seed pearls. She belonged to the first generation of young women who saved their money and paid for their own weddings—far fancier than their parents could have afforded.

On her last evening, the friend from the post office came to drive her away, with her clothes and her books and the things she had made for her trousseau and the gifts her pupils and others had given her. There was great fuss and laughter about getting everything loaded into the car. Flora came out and helped. This getting married is even more of a nuisance than I thought, said Flora, laughing. She gave my mother a dresser scarf, which she had crocheted in secret. Nurse Atkinson could not be shut out of an important occasion—she presented a spray bottle of cologne. Flora stood on the slope at the side of the house to wave goodbye. She had been invited to the wedding, but of course she had said she could not come, she could not "go out" at such a time. The last my mother ever saw of her was this solitary, energetically waving figure in her housecleaning apron and bandanna, on the green slope by the black-walled house, in the evening light.

"Well, maybe now she'll get what she should've got the first time round," the friend from the post office said. "Maybe now they'll be able to get married. Is she too old to start a family? How old is she, anyway?"

My mother thought that this was a crude way of talking about Flora and replied that she didn't know. But she had to admit to herself that she had been thinking the very same thing.

When she was married and settled in her own home, three hundred miles away, my mother got a letter from Flora. Ellie was dead. She had died firm in her faith, Flora said, and grateful for her release. Nurse Atkinson was staying on for a little while, until it was time for her to go off to her next case. This was late in the summer.

News of what happened next did not come from Flora. When she wrote at Christmas, she seemed to take for granted that information would have gone ahead of her.

"You have in all probability heard," wrote Flora, "that Robert and Nurse Atkinson have been married. They are living on

here, in Robert's part of the house. They are fixing it up to suit
themselves. It is very impolite of me to call her Nurse Atkinson,
as I see I have done. I ought to have called her Audrey."

Of course the post-office friend had written, and so had
others. It was a great shock and scandal and a matter that excited
the district—the wedding as secret and surprising as Robert's first
one had been (though surely not for the same reason), Nurse
Atkinson permanently installed in the community, Flora losing
out for the second time. Nobody had been aware of any court-
ship, and they asked how the woman could have enticed him.
Did she promise children, lying about her age?

The surprises were not to stop with the wedding. The bride
got down to business immediately with the "fixing up" that Flora
mentioned. In came the electricity and then the telephone. Now
Nurse Atkinson—she would always be called Nurse Atkinson—
was heard on the party line lambasting painters and paperhangers
and delivery services. She was having everything done over. She
was buying an electric stove and putting in a bathroom, and who
knew where the money was coming from? Was it all hers, got in
her deathbed dealings, in shady bequests? Was it Robert's, was
he claiming his share? Ellie's share, left to him and Nurse Atkinson to enjoy themselves with, the shameless pair?

All these improvements took place on one side of the house
only. Flora's side remained just as it was. No electric lights there,
no fresh wallpaper or new venetian blinds. When the house was
painted on the outside—cream with dark-green trim—Flora's
side was left bare. This strange open statement was greeted at
first with pity and disapproval, then with less sympathy, as a sign
of Flora's stubbornness and eccentricity (she could have bought
her own paint and made it look decent), and finally as a joke.
People drove out of their way to see it.

There was always a dance given in the schoolhouse for a
newly married couple. A cash collection—called "a purse of
money"—was presented to them. Nurse Atkinson sent out word
that she would not mind seeing this custom followed, even

though it happened that the family she had married into was opposed to dancing. Some people thought it would be a disgrace to gratify her, a slap in the face to Flora. Others were too curious to hold back. They wanted to see how the newlyweds would behave. Would Robert dance? What sort of outfit would the bride show up in? They delayed a while, but finally the dance was held, and my mother got her report.

The bride wore the dress she had worn at her wedding, or so she said. But who would wear such a dress for a wedding at the manse? More than likely it was bought specially for her appearance at the dance. Pure-white satin with a sweetheart neckline, idiotically youthful. The groom was got up in a new dark-blue suit, and she had stuck a flower in his buttonhole. They were a sight. Her hair was freshly done to blind the eye with brassy reflections, and her face looked as if it would come off on a man's jacket, should she lay it against his shoulder in the dancing. Of course she did dance. She danced with every man present except the groom, who sat scrunched into one of the school desks along the wall. She danced with every man present—they all claimed they had to do it, it was the custom—and then she dragged Robert out to receive the money and to thank everybody for their best wishes. To the ladies in the cloakroom she even hinted that she was feeling unwell, for the usual newlywed reason. Nobody believed her, and indeed nothing ever came of this hope, if she really had it. Some of the women thought that she was lying to them out of malice, insulting them, making them out to be so credulous. But nobody challenged her, nobody was rude to her—maybe because it was plain that she could summon a rudeness of her own to knock anybody flat.

Flora was not present at the dance.

"My sister-in-law is not a dancer," said Nurse Atkinson. "She is stuck in the olden times." She invited them to laugh at Flora, whom she always called her sister-in-law, though she had no right to do so.

My mother wrote a letter to Flora after hearing about all

these things. Being removed from the scene, and perhaps in a flurry of importance due to her own newly married state, she may have lost sight of the kind of person she was writing to. She offered sympathy and showed outrage, and said blunt disparaging things about the woman who had—as my mother saw it—dealt Flora such a blow. Back came a letter from Flora saying that she did not know where my mother had been getting her information, but that it seemed she had misunderstood, or listened to malicious people, or jumped to unjustified conclusions. What happened in Flora's family was nobody else's business, and certainly nobody needed to feel sorry for her or angry on her behalf. Flora said that she was happy and satisfied in her life, as she always had been, and she did not interfere with what others did or wanted, because such things did not concern her. She wished my mother all happiness in her marriage and hoped that she would soon be too busy with her own responsibilities to worry about the lives of people that she used to know.

This well-written letter cut my mother, as she said, to the quick. She and Flora stopped corresponding. My mother did become busy with her own life and finally a prisoner in it.

But she thought about Flora. In later years, when she sometimes talked about the things she might have been, or done, she would say, "If I could have been a writer—I do think I could have been; I could have been a writer—then I would have written the story of Flora's life. And do you know what I would have called it? 'The Maiden Lady.' "

The Maiden Lady. She said these words in a solemn and sentimental tone of voice that I had no use for. I knew, or thought I knew, exactly the value she found in them. The stateliness and mystery. The hint of derision turning to reverence. I was fifteen or sixteen years old by that time, and I believed that I could see into my mother's mind. I could see what she would do with Flora, what she had already done. She would make her into a noble figure, one who accepts defection, treachery, who forgives and stands aside, not once but twice. Never a moment of complaint. Flora goes about her cheerful labors, she cleans the house and shovels out the cow byre, she removes some bloody mess from her sister's bed, and when at last the future seems to open up for her—Ellie will die and Robert will beg forgiveness and Flora will silence him with the proud gift of herself—it is time for Audrey Atkinson to drive into the yard and shut Flora out again, more inexplicably and thoroughly the second time than the first. She must endure the painting of the house, the electric lights, all the prosperous activity next door. "Make-Believe Ballroom," "Amos 'n' Andy." No more Scottish comedies or ancient sermons. She must see them drive off to the dance—her old lover and that coldhearted, stupid, by no means beautiful woman in the white satin wedding dress. She is mocked. (And of course she has made over the farm to Ellie and Robert, of course he has inherited it, and now everything belongs to Audrey Atkinson.) The wicked flourish. But it is all right. It is all right—the elect are veiled in patience and humility and lighted by a certainty that events cannot disturb.

That was what I believed my mother would make of things. In her own plight her notions had turned mystical, and there was sometimes a hush, a solemn thrill in her voice that grated on me, alerted me to what seemed a personal danger. I felt a great fog of platitudes and pieties lurking, an incontestable crippled-mother power, which could capture and choke me. There would be no end to it. I had to keep myself sharp-tongued and cynical, arguing and deflating. Eventually I gave up even that recognition and opposed her in silence.

This is a fancy way of saying that I was no comfort and poor company to her when she had almost nowhere else to turn.

I had my own ideas about Flora's story. I didn't think that I could have written a novel but that I would write one. I would take a different tack. I saw through my mother's story and put in what she left out. My Flora would be as black as hers was white. Rejoicing in the bad turns done to her and in her own forgiveness, spying on the shambles of her sister's life. A Presbyterian witch, reading out of her poisonous book. It takes a rival ruthlessness, the comparatively innocent brutality of the thickskinned nurse, to drive her back, to flourish in her shade. But she is driven back; the power of sex and ordinary greed drive her back and shut her up in her own part of the house with the coal-oil lamps. She shrinks, she caves in, her bones harden and her joints thicken, and—oh, this is it, this is it, I see the bare beauty of the ending I will contrive!—she becomes crippled herself, with arthritis, hardly able to move. Now Audrey Atkinson comes into her full power—she demands the whole house. She wants those partitions knocked out that Robert put up with Flora's help when he married Ellie. She will provide Flora with a room, she will take care of her. (Audrey Atkinson does not wish to be seen as a monster, and perhaps she really isn't one.) So one day Robert carries Flora—for the first and last time he carries her in his arms—to the room that his wife Audrey has prepared for her. And once Flora is settled in her well-lit, well-heated corner Audrey Atkinson undertakes to clean out the newly vacated rooms, Flora's rooms. She carries a heap of old books out into the yard. It's spring again, housecleaning time, the season when Flora herself performed such feats, and now the pale face of Flora appears behind the new net curtains. She has dragged herself from her corner, she sees the light-blue sky with its high skidding clouds over the watery fields, the contending crows, the flooded creeks, the reddening tree branches. She sees the smoke rise out of the incinerator in the yard, where her books are burning. Those smelly old books, as Audrey has called them. Words and pages, the ominous dark spines. The elect, the damned, the slim hopes, the mighty torments—up in smoke. There was the ending.

To me the really mysterious person in the story, as my mother told it, was Robert. He never has a word to say. He gets engaged to Flora. He is walking beside her along the river when Ellie leaps out at them. He finds Ellie's thistles in his bed. He does the carpentry made necessary by his and Ellie's marriage. He listens or does not listen while Flora reads. Finally he sits scrunched up in the school desk while his flashy bride dances by with all the men.

So much for his public acts and appearances. But he was the one who started everything, in secret. He *did it to* Ellie. He did it to that skinny wild girl at a time when he was engaged to her sister, and he did it to her again and again when she was nothing but a poor botched body, a failed childbearer, lying in bed.

He must have done it to Audrey Atkinson, too, but with less disastrous results.

Those words, *did it to*—the words my mother, no more than Flora, would never bring herself to speak—were simply exciting to me. I didn't feel any decent revulsion or reasonable indignation. I refused the warning. Not even the fate of Ellie could put me off. Not when I thought of that first encounter—the desperation of it, the ripping and striving. I used to sneak longing looks at men in those days. I admired their wrists and their necks and any bit of their chests a loose button let show, and even their ears and their feet in shoes. I expected nothing reasonable of them, only to be engulfed by their passion. I had similar thoughts about Robert.

What made Flora evil in my story was just what made her admirable in my mother's—her turning away from sex. I fought against everything my mother wanted to tell me on this subject; I despised even the drop in her voice, the gloomy caution, with which she approached it. My mother had grown up in a time and in a place where sex was a dark undertaking for women. She knew that you could die of it. So she honored the decency, the prudery, the frigidity, that might protect you. And I grew up in horror of that very protection, the dainty tyranny that seemed to me to extend to all areas of life, to enforce tea parties and white gloves and all other sorts of tinkling inanities. I favored bad words and a breakthrough, I teased myself with the thought of a man's recklessness and domination. The odd thing is that my mother's ideas were in line with some progressive notions of her times, and mine echoed the notions that were favored in my time. This in spite of the fact that we both believed ourselves independent, and lived in backwaters that did not register such changes. It's as if tendencies that seem most deeply rooted in our minds, most private and singular, have come in as spores on the prevailing wind, looking for any likely place to land, any welcome.

Not long before she died, but when I was still at home, my mother got a letter from the real Flora. It came from that town near the farm, the town that Flora used to ride to, with Robert, in the cart, holding on to the sacks of wool or potatoes.

Flora wrote that she was no longer living on the farm.

"Robert and Audrey are still there," she wrote. "Robert has some trouble with his back but otherwise he is very well. Audrey has poor circulation and is often short of breath. The doctor says she must lose weight but none of the diets seem to work. The farm has been doing very well. They are out of sheep entirely and into dairy cattle. As you may have heard, the chief thing now-adays is to get your milk quota from the government and then you are set. The old stable is all fixed up with milking machines and the latest modern equipment, it is quite a marvel. When I go out there to visit I hardly know where I am."

She went on to say that she had been living in town for some years now, and that she had a job clerking in a store. She must have said what kind of a store this was, but I cannot now remember. She said nothing, of course, about what had led her to this decision—whether she had in fact been put off her own farm, or had sold out her share, apparently not to much advantage. She stressed the fact of her friendliness with Robert and Audrey. She said her health was good.

"I hear that you have not been so lucky in that way," she wrote. "I ran into Cleta Barnes who used to be Cleta Stapleton at the post office out at home, and she told me that there is some problem with your muscles and she said your speech is affected too. This is sad to hear but they can do such wonderful things nowadays so I am hoping that the doctors may be able to help you."

An unsettling letter, leaving so many things out. Nothing in it about God's will or His role in our afflictions. No mention of whether Flora still went to that church. I don't think my mother ever answered. Her fine legible handwriting, her schoolteacher's writing, had deteriorated, and she had difficulty holding a pen. She was always beginning letters and not finishing them. I would find them lying around the house. My *dearest Mary*, they began. My *darling Ruth, My dear little Joanne (though I realize you are not little anymore), My dear old friend Cleta, My lovely Margaret.* These women were friends from her teaching days, her Normal School days, and from high school. A few were former pupils. I have friends all over the country, she would say defiantly. I have dear, dear friends.

I remember seeing one letter that started out: *Friend of my Youth.* I don't know whom it was to. They were all friends of her youth. I don't recall one that began with My *dear and most admired Flora.* I would always look at them, try to read the salutation and the few sentences she had written, and because I could not bear to feel sadness I would feel an impatience with the flowery language, the direct appeal for love and pity. She would get more of that, I thought (more from myself, I meant), if she could manage to withdraw with dignity, instead of reaching out all the time to cast her stricken shadow.

I had lost interest in Flora by then. I was always thinking of stories, and by this time I probably had a new one on my mind.

But I have thought of her since. I have wondered what kind of a store. A hardware store or a five-and-ten, where she has to wear a coverall, or a drugstore, where she is uniformed like a nurse, or a Ladies' Wear, where she is expected to be genteelly fashionable? She might have had to learn about food blenders or chain saws, negligees, cosmetics, even condoms. She would have to work all day under electric lights, and operate a cash register.

Would she get a permanent, paint her nails, put on lipstick? She must have found a place to live—a little apartment with a kitchenette, overlooking the main street, or a room in a boarding house. How could she go on being a Cameronian? How could she get to that out-of-the-way church unless she managed to buy a car and learned to drive it? And if she did that she might drive not only to church but to other places. She might go on holidays. She might rent a cottage on a lake for a week, learn to swim, visit a city. She might eat meals in a restaurant, possibly in a restaurant where drinks were served. She might make friends with women who were divorced.

She might meet a man. A friend's widowed brother, perhaps. A man who did not know that she was a Cameronian or what Cameronians were. Who knew nothing of her story. A man who had never heard about the partial painting of the house or the two betrayals, or that it took all her dignity and innocence to keep her from being a joke. He might want to take her dancing, and she would have to explain that she could not go. He would be surprised but not put off—all that Cameronian business might seem quaint to him, almost charming. So it would to everybody. She was brought up in some weird religion, people would say. She lived a long time out on some godforsaken farm. She is a little bit strange but really quite nice. Nice-looking, too. Especially since she went and got her hair done.

I might go into a store and find her.

No, no. She would be dead a long time now.

But suppose I had gone into a store—perhaps a department store. I see a place with the brisk atmosphere, the straightforward displays, the old-fashioned modern look of the fifties. Suppose a tall, handsome woman, nicely turned out, had come to wait on me, and I had known, somehow, in spite of the sprayed and puffed hair and the pink or coral lips and fingernails—I had known that this was Flora. I would have wanted to tell her that I knew, I knew her story, though we had never met. I imagine myself trying to tell her. (This is a dream now, I understand it as a dream.) I imagine her listening, with a pleasant composure. But she shakes her head. She smiles at me, and in her smile there is a degree of mockery, a faint, self-assured malice. Weariness, as well. She is not surprised that I am telling her this, but she is weary of it, of me and my idea of her, my information, my notion that I can know anything about her.

Of course it's my mother I'm thinking of, my mother as she was in those dreams, saying, It's nothing, just this little tremor; saying with such astonishing lighthearted forgiveness, Oh, I knew you'd come someday. My mother surprising me, and doing it almost indifferently. Her mask, her fate, and most of her affliction taken away. How relieved I was, and happy. But I now recall that I was disconcerted as well. I would have to say that I felt slightly cheated. Yes. Offended, tricked, cheated, by this welcome turnaround, this reprieve. My mother moving rather carelessly out of her old prison, showing options and powers I never dreamed she had, changes more than herself. She changes the bitter lump of love I have carried all this time into a phantom—something useless and uncalled for, like a phantom pregnancy.

The Cameronians, I have discovered, are or were an uncompromising remnant of the Covenanters—those Scots who in the seventeenth century bound themselves, with God, to resist prayer books, bishops, any taint of popery or interference by the King. Their name comes from Richard Cameron, an outlawed, or "field," preacher, soon cut down. The Cameronians—for a long time they have preferred to be called the Reformed Presbyterians—went into battle singing the seventy-fourth and the seventy-eighth Psalms. They hacked the haughty Bishop of St. Andrews to death on the highway and rode their horses over his body. One of their ministers, in a mood of firm rejoicing at his own hanging, excommunicated all the other preachers in the world.

Five Points

While they drink vodka and orange juice in the trailer park on the cliffs above Lake Huron, Neil Bauer tells Brenda a story. It happened a long way away, in Victoria, British Columbia, where Neil grew up. Neil is not much younger than Brenda—less than three years—but it sometimes feels to her like a generation gap, because she grew up here, and stayed here, marrying Cornelius Zendt when she was twenty years old, and Neil grew up on the West Coast, where things were very different, and he left home at sixteen to travel and work all over.

What Brenda has seen of Victoria, in pictures, is flowers and horses. Flowers spilling out of baskets hanging from old-fashioned lampposts, filling grottoes and decorating parks; horses carrying wagonloads of people to look at the sights.

"That's all just tourist shit," Neil says. "About half the place is nothing but tourist shit. That's not where I'm talking about."

He is talking about Five Points, which was—is—a section, or maybe just a corner, of the city, where there was a school and a drugstore and a Chinese grocery and a candy store. When Neil was in public school, the candy store was run by a grouchy old woman with painted-on eyebrows. She used to let her cat sprawl in the sun in the window. After she died, some new people, Europeans, not Poles or Czechs but from some smaller country—Croatia; is that a country?—took over the candy store and changed it. They cleared out all the stale candy and the balloons that wouldn't blow up and the ballpoint pens that wouldn't write and the dead Mexican jumping beans. They painted the place top to bottom and put in a few chairs and tables. They still sold candy—in clean jars now, instead of cat-pissed cardboard boxes—and rulers and erasers. But they also started to operate as a kind of neighborhood café, with coffee and soft drinks and homemade cakes.

The wife, who made the cakes, was very shy and fussy, and if you came up and tried to pay her she would call for her husband in Croatian, or whatever—let's say it was Croatian—in such a startled way you'd think that you'd broken into her house and interrupted her private life. The husband spoke English pretty well. He was a little bald guy, polite and nervous, a chain-smoker, and she was a big, heavy woman with bent shoulders, always wearing an apron and a cardigan sweater. He washed the windows and swept off the sidewalk and took the money, and she baked the buns and cakes and made things that people had never seen before but that quickly became popular, like pierogi and poppy-seed loaf.

Their two daughters spoke English just like Canadians, and went to the convent school. They showed up in their school uniforms in the late afternoon and got right to work. The younger one washed the coffee cups and glasses and wiped the tables, and the older one did everything else. She waited on customers, worked the cash register, filled the trays, and shooed away the little kids who were hanging around not buying anything. When the younger one finished washing up, she would sit in the back room doing her homework, but the older one never sat down. If there was nothing to do at the moment, she just stood by the cash register, watching.

The younger one was called Lisa, the older one Maria. Lisa was small and nice enough looking—just a little kid. But Maria, by the age of maybe thirteen, had big, saggy breasts and a rounded-out stomach and thick legs. She wore glasses, and her hair was done in braids around her head. She looked about fifty years old.

And she acted it, the way she took over the store. Both parents seemed willing to take a back seat to her. The mother retreated to the back room, and the father became a handyman-helper. Maria understood English and money and wasn't fazed by anything. All the little kids said, "Ugh, that Maria—isn't she *gross?*" But they were scared of her. She looked like she already knew all about running a business.

Brenda and her husband also run a business. They bought a farm just south of Logan and filled the barn with used appliances (which Cornelius knows how to fix) and secondhand furniture and all the other things—the dishes, pictures, knives and forks and ornaments and jewelry—that people like to poke through and think they're buying cheap. It's called Zendt's Furniture Barn. Locally, a lot of people refer to it as the Used Furniture on the Highway.

They didn't always do this. Brenda used to teach nursery school, and Cornelius, who is twelve years older than she is, worked in the salt mine at Walley, on the lake. After his accident they had to think of something he could do sitting down most of the time, and they used the money they got to buy a worn-out farm with good buildings. Brenda quit her job, because there was too much for Cornelius to handle by himself. There are hours in the day and sometimes whole days when he has to lie down and watch television, or just lie on the living room floor, coping with the pain.

In the evenings Cornelius likes to drive over to Walley. Brenda never offers—she waits for him to say, "Why don't you drive?" if he doesn't want the movement of his arms or legs to jar his back. The kids used to go along, but now that they're in high school—Lorna in grade eleven and Mark in grade nine—they usually don't want to. Brenda and Cornelius sit in the parked van and look at the sea gulls lining up out on the breakwater, the grain elevators, the great green-lighted shafts and ramps of the mine where Cornelius used to work, the pyramids of coarse gray salt. Sometimes there is a long lake boat in port. Of course, there are pleasure boats in the summer, wind surfers out on the water, people fishing off the pier. The time of the sunset is posted daily on a board on the beach then; people come especially to watch it. Now, in October, the board is bare and the lights are turned on along the pier—one or two diehards are still fishing—and the water is choppy and cold-looking, the harbor entirely business-like.

There is still work going on on the beach. Since early last spring, boulders have been set up in some places, sand has been poured down in others, a long rocky spit has been constructed, all making a protected curve of beach, with a rough road along it, on which they drive. Never mind Cornelius's back—he wants to see. Trucks, earthmovers, bulldozers have been busy all day, and they are still sitting there, temporarily tame and useless monsters, in the evening. This is where Neil works. He drives these things—he hauls the rocks around, clears the space, and makes the road for Brenda and Cornelius to drive on. He works for the Fordyce Construction Company, from Logan, which has the contract.

Cornelius looks at everything. He knows what the boats are loading (soft wheat, salt, corn) and where they're going, he understands how the harbor is being deepened, and he always wants to get a look at the huge pipe running at an angle onto the beach and crossing it, finally letting out water and sludge and rocks from the lake bottom that have never before seen the light of day. He goes and stands beside this pipe to listen to the commotion inside it, the banging and groaning of the rocks and water rushing on their way. He asks what a rough winter will do to all this changing and arranging if the lake just picks up the rocks and beach and flings them aside and eats away at the clay cliffs, as before.

Brenda listens to Cornelius and thinks about Neil. She derives pleasure from being in the place where Neil spends his days. She likes to think of the noise and the steady strength of these machines and of the men in the cabs bare-armed, easy with this power, as if they knew naturally what all this roaring and chomping up the shore was leading to. Their casual, good-humored authority. She loves the smell of work on their bodies, the language of it they speak, their absorption in it, their disregard of her. She loves to get a man fresh from all that.

When she is down there with Cornelius and hasn't seen Neil for a while, she can feel uneasy and forlorn, as if this might be a world that could turn its back on her. Just after she has been with Neil, it's her kingdom—but what isn't, then? The night before they are to meet—last night, for instance—she should be feeling happy and expectant, but to tell the truth the last twenty-four hours, even the last two or three days, seem too full of pitfalls, too momentous, for her to feel anything much but caution and anxiety. It's a countdown—she actually counts the hours. She has a tendency to fill them with good deeds—cleaning jobs around the house that she was putting off, mowing the lawn, doing a reorganization at the Furniture Barn, even weeding the rock garden. The morning of the day itself is when the hours pass most laggingly and are full of dangers. She always has a story about where she's supposed to be going that afternoon, but her expedition can't be an absolutely necessary one—that would be calling too much attention to it—so there's the chance, always, that something will come up to make Cornelius say, "Can't you put that off till later in the week? Can't you do it some other day?" It's not so much that she wouldn't then be able to get in touch with Neil that bothers her. Neil would wait an hour or so, then figure out what had happened. It's that she thinks she couldn't bear it. To be so close, then have to do without. Yet she doesn't feel any physical craving during those last torturing hours; even her secret preparations—her washing, shaving, oiling, and perfuming—don't arouse her. She stays numb, harassed by details, lies, arrangements, until the moment when she actually sees Neil's car. The fear that she won't be able to get away is succeeded, during the fifteen-minute drive, by the fear that he won't show up, in that lonely, dead-end spot in the swamp which is their meeting place. What she's looking forward to, during those last hours, gets to be less of a physical thing—so that missing it would be like missing not a meal you're hungry for but a ceremony on which your life or salvation depended.

By the time Neil was an older teenager—but not old enough to get into bars, still hanging around at the Five Points Confectionery (the Croatians kept the old name for it)—the change had arrived, which everybody who was alive then remembers. (That's what Neil thinks, but Brenda says, "I don't know—as far as I was concerned, all that was just sort of going on someplace else.") Nobody knew what to do about it, nobody was prepared. Some schools were strict about long hair (on boys), some thought it best to let that go and concentrate on serious things. Just hold it back with an elastic band was all they asked. And what about clothes? Chains and seed beads, rope sandals, Indian cotton, African patterns, everything all of a sudden soft and loose and bright. In Victoria the change may not have been contained so well as in some other places. It spilled over. Maybe the climate softened people up, not just young people. There was a big burst of paper flowers and marijuana fumes and music (the stuff that seemed so wild then, Neil says, and seems so tame now), and that music rolling out of downtown windows hung with dishonored flags, over the flower beds in Beacon Hill Park to the yellow broom on the sea cliffs to the happy beaches looking over at the magic peaks of the Olympics. Everybody was in on the act.

University professors wandered around with flowers behind their ears, and people's mothers turned up in those outfits. Neil and his friends had contempt for these people, naturally—these hip oldsters, toe-dippers. Neil and his friends took the world of drugs and music seriously.

When they wanted to do drugs, they went outside the Confectionery. Sometimes they went as far as the cemetery and sat on the seawall. Sometimes they sat beside the shed that was in back of the store. They couldn't go in; the shed was locked. Then they went back inside the Confectionery and drank Cokes and ate hamburgers and cheeseburgers and cinnamon buns and cakes, because they got very hungry. They leaned back on their chairs and watched the patterns move on the old pressed-tin ceiling, which the Croatians had painted white. Flowers, towers, birds, and monsters detached themselves, swam overhead.

"What were you taking?" Brenda says.

"Pretty good stuff, unless we got sold something rotten. Hash, acid, mescaline sometimes. Combinations sometimes. Nothing too serious."

"All I ever did was smoke about a third of a joint on the beach when at first I wasn't even sure what it was, and when I got home my father slapped my face."

(That's not the truth. It was Cornelius. Cornelius slapped her face. It was before they were married, when Cornelius was working nights in the mine and she would sit around on the beach after dark with some friends of her own age. Next day she told him, and he slapped her face.)

All they did in the Confectionery was eat, and moon around, happily stoned, and play stupid games, such as racing toy cars along the tabletops. Once, a guy lay down on the floor and they squirted ketchup at him. Nobody cared. The daytime customers—the housewives buying bakery goods and the pensioners killing time with a coffee—never came in at night. The mother and Lisa had gone home on the bus, to wherever they lived. Then even the father started going home, a little after suppertime. Maria was left in charge. She didn't care what they did, as long as they didn't do damage and as long as they paid.

This was the world of drugs that belonged to the older boys, that they kept the younger boys out of. It was a while before they noticed that the younger ones had something, too. They had some secret of their own. They were growing insolent and self-important. Some of them were always pestering the older boys to let them buy drugs. That was how it became evident that they had quite a bit of unexplained money.

Neil had—he has—a younger brother named Jonathan. Very straight now, married, a teacher. Jonathan began dropping hints; other boys did the same thing, they couldn't keep the secret to themselves, and pretty soon it was all out in the open. They were getting their money from Maria. Maria was paying them to have sex with her. They did it in the back shed after she closed the store up at night. She had the key to the shed.

She also had the day-to-day control of the money. She emptied the till at night, she kept the books. Her parents trusted her to do this. Why not? She was good at arithmetic, and she was devoted to the business. She understood the whole operation better than they did. It seemed that they were very uncertain and superstitious about money, and they did not want to put it in the bank. They kept it in a safe or maybe just a strongbox some-where, and got it as they needed it. They must have felt they couldn't trust anybody, banks or anybody, outside of the family. What a godsend Maria must have seemed to them—steady and smart, not pretty enough to be tempted to put her hopes or energies into anything but the business. A pillar, Maria.

She was a head taller and thirty or forty pounds heavier than those boys she paid.

There are always a few bad moments after Brenda turns off the highway—where she has some excuse to be driving, should any-one see her—and onto the side road. The van is noticeable, unmistakable. But once she has taken the plunge, driving where she shouldn't be, she feels stronger. When she turns onto the dead-end swamp road, there's no excuse possible. Spotted here, she's finished. She has about half a mile to drive out in the open before she gets to the trees. She'd hoped that they would plant corn, which would grow tall and shelter her, but they hadn't, they'd planted beans. At least the roadsides here hadn't been sprayed; the grass and weeds and berry bushes had grown tall, though not tall enough to hide a van. There was goldenrod and milkweed, with the pods burst open, and dangling bunches of bright, poisonous fruit, and wild grapevine flung over every-thing, even creeping onto the road. And finally she was in, she was into the tunnel of trees. Cedar, hemlock, farther back in the wetter ground the wispy-looking tamarack, lots of soft maples with leaves spotty yellow and brown. No standing water, no black pools, even far back in the trees. They'd had luck, with the dry summer and fall. She and Neil had had luck, not the farmers. If it had been a wet year, they could never have used this place. The hard ruts she eases the van through would have been slick mud and the turnaround spot at the end a soggy sinkhole.

That's about a mile and a half in. There are some tricky spots to drive—a couple of bumpy little hills rising out of the swamp, and a narrow log bridge over a creek where she can't see any water, just choking, yellowy cress and nettles, sucking at dry mud.

Neil drives an old blue Mercury—dark blue that can turn into a pool, a spot of swampy darkness under the trees. She strains to see it. She doesn't mind getting there a few minutes ahead of him, to compose herself, brush out her hair and check her face and spray her throat with purse cologne (sometimes between her legs as well). More than a few minutes makes her nervous. She isn't afraid of wild dogs or rapists or eyes watching her out of thickets—she used to pick berries in here when she was a child; that's how she knew about the place. She is afraid of what may not be there, not what is. The absence of Neil, the possibility of his defection, his sudden denial of her. That can turn any place, any thing, ugly and menacing and stupid. Trees or gardens or parking meters or coffee tables—it wouldn't matter. Once, he didn't come; he was sick: food poisoning or the most incredible hangover of his life—something terrible, he told her on the phone that night—and she had to pretend it was somebody calling to sell them a sofa. She never forgot the wait, the draining of hope, the heat and the bugs—it was in July—and her body oozing sweat, here on the seat of the van, like some sickly admission of defeat.

He is there, he's there first; she can see one eye of the Mercury in the deep cedar shade. It's like hitting water when you're dead of heat and scratched and bitten all over from picking berries in the summer bush—the lapping sweetness of it, the cool kindness soaking up all your troubles in its sudden depths. She gets the van parked and fluffs out her hair and jumps out, tries the door to show it's locked, else he'll send her running back, just like Cornelius—are you sure you locked the van? She walks across the little sunny space, the leaf-scattered ground, seeing herself walk, in her tight white pants and turquoise top and low-slung white belt and high heels, her bag over her shoulder. A shapely woman, with fair, freckled skin and blue eyes rimmed with blue shadow and liner, screwed up appealingly against any light. Her reddish-blond hair—touched up yesterday—catching the sun like a crown of petals. She wears heels just for this walk, just for this moment of crossing the road with his eyes on her, the extra bit of pelvic movement and leg length they give her.

Often, often, they've made love in his car, right here at their meeting place, though they always keep telling each other to wait. Stop; wait till we get to the trailer. "Wait" means the opposite of what it says, after a while. Once, they started as they drove. Brenda slipped off her pants and pulled up her loose summer skirt, not saying a word, looking straight ahead, and they ended up stopping beside the highway, taking a shocking risk. Now when they pass this spot, she always says something like "Don't go off the road here," or "Somebody should put up a warning sign."

"Historical marker," Neil says.

They have a history of passion, the way families have a history, or people who have gone to school together. They don't have much else. They've never eaten a meal with each other, or seen a movie. But they've come through some complicated adventures together, and dangers—not just of the stopping-on-the-highway kind. They've taken risks, surprising each other, always correctly. In dreams you can have the feeling that you've had this dream before, that you have this dream over and over again, and you know that it's really nothing that simple. You know that there's a whole underground system that you call "dreams," having nothing better to call them, and that this system is not like roads or tunnels but more like a live body network, all coiling and stretching, unpredictable but finally familiar—where you are now, where you've always been. That was the way it was with them and sex, going somewhere like that, and they understood the same things about it and trusted each other, so far.

Another time on the highway, Brenda saw a white convertible approaching, an old white Mustang convertible with the top down—this was in the summer—and she slid to the floor.

"Who's in that car?" she said. "Look! Quick! Tell me."

"Girls," Neil said. "Four or five girls. Out looking for guys."

"My daughter," Brenda said, scrambling up again. "Good thing I wasn't wearing my seat belt."

"You got a daughter old enough to drive? You got a daughter owns a convertible?"

"Her friend owns it. Lorna doesn't drive yet. But she could—she's sixteen."

She felt there were things in the air then that he could have said, that she hoped he wouldn't. The things men feel obliged to say about young girls.

"You could have one that age yourself," she said. "Maybe you do and don't know it. Also, she lied to me. She said she was going to play tennis."

Again he didn't say anything she hoped not to hear, any sly reminder about lies. A danger past.

All he said was, "Easy. Take it easy. Nothing happened."

She had no way of knowing how much he understood of her feelings at that moment, or if he understood anything. They almost never mentioned that part of her life. They never mentioned Cornelius, though he was the one Neil talked to the first time he came to the Furniture Barn. He came to look for a bicycle—just a cheap bike to ride on the country roads. They had no bikes around at that time, but he stayed and talked to Cornelius for a while, about the kind he wanted, ways of repairing or improving that kind, how they should watch out for one. He said he would drop by again. He did that, very soon, and only Brenda was there. Cornelius had gone to the house to lie down; it was one of his bad days. Neil and Brenda made everything clear to each other then, without saying anything definite. When he phoned and asked her to have a drink with him, in a tavern on the lakeshore road, she knew what he was asking and she knew what she would answer.

She told him she hadn't done anything like this before. That was a lie in one way and in another way true.

During store hours, Maria didn't let one sort of transaction interfere with another. Everybody paid as usual. She didn't behave any differently; she was still in charge. The boys knew that they had some bargaining power, but they were never sure how much. A dollar. Two dollars. Five. It wasn't as if she had to depend on one or two of them. There were always several friends outside, waiting and willing, when she took one of them into the shed before she caught the bus home. She warned them that she would stop dealing with them if they talked, and for a while they believed her. She didn't hire them regularly at first, or all that often.

That was at first. Over a few months' time, things began to change. Maria's needs increased. The bargaining got to be more open and obstreperous. The news got out. Maria's powers were being chipped, then hammered, away.

Come on, Maria, give me a ten. Me, too. Maria, give me a ten, too. Come on, Maria, you know me.

Twenty, Maria. Give me twenty. Come on. Twenty bucks. You owe me, Maria. Come on, now. You don't want me to tell. Come on, Maria.

A twenty, a twenty, a twenty. Maria is forking over. She is going to the shed every night. And if that isn't bad enough for her, some boys start refusing. They want the money first. They take the money and then they say no. They say she never paid them. She paid them, she paid them in front of witnesses, and all the witnesses deny that she did. They shake their heads, they taunt her. *No. You never paid him. I never saw you. You pay me now and I'll go. I promise I will. I'll go. You pay me twenty, Maria.*

And the older boys, who have learned from their younger brothers what is going on, are coming up to her at the cash register and saying, "How about me, Maria? You know me, too. Come on, Maria, how about a twenty?" Those boys never go to the shed with her, never. Did she think they would? They never even promise, they just ask her for money. *You know me a long time, Maria.* They threaten, they wheedle. *Aren't I your friend, too, Maria?*

Nobody was Maria's friend.

Maria's matronly, watchful calm was gone—she looked wild and sullen and mean. She gave them looks full of hate, but she continued giving them money. She kept handing over the bills. Not even trying to bargain, or to argue or refuse, anymore. In a rage she did it—a silent rage. The more they taunted her, the more readily the twenty-dollar bills flew out of the till. Very little, perhaps nothing, was done to earn them now.

They're stoned all the time, Neil and his friends. All the time, now that they have this money. They see sweet streams of atoms flowing in the Formica tabletops. Their colored souls are shooting out under their fingernails. Maria has gone crazy, the store is bleeding money. How can this go on? How is it going to end? Maria must be into the strongbox now; the till at the end of the day wouldn't have enough for her. And all the time her mother keeps on baking buns and making pierogi, and the father keeps sweeping the sidewalk and greeting the customers. Nobody has told them. They go on just the same.

They had to find out on their own. They found a bill that Maria hadn't paid—something like that, somebody coming in with an unpaid bill—and they went to get the money to pay it, and they found that there was no money. The money wasn't where they kept it, in the safe or strongbox or wherever, and it wasn't anywhere else—the money was gone. That was how they found out.

Maria had succeeded in giving away everything. All they had saved, all their slowly accumulated profits, all the money on which they operated their business. Truly, everything. They could not pay the rent now, they could not pay the electricity bill or their suppliers. They could not keep on running the Confectionery. At least they believed they couldn't. Maybe they simply had not the heart to go on.

The store was locked. A sign went up on the door: "CLOSED UNTIL FURTHER NOTICE." Nearly a year went by before the place was reopened. It had been turned into a laundromat.

People said it was Maria's mother, that big, meek, bent-over woman, who insisted on bringing charges against her daughter. She was scared of the English language and the cash register, but she brought Maria into court. Of course, Maria could only be charged as a juvenile, and she could only be sent to a place for young offenders, and nothing could be done about the boys at all. They all lied anyway—they said it wasn't them. Maria's parents must have found jobs, they must have gone on living in

Victoria, because Lisa did. She still swam at the Y, and in a few years she was working at Eaton's, in Cosmetics. She was very glamorous and haughty by that time.

Neil always has vodka and orange juice for them to drink. That's Brenda's choice. She read somewhere that orange juice replenishes the vitamin C that the liquor leeches away, and she hopes the vodka really can't be detected on your breath. Neil tidies up the trailer, too—or so she thinks, because of the paper bag full of beer cans leaning against the cupboard, a pile of newspapers pushed together, not really folded, a pair of socks kicked into a corner. Maybe his housemate does it. A man called Gary, whom Brenda has never met or seen a picture of, and wouldn't know if they met on the street. Would he know her? He knows she comes here, he knows when; does he even know her name? Does he recognize her perfume, the smell of her sex, when he comes home in the evening? She likes the trailer, the way nothing in it has been made to look balanced or permanent. Things set down just wherever they will be convenient. No curtains or placemats, not even a pair of salt and pepper shakers—just the salt box and pepper tin, the way they come from the store. She loves the sight of Neil's bed—badly made, with a rough plaid blanket and a flat pillow, not a marriage bed or a bed of illness, comfort, complication. The bed of his lust and sleep, equally strenuous and oblivious. She loves the life of his body, so sure of its rights. She wants commands from him, never requests. She wants to be his territory.

It's only in the bathroom that the dirt bothers her a bit, like anybody else's dirt, and she wishes they'd done a better job of cleaning the toilet and the washbasin.

They sit at the table to drink, looking out through the trailer window at the steely, glittering, choppy water of the lake. Here the trees, exposed to lake winds, are almost bare. Birch bones and poplars stiff and bright as straw frame the water. There may be snow in another month. Certainly in two months. The seaway will close, the lake boats will be tied up for the winter, there'll be a wild landscape of ice thrown up between the shore and the open water. Neil says he doesn't know what he'll do, once the work on the beach is over. Maybe stay on, try to get another job. Maybe go on unemployment insurance for a while, get a snowmobile, enjoy the winter. Or he could go and look for work somewhere else, visit friends. He has friends all over the continent of North America and out of it. He has friends in Peru.

"So what happened?" Brenda says. "Don't you have any idea what happened to Maria?"

Neil says no, he has no idea.

The story won't leave Brenda alone; it stays with her like a coating on the tongue, a taste in the mouth.

"Well, maybe she got married," she says. "After she got out. Lots of people get married who are no beauties. That's for sure. She might've lost weight and be looking good even."

"Sure," says Neil. "Maybe have guys paying her, instead of the other way round."

"Or she might still be just sitting in one of those places. One of those places where they put people."

Now she feels a pain between her legs. Not unusual after one of these sessions. If she were to stand up at this moment, she'd feel a throb there, she'd feel the blood flowing back down through all the little veins and arteries that have been squashed and bruised, she'd feel herself throbbing like a big swollen blister.

She takes a long drink and says, "So how much money did you get out of her?"

"I never got anything," Neil says. "I just knew these other guys who did. It was my brother Jonathan made the money off her. I wonder what he'd say if I reminded him now."

"Older guys, too—you said older guys, too. Don't tell me you just sat back and watched and never got your share."

"That's what I *am* telling you. I never got anything."

Brenda clicks her tongue, tut-tut, and empties her glass and moves it around on the table, looking skeptically at the wet circles.

"Want another?" Neil says. He takes the glass out of her hand.

"I've got to go," she says. "Soon." You can make love in a hurry if you have to, but you need time for a fight. Is that what they're starting on? A fight? She feels edgy but happy. Her happiness is tight and private, not the sort that flows out from you and fuzzes everything up and makes you good-naturedly careless about what you say. The very opposite. She feels light and sharp and unconnected. When Neil brings her back a full glass, she takes a drink from it at once, to safeguard this feeling.

"You've got the same name as my husband," she says. "It's funny I never thought of that before."

She has thought of it before. She just hasn't mentioned it, knowing it's not something Neil would like to hear.

"Cornelius isn't the same as Neil," he says.

"It's Dutch. Some Dutch people shorten it to Neil."

"Yeah, but I'm not Dutch, and I wasn't named Cornelius, just Neil."

"Still, if his had been shortened you'd be named the same."

"His isn't shortened."

"I never said it was. I said if it had been."

"So why say that if it isn't?"

He must feel the same thing she does—the slow but irresistible rise of a new excitement, the need to say, and hear, dire things. What a sharp, releasing pleasure there is in the first blow, and what a dazzling temptation ahead—destruction. You don't stop to think why you want that destruction. You just do.

"Why do we have to drink every time?" Neil says abruptly. "Do we want to turn ourselves into alcoholics or something?"

Brenda takes a quick sip and pushes her glass away. "Who has to drink?" she says.

She thinks he means they should drink coffee, or Cokes. But he gets up and goes to the dresser where he keeps his clothes, opens a drawer, and says, "Come over here."

"I don't want to look at any of that stuff," she says.

"You don't even know what it is."

"Sure I do."

Of course she doesn't—not specifically.

"You think it's going to bite you?"

Brenda drinks again and keeps looking out the window. The sun is getting down in the sky already, pushing the bright light across the table to warm her hands.

"You don't approve," Neil says.

"I don't approve or disapprove," she says, aware of having lost some control, of not being as happy as she was. "I don't care what you do. That's you."

"I don't approve or disapprove," says Neil, in a mincing voice. "Don't care what you do."

That's the signal, which one or the other had to give. A flash of hate, pure meanness, like the glint of a blade. The signal that the fight can come out into the open. Brenda takes a deep drink, as if she very much deserved it. She feels a desolate satisfaction. She stands up and says, "Time for me to go."

"What if I'm not ready to go yet?" Neil says.

"I said me, not you."

"Oh. You got a car outside?"

"I can walk."

"That's five miles back to where the van is."

"People have walked five miles."

"In shoes like that?" says Neil. They both look at her yellow shoes, which match the appliquéd-satin birds on her turquoise sweater. Both things bought and worn for him!

"You didn't wear those shoes for walking," he says. "You wore them so every step you took would show off your fat arse."

She walks along the lakeshore road, in the gravel, which bruises her feet through the shoes and makes her pay attention to each step, lest she should twist an ankle. The afternoon is now too

cold for just a sweater. The wind off the lake blows at her sideways, and every time a vehicle passes, particularly a truck, an
eddy of stiff wind whirls around her and grit blows into her face.
Some of the trucks slow down, of course, and some cars do, too,
and men yell at her out of the windows. One car skids onto the
gravel and stops ahead of her. She stands still, she cannot think
what else to do, and after a moment he churns back onto the
pavement and she starts walking again.

That's all right, she's not in any real danger. She doesn't
even worry about being seen by someone she knows. She feels
too free to care. She thinks about the first time Neil came to the
Furniture Barn, how he put his arm around Samson's neck and
said, "Not much of a watchdog you got here, Ma'am." She
thought the "Ma'am" was impudent, phony, out of some old
Elvis Presley movie. And what he said next was worse. She
looked at Samson, and she said, "He's better at night." And Neil
said, "So am I." Impudent, swaggering, conceited, she thought.
And he's not young enough to get away with it. Her opinion
didn't even change so much the second time. What happened
was that all that became just something to get past. It was something she could let him know he didn't have to do. It was her job
to take his gifts seriously, so that he could be serious, too, and
easy and grateful. How was she sure so soon that what she didn't
like about him wasn't real?

When she's in the second mile, or maybe just the second
half of the first mile, the Mercury catches up to her. It pulls
onto the gravel across the road. She goes over and gets in. She
doesn't see why not. It doesn't mean that she is going to talk to
him, or be with him any longer than the few minutes it will take
to drive to the swamp road and the van. His presence doesn't
need to weigh on her any more than the grit blowing beside the
road.

She winds the window all the way down so that there
will be a rush of chilly wind across anything he may have to
say.

"I want to beg your pardon for the personal remarks," he says.

"Why?" she says. "It's true. It is fat."

"No."

"It is," she says, in a tone of bored finality that is quite sincere. It shuts him up for a few miles, until they've turned down the swamp road and are driving in under the trees.

"If you thought there was a needle there in the drawer, there wasn't."

"It isn't any of my business what there was," she says.

"All that was in there was some Percs and Quaaludes and a little hash."

She remembers a fight she had with Cornelius, one that almost broke their engagement. It wasn't the time he slapped her for smoking marijuana. They made that up quickly. It wasn't about anything to do with their own lives. They were talking about a man Cornelius worked with at the mine, and his wife, and their retarded child. This child was just a vegetable, Cornelius said; all it did was gibber away in a sort of pen in a corner of the living room and mess its pants. It was about six or seven years old, and that was all it would ever do. Cornelius said he believed that if anybody had a child like that they had a right to get rid of it. He said that was what he would do. No question about it. There were a lot of ways you could do it and never get caught, and he bet that was what a lot of people did. He and Brenda had a terrible fight about this. But all the time they were arguing and fighting Brenda suspected that this was not something Cornelius would really do. It was something he had to say he would do. To her. To her, he had to insist that he would do it. And this actually made her angrier at him than she would have been if she believed he was entirely and brutally sincere. He wanted her to argue with him about this. He wanted her protest, her horror, and why was that? Men wanted you to make a fuss, about disposing of vegetable babies or taking drugs or driving a car like a bat out of hell, and why was that? So they could have your marshmallow sissy goodness to preen against, with their hard showoff badness? So that they finally could give in to you, growling, and not have to be so bad and reckless anymore? Whatever it was, you got sick of it.

In the mine accident, Cornelius could have been crushed to death. He was working the night shift when it happened. In the great walls of rock salt an undercut is made, then there are holes drilled for explosives, and the charges are fitted in; an explosion goes off every night at five minutes to midnight. The huge slice of salt slides loose, to be started on its journey to the surface. Cornelius was lifted up in a cage on the end of the arm of the scaler. He was to break off the loose material on the roof and fix in the bolts that held it for the explosion. Something went wrong with the hydraulic controls he was operating—he stalled, tried for a little power and got a surge that lifted him, so that he saw the rock ceiling closing down on him like a lid. He ducked, the cage halted, a rocky outcrop struck him in the back.

He had worked in the mine for seven years before that and hardly ever spoke to Brenda about what it was like. Now he tells her. It's a world of its own, he says—caverns and pillars, miles out under the lake. If you get in a passage where there are no machines to light the gray walls, the salt-dusty air, and you turn your headlamp off, you can find out what real darkness is like, the darkness people on the surface of the earth never get to see. The machines stay down there forever. Some are assembled down there, taken down in parts; all are repaired there; and finally they're ransacked for usable parts, then piled into a dead-end passage that is sealed up—a tomb for these underground machines. They make a ferocious noise all the time they're working; the noise of the machines and the ventilating fans cuts out any human voice. And now there's a new machine that can do what Cornelius went up in the cage to do. It can do it by itself, without a man.

Brenda doesn't know if he misses being down there. He says

he doesn't. He says he just can't look at the surface of the water without seeing all that underneath, which nobody who hasn't seen it could imagine.

Neil and Brenda drive along under the trees, where suddenly you could hardly feel the wind at all.

"Also, I did take some money," Neil says. "I got forty dollars, which, compared to what some guys got, was just nothing. I swear that's all, forty dollars. I never got any more."

She doesn't say anything.

"I wasn't looking to confess it," he says. "I just wanted to talk about it. Then what pisses me off is I lied anyway."

Now that she can hear his voice better, she notices that it's nearly as flat and tired as her own. She sees his hands on the wheel and thinks what a hard time she would have describing what he looks like. At a distance—in the car, waiting for her—he's always been a bright blur, his presence a relief and a promise. Close up, he's been certain separate areas—silky or toughened skin, wiry hair or shaved prickles, smells that are unique or shared with other men. But it's chiefly an energy, a quality of his self that she can see in his blunt, short fingers or the tanned curve of his forehead. And even to call it energy is not exact—it's more like the sap of him, rising from the roots, clear and on the move, filling him to bursting. That's what she has set herself to follow—the sap, the current, under the skin, as if that were the one true thing.

If she turned sideways now, she would see him for what he is—that tanned curved forehead, the receding fringe of curly brown hair, heavy eyebrows with a few gray hairs in them, deep-set light-colored eyes, and a mouth that enjoys itself, rather sulky and proud. A boyish man beginning to age—though he still feels light and wild on top of her, after Cornelius's bulk settling down possessively, like a ton of blankets. A responsibility, Brenda feels then. Is she going to feel the same about this one?

Neil turns the car around, he points it ready to drive back, and it's time for her to get out and go across to the van. He takes his hands off the wheel with the engine running, flexes his fingers, then grabs the wheel hard again—hard enough, you'd think, to squeeze it to pulp. "Christ, don't get out yet!" he says. "Don't get out of the car!"

She hasn't even put a hand on the door, she hasn't made a move to leave. Doesn't he know what's happening? Maybe you need the experience of a lot of married fights to know it. To know that what you think—and, for a while, hope—is the absolute end for you can turn out to be only the start of a new stage, a continuation. That's what's happening, that's what has happened. He has lost some of his sheen for her; he may not get it back. Probably the same goes for her, with him. She feels his heaviness and anger and surprise. She feels that also in herself. She thinks that up till now was easy.

Meneseteung

Columbine, bloodroot,
And wild bergamot,
Gathering armfuls,
Giddily we go.

Offerings the book is called. Gold lettering on a dull-blue cover. The author's full name underneath: Almeda Joynt Roth. The local paper, the *Vidette*, referred to her as "our poetess." There seems to be a mixture of respect and contempt, both for her calling and for her sex—or for their predictable conjuncture. In the front of the book is a photograph, with the photographer's name in one corner, and the date: 1865. The book was published later, in 1873.

The poetess has a long face; a rather long nose; full, sombre dark eyes, which seem ready to roll down her cheeks like giant tears; a lot of dark hair gathered around her face in droopy rolls and curtains. A streak of gray hair plain to see, although she is, in this picture, only twenty-five. Not a pretty girl but the sort of woman who may age well, who probably won't get fat. She wears a tucked and braid-trimmed dark dress or jacket, with a lacy, floppy arrangement of white material—frills or a bow—filling the deep V at the neck. She also wears a hat, which might be made of velvet, in a dark color to match the dress. It's the untrimmed, shapeless hat, something like a soft beret, that makes me see artistic intentions, or at least a shy and stubborn eccentricity, in this young woman, whose long neck and forward-inclining head indicate as well that she is tall and slender and somewhat awkward. From the waist up, she looks like a young nobleman of another century. But perhaps it was the fashion.

"In 1854," she writes in the preface to her book, "my father brought us—my mother, my sister Catherine, my brother William, and me—to the wilds of Canada West (as it then was). My father was a harness-maker by trade, but a cultivated man who could quote by heart from the Bible, Shakespeare, and the writings of Edmund Burke. He prospered in this newly opened land and was able to set up a harness and leather-goods store, and after a year to build the comfortable house in which I live (alone) today. I was fourteen years old, the eldest of the children, when we came into this country from Kingston, a town whose handsome streets I have not seen again but often remember. My sister was eleven and my brother nine. The third summer that we lived here, my brother and sister were taken ill of a prevalent fever and died within a few days of each other. My dear mother did not regain her spirits after this blow to our family. Her health declined, and after another three years she died. I then became housekeeper to my father and was happy to make his home for twelve years, until he died suddenly one morning at his shop.

"From my earliest years I have delighted in verse and I have occupied myself—and sometimes allayed my griefs, which have been no more, I know, than any sojourner on earth must encounter—with many floundering efforts at its composition. My fingers, indeed, were always too clumsy for crochetwork, and those dazzling productions of embroidery which one sees often today—the overflowing fruit and flower baskets, the little Dutch boys, the bonneted maidens with their watering cans—have likewise proved to be beyond my skill. So I offer instead, as the product of my leisure hours, these rude posies, these ballads, couplets, reflections."

Titles of some of the poems: "Children at Their Games," "The Gypsy Fair," "A Visit to My Family," "Angels in the Snow," "Champlain at the Mouth of the Meneseteung," "The Passing of the Old Forest," and "A Garden Medley." There are other, shorter poems, about birds and wildflowers and snow-storms. There is some comically intentioned doggerel about what people are thinking about as they listen to the sermon in church.

"Children at Their Games": The writer, a child, is playing with her brother and sister—one of those games in which children on different sides try to entice and catch each other. She plays on in the deepening twilight, until she realizes that she is alone, and much older. Still she hears the (ghostly) voices of her brother and sister calling. *Come over, come over, let Meda come over.* (Perhaps Almeda was called Meda in the family, or perhaps she shortened her name to fit the poem.)

"The Gypsy Fair": The Gypsies have an encampment near the town, a "fair," where they sell cloth and trinkets, and the writer as a child is afraid that she may be stolen by them, taken away from her family. Instead, her family has been taken away from her, stolen by Gypsies she can't locate or bargain with.

"A Visit to My Family": A visit to the cemetery, a one-sided conversation.

"Angels in the Snow": The writer once taught her brother and sister to make "angels" by lying down in the snow and moving their arms to create wing shapes. Her brother always jumped up carelessly, leaving an angel with a crippled wing. Will this be made perfect in Heaven, or will he be flying with his own makeshift, in circles?

"Champlain at the Mouth of the Meneseteung": This poem celebrates the popular, untrue belief that the explorer sailed down the eastern shore of Lake Huron and landed at the mouth of the major river.

"The Passing of the Old Forest": A list of all the trees—

their names, appearance, and uses—that were cut down in the original forest, with a general description of the bears, wolves, eagles, deer, waterfowl.

"A Garden Medley": Perhaps planned as a companion to the forest poem. Catalogue of plants brought from European countries, with bits of history and legend attached, and final Canadianness resulting from this mixture.

The poems are written in quatrains or couplets. There are a couple of attempts at sonnets, but mostly the rhyme scheme is simple—*a b a b* or *a b c b*. The rhyme used is what was once called "masculine" ("shore"/"before"), though once in a while it is "feminine" ("quiver"/"river"). Are those terms familiar anymore? No poem is unrhymed.

II

> *White roses cold as snow*
> *Bloom where those "'angels" lie.*
> *Do they but rest below*
> *Or, in God's wonder, fly?*

In 1879, Almeda Roth was still living in the house at the corner of Pearl and Dufferin streets, the house her father had built for his family. The house is there today; the manager of the liquor store lives in it. It's covered with aluminum siding; a closed-in porch has replaced the veranda. The woodshed, the fence, the gates, the privy, the barn—all these are gone. A photograph taken in the eighteen-eighties shows them all in place. The house and fence look a little shabby, in need of paint, but perhaps that is just because of the bleached-out look of the brownish photograph. The lace-curtained windows look like white eyes. No big shade tree is in sight, and, in fact, the tall elms that overshadowed the town until the nineteen-fifties, as well as the maples that shade it now, are skinny young trees with rough fences around them to protect them from the cows. Without the shelter of those trees, there is a great exposure—back yards, clotheslines, woodpiles, patchy sheds and barns and privies—all bare, exposed, provisional-looking. Few houses would have anything like a lawn, just a patch of plantains and anthills and raked dirt. Perhaps petunias growing on top of a stump, in a round box. Only the main street is gravelled; the other streets are dirt roads, muddy or dusty according to season. Yards must be fenced to keep animals out. Cows are tethered in vacant lots or pastured in back yards, but sometimes they get loose. Pigs get loose, too, and dogs roam free or nap in a lordly way on the boardwalks. The town has taken root, it's not going to vanish, yet it still has some of the look of an encampment. And, like an encampment, it's busy all the time—full of people, who, within the town, usually walk wherever they're going; full of animals, which leave horse buns, cow pats, dog turds that ladies have to hitch up their skirts for; full of the noise of building and of drivers shouting at their horses and of the trains that come in several times a day.

I read about that life in the *Vidette*.

The population is younger than it is now, than it will ever be again. People past fifty usually don't come to a raw, new place. There are quite a few people in the cemetery already, but most of them died young, in accidents or childbirth or epidemics. It's youth that's in evidence in town. Children—boys—rove through the streets in gangs. School is compulsory for only four months a year, and there are lots of occasional jobs that even a child of eight or nine can do—pulling flax, holding horses, delivering groceries, sweeping the boardwalk in front of stores. A good deal of time they spend looking for adventures. One day they follow an old woman, a drunk nicknamed Queen Aggie. They get her into a wheelbarrow and trundle her all over town, then dump her into a ditch to sober her up. They also spend a lot of time around the railway station. They jump on shunting cars and dart between them and dare each other to take chances, which once in a while result in their getting maimed or killed. And they keep an eye out for any strangers coming into town. They follow them, offer to carry their bags, and direct them (for a five-cent piece) to a hotel. Strangers who don't look so prosperous are taunted and tormented. Speculation surrounds all of them—it's like a cloud of flies. Are they coming to town to start up a new business, to persuade people to invest in some scheme, to sell cures or gimmicks, to preach on the street corners? All these things are possible any day of the week. Be on your guard, the *Vidette* tells people. These are times of opportunity and danger. Tramps, confidence men, hucksters, shysters, plain thieves are travelling the roads, and particularly the railroads. Thefts are announced: money invested and never seen again, a pair of trousers taken from the clothesline, wood from the woodpile, eggs from the henhouse. Such incidents increase in the hot weather.

Hot weather brings accidents, too. More horses run wild then, upsetting buggies. Hands caught in the wringer while doing the washing, a man lopped in two at the sawmill, a leaping boy killed in a fall of lumber at the lumberyard. Nobody sleeps well. Babies wither with summer complaint, and fat people can't catch their breath. Bodies must be buried in a hurry. One day a man goes through the streets ringing a cowbell and calling, "Repent! Repent!" It's not a stranger this time, it's a young man who works at the butcher shop. Take him home, wrap him in cold wet cloths, give him some nerve medicine, keep him in bed, pray for his wits. If he doesn't recover, he must go to the asylum.

Almeda Roth's house faces on Dufferin Street, which is a street of considerable respectability. On this street, merchants, a mill owner, an operator of salt wells have their houses. But Pearl Street, which her back windows overlook and her back gate opens onto, is another story. Workmen's houses are adjacent to hers. Small but decent row houses—that is all right. Things deteriorate toward the end of the block, and the next, last one becomes dismal. Nobody but the poorest people, the unrespectable and undeserving poor, would live there at the edge of a boghole (drained since then), called the Pearl Street Swamp. Bushy and luxuriant weeds grow there, makeshift shacks have been put up, there are piles of refuse and debris and crowds of runty children, slops are flung from doorways. The town tries to compel these people to build privies, but they would just as soon go in the bushes. If a gang of boys goes down there in search of adventure, it's likely they'll get more than they bargained for. It is said that even the town constable won't go down Pearl Street on a Saturday night. Almeda Roth has never walked past the row housing. In one of those houses lives the young girl Annie, who helps her with her housecleaning. That young girl herself, being a decent girl, has never walked down to the last block or the swamp. No decent woman ever would.

But that same swamp, lying to the east of Almeda Roth's house, presents a fine sight at dawn. Almeda sleeps at the back of the house. She keeps to the same bedroom she once shared with her sister Catherine—she would not think of moving to the large front bedroom, where her mother used to lie in bed all day, and which was later the solitary domain of her father. From her window she can see the sun rising, the swamp mist filling with light, the bulky, nearest trees floating against that mist and the trees behind turning transparent. Swamp oaks, soft maples, tamarack, bitternut.

III

Here where the river meets the
inland sea,
Spreading her blue skirts from the
solemn wood,
I think of birds and beasts and
vanished men,
Whose pointed dwellings on these
pale sands stood.

One of the strangers who arrived at the railway station a few years ago was Jarvis Poulter, who now occupies the next house to

Almeda Roth's—separated from hers by a vacant lot, which he has bought, on Dufferin Street. The house is plainer than the Roth house and has no fruit trees or flowers planted around it. It is understood that this is a natural result of Jarvis Poulter's being a widower and living alone. A man may keep his house decent, but he will never—if he is a proper man—do much to decorate it. Marriage forces him to live with more ornament as well as sentiment, and it protects him, also, from the extremities of his own nature—from a frigid parsimony or a luxuriant sloth, from squalor, and from excessive sleeping or reading, drinking, smoking, or freethinking.

In the interests of economy, it is believed, a certain estimable gentleman of our town persists in fetching water form the public tap and supplementing his fuel supply by picking up the loose coal along the railway track. Does he think to repay the town or the railway company with a supply of free salt?

This is the *Vidette*, full of shy jokes, innuendo, plain accusation that no newspaper would get away with today. It's Jarvis Poulter they're talking about—though in other passages he is spoken of with great respect, as a civil magistrate, an employer, a churchman. He is close, that's all. An eccentric, to a degree. All of which may be a result of his single condition, his widower's life. Even carrying his water from the town tap and filling his coal pail along the railway track. This is a decent citizen, prosperous: a tall—slightly paunchy?—man in a dark suit with polished boots. A beard? Black hair streaked with gray. A severe and self-possessed air, and a large pale wart among the bushy hairs of one eyebrow? People talk about a young, pretty, beloved wife, dead in childbirth or some horrible accident, like a house fire or a railway disaster. There is no ground for this, but it adds interest. All he has told them is that his wife is dead.

He came to this part of the country looking for oil. The first oil well in the world was sunk in Lambton County, south of here, in the eighteen-fifties. Drilling for oil, Jarvis Poulter discovered salt. He set to work to make the most of that. When he walks home from church with Almeda Roth, he tells her about his salt wells. They are twelve hundred feet deep. Heated water is pumped down into them, and that dissolves the salt. Then the brine is pumped to the surface. It is poured into great evaporator pans over slow, steady fires, so that the water is steamed off and the pure, excellent salt remains. A commodity for which the demand will never fail.

"The salt of the earth," Almeda says.

"Yes," he says, frowning. He may think this disrespectful. She did not intend it so. He speaks of competitors in other towns who are following his lead and trying to hog the market. Fortunately, their wells are not drilled so deep, or their evaporating is not done so efficiently. There is salt everywhere under this land, but it is not so easy to come by as some people think.

Does this not mean, Almeda says, that there was once a great sea?

Very likely, Jarvis Poulter says. Very likely. He goes on to tell her about other enterprises of his—a brickyard, a limekiln. And he explains to her how this operates, and where the good clay is found. He also owns two farms, whose woodlots supply the fuel for his operations.

Among the couples strolling home from church on a recent, sunny Sabbath morning we noted a certain salty gentleman and literary lady, not perhaps in their first youth but by no means blighted by the frosts of age. May we surmise?

This kind of thing pops up in the *Vidette* all the time.

May they surmise, and is this courting? Almeda Roth has a bit of money, which her father left her, and she has her house. She is not too old to have a couple of children. She is a good enough housekeeper, with the tendency toward fancy iced cakes and decorated tarts that is seen fairly often in old maids. (Honorable mention at the Fall Fair.) There is nothing wrong with her looks, and naturally she is in better shape than most married women of her age, not having been loaded down with work and children. But why was she passed over in her earlier, more marriageable years, in a place that needs women to be partnered and fruitful? She was a rather gloomy girl—that may have been the trouble. The deaths of her brother and sister, and then of her mother, who lost her reason, in fact, a year before she died, and lay in her bed talking nonsense—those weighed on her, so she was not lively company. And all that reading and poetry—it seemed more of a drawback, a barrier, an obsession, in the young girl than in the middle-aged woman, who needed something, after all, to fill her time. Anyway, it's five years since her book was published, so perhaps she has got over that. Perhaps it was the proud, bookish father encouraging her?

Everyone takes it for granted that Almeda Roth is thinking of Jarvis Poulter as a husband and would say yes if he asked her. And she is thinking of him. She doesn't want to get her hopes up too much, she doesn't want to make a fool of herself. She would like a signal. If he attended church on Sunday evenings, there would be a chance, during some months of the year, to walk home after dark. He would carry a lantern. (There is as yet no street lighting in town.) He would swing the lantern to light the way in front of the lady's feet and observe their narrow and delicate shape. He might catch her arm as they step off the boardwalk. But he does not go to church at night.

Nor does he call for her, and walk with her *to* church on Sunday mornings. That would be a declaration. He walks her home, past his gate as far as hers; he lifts his hat then and leaves her. She does not invite him to come in—a woman living alone could never do such a thing. As soon as a man and woman of almost any age are alone together within four walls, it is assumed that anything may happen. Spontaneous combustion, instant fornication, an attack of passion. Brute instinct, triumph of the senses. What possibilities men and women must see in each other to infer such dangers. Or, believing in the dangers, how often they must think about the possibilities.

When they walk side by side, she can smell his shaving soap, the barber's oil, his pipe tobacco, the wool and linen and leather smell of his manly clothes. The correct, orderly, heavy clothes are like those she used to brush and starch and iron for her father. She misses that job—her father's appreciation, his dark, kind authority. Jarvis Poulter's garments, his smell, his movements all cause the skin on the side of her body next to him to tingle hopefully, and a meek shiver raises the hairs on her arms. Is this to be taken as a sign of love? She thinks of him coming into her—*their*—bedroom in his long underwear and his hat. She knows this outfit is ridiculous, but in her mind he does not look so; he has the solemn effrontery of a figure in a dream. He comes into the room and lies down on the bed beside her, preparing to take her in his arms. Surely he removes his hat? She doesn't know, for at this point a fit of welcome and submission overtakes her, a buried gasp. He would be her husband.

One thing she has noticed about married women, and that is how many of them have to go about creating their husbands. They have to start ascribing preferences, opinions, dictatorial ways. Oh, yes, they say, my husband is very particular. He won't touch turnips. He won't eat fried meat. (Or he will only eat fried meat.) He likes me to wear blue (brown) all the time. He can't stand organ music. He hates to see a woman go out bareheaded. He would kill me if I took one puff of tobacco. This way, bewildered, sidelong-looking men are made over, made into husbands, heads of households. Almeda Roth cannot imagine herself doing that. She wants a man who doesn't have to be made, who is firm already and determined and mysterious to her. She does not look for companionship. Men—except for her father—seem to her deprived in some way, incurious. No doubt that is necessary, so that they will do what they have to do. Would she herself, knowing that there was salt in the earth, discover how to get it out and sell it? Not likely. She would be thinking about the ancient sea. That kind of speculation is what Jarvis Poulter has, quite properly, no time for.

Instead of calling for her and walking her to church, Jarvis Poulter might make another, more venturesome declaration. He could hire a horse and take her for a drive out to the country. If he did this, she would be both glad and sorry. Glad to be beside him, driven by him, receiving this attention from him in front of the world. And sorry to have the countryside removed for her— filmed over, in a way, by his talk and preoccupations. The countryside that she has written about in her poems actually takes diligence and determination to see. Some things must be disregarded. Manure piles, of course, and boggy fields full of high, charred stumps, and great heaps of brush waiting for a good day for burning. The meandering creeks have been straightened, turned into ditches with high, muddy banks. Some of the crop fields and pasture fields are fenced with big, clumsy uprooted stumps; others are held in a crude stitchery of rail fences. The trees have all been cleared back to the woodlots. And the woodlots are all second growth. No trees along the roads or lanes or around the farmhouses, except a few that are newly planted, young and weedy-looking. Clusters of log barns—the grand barns that are to dominate the countryside for the next hundred years are just beginning to be built—and mean-looking log houses, and every four or five miles a ragged little settlement with a church and school and store and a blacksmith shop. A raw countryside just wrenched from the forest, but swarming with people. Every hundred acres is a farm, every farm has a family, most families have ten or twelve children. (This is the country that will send out wave after wave of settlers—it's already starting to send them—to northern Ontario and the West.) It's true that you can gather wildflowers in spring in the woodlots, but you'd have to walk through herds of horned cows to get to them.

IV

The Gypsies have departed.
Their camping-ground is bare.
Oh, boldly would I bargain now
At the Gypsy Fair.

Almeda suffers a good deal from sleeplessness, and the doctor has given her bromides and nerve medicine. She takes the bromides, but the drops gave her dreams that were too vivid and disturbing, so she has put the bottle by for an emergency. She told the doctor her eyeballs felt dry, like hot glass, and her joints ached. Don't read so much, he said, don't study; get yourself good and tired out with housework, take exercise. He believes that her troubles would clear up if she got married. He believes this in spite of the fact that most of his nerve medicine is prescribed for married women.

So Almeda cleans house and helps clean the church, she lends a hand to friends who are wallpapering or getting ready for a wedding, she bakes one of her famous cakes for the Sunday-school picnic. On a hot Saturday in August, she decides to make some grape jelly. Little jars of grape jelly will make fine Christmas presents, or offerings to the sick. But she started late in the day and the jelly is not made by nightfall. In fact, the hot pulp has just been dumped into the cheesecloth bag to strain out the juice. Almeda drinks some tea and eats a slice of cake with butter (a childish indulgence of hers), and that's all she wants for supper. She washes her hair at the sink and sponges off her body to be clean for Sunday. She doesn't light a lamp. She lies down on the bed with the window wide open and a sheet just up to her waist, and she does feel wonderfully tired. She can even feel a little breeze.

When she wakes up, the night seems fiery hot and full of threats. She lies sweating on her bed, and she has the impression that the noises she hears are knives and saws and axes—all angry implements chopping and jabbing and boring within her head. But it isn't true. As she comes further awake, she recognizes the sounds that she has heard sometimes before—the fracas of a summer Saturday night on Pearl Street. Usually the noise centers on a fight. People are drunk, there is a lot of protest and encouragement concerning the fight, somebody will scream, "Murder!" Once, there was a murder. But it didn't happen in a fight. An old man was stabbed to death in his shack, perhaps for a few dollars he kept in the mattress.

She gets out of bed and goes to the window. The night sky is clear, with no moon and with bright stars. Pegasus hangs straight ahead, over the swamp. Her father taught her that constellation—automatically, she counts its stars. Now she can make out distinct voices, individual contributions to the row. Some people, like herself, have evidently been wakened from sleep. "Shut up!" they are yelling. "Shut up that caterwauling or I'm going to come down and tan the arse off yez!"

But nobody shuts up. It's as if there were a ball of fire rolling up Pearl Street, shooting off sparks—only the fire is noise; it's yells and laughter and shrieks and curses, and the sparks are voices that shoot off alone. Two voices gradually distinguish themselves—a rising and falling howling cry and a steady throbbing, low-pitched stream of abuse that contains all those words which Almeda associates with danger and depravity and foul smells and disgusting sights. Someone—the person crying out, "Kill me! Kill me now!"—is being beaten. A woman is being beaten. She keeps crying, "Kill me! Kill me!" and sometimes her mouth seems choked with blood. Yet there is something taunting and triumphant about her cry. There is something theatrical about it. And the people around are calling out, "Stop it! Stop that!" or "Kill her! Kill her!" in a frenzy, as if at the theatre or a sporting match or a prizefight. Yes, thinks Almeda, she has noticed that before—it is always partly a charade with these people; there is a clumsy sort of parody, an exaggeration, a missed connection. As if anything they did—even a murder—might be something they didn't quite believe but were powerless to stop.

Now there is the sound of something thrown—a chair, a plank?—and of a woodpile or part of a fence giving way. A lot of newly surprised cries, the sound of running, people getting out of the way, and the commotion has come much closer. Almeda can see a figure in a light dress, bent over and running. That will be the woman. She has got hold of something like a stick of wood or a shingle, and she turns and flings it at the darker figure running after her.

"Ah, go get her!" the voices cry. "Go baste her one!"

Many fall back now; just the two figures come on and grapple, and break loose again, and finally fall down against Almeda's fence. The sound they make becomes very confused—gagging, vomiting, grunting, pounding. Then a long, vibrating, choking sound of pain and self-abasement, self-abandonment, which could come from either or both of them.

Almeda has backed away from the window and sat down on the bed. Is that the sound of murder she has heard? What is to be done, what is she to do? She must light a lantern, she must go downstairs and light a lantern—she must go out into the yard, she must go downstairs. Into the yard. The lantern. She falls over on her bed and pulls the pillow to her face. In a minute. The stairs, the lantern. She sees herself already down there, in the back hall, drawing the bolt of the back door. She falls asleep.

She wakes, startled, in the early light. She thinks there is a big crow sitting on her windowsill, talking in a disapproving but unsurprised way about the events of the night before. "Wake up and move the wheelbarrow!" it says to her, scolding, and she understands that it means something else by "wheelbarrow"—something foul and sorrowful. Then she is awake and sees that there is no such bird. She gets up at once and looks out the window.

Down against her fence there is a pale lump pressed—a body.

Wheelbarrow.

She puts a wrapper over her nightdress and goes downstairs. The front rooms are still shadowy, the blinds down in the kitchen. Something goes *plop, plup,* in a leisurely, censorious way, reminding her of the conversation of the crow. It's just the grape juice, straining overnight. She pulls the bolt and goes out the back door. Spiders have draped their webs over the doorway in the night, and the hollyhocks are drooping, heavy with dew. By the fence, she parts the sticky hollyhocks and looks down and she can see.

A woman's body heaped up there, turned on her side with her face squashed down into the earth. Almeda can't see her face. But there is a bare breast let loose, brown nipple pulled long like a cow's teat, and a bare haunch and leg, the haunch showing a bruise as big as a sunflower. The unbruised skin is grayish, like a plucked, raw drumstick. Some kind of nightgown or all-purpose dress she has on. Smelling of vomit. Urine, drink, vomit.

Barefoot, in her nightgown and flimsy wrapper, Almeda runs away. She runs around the side of her house between the apple trees and the veranda; she opens the front gate and flees down Dufferin Street to Jarvis Poulter's house, which is the nearest to hers. She slaps the flat of her hand many times against the door.

"There is the body of a woman," she says when Jarvis Poulter appears at last. He is in his dark trousers, held up with braces, and his shirt is half unbuttoned, his face unshaven, his hair standing up on his head. "Mr. Poulter, excuse me. A body of a woman. At my back gate."

He looks at her fiercely. "Is she dead?"

His breath is dank, his face creased, his eyes bloodshot.

"Yes. I think murdered," says Almeda. She can see a little of his cheerless front hall. His hat on a chair. "In the night I woke up. I heard a racket down on Pearl Street," she says, struggling to keep her voice low and sensible. "I could hear this—pair. I could hear a man and a woman fighting."

He picks up his hat and puts it on his head. He closes and

locks the front door, and puts the key in his pocket. They walk along the boardwalk and she sees that she is in her bare feet. She holds back what she feels a need to say next—that she is responsible, she could have run out with a lantern, she could have screamed (but who needed more screams?), she could have beat the man off. She could have run for help then, not now.

They turn down Pearl Street, instead of entering the Roth yard. Of course the body is still there. Hunched up, half bare, the same as before.

Jarvis Poulter doesn't hurry or halt. He walks straight over to the body and looks down at it, nudges the leg with the toe of his boot, just as you'd nudge a dog or a sow.

"You," he says, not too loudly but firmly, and nudges again.

Almeda tastes bile at the back of her throat.

"Alive," says Jarvis Poulter, and the woman confirms this. She stirs, she grunts weakly.

Almeda says, "I will get the doctor." If she had touched the woman, if she had forced herself to touch her, she would not have made such a mistake.

"Wait," says Jarvis Poulter. "Wait. Let's see if she can get up."

"Get up, now," he says to the woman. "Come on. Up, now. Up."

Now a startling thing happens. The body heaves itself onto all fours, the head is lifted—the hair all matted with blood and vomit—and the woman begins to bang this head, hard and rhythmically, against Almeda Roth's picket fence. As she bangs her head, she finds her voice and lets out an openmouthed yowl, full of strength and what sounds like an anguished pleasure.

"Far from dead," says Jarvis Poulter. "And I wouldn't bother the doctor."

"There's blood," says Almeda as the woman turns her smeared face.

"From her nose," he says. "Not fresh." He bends down and catches the horrid hair close to the scalp to stop the head-banging.

"You stop that, now," he says. "Stop it. Gwan home, now. Gwan home, where you belong." The sound coming out of the woman's mouth has stopped. He shakes her head slightly, warning her, before he lets go of her hair. "Gwan home!"

Released, the woman lunges forward, pulls herself to her feet. She can walk. She weaves and stumbles down the street, making intermittent, cautious noises of protest. Jarvis Poulter watches her for a moment to make sure that she's on her way. Then he finds a large burdock leaf, on which he wipes his hand. He says, "There goes your dead body!"

The back gate being locked, they walk around to the front. The front gate stands open. Almeda still feels sick. Her abdomen is bloated; she is hot and dizzy.

"The front door is locked," she says faintly. "I came out by the kitchen." If only he would leave her, she could go straight to the privy. But he follows. He follows her as far as the back door and into the back hall. He speaks to her in a tone of harsh joviality that she has never before heard from him. "No need for alarm," he says. "It's only the consequences of drink. A lady oughtn't to be living alone so close to a bad neighborhood." He takes hold of her arm just above the elbow. She can't open her mouth to speak to him, to say thank you. If she opened her mouth, she would retch.

What Jarvis Poulter feels for Almeda Roth at this moment is just what he has not felt during all those circumspect walks and all his own solitary calculations of her probable worth, undoubted respectability, adequate comeliness. He has not been able to imagine her as a wife. Now that is possible. He is sufficiently stirred by her loosened hair—prematurely gray but thick and soft—her flushed face, her light clothing, which nobody but a husband should see. And by her indiscretion, her agitation, her foolishness, her need?

"I will call on you later," he says to her. "I will walk with you to church."

At the corner of Pearl and Dufferin streets last Sunday morning there was discovered, by a lady resident there, the body of a certain woman of Pearl Street, thought to be dead but only, as it turned out, dead drunk. She was roused from her heavenly—or otherwise—stupor by the firm persuasion of Mr. Poulter, a neighbour and a Civil Magistrate, who had been summoned by the lady resident. Incidents of this sort, unseemly, troublesome, and disgraceful to our town, have of late become all too common.

V

I sit at the bottom of sleep,
As on the floor of the sea.
And fanciful Citizens of the Deep
Are graciously greeting me.

As soon as Jarvis Poulter has gone and she has heard her front gate close, Almeda rushes to the privy. Her relief is not complete, however, and she realizes that the pain and fullness in her lower body come from an accumulation of menstrual blood that has not yet started to flow. She closes and locks the back door. Then, remembering Jarvis Poulter's words about church, she writes on a piece of paper, "I am not well, and wish to rest today." She sticks this firmly into the outside frame of the little window in the front door. She locks that door, too. She is trembling, as if from a great shock or danger. But she builds a fire, so that she can make tea. She boils water, measures the tea leaves, makes a large pot of tea, whose steam and smell sicken her further. She pours out a cup while the tea is still quite weak and adds to it several dark drops of nerve medicine. She sits to drink it without raising the kitchen blind. There, in the middle of the floor, is the cheesecloth bag hanging on its broom handle between the two chairbacks. The grape pulp and juice has stained the swollen cloth a dark purple. *Plop, plup*, into the basin beneath. She can't sit and look at such a thing. She takes her cup, the teapot, and the bottle of medicine into the dining room.

She is still sitting there when the horses start to go by on the way to church, stirring up clouds of dust. The roads will be getting hot as ashes. She is there when the gate is opened and a man's confident steps sound on her veranda. Her hearing is so sharp she seems to hear the paper taken out of the frame and unfolded—she can almost hear him reading it, hear the words in his mind. Then the footsteps go the other way, down the steps. The gate closes. An image comes to her of tombstones—it makes her laugh. Tombstones are marching down the street on their little booted feet, their long bodies inclined forward, their expressions preoccupied and severe. The church bells are ringing.

Then the clock in the hall strikes twelve and an hour has passed.

The house is getting hot. She drinks more tea and adds more medicine. She knows that the medicine is affecting her. It is responsible for her extraordinary languor, her perfect immobility, her unresisting surrender to her surroundings. That is all right. It seems necessary.

Her surroundings—some of her surroundings—in the dining room are these: walls covered with dark-green garlanded wallpaper, lace curtains and mulberry velvet curtains on the windows, a table with a crocheted cloth and a bowl of wax fruit, a pinkish-gray carpet with nosegays of blue and pink roses, a sideboard spread with embroidered runners and holding various patterned plates and jugs and the silver tea things. A lot of things to watch. For every one of these patterns, decorations seems charged with life, ready to move and flow and alter. Or possibly to explode. Almeda Roth's occupation throughout the day is to keep an eye on them. Not to prevent their alteration so much as to catch them at it—to understand it, to be a part of it. So much is going on in this room that there is no need to leave it. There is not even the thought of leaving it.

Of course, Almeda in her observations cannot escape words. She may think she can, but she can't. Soon this glowing and swelling begins to suggest words—not specific words but a flow of words somewhere, just about ready to make themselves known to her. Poems, even. Yes, again, poems. Or one poem. Isn't that the idea—one very great poem that will contain everything and, oh, that will make all the other poems, the poems she has written, inconsequential, mere trial and error, mere rags? Stars and flowers and birds and trees and angels in the snow and dead children at twilight—that is not the half of it. You have to get in the obscene racket on Pearl Street and the polished toe of Jarvis Poulter's boot and the plucked-chicken haunch with its blue-black flower. Almeda is a long way now from human sympathies or fears or cozy household considerations. She doesn't think about what could be done for that woman or about keeping Jarvis Poulter's dinner warm and hanging his long underwear on the line. The basin of grape juice has overflowed and is running over her kitchen floor, staining the boards of the floor, and the stain will never come out.

She has to think of so many things at once—Champlain and the naked Indians and the salt deep in the earth, but as well as the salt the money, the money-making intent brewing forever in heads like Jarvis Poulter's. Also the brutal storms of winter and the clumsy and benighted deeds on Pearl Street. The changes of climate are often violent, and if you think about it there is no peace even in the stars. All this can be borne only if it is channelled into a poem, and the word "channelled" is appropriate, because the name of the poem will be—it *is*—"The Meneseteung." The name of the poem is the name of the river. No, in fact it is the river, the Meneseteung, that is the poem—with its deep holes and rapids and blissful pools under the summer trees and its grinding blocks of ice thrown up at the end of winter and its desolating spring floods. Almeda looks deep, deep into the river of her mind and into the tablecloth, and she sees the crocheted roses floating. They look bunchy and foolish, her mother's crocheted roses—they don't look much like real flowers. But their effort, their floating independence, their pleasure in their silly selves do seem to her so admirable. A hopeful sign. *Meneseteung.*

She doesn't leave the room until dusk, when she goes out to the privy again and discovers that she is bleeding, her flow has started. She will have to get a towel, strap it on, bandage herself up. Never before, in health, has she passed a whole day in her nightdress. She doesn't feel any particular anxiety about this. On her way through the kitchen, she walks through the pool of grape juice. She knows that she will have to mop it up, but not yet, and she walks upstairs leaving purple footprints and smelling her escaping blood and the sweat of her body that has sat all day in the closed hot room.

No need for alarm.

For she hasn't thought that crocheted roses could float away or that tombstones could hurry down the street. She doesn't mistake that for reality, and neither does she mistake anything else for reality, and that is how she knows that she is sane.

VI

I dream of you by night,
I visit you by day.
Father, Mother,
Sister, Brother,
Have you no word to say?

April 22, 1903. At her residence, on Tuesday last, between three and four o'clock in the afternoon, there passed away a lady of talent and refinement whose pen, in days gone by, enriched our local literature with a volume of sensitive, eloquent verse. It is a sad misfortune that in later years the mind of this fine person had become somewhat clouded and her behaviour, in consequence, somewhat rash and unusual. Her attention to decorum and to the care and adornment of her person had suffered, to the degree that she had become, in the eyes of those unmindful of her former pride and daintiness, a familiar eccentric, or even, sadly, a figure of fun. But now all such lapses pass from memory and what is recalled is her excellent published verse, her labours in former days in the Sunday school, her dutiful care of her parents, her noble womanly nature, charitable concerns, and unfailing religious faith. Her last illness was of mercifully short duration. She caught cold, after having become thoroughly wet from a ramble in the Pearl Street bog. (It has been said that some urchins chased her into the water, and such is the boldness and cruelty of some of our youth, and their observed persecution of this lady, that the tale cannot be entirely discounted.) The cold developed into pneumonia, and she died, attended at the last by a former neighbour, Mrs. Bert (Annie) Friels, who witnessed her calm and faithful end.

January, 1904. One of the founders of our community, an early maker and shaker of this town, was abruptly removed from our midst on Monday morning last, whilst attending to his correspondence in the office of his company. Mr. Jarvis Poulter possessed a keen and lively commercial spirit, which was instrumental in the creation of not one but several local enterprises, bringing the benefits of industry, productivity, and employment to our town.

So the *Vidette* runs on, copious and assured. Hardly a death goes undescribed, or a life unevaluated.

I looked for Almeda Roth in the graveyard. I found the family stone. There was just one name on it—Roth. Then I noticed two flat stones in the ground, a distance of a few feet—six feet?—from the upright stone. One of these said "Papa," the other "Mama." Farther out from these I found two other flat stones, with the names William and Catherine on them. I had to clear away some overgrowing grass and dirt to see the full name of Catherine. No birth or death dates for anybody, nothing about being dearly beloved. It was a private sort of memorializing, not for the world. There were no roses, either—no sign of a rose-bush. But perhaps it was taken out. The grounds keeper doesn't like such things; they are a nuisance to the lawnmower, and if there is nobody left to object he will pull them out.

I thought that Almeda must have been buried somewhere else. When this plot was bought—at the time of the two children's deaths—she would still have been expected to marry, and to lie finally beside her husband. They might not have left room for her here. Then I saw that the stones in the ground fanned out from the upright stone. First the two for the parents, then the two for the children, but these were placed in such a way that there was room for a third, to complete the fan. I paced out from "Catherine" the same number of steps that it took to get from "Catherine" to "William," and at this spot I began pulling grass and scrabbling in the dirt with my bare hands. Soon I felt the stone and knew that I was right. I worked away and got the whole stone clear and I read the name "Meda." There it was with the others, staring at the sky.

I made sure I had got to the edge of the stone. That was all the name there was—Meda. So it was true that she was called by that name in the family. Not just in the poem. Or perhaps she chose her name from the poem, to be written on her stone.

I thought that there wasn't anybody alive in the world but me who would know this, who would make the connection. And I would be the last person to do so. But perhaps this isn't so. People are curious. A few people are. They will be driven to find things out, even trivial things. They will put things together. You see them going around with notebooks, scraping the dirt off gravestones, reading microfilm, just in the hope of seeing this trickle in time, making a connection, rescuing one thing from the rubbish.

And they may get it wrong, after all. I may have got it wrong. I don't know if she ever took laudanum. Many ladies did. I don't know if she ever made grape jelly.

Hold Me Fast, Don't Let Me Pass

Ruins of "Kirk of the Forest." Old graveyard, William Wallace declared Guardian of Scotland here, 1298.

Courthouse where Sir Walter Scott dispensed judgment, 1799–1832. Philiphaugh? 1945.

Gray town. Some old gray stone like Edinburgh. Also grayish-brown stucco, not so old. Library once the jail (gaol).

Country around very hilly, almost low mountains. Colors tan, lilac, gray. Some dark patches, look like pine. Reforestation? Woods at edge of town, oak, beech, birch, holly. Leaves turned, golden-brown. Sun out, but raw wind and damp feels like coming out of the ground. Nice clean little river.

One gravestone sunk deep, crooked, name, date, etc., all gone, just skull and crossbones. Girls with pink hair going by, smoking.

Hazel struck out the word "judgment" and wrote in "justice." Then she struck out "lilac," which seemed too flimsy a word to describe the gloomy, beautiful hills. She didn't know what to write in its place.

She had pressed the button beside the fireplace, hoping to order a drink, but nobody had come.

Hazel was cold in this room. When she checked into the Royal Hotel, earlier in the afternoon, a woman with a puff of gilt hair and a smooth, tapered face had given her the once-over, told her what time they served dinner, and pointed out the upstairs lounge as the place where she was to sit—ruling out, in this way, the warm and noisy pub downstairs. Hazel wondered if women guests were considered too respectable to sit in the pub. Or was she not respectable enough? She was wearing corduroy pants and tennis shoes and a windbreaker. The gilt-haired woman wore a trim pale-blue suit with glittery buttons, white lacy nylons, and high-heeled shoes that would have killed Hazel in half an hour. When she came in after a couple of hours' walk, she thought about putting on her one dress but decided not to be intimidated. She did change into a pair of black velvet pants and a silk shirt, to show she was making some effort, and she brushed and repinned her hair, which was gray as much as fair now, and fine enough to have got into an electric tangle in the wind.

Hazel was a widow. She was in her fifties, and she taught biology in the high school in Walley, Ontario. This year she was on a leave of absence. She was a person you would not be surprised to find sitting by herself in a corner of the world where she didn't belong, writing things in a notebook to prevent the rise of panic. She had found that she was usually optimistic in the morning but that panic was a problem at dusk. This sort of panic had nothing to do with money or tickets or arrangements or whatever dangers she might encounter in a strange place. It had to do with a falling-off of purpose, and the question why am I here? One could as reasonably ask that question at home, and some people do, but generally enough is going on there to block it out.

Now she noticed the date that she'd written beside "Philiphaugh": 1945. Instead of 1645. She thought that she must have been influenced by the style of this room. Glass-brick windows, dark-red carpet with a swirly pattern, cretonne curtains with red flowers and green leaves on a beige background. Blocky, dusty, dark upholstered furniture. Floor lamps. All of this could have been here when Hazel's husband, Jack, used to come to this hotel, during the war. Something must have been in the fire-place then—a gas fire, or else a real grate, for coal. Nothing was there now. And the piano had probably been kept open, in tune, for dancing. Or else they'd had a gramophone, with 78s. The room would have been full of servicemen and girls. She could see the girls' dark lipstick and rolled-up hair and good crêpe dresses with their sweetheart necklines or detachable white-lace collars. The men's uniforms would be stiff and scratchy against the girls' arms and cheeks, and they would have a sour, smoky, exciting smell. Hazel was fifteen when the war ended, so she did not get to many parties of that sort. And even when she did get to one, she was too young to be taken seriously, and had to dance with other girls or maybe a friend's older brother. The smell and feel of a uniform must have been just something she imagined.

Walley is a lake port. Hazel grew up there and so did Jack, but she never knew him, or saw him to remember, until he turned up at a high-school dance escorting the English teacher, who was one of the chaperones. By that time Hazel was seven-teen. When Jack danced with her, she was so nervous and ex-cited that she shook. He asked her what the matter was, and she had to say that she thought she was getting the flu. Jack nego-tiated with the English teacher and took Hazel home.

They were married when Hazel was eighteen. In the first four years of marriage they had three children. No more after that. (Jack told people that Hazel had found out what was caus-ing it.) Jack had gone to work for an appliance-sales-and-repair business as soon as he got out of the Air Force. The business belonged to a friend of his who had not gone overseas. Until the day of his death Jack worked in that place, more or less at the same job. Of course, he had to learn about new things, like microwave ovens.

After she had been married for about fifteen years, Hazel started to take extension courses. Then she commuted to a col-lege fifty miles away, as a full-time student. She got her degree and became a teacher, which was what she had meant to do before she got married.

Jack must have been in this room. He could easily have looked at these curtains, sat in this chair.

A man came in, at last, to ask what she would like to drink. Scotch, she said. That made him smile.

"*Whisky*'ll do it."

Of course. You don't ask for Scotch whisky in Scotland.

Jack was stationed near Wolverhampton, but he used to come up here on his leaves. He came to look up, and then to stay with, the only relative in Britain that he knew of—a cousin of his mother's, a woman named Margaret Dobie. She was not married, she lived alone; she was middle-aged then, so she would be quite old now, if indeed she was still alive. Jack didn't keep up with her after he went back to Canada—he was not a letter writer. He talked about her, though, and Hazel found her name and address when she was going through his things. She wrote Margaret Dobie a letter, just to say that Jack had died and that he had often mentioned his visits to Scotland. The letter was never answered.

Jack and this cousin seemed to have hit it off. He stayed with her in a large, cold, neglected house on a hilly farm, where she lived with her dogs and sheep. He borrowed her motorbike and rode around the countryside. He rode into town, to this very hotel, to drink and make friends or get into scraps with other servicemen or go after girls. Here he met the hotelkeeper's daughter Antoinette.

Antoinette was sixteen, too young to be allowed to go to parties or to be permitted in the bar. She had to sneak out to meet Jack behind the hotel or on the path along the river. A most delectable, heedless, soft, and giddy sort of girl. *Little Antoinette.* Jack talked about her in front of Hazel and to Hazel as easily as if he had known her not just in another country but in another world. Your Blond Bundle, Hazel used to call her. She imagined Antoinette wearing some sort of woolly pastel sleeper outfit, and she thought that she would have had silky, babyish hair, a soft, bruised mouth.

Hazel herself was a blonde when Jack first met her, though not a giddy one. She was shy and prudish and intelligent. Jack triumphed easily over the shyness and the prudery, and he was not as irritated as most men were, then, by the intelligence. He took it as a kind of joke.

Now the man was back, with a tray. On the tray were two whiskies and a jug of water.

He served Hazel her drink and took the other drink himself. He settled into the chair opposite her.

So he wasn't the barman. He was a stranger who had bought her a drink. She began to protest.

"I rang the bell," she said. "I thought you had come because I rang the bell."

"That bell is useless," he said with satisfaction. "No. Antoinette told me she had put you in here, so I thought I'd come and inquire if you were thirsty."

Antoinette.

"Antoinette," Hazel said. "Is that the lady I was speaking to this afternoon?" She felt a drop inside: her heart or her stomach or her courage—whatever it is that drops.

"Antoinette," he said. "That's the lady."

"And is she the manager of the hotel?"

"She is the owner of the hotel."

The problem was just the opposite of what she had expected. It was not that people had moved away and the buildings were gone and had left no trace. Just the opposite. The very first person that she had spoken to that afternoon had been Antoinette.

She should have known, though—she should have known that such a tidy woman, Antoinette, wouldn't employ this fellow as a barman. Look at his baggy brown pants and the burn hole in the front of his V-neck sweater. Underneath the sweater was a dingy shirt and tie. But he didn't look ill cared for or downhearted. Instead, he looked like a man who thought so well of himself that he could afford to be a bit slovenly. He had a stocky, strong body, a square, flushed face, fluffy white hair springing up in a vigorous frill around his forehead. He was pleased that she had mistaken him for the barman, as if that might be a kind of trick he'd played on her. In the classroom she would have picked him for a possible troublemaker, not the rowdy, or the silly, or the positively sneering and disgusted kind, but the kind who sits at the back of the class, smart and indolent, making remarks you can't quite be sure of. Mild, shrewd, determined subversion—one of the hardest things to root out of a classroom. What you have to do—Hazel had said this to younger teachers, or those who tended to get discouraged more easily than she did—what you have to do is find some way of firing up their intelligence. Make it a tool, not a toy. The intelligence of such a person is underemployed.

What did she care about this man anyway? All the world is not a classroom. I've got your number, she said to herself; but I don't have to do anything about it.

She was thinking about him to keep her mind off Antoinette.

He told her that his name was Dudley Brown and that he was a solicitor. He said that he lived here (she took that to mean he had a room in the hotel) and that his office was just down the street. A permanent guest—a widower, then, or a bachelor. She thought a bachelor. That twinkly, edgy air of satisfaction didn't usually survive married life.

Too young, in spite of the white hair, a few years too young, to have been in the war.

"So have you come over here looking for your roots?" he said. He gave the word its most exaggerated American pronunciation.

"I'm Canadian," Hazel said quite pleasantly. "We don't say 'roots' that way."

"Ah, I beg your pardon," he said. "I'm afraid we do that. We do tend to lump you all together, you and the Americans."

Then she started to tell him her business—why not? She

told him that her husband had been here during the war and that they had always planned to make this trip together, but they hadn't, and her husband had died, and now she had come by herself. This was only half true. She had often suggested such a trip to Jack, but he had always said no. She thought this was because of her—he didn't want to do it with her. She took things more personally than she ought to have done, for a long time. He probably meant just what he said. He said, "No, it wouldn't be the same."

He was wrong if he meant that people wouldn't be in place, right where they used to be. Even now, when Dudley Brown asked the name of the cousin in the country and Hazel said Margaret Dobie, Miss Dobie, but in all probability she's dead, the man just laughed. He laughed and shook his head and said, Oh, no, by no means, indeed not.

"Maggie Dobie is far from dead. She's a very old lady, certainly, but I don't believe she's got any thought of dying. She lives out on the same land she's always lived on, though it's a different house. She's pretty sound."

"She didn't answer my letter."

"Ah. She wouldn't."

"Then I guess she wouldn't want a visitor, either?"

She almost wanted him to say no. *Miss Dobie is very much the recluse, I'm afraid. No, no visitors.* Why, when she'd come so far?

"Well, if you drove up on your own, I don't know, that would be one thing," Dudley Brown said. "I don't know how she would take it. But if I was to ring up and explain about you, and then we took a run out, then I think you'd be made most welcome. Would you care to? It's a lovely drive out, too. Pick a day when it isn't raining."

"That would be very kind."

"Ah, it isn't far."

In the dining room, Dudley Brown ate at one little table, and Hazel at another. This was a pretty room, with blue walls and deep-set windows looking out over the town square. Hazel sensed none of the gloom and neglect that prevailed in the lounge. Antoinette served them. She offered the vegetables in silver serving dishes with rather difficult implements. She was very correct, even disdainful. When not serving, she stood by the sideboard, alert, upright, hair stiff in its net of spray, suit spotless, feet slim and unswollen in the high-heeled shoes.

Dudley said that he would not eat the fish. Hazel, too, had refused it.

"You see, even the Americans," Dudley said. "Even the Americans won't eat that frozen stuff. And you'd think they'd be used to it; they have everything frozen."

"I'm Canadian," Hazel said. She thought he'd apologize, remembering he'd been told this once already. But neither he nor Antoinette paid any attention to her. They had embarked on an argument whose tone of practiced acrimony made them sound almost married.

"Well, I wouldn't eat anything else," Antoinette said. "I wouldn't eat any fish that hadn't been frozen. And I wouldn't serve it. Maybe it was all right in the old days, when we didn't have all the chemicals we have now in the water, and all the pollution. The fish now are so full of pollution that we need the freezing to kill it. That's right, isn't it?" she said, turning to include Hazel. "They know all about that in America."

"I just preferred the roast," Hazel said.

"So your only safe fish is a frozen one," Antoinette said, ignoring her. "And another thing: they take all of the best fish for freezing. The rejects is all that is left to sell fresh."

"Give me your rejects, then," Dudley said. "Let me chance it with the chemicals."

"More fool you. I wouldn't put a bite of fresh fish in my mouth."

"You wouldn't get a chance to. Not around here."

While the law was being laid down in this way about the fish, Dudley Brown once or twice caught Hazel's eye. He kept a very straight face, which indicated, more than a smirk would have done, a settled mixture of affection and contempt. Hazel kept looking at Antoinette's suit. Antoinette's suit made her think of Joan Crawford. Not the style of the suit but its perfect condition. She had read an interview with Joan Crawford, years ago, that described many little tricks Joan Crawford had for keeping hair, clothes, footwear, fingernails in a most perfect condition. She remembered something about the way to iron seams. Never iron seams open. Antoinette looked like a woman who would have all that down pat.

She hadn't, after all, expected to find Antoinette still babyish and boisterous and charming. Far from it. Hazel had imagined—and not without satisfaction—a dumpy woman wearing false teeth. (Jack used to recall Antoinette's habit of popping caramels into her mouth between kisses, and making him wait until she'd sucked the sweetness out of the last shred.) A good-natured soul, chatty, humdrum, a waddly little grandmother—that was what she had thought would be left of Antoinette. And here was this pared-down, vigilant, stupid-shrewd woman, sprayed and painted and preserved to within an inch of her life. Tall, too. It wasn't likely she'd been any kind of cozy bundle, even at sixteen.

But how much would you find in Hazel of the girl Jack had taken home from the dance? How much of Hazel Joudry, a pale, squeaky-voiced girl who held her fair hair back with two bows of pink celluloid, in Hazel Curtis? Hazel was thin, too—wiry, not brittle like Antoinette. She had muscles that came from gardening and hiking and cross-country skiing. These activities had also dried and wrinkled and roughened her skin, and at some point she'd stopped bothering about it. She threw out all the colored pastes and pencils and magic unguents she had bought in moments of bravado or despair. She let her hair grow out whatever color it liked and pinned it up at the back of her head. She broke open the shell of her increasingly doubtful and expensive prettiness; she got out. Years before Jack died, even, she did that. It had something to do with how she took hold of her life. She has said and thought that there came a time when she had to take hold of her life, and she has urged the same course on others. She urges action, exercise, direction. She doesn't mind letting people know that when she was in her thirties she had what used to be called a nervous breakdown. For nearly two months she was unable to leave the house. She stayed in bed much of the time. She crayoned the pictures in children's coloring books. That was all she could do to control her fear and unfocussed grief. Then she took hold. She sent for college catalogues. What got her going again? She doesn't know. She has to say she doesn't know. Maybe she just got bored, she has to say. Maybe she just got bored, having her breakdown.

She knew that when she had got out of bed (this is what she doesn't say), she was leaving some part of herself behind. She suspected that this was a part that had to do with Jack. But she didn't think then that any abandonment had to be permanent. Anyway, it couldn't be helped.

When he had finished his roast and vegetables, Dudley got up abruptly. He nodded to Hazel and said to Antoinette, "I'm off now, my lamb." Did he really say that—"lamb"? Whatever it was, it had the satirical inflection that an endearment would need between him and Antoinette. Perhaps he said "lass." People did say "lass" here. The driver on the bus from Edinburgh had said it to Hazel, that afternoon.

Antoinette served Hazel a piece of apricot flan and started immediately to fill her in on Dudley. People were supposed to be so reserved in Britain—that was what Hazel had been led to believe, by her reading, if not by Jack—but it didn't always seem to be the case.

"Off to see his mother before she's tucked up for the night," Antoinette said. "Always off home early on a Sunday night."

"He doesn't live here?" Hazel said. "I mean, in the hotel?"

"He didn't say that, did he?" said Antoinette. "I'm sure he didn't say that. He has his own home. He has a lovely home. He shares it with his mother. She's in bed all the time now—she's

one of those ones who have to have everything done for them.
He's got a day nurse for her and a night nurse, too. But he always
looks in and has a chat Sunday nights, even if she doesn't know
him from Adam. He must have meant that he gets his meals
here. He couldn't expect the nurse to get his meals. She wouldn't
do it, anyway. They won't do anything extra at all for you now.
They want to know just what they're supposed to do, and they
won't do a tick more. It's just the same with what I get here. If
I say to them, 'Sweep the floor,' and I don't say, 'Put up the
broom when you're finished,' they'll just leave the broom lying."

Now is the time, Hazel thought. She wouldn't be able to say
it if she put if off longer.

"My husband used to come here," she said. "He used to
come here during the war."

"Well, that's a long time ago, isn't it? Would you like your
coffee now?"

"Please," Hazel said. "He came here first on account of
having a relative here. A Miss Dobie. Mr. Brown seemed to
know who she would be."

"She's quite an elderly person," Antoinette said—
disapprovingly, Hazel thought. "She lives away up in the valley."

"My husband's name was Jack." Hazel waited, but she didn't
get any response. The coffee was bad, which was a surprise, since
the rest of the meal had been so good.

"Jack Curtis," she said. "His mother was a Dobie. He used
to come here on his leaves and stay with this cousin and he
would come into town in the evenings. He used to come here, to
the Royal Hotel."

"It was a busy place during the war," Antoinette said. "Or
so they tell me."

"He would talk about the Royal Hotel and he mentioned
you, too," Hazel said. "I was surprised when I heard your name.
I didn't think you'd still be here."

"I haven't been here the whole time," Antoinette said—as
if to suppose that she had been would be to insult her. "I lived

in England while I was married. That's why I don't talk the way they do around here."

"My husband is dead," Hazel said. "He mentioned you. He said your father owned the hotel. He said you were a blonde."

"I still am," Antoinette said. "My hair is just the same color it always was; I never have had to do anything to it. I can't remember the war years very well. I was such a wee little girl at the time. I don't think I was born when the war started. When did the war start? I was born in 1940."

Two lies in one speech, hardly any doubt about it. Blatant, smooth-faced, deliberate, self-serving lies. But how could Hazel tell if Antoinette was lying about not knowing Jack? Antoinette would have no choice but to say that, given the lie she must have told all the time about her age.

For the next three days it rained, off and on. When it wasn't raining, Hazel walked around the town, looking at the exploded cabbages in kitchen gardens, the unlined flowered window curtains, and even at such things as a bowl of waxed fruit on the table in a cramped, polished dining room. She must have thought that she was invisible, the way she slowed down and peered. She got used to the houses' being all strung together. At the turn of the street she might get a sudden, misty view of the enthralling hills. She walked along the river and got into a wood that was all beech trees, with bark like elephant skin and bumps like swollen eyes. They gave a kind of gray light to the air.

When the rains came, she stayed in the library, reading history. She read about the old monasteries that were here in Selkirk County once, and the Kings with their Royal Forest, and all the fighting with the English. Flodden Field. She knew some things already from the reading she had done in the Encyclopaedia Britannica before she ever left home. She knew who William Wallace was, and that Macbeth killed Duncan in battle instead of murdering him in bed.

Dudley and Hazel had a whisky in the lounge now, every

night before dinner. An electric radiator had appeared, and was set up in front of the fireplace. After dinner Antoinette sat with them. They all had their coffee together. Later in the evening Dudley and Hazel would have another whisky. Antoinette watched television.

"What a long history," said Hazel politely. She told Dudley something of what she'd read and looked at. "When I first saw the name Philiphaugh on that building across the street I didn't know what it meant."

"At Philiphaugh the fray began," Dudley said, obviously quoting. "Do you know now?"

"The Covenanters," Hazel said.

"Do you know what happened after the battle of Philiphaugh? The Covenanters hanged all their prisoners. Right out there in the town square, under the dining-room windows. Then they butchered all the women and children on the field. A lot of families travelled with Montrose's army, because so many of them were Irish mercenaries. Catholics, of course. No—they didn't butcher all of them. Some they marched up toward Edinburgh. But on the way they decided to march them off a bridge."

He told her this in a most genial voice, with a smile. Hazel had met this smile before and she had never been sure what it meant. Was a man who smiled in this way daring you not to believe, not to acknowledge, not to agree, that this was how things must be, forever?

Jack was a hard person to argue with. He put up with all kinds of nonsense—from customers, from the children, probably from Hazel as well. But he would get angry every year on Remembrance Day, because the local paper would run some lugubrious story about the war.

"NOBODY WINS IN A WAR" was the headline of one such story. Jack threw the paper on the floor.

"Holy Christ! Do they think it'd be all the same if *Hitler* had won?"

He was angry, too, when he saw the Peace Marchers on television, though he usually didn't say anything, just hissed at the screen in a controlled, fed-up way. As far as Hazel could see, what he thought was that a lot of people—women, of course, but, as time went on, more and more men, too—were determined to spoil the image of the best part of his life. They were spoiling it with pious regrets and reproofs and a certain amount of out-and-out lying. None of them would admit that any of the war was fun. Even at the Legion you were supposed to put on a long face about it; you weren't supposed to say anymore that you wouldn't have missed it for the world.

When they were first married, Jack and Hazel used to go to dances, or to the Legion, or just to other couples' houses, and sooner or later the men would begin telling their stories about the war. Jack did not tell the most stories, or the longest, and his were never thick with heroics and death staring you in the face. Usually he talked about things that were funny. But he was on top then, because he had been a bomber pilot, which was one of the most admired things for a man to have been. He had flown two full tours of operations ("ops"—even the women referred to "ops"). That is, he had flown on fifty bombing raids.

Hazel used to sit with the other young wives and listen, meek and proud and—in her case, at least—distracted by desire. These husbands came to them taut with proved courage. Hazel pitied women who had given themselves to lesser men.

Ten or fifteen years later the same women sat with strained faces or caught one another's eyes or even absented themselves (Hazel did, sometimes) when the stories were being told. The band of men who told these stories had shrunk, and it shrank further. But Jack was still at the center of it. He grew more descriptive, thoughtful, some might say long-winded. He recalled now the noise of the planes at the American airfield close by, the mighty sound of them warming up in the early dawn and then taking off, three by three, flying out over the North Sea in their great formations. The Flying Fortresses. The Americans bombed by day, and their planes never flew alone. Why not?

"They didn't know how to navigate," Jack said. "Well, they did, but not the way we navigated." He was proud of an extra skill, or foolhardiness, that he would not bother to explain. He told how the R.A.F. planes lost sight of one another almost at once and flew for six or seven hours alone. Sometimes the voice that directed them, over the radio, was a German voice with a perfect English accent, providing deadly false information. He told about planes appearing out of nowhere, gliding above or beneath you, and of the death of planes in dreamlike flashes of light. It was nothing like the movies, nothing so concentrated or organized—nothing made sense. Sometimes he had thought he could hear a lot of voices, or instrumental music, weird but familiar, just beyond or inside the noises of the plane.

Then he seemed to come back to earth—in more ways than one—and he told his stories about leaves and drunks, fights in the blackout outside pubs, practical jokes in the barracks.

On the third night Hazel thought that she had better speak to Dudley about the trip to see Miss Dobie. The week was passing, and the idea of the visit didn't alarm her so much, now that she'd got a little used to being here.

"I'll ring up in the morning," Dudley said. He seemed glad to have been reminded. "I'll see if it would suit her. There's a chance of the weather's clearing, too. Tomorrow or the next day we'll go."

Antoinette was watching a television show in which couples selected each other, by a complicated ritual, for a blind date, and then came back the next week to tell how everything went. She laughed outright at disastrous confessions.

Antoinette used to run out to meet Jack with nothing but

her nightie on under her coat. Her daddy would have tanned her, Jack used to say. Tanned us both.

"I'll drive you out, then, to see Miss Dobie," Antoinette said to Hazel at breakfast. "Dudley's got too much on."

Hazel said, "No, no, it's all right, if Dudley is too busy."

"It's all set up now," Antoinette said. "But we'll go a bit earlier than Dudley planned. I thought later this morning, before lunch. I just have a couple of things to see about first."

So they set out in Antoinette's car, around half past eleven. The rain had stopped, the clouds had whitened, the oak and beech trees were dripping last night's rainwater with the stirring of their gold and rusty leaves. The road went between low stone walls. It crossed the clear, hard-flowing little river.

"Miss Dobie has a nice house," Antoinette said. "It's a nice little bungalow. It's on a corner of the old farm. When she sold off the farm, she kept one corner of it and built herself a little bungalow. Her other old house was all gone to rookery."

Hazel had a clear picture in her mind of that other, old house. She could see the big kitchen, roughly plastered, with its uncurtained windows. The meat safe, the stove, the slick horse-hair couch. A great quantity of pails and implements and guns, fishing rods, oilcans, lanterns, baskets. A battery radio. On a backless chair a big husky woman, in trousers, would be sitting, oiling a gun or cutting up seed potatoes or gutting a fish. There was not a thing she couldn't do herself, Jack had said, providing Hazel with this picture. He put himself in it as well. He had sat on the steps outside the kitchen door, on days of hazy radiance like today's—except that the grass and the trees had been green—and he passed the time fooling with the dogs or trying to get the muck off the shoes he had borrowed from his hostess.

"Jack borrowed Miss Dobie's shoes once," she said to Antoinette. "She had big feet, apparently. She always wore men's shoes. I don't know what had happened to his. Maybe he just had boots. Anyway, he wore her shoes to a dance and he went down to the river, I don't know what for"—it was to meet a girl, of course, probably to meet Antoinette—"and he got the shoes soaked, covered with muck. He was so drunk he didn't take anything off when he went to bed, just passed out on top of the quilt. Miss Dobie did not say a word about it. Next night he came home late again and he crawled into bed in the dark, and a pailful of cold water hit him in the face! She'd rigged up this arrangement of weights and ropes, so that when the springs of the bed sagged under him, the pail would be tipped over and the water would hit him like that, to serve him right."

"She mustn't have minded going to a lot of trouble," Antoinette said. Then she said they would stop for lunch. Hazel had thought that the whole point of leaving when they did had been to get the visit over with early, because Antoinette was short of time. But now, apparently, they were taking care not to arrive too soon.

They stopped at a pub that had a famous name. Hazel had read about a duel fought there; it was mentioned in an old ballad. But the pub now seemed ordinary, and was run by an Englishman who was in the middle of redecorating. He heated their sandwiches in a microwave oven.

"I wouldn't give one of those houseroom," Antoinette said. "They irrigate your food."

She began to talk about Miss Dobie and the girl Miss Dobie had to look after her.

"Well, she's hardly a girl anymore. Her name is Judy Armstrong. She was one of those what-do-you-call-thems—orphans. She went to work for Dudley's mother. She worked there for a while, and then she got herself in trouble. The result was she had a baby. The way they often do. She couldn't stay in town so easily after that, so it was fortunate Miss Dobie was just getting in the way of needing somebody. Judy and her child went out there, and it turned out to be the best arrangement all round."

They delayed at the pub until Antoinette judged that Judy and Miss Dobie would be ready for them.

The valley narrowed in. Miss Dobie's house was close to the road, with hills rising steeply behind it. In front was a shining laurel hedge and some wet bushes, all red-leaved or dripping with berries. The house was stuccoed, with stones set here and there in a whimsical suburban style.

A young woman stood in the doorway. Her hair was glorious—a ripply fan of red hair, shining over her shoulders. She was wearing a rather odd dress for the time of day—a sort of party dress of thin, silky brown material, shot through with gold metallic thread. She must have been chilly in it—she had her arms crossed, squeezing her breasts.

"Here we are, then, Judy," Antoinette said, speaking heartily as if to a slightly deaf or mutinous person. Dudley couldn't come. He was too busy. This is the lady he told you about on the phone."

Judy blushed as she shook hands. Her eyebrows were very fair, almost invisible, giving her dark-brown eyes an undefended look. She seemed dismayed by something—was it the fact of visitors, or just the flamboyance of her own spread-out hair? But she was the one who must have brushed it to this gloss and arranged it on show.

Antoinette asked her if Miss Dobie was well.

A clot of phlegm thickened Judy's voice as she tried to answer. She cleared her throat and said, "Miss Dobie's kept well all this year."

Now there was some awkwardness about getting their coats off—Judy not knowing quite when to reach for them, or how to direct Antoinette and Hazel where to go. But Antoinette took charge and led the way down the hall to the sitting room, which was full of patterned upholstery, brass and china ornaments, pampas grass, peacock feathers, dried flowers, clocks and pictures and cushions. In the midst of this an old woman sat in a high-backed chair, against the light of the windows, waiting for them. Though she was old, she was not at all shrivelled. She had thick arms and legs and a bushy halo of white hair. Her skin was brown, like the skin of a russet apple, and she had large purplish pouches under her eyes. But the eyes themselves were bright and shifty, as if some intelligence there looked out just when it wanted to—something as quick and reckless as a squirrel darting back and forth behind this heavy, warty, dark old face.

"So you are the lady from Canada," she said to Antoinette. She had a strong voice. Spots on her lips were like blue-black grapes.

"No, that's not me," Antoinette said. "I'm from the Royal Hotel, and you've met me before. I'm the friend of Dudley Brown's." She took a bottle of wine—it was Madeira—out of her bag and presented it, as a credential. "This is the kind you like, isn't it?"

"All the way from Canada," Miss Dobie said, taking possession of the bottle. She still wore men's shoes—she was wearing them now, unlaced.

Antoinette repeated what she had said before, in a louder voice, and introduced Hazel.

"Judy! Judy, you know where the glasses are!" Miss Dobie said. Judy was just coming in with a tray. On it was a stack of cups and saucers, a teapot, a plate of sliced fruitcake, milk, and sugar. The demand for the glasses seemed to throw her off course, and she looked around distractedly. Antoinette relieved her of the tray.

"I think she'd like a taste of the wine first, Judy," Antoinette said. "Isn't this nice! Did you make the cake yourself? May I take a piece back to Dudley when we go? He's so fond of fruitcake. He'll believe it was made for him. That can't be true, since he only called this morning and fruitcake takes a lot longer than that, doesn't it? But he'll never know the difference."

"I know who you are now," Miss Dobie said. "You're the woman from the Royal Hotel. Did you and Dudley Brown ever get married?"

"I am already married," Antoinette said irritably. "I would get a divorce, but I don't know where my husband is." Her voice quickly smoothed out, so that she ended up seeming to reassure Miss Dobie. "Perhaps in time."

"So that's why you went to Canada," Miss Dobie said.

Judy came in with some wineglasses. Anybody could see that her hands were too unsteady to pour the wine. Antoinette got the bottle out of Miss Dobie's clasp and held a wineglass up to the light.

"If you could just fetch me a napkin, Judy," Antoinette said. "Or a clean tea towel. Mind it's a clean one!"

"My husband, Jack," Hazel broke in resolutely, speaking to Miss Dobie—"my husband, Jack Curtis, was in the Air Force, and he used to visit you during the war."

Miss Dobie picked this up all right.

"Why would your husband want to visit me?"

"He wasn't my husband then. He was quite young then. He was a cousin of yours. From Canada. Jack Curtis, Curtis. But you may have had a lot of different relatives visiting you, over the years."

"We never had visitors. We were too far off the beaten track," Miss Dobie said firmly. "I lived at home with Mother and Father and then I lived with Mother and then I lived alone. I gave up on the sheep and went to work in town. I worked at the post office."

"That's right, she did," Antoinette said thoughtfully, handing round the wine.

"But I never lived in town," Miss Dobie said, with an obscure, vengeful-sounding pride. "No. I rode in every day, all that way on the motorbike."

"Jack mentioned your motorbike," Hazel said, to encourage her.

"I lived in the old house then. Terrible people live there now."

She held out her glass for more wine.

"Jack used to borrow your motorbike," Hazel said. "And he went fishing with you, and when you cleaned the fish, the dogs ate the fish heads."

"Ugh," Antoinette said.

"I'm thankful I can't see it from here," Miss Dobie said.

"The house," Antoinette explained, in a regretful under-
tone. "The couple that live in it are not married. They have
fixed it up but they are not married." And, as if naturally reminded, she said to Judy, "How is Tania?"

"She's fine," said Judy, who was not having any wine. She
lifted the plate of fruitcake and set it down. "She goes to kindergarten now."

"She goes on the bus," Miss Dobie said. "The bus comes
and picks her up right at the door."

"Isn't that nice," Antoinette said.

"And it brings her back," Miss Dobie continued impres-
sively. "It brings her back right to the door."

"Jack said you had a dog that ate porridge," Hazel said.
"And that one time he borrowed your shoes. I mean Jack did.
My husband."

Miss Dobie seemed to brood over this for a little while.
Then she said, "Tania has the red hair."

"She has her mother's hair," Antoinette said. "And her
mother's brown eyes. She is Judy all over again."

"She is illegitimate," Miss Dobie said, with the air of somebody sweeping aside a good deal of nonsense. "But Judy brings
her up well. Judy is a good worker. I am glad to see that they have
a home. It is the innocent ones, anyway, that get caught."

Hazel thought that this would finish Judy off completely,
send her running to the kitchen. Instead, she seemed to come to
a decision. She got up and handed around the cake. The flush
had never left her face or her neck or the part of her chest left
bare by the party dress. Her skin was burning as if she had been
slapped, and her expression, as she bent to each of them with the
plate, was that of a child who was furiously, bitterly, contemp-
tuously holding back a howl. Miss Dobie spoke to Hazel. She
said, "Can you say any recitations?"

Hazel had to think for a moment to remember what a recitation was. Then she said that she could not.

"I will say one, if you like," Miss Dobie said.

She put down her empty glass and straightened her shoulders and placed her feet together.

"Excuse my not rising," she said.

She began to speak in a voice that seemed strained and faltering at first but that soon became dogged and preoccupied. Her Scottish pronunciation thickened. She paid less attention to the content of the poem than to the marathon effort of getting it out in the right order—word after word, line after line, verse after verse. Her face darkened further with the effort. But the recitation was not wholly without expression; it was not like those numbing presentations of "memory work" that Hazel remembered having to learn at school. It was more like the best scholar's offering at the school concert, a kind of willing public martyrdom, with every inflection, every gesture, rehearsed and ordained.

Hazel started picking up bits and pieces. A rigmarole about fairies, some boy captured by the fairies, then a girl called Fair Jennet falling in love with him. Fair Jennet was giving back talk to her father and wrapping herself in her mantle green and going to meet her lover. Then it seemed to be Halloween and the dead of night, and a great charge of fairies came on horseback. Not dainty fairies, by any means, but a fierce lot who rode through the night making a horrid uproar.

> "Fair Jennet stood, with mind unmoved,
> The dreary heath upon;
> And louder, louder wax'd the sound,
> As they came riding on!"

Judy sat with the cake plate in her lap and ate a large slice of fruitcake. Then she ate another—still with a fiery, unforgiving face. When she had bent to offer the cake, Hazel had smelled her body—not a bad smell, but nevertheless a smell that washing and deodorizing had made uncommon. It poured out hotly from between the girl's flushed breasts.

Antoinette, not bothering to be very quiet, possessed herself of a tiny brass ashtray, got her cigarettes out of her bag, and began to smoke. (She said she allowed herself three cigarettes a day.)

> *"And first gaed by the black black steed,*
> *And then gaed by the brown;*
> *But fast she gript the milk-white steed,*
> *And pu'd the rider down!"*

Hazel thought that there was no use asking anymore about Jack. Somebody around here probably remembered him—somebody who had seen him go down the road on the motorbike or talked to him one night in the pub. But how was she to find that person? It was probably true that Antoinette had forgotten him. Antoinette had enough on her mind, with what was going on now. As for what was on Miss Dobie's mind, that seemed to be picked out of the air, all willfulness and caprice. An elf-man in her yammering poem took precedence now.

> *"They shaped him in Fair Jennet's arms,*
> *An esk, but and an adder;*
> *She held him fast in every shape,*
> *To be her bairn's father!"*

A note of gloomy satisfaction in Miss Dobie's voice indicated that the end might be in sight. What was an eskbut? Never mind, Jennet was wrapping her lover up in her mantle green, a "mother-naked man," and the Queen of the Fairies was lamenting his loss, and just about at the point where the audience might be afraid that some new development was under way—for Miss Dobie's voice had gone resigned again, and speeded up a bit as if for a long march—the recitation was over.

"Good Lord," Antoinette said when she was sure. "How ever do you keep all that in your head? Dudley does it, too. You and Dudley, you are a pair!"

Judy began a clattering, distributing cups and saucers. She started to pour out the tea. Antoinette let her get that far before stopping her.

"That's going to be a bit strong by now, isn't it, dear?" Antoinette said. "I'm afraid too strong for me. We have to be getting back anyway, really. Miss Dobie'll be wanting her rest, after all that."

Judy picked up the tray without protest and headed for the kitchen. Hazel went after her, carrying the cake plate.

"I think Mr. Brown meant to come," she said to Judy quietly. "I don't think he knew that we were leaving as early as we did."

"Oh, aye," said that bitter, rosy girl, as she splashed the poured tea down the sink.

"If you wouldn't mind opening my bag," Antoinette said, "and getting me out another cigarette? I have to have another cigarette. If I look down to do it myself, I'll feel sick. I've got a headache coming, from that moaning and droning."

The sky had darkened again, and they were driving through a light rain.

"It must be a lonely life for her," Hazel said. "For Judy."

"She's got Tania."

The last thing that Antoinette had done, as they were leaving, was to press some coins into Judy's hand.

"For Tania," she'd said.

"She might like to get married," Hazel said. "But would she meet anybody out there to marry?"

"I don't know how easy it'd be for her to meet anybody anywhere," Antoinette said. "Being in the position she is in."

"It doesn't matter so much nowadays," Hazel said. "Girls have children first and get married later. Movie stars, ordinary girls, too. All the time. It doesn't matter."

"I would say it matters around here," Antoinette said. "We

aren't movie stars around here. A man would have to think twice. He'd have to think about his family. It'd be an insult to his mother. It would be even if she was past knowing anything about it. And if you make your living dealing with the public, you have to think about that, too."

She was pulling the car off the road. She said, "Excuse me," and got out and walked over to the stone wall. She bent forward. Was she weeping? No. She was vomiting. Her shoulders were hunched and quivering. She vomited neatly over the wall into the fallen leaves of the oak forest. Hazel opened the car door and started toward her, but Antoinette waved her back with one hand.

The helpless and intimate sound of vomiting, in the stillness of the country, the misty rain.

Antoinette leaned down and held on to the wall for a moment. Then she straightened up and came back to the car and wiped herself off with tissues, shakily but thoroughly.

"I get that," she said, "with the kind of headaches I get."

Hazel said, "Do you want me to drive?"

"You aren't used to this side of the road."

"I'll go carefully."

They changed places—Hazel was rather surprised that Antoinette had agreed—and Hazel drove slowly, while Antoinette sat with her eyes closed most of the time and her hands against her mouth. Her skin showed gray through the pink makeup. But near the edge of town she opened her eyes and dropped her hands and said something like "This is Cathaw."

They were going past a low field by the river. "Where in that poem," Antoinette said—speaking hastily, as one might if one was afraid of being overtaken by further vomiting—"the girl goes out and loses her maidenhead, and so on."

The field was brown and soggy and surrounded by what looked like council housing.

Hazel was surprised to recall a whole verse now. She could hear Miss Dobie's voice chanting it hard at them.

> "Now, gowd rings ye may buy, maidens,
> Green mantles ye may spin;
> But, gin ye lose your maidenheid,
> Ye'll ne'er get that agen!"

A ton of words Miss Dobie had, to bury anything.

"Antoinette isn't well," Hazel said to Dudley Brown when she came into the lounge that evening. "She has a sick headache. We drove out today to see Miss Dobie."

"She left me a note to that effect," Dudley said, setting out the whisky and water.

Antoinette was in bed. Hazel had helped her get there, because she was too dizzy to manage by herself. Antoinette got into bed in her slip and asked for a facecloth, so that she could remove what was left of her makeup and not spoil the pillowcase. Then she asked for a towel, in case she should be sick again. She told Hazel how to hang up her suit—still the same one, and still miraculously unspotted—on its padded hanger. Her bedroom was mean and narrow. It looked out on the stucco wall of the bank next door. She slept on a metal-frame cot. On the dresser was displayed all the paraphernalia that she used to color her hair. Would she be upset when she realized that Hazel must have seen it? Probably not. She might have forgotten that lie already. Or she might be prepared to go on lying—like a queen, who makes whatever she says the truth.

"She had the woman from the kitchen go up to see about dinner," Hazel said. "It'll be on the sideboard, and we're to help ourselves."

"Help ourselves to this first," Dudley said. He had brought the whisky bottle.

"Miss Dobie was not able to remember my husband."

"Was she not?"

"A girl was there. A young woman, rather. Who looks after Miss Dobie."

"Judy Armstrong," Dudley said.

She waited to see if he could keep himself from asking more, if he could force himself to change the subject. He couldn't. "Has she still got her wonderful red hair?"

"Yes," Hazel said. "Did you think she would have shaved it off?"

"Girls do terrible things to their hair. I see sights every day. But Judy is not that sort."

"She served a very nice dark fruitcake," Hazel said. "Antoinette mentioned bringing a piece home to you. But I think she forgot. I think she was already feeling ill when we left."

"Perhaps the cake was poisoned," Dudley said. "The way it often is, in the stories."

"Judy ate two slices herself, and I ate some and Miss Dobie ate some, so I don't think so."

"Perhaps only Antoinette's."

"Antoinette didn't have any. Just some wine, and a cigarette."

After a silent moment Dudley said, "How did Miss Dobie entertain you?"

"She recited a long poem."

"Aye, she'll do that. Ballads, they're rightly called, not poems. Do you recall which one it was?"

The lines that came into Hazel's mind were those concerning the maidenhead. But she rejected them as being too crudely malicious and tried to find others.

"First dip me in a stand of milk?" she said tentatively. "Then in a stand of water?"

"But hold me fast, don't let me pass," Dudley cried, very pleased. "I'll be your bairn's father!"

Quite as tactless as the first lines she had thought of, but he did not seem to mind. Indeed, he threw himself back in his chair, looking released, and lifted his head and started reciting—

the same poem that Miss Dobie had recited, but spoken with calm relish now, and with style, in a warm, sad, splendid male voice. His accent broadened, but, having absorbed a good deal of the poem once already, almost against her will, Hazel was able to make out every word. The boy captured by fairies, living a life of adventures and advantages—not able to feel pain, for one thing—but growing wary as he gets older, scared of "paying the teint to hell," and longing for a human climate, so seducing a bold girl and instructing her how she can get him free. She has to do it by holding on to him, holding on no matter what horror the fairies can change him into, holding on until all their tricks are exhausted, and they let him go. Of course Dudley's style was old-fashioned, of course he mocked himself, a little. But that was only on the surface. This reciting was like singing. You could parade your longing without fear of making a fool of yourself.

> "They shaped him in her arms at last,
> A mother-naked man;
> She wrapt him in her green mantle,
> And so her true love wan!"

You and Miss Dobie, you are a pair.

"We saw the place where she went to meet him," Hazel said. "On the way back, Antoinette showed it to me. Down by the river." She thought that it was a wonder to be here, in the middle of these people's lives, seeing what she'd seen of their scheming, their wounds. Jack was not here, Jack was not here after all, but she was.

"Carterhaugh?" Dudley said, sounding scornful and excited. "That's not down by the river! Antoinette doesn't know what she's talking about! That's the high field, it overlooks the river. That's where the fairy rings were. Fungi. If the moon were out, we could drive out tonight and look at it."

Hazel could feel something, as if a cat had jumped into her lap. Sex. She felt her eyes widen, her skin tighten, her limbs settle, attentively. But the moon was not going to be out—that was the other thing his tone made clear. He poured out more whisky, and it wasn't in aid of a seduction. All the faith and energy, the adeptness, the forgetfulness that is necessary to manage even a tiny affair—Hazel knew, for she'd had two tiny affairs, one at college and one at a teachers' conference—all that was beyond them at present. They would let the attraction wash over them and ebb away. Antoinette would have been willing, Hazel was sure of that. Antoinette would have tolerated someone who was going away, who didn't really matter, who was only a sort of American. That was another thing to make them draw back—Antoinette's acceptance. That was enough to make them thoughtful, fastidious.

"The little girl," Dudley said, in a quieter voice. "Was she there?"

"No. She goes to kindergarten." Hazel thought how little was required, really—a recitation—to turn her mind from needling to comforting.

"Does she? What a name that child has got. Tania."

"That's not so odd a name," Hazel said. "Not nowadays."

"I know. They all have outlandish international names, like Tania and Natasha and Erin and Solange and Carmen. No one has family names. Those girls with the rooster hair I see on the streets. They pick the names. They're the mothers."

"I have a granddaughter named Brittany," Hazel said. "And I have heard of a little girl called Cappuccino."

"Cappuccino! Is that true? Why don't they call one Cassoulet? Fettucini? Alsace-Lorraine?"

"They probably do."

"Schleswig-Holstein! There's a good name for you!"

"But when did you see her last?" Hazel said. "Tania?"

"I don't see her," Dudley said. "I don't go out there. We have financial matters, but I don't go out."

Well, you ought to go, she was about to say to him. You must go, and not make stupid arrangements that Antoinette can step in and spoil, as she did today. He was the one, however, who spoke first. He leaned across and spoke to her with slightly drunken sincerity.

"What am I to do? I can't make two women happy."

A statement that might have been thought fatuous, conceited, evasive.

Yet it was true. Hazel was stopped. It was true. At first the claim seemed to be all Judy's, because of her child and her loneliness and her lovely hair. But why did Antoinette have to lose out, just because she had been in the running for a long time, could calculate, and withstand defections, and knew how to labor at her looks? Antoinette must have been useful and loyal and perhaps privately tender. And she didn't even ask for a man's whole heart. She might shut her eyes to a secret visit once in a while. (She'd be sick, though; she'd have to turn her head away and vomit.) Judy wouldn't put up with that at all. She'd be bursting with ballad fervor, all vows and imprecations. He couldn't bear such suffering, such railing. So had Antoinette foiled him today for his own good? That was the way she must see it—the way he might see it, too, after a little while. Even now, perhaps—now that the ballad had stirred and eased his heart.

Jack had said something like that once. Not about two women, but about making a woman—well, it was Hazel—happy. She thought back to what he had said. *I could make you very happy.* He meant that he could give her an orgasm. It was something men said then, when they were trying to persuade you, and that was what they meant. Perhaps they still said it. Probably they were not so indirect nowadays. And he had been quite right about what he promised. But nobody had said that to Hazel before, and she was amazed, taking the promise at face value. It seemed rash and sweeping to her, dazzling but presumptuous. She had to try to see herself, then, as somebody who could be *made happy.* The whole worrying, striving, complicated bundle of Hazel—was that something that could just be picked up and *made happy*?

One day, about twenty years later, she was driving down the main street of Walley and she saw Jack. He was looking out the front window of the appliance store. He wasn't looking in her direction, he didn't see the car. This was while she was going to college. She had errands to do, classes to get to, papers, labs, housework. She could notice things only if she was halted for a minute or two, as she was now, waiting for the light. She noticed Jack—how slim and youthful he looked, in his slacks and pullover—how gray and insubstantial. She didn't have anything like a clear intimation that he was going to die there, in the store. (He did die there; he slumped over while talking to a customer—but that was years later.) She didn't take account, all at once, of what his life had become—two or three nights a week at the Legion, the other nights spent lying on the sofa from supper to bedtime, watching television, drinking. Three drinks, four. Never mean, never noisy, he never passed out. He rinsed his glass at the kitchen sink before he went to bed. A life of chores, routines, seasons, pleasantries. All she saw was the stillness about him, a look you could have called ghostly. She saw that his handsomeness—a particular Second World War handsomeness, she felt, with a wisecracking edge to it and a proud passivity—was still intact but drained of power. A ghostly sweetness was what he showed her, through the glass.

She could be striving toward him, now as much as then. Full of damaging hopes, and ardor, and accusations. She didn't let herself then—she thought about an exam, or groceries. And if she let herself now, it would be like testing the pain in a lost limb. A quick test, a twinge that brings the whole shape into the air. That would be enough.

She was a little drunk herself by this time, and she thought of saying to Dudley Brown that perhaps he *was* making those two women happy. What could she mean by that? Maybe that he was giving them something to concentrate on. A hard limit that you might someday get past in a man, a knot in his mind you might undo, a stillness in him you might jolt, or an absence you might make him regret—that sort of thing will make you pay attention, even when you think you've taught yourself not to. Could it be said to make you happy?

Meanwhile, what makes a man happy?

It must be something quite different.

Oranges and Apples

"I hired a looker from out Shawtown," Murray's father said. "She's a Delaney, but so far she doesn't seem to have any bad habits. I put her in Men's Wear."

This was in the spring of 1955. Murray was just out of college. He'd come home and seen at once what fate was waiting for him. Anybody could see it, written on his father's darkened, scooped-out face, rising almost daily in his father's stomach—the hard loaf that would kill before winter. In six months Murray would be in charge, sitting in the little lookout office that hung like a cage at the back of the store, over Linoleum.

Zeigler's then was still called Zeigler's Department Store. It was about the same age as the town itself. The present building— three stories high, red brick, the name in angled gray brick letters that had always looked, to Murray, puzzlingly jaunty and Oriental—had gone up in 1880, replacing an earlier building of wood. The store did not deal in groceries or hardware anymore, but they still had Men's, Ladies', and Children's Wear, Dry Goods, Boots and Shoes, Draperies, Housewares, Furniture.

Murray strolled by to have a look at the looker. He found her penned behind rows of cellophaned shirts. Barbara. She was tall and well developed, as his father in a lowered and regretful voice had said. Her thick black hair did not curl or lie flat—it sprang up like a crest from her wide white forehead. Her eyebrows were thick and black as well, and glossy. Murray found out later that she put Vaseline on them, and plucked out the hairs that would have met above her nose.

Barbara's mother had been the mainstay of a back-country farm. When she died, the family migrated to Shawtown, which was a rackety half-rural settlement on the edge of Walley. Barbara's father did odd jobs, and her two brothers had got into trouble with cars and breaking and entering. One later disappeared. The other married a managing sort of girl and settled down. It was that one who was coming into the store at this time and hanging around, on the pretext of visiting Barbara.

"Watch out for him," Barbara told the other clerks. "He's a jerk, but he knows how to stick things to his fingers."

Hearing about this, Murray was impressed by her lack of family feeling. He was an only child, not spoiled but favored, and he felt himself bound by many ties of obligation, decency, and love. As soon as he got home from college, he had to go around greeting all the people who worked in the store, most of whom he'd known since childhood. He had to chat and smile on the streets of Walley, affable as a crown prince.

Barbara's brother was caught with a pair of socks in one pocket and a package of curtain hooks in the other.

"What do you think he wanted the curtain hooks for?" Murray asked Barbara. He was anxious to make a joke of this, showing her how nothing was held against her on her brother's account.

"How should I know?" said Barbara.

"Maybe he needs counselling," said Murray. He had taken some sociology courses, because he had hoped at one time to become a United Church minister.

Barbara said, "Maybe he needs to be hanged."

Murray fell in love with her then, if he was not in love

already. Here is a noble girl, he thought. A bold black-and-white lily out of the Swamp Irish—Lorna Doone with a rougher tongue and a stronger spine. Mother won't like her, he thought. (About that he was entirely right.) He was happier than he'd been at any time since he lost his faith. (That was an unsatisfactory way of putting it. It was more as if he'd come into a closed-off room or opened a drawer and found that his faith had dried up, turned to a mound of dust in the corner.)

He always said that he made up his mind at once to get Barbara, but he used no tactics beyond an open display of worship. A capacity for worship had been noticeable in him all through his school days, along with his good nature and a tendency to befriend underdogs. But he was sturdy enough—he had enough advantages of his own—that it hadn't got him any serious squelching. Minor squelches he was able to sustain.

Barbara refused to ride on a float as the Downtown Merchants' contestant for the Queen of the Dominion Day Parade.

"I absolutely agree with you," said Murray. "Beauty contests are degrading."

"It's the paper flowers," said Barbara. "They make me sneeze."

Murray and Barbara live now at Zeigler's Resort, twenty-five miles or so northwest of Walley. The land here is rough and hilly. The farmers abandoned it around the turn of the century and let it go back to bush. Murray's father bought two hundred acres of it and built a primitive cabin and called the place his hunting camp. When Murray lost the store in Walley, and the big house and the little house on the lot behind the store, he came up here with Barbara and their two small children. He drove a school bus to get some cash income, and worked all the rest of the time building eight new cabins and renovating the one that was there, to serve as the lodge and as living quarters for his family. He learned carpentry, masonry, wiring, plumbing. He cut down trees and dammed the creek and cleaned the creek bed and trucked in sand, to make a swimming pond and a beach. For obvious reasons (as he says), Barbara handled the finances.

Murray says that his is a common story. Does it deserve to be called a classic? "My great-grandfather got the business going. My grandfather established it in all its glory. My father preserved it. And I lost it."

He doesn't mind telling people. Not that he waylays them and unburdens himself immediately. Guests are used to seeing him always at work. Repairing the dock, painting the rowboat, hauling in groceries, digging up drains, he looks so competent and unfrazzled, so cheerfully committed to whatever job he's doing, that they take him for a farmer turned to resort-keeping. He has the kind of patience and uninquisitive friendliness, the unathletic but toughened and serviceable body, the sunburned face, the graying boyishness that they might expect of a country man. But the same guests come back year after year, and sometimes they become friends who are invited on their last night to eat dinner at the family table. (It is considered an achievement, among the regulars, to become friends with stately Barbara. Some never manage it.) Then they may get to hear Murray's story.

"My grandfather used to go up on the roof of our building in Walley," Murray says. "He went up on the roof and he threw down money. Every Saturday afternoon. Quarters, dimes, nickels—five-cent pieces, I guess you called them then. It drew the crowds. The men who started Walley were flashy fellows. They weren't well educated. They weren't genteel. They thought they were building Chicago."

Then something different happened, he says. In came the ladies and the rectors and the grammar school. Out with the saloons and in with the garden parties. Murray's father was an elder of St. Andrew's; he stood for the Conservative Party.

"Funny—we used to say 'stood for' instead of 'ran for.' The store was an institution by that time. Nothing changed for decades. The old display cases with curved glass tops, and the change zinging overhead in those metal cylinders. The whole town was like that, into the fifties. The elm trees weren't dead yet. They'd started. In the summer there were the old cloth awnings all around the square."

When Murray decided to modernize, he went all out. It was 1965. He had the whole building covered in white stucco, the windows blocked in. Just little, classy, eye-level windows left along the street, as if intended to display the Crown jewels. The name Zeigler's—just that—written across the stucco in flowing script, pink neon. He chucked the waist-high counters and carpeted the varnished floors and put in indirect lighting and lots of mirrors. A great skylight over the staircase. (It leaked, had to be repaired, was taken out before the second winter.) Indoor trees and bits of pools and a kind of fountain in the ladies' room.

Insanity.

Meanwhile the mall had opened south of town. Should Murray have gone out there? He was too mired in debt to move. Also, he had become a downtown promoter. He had not only changed the image of Zeigler's, he had changed himself, becoming a busy loudmouth on the municipal scene. He served on committees. He was on the building committee. That was how he discovered that a man from Logan, a dealer and developer, was getting government money for restoring old buildings when the fact of the matter was that he was tearing the old buildings down and preserving only a remnant of the foundation to incorporate into his new, ugly, badly built, profitable apartment blocks.

"Aha—corruption," says Murray when he recalls this. "Let the people know! I ranted to the newspaper. I practically ranted on the street corners. What did I think? Did I think the people *didn't* know? It must have been a death wish. It was a death wish. I got to be such a ranter and public entertainment that I was turfed off the committee. I'd lost credibility. They said so. I'd also lost the store. I'd lost it to the bank. Plus the big house my grandfather built and the little house on the same lot, where

Barbara and I and the kids were living. The bank couldn't get at them, but I sold them off, to get square—that was the way I wanted to do it. Lucky thing my mother died before the crash came."

Sometimes Barbara excuses herself while Murray is talking. She could be going to get more coffee, she might come back in a moment. Or she might take the dog, Sadie, and go for a walk down to the pond, in among the pale trunks of the birch and poplar trees and under the droopy hemlocks. Murray doesn't bother explaining, though he listens, without appearing to do so, to hear her come back. Anybody who becomes their friend has to understand how Barbara balances contact with absences, just as they have to understand that Barbara doesn't want to *do* anything. She does plenty, of course. She does the cooking, she manages the resort. But when people find out how much she has read, and that she's never been to college, they sometimes suggest that she should go, she should get a degree.

"What for?" says Barbara.

And it turns out that she doesn't want to be a teacher, or a scholar, or a librarian, or an editor, or to make television documentaries, or review books, or write articles. The list of things that Barbara doesn't want to do is as long as your arm. Apparently she wants to do what she does—read, and go for walks, eat and drink with pleasure, tolerate some company. And unless people can value this about her—her withdrawals, her severe indolence (she has an air of indolence even when she's cooking an excellent dinner for thirty people)—they don't remain among the company she tolerates.

When Murray was busy renovating and borrowing money and involving himself in municipal life, Barbara was reading. She had always read, but now she let it take up more and more of her time. The children had started to school. Some days Barbara never left the house. There was always a coffee cup by her chair, and a pile of fat dusty books from the library, *Remembrance of Things Past, Joseph and His Brothers,* books by lesser

Russians whom Murray had never heard of. Barbara has a real mania for reading, his mother said—isn't she worried about bringing all those books from the library into the house? You never know who has been handling them.

Reading such heavy books, Barbara grew heavier herself. She did not get really fat, but she put on twenty or twenty-five pounds, well distributed over her tall, never delicate frame. Her face changed, too—flesh blurred its firm lines, making her look softer and in a way younger. Her cheeks puffed out and her mouth looked more secretive. Sometimes she had—she still has—the expression of a self-absorbed and rather willful little girl. Nowadays she reads skimpy-looking books by Czechs or Japanese or Rumanians, but she is still heavy. Her hair is still long, too, and black, except around the face, where it has gone white, as if a piece of veiling had been thrown over it.

Murray and Barbara are driving down out of the hills, from twisting, hilly roads to the flat, straight grid of the farmland. They are driving to Walley, for a special reason. Two weeks ago Barbara discovered a lump in the flesh of one of her buttocks. She was drying herself after coming out of the pond—it was the last swim, the last spurt of warm weather of the year. The lump was about the size of a marble. "If I wasn't so fat, I'd probably have found it sooner," she said, without particular regret or alarm. She and Murray spoke of the lump as they would of a bad tooth—a nuisance that had to be dealt with. She had it removed in the hospital in Walley. Then there had to be a biopsy.

"Is it possible to have cancer of the buttock?" she asked the doctor. "What an undignified thing!"

The doctor said that the lump could be a floater—malignant cells that had their origin somewhere else in the body. A sealed message. And they could remain a mystery—bad cells whose home base could never be found. If indeed they proved to be bad cells at all. "The future is unclear till we know," said the doctor.

Yesterday the doctor's receptionist phoned and said that the results were in. She made an appointment for Barbara to see the doctor in his office in Walley that afternoon.

"Is that all?" Murray said.

"All what?"

"Is that all she said?"

"She's just the receptionist. That's all she's supposed to say."

They are driving between walls of corn. The stalks are eight or nine feet high. Any day now the farmers will start to cut them. The sun is low enough even by midafternoon to shine through the cornstalks and turn them to coppery gold. They drive through an orderly radiance, mile after mile.

Last night they stayed up late; they watched an old, old movie, *The Trail of the Lonesome Pine*. Murray had seen it when he was a child, in the Roxy Theatre, in Walley. All he had remembered was the part about Buddy getting killed and Henry Fonda chipping out the pine-tree coffin.

Thinking about that, he starts to sing. " 'Oh, they cut down the old pine tree, and they hauled it away to the mill.' I always thought," he says, interrupting himself, "that that song came from that movie."

Barbara continues singing. " 'To make a coffin of pine, for that sweetheart of mine.' " Then she says, "Don't be squeamish."

"I wasn't," says Murray. "I forgot what came next."

"Don't come and sit in the waiting room. It's awful. Go down to the beach and wait for me. I'll come down the Sunset Steps."

They have to drive past the farm where Beatrice Sawicky used to keep horses. At one time she had a riding school. That didn't last very long. She boarded horses then, and she must have made a living out of that, because she kept at it, she stayed there, until four or five years ago, when she sold out and, presumably, moved away. They didn't know where she would go;

they had seen her a few times in town but never talked to her. When they used to drive past, and saw the horses in the fields, one or the other of them would say, "I wonder what happened to Victor." Not every time they passed, but about once a year, one of them would say that, and the other would answer, "God knows," or something of the sort. But they haven't bothered saying it since Beatrice and the horses left.

The first time that Victor Sawicky came into the store, he scattered the clerks—so Murray said to Barbara—like a cat among the pigeons. And, in fact, many of the clerks whom Murray had inherited with the store did look like pigeons—they were gray-haired maiden ladies whom maidenhood had not kept from growing stout and bosomy. It was easy to imagine a clammy dew of alarm between those bosoms at the sight of Victor. One of the women came pattering up the ramp to Murray's little office to tell him that there was a foreigner and that none of them could make out what it was he wanted.

He wanted work clothes. It wasn't so difficult to tell what he was saying. (After all, he had lived for several years in England.) It was not the Polish accent that dismayed the clerks in Zeigler's store, it was Victor's looks. Murray put Victor immediately into the same class of human beings as Barbara, but of the two he found Victor far the more splendid and disturbing. He had been able to look at Barbara and think, That is a rare girl. But she was still a girl, and he wanted to sleep with her. (He had been married to her now for seven years.) Victor drew his attention as a sleek and princely animal might—say, a golden palomino, bold but high-strung, shy about the stir he created. You'd try to say something soothing but deferential and stroke his shining neck, if he'd let you.

Murray said, "Work clothes."

Victor was tall and light-boned and looked polished. In the coffee shop of the British Exchange Hotel, where he and Murray got in the habit of going, a waitress said to him one day, "You mind telling me? Because we kind of have a bet going on? How tall are you?"

"I am six feet and five inches," said Victor.

"Is that all? We had you going up as high as seven feet."

His skin was a pale-olive color, his hair a dark blond, his eyes a light, bright blue. The eyes protruded a little, and the eyelids never lifted quite all the way. His teeth were large and stained, like his fingers, from nicotine. He smoked all the time. He was smoking while he gave his puzzled consideration to the overalls in Zeigler's store. They were all too short in the legs.

He said that he and his wife, who was English, had bought a farm just on the edge of town. Murray wanted to talk to him without the clerks hanging around in amazement, so he took him along the street, for the first time, to the British Exchange. He knew the farm Victor was talking about, and he didn't think much of it. But Victor said that they were not intending to farm it. They were going to keep horses and run a riding school. Victor asked Murray's opinion about whether or not this would be a success. Were there enough little rich girls around? "I think if you have a riding school you must have the little rich girls. They are the ones for the horse riding."

"You could advertise in the city papers, and they could come in the summers," Murray said.

"Of course. To the camp. To the horse camp. Here and in the United States they always go in summer to the camp, isn't that so?"

Victor seemed delighted with this idea. Everything was absurd to him, everything acceptable. The winters—is it true that there is frost from October to May? Does the snow actually reach to the windowsills? Can one drink the well water without boiling, or is there a danger of catching typhoid fever? What kind of trees, cut down, will provide the best heat in the stove?

Murray could not remember afterward which questions came the first day, or if there was ever a boundary between the practical questions and the more general or personal. He didn't think there was—they came all mixed up together. When Victor wondered about anything, he asked. When were those buildings put up? What is the people's main religion and are they very serious about it? Who is that important-looking man, that sad-looking woman? What do the people work at? Are there agitators, free-thinkers, very rich people, Communists? What sort of crimes are committed, when was the last time there was a murder, is there a certain amount of adultery? Did Murray play golf, did he own a pleasure boat, did his employees call him sir? (Not much, and no, and no.) Victor's blue eyes continued to shine with pleasure, whatever the question, whatever the answer. He stretched his long legs out of the coffee-shop booth and clasped his hands behind his head. He luxuriated, taking everything in. Soon Murray was telling him about how his grandfather threw coins down into the street, and about his father's dark suits and silk-backed vests, and his own notions of becoming a minister.

"But you did not?"

"I lost my faith." Murray always felt he had to grin when he said this. "That is—"

"I know what it is."

When he came to find Murray at the store, Victor would not ask any of the clerks if he could see him but would go straight up to the office, up the ramp to the little cage. It had wrought-iron walls around it, about as high as Murray was—about five-nine. Victor would try to come up stealthily, but of course his presence would have already disturbed the store, stirring up ripples of attention, misgiving, excitement. Murray usually knew when he was coming but pretended not to. Then Victor, for a surprise, would rest his gleaming head on the top of the wall, his neck held between two of the pointed, decorative spikes. He grinned at the idiotic effect.

Murray found this inexpressibly flattering.

Victor had a history of his own, of course. He was ten years older than Murray; he had been nineteen when the war broke out. He was a student then, in Warsaw. He had been taking flying lessons, but did not yet have his pilot's license. Nevertheless he went out to the airstrip where the planes of the Polish Air Force were sitting—he and some of his friends went out there almost as a prank, on the morning of the German invasion, and almost as a prank they took some of the planes into the air, and then they flew them to Sweden. After that, he got to England and joined the Polish Air Force, which was attached to the Royal Air Force. He flew on many raids, and was shot down over France. He bailed out; he hid in the woods, he ate raw potatoes from the fields, he was helped by the French Underground and made his way to the Spanish border. He got back to England. And he found to his great disappointment that he was not to be allowed to fly again. He knew too much. If he should be shot down again and captured and interrogated, he knew too much. He was so disappointed, so restless, he made such a nuisance of himself, that he was given another job—he was sent to Turkey, on a more or less secret mission, to be part of a network that helped Poles, and others, who were escaping through the Balkans.

That was what he had been doing while Murray and his friends had been building model airplanes and fixing up a kind of cockpit in the bicycle shed at school, so that they could pretend to be bombing Germany.

"But do you believe all that stuff, really?" Barbara said.

"They did fly Polish planes to Sweden before the Germans could get them," Murray said stubbornly. "And people did get shot down over France and escape."

"Do you think anybody as conspicuous as Victor could escape? Do you think anybody that conspicuous would ever get sent on a secret mission? You have to look more like Alec Guinness to get sent on a secret mission."

"Maybe he's so conspicuous he looks innocent," Murray said. "Maybe he'd look like the last person on earth to be sent on a secret mission and that would be the very reason nobody would suspect."

Perhaps for the first time, he thought that Barbara's cynicism was automatic and irritating. It was like a quirk she had, a tic.

They had this conversation after Victor and Beatrice had come to dinner. Murray had been anxious for Victor and Barbara to meet. He wanted to present them to each other, almost to show them off to each other. But when the opportunity arrived they were not at their best. Each seemed standoffish, lukewarm, nervous, ironical.

The day of the dinner party, in late May, had been freakishly cold and rainy. The children—Felicity was five then, and Adam three—had been playing indoors all day, getting in Barbara's way, messing up the living room, which she had cleaned, and by bedtime they weren't tired enough to settle down. The long, light evening was no help. There were many calls for drinks of water, reports of a stomachache, complaints about a dog that had almost bitten Felicity last week. Finally, Adam raced into the living room wearing only his pajama top, shouting, "I want a bicky, I want a bicky!" "Bicky" was a baby word for "biscuit," which he didn't normally use anymore. It seemed very likely that he had been inspired to this performance and probably rehearsed in it by Felicity. Murray scooped him up and carried him into the children's room and whacked his conveniently bare bottom. Then he whacked Felicity's once for good measure and returned to the dining room rubbing his hands together, playing a role he detested, that of the hearty disciplinarian. The bedroom door stayed shut, but it could not shut out a prolonged and vengeful howling.

Everything had gone wrong from the start with this visit. Murray had opened the door and said expansively, " 'The chestnut casts his flambeaux, and the flowers stream from the hawthorn on the wind away!' "—referring to the weather, and thinking that Beatrice would appreciate an English poem. Victor, smiling distractedly, said, "What? What do you say?" And Beatrice said, "It's a poem," just as if somebody had asked,

"What's that running across the road?" and she had replied, "It's a groundhog."

Victor's gaiety remained muted. His large, bright-eyed grin, his laughter seemed misplaced and forced, without energy. Even his skin looked dull and putty-colored. He was like the statue of a prince in a story Murray remembered, a children's story. The prince has his jewel eyes plucked out to be sold to help the poor, and finally gives all his gold-leaf skin to serve the same purpose. A little swallow helps him when he is blind, and remains his only friend.

The whole house smelled of the cooking. Barbara had done a pork roast. She had made the potatoes according to a new recipe, slicing them and cooking them in the oven in a buttered dish. They seemed greasy to Murray, and slightly on the raw side. The other vegetables were overcooked, because she had been so harassed in the kitchen, distracted by the children. The pecan pie was too rich a dessert for the meal, and the crust was too brown. Beatrice did not even try it. Beatrice did not finish the potatoes on her plate. She did not laugh when Adam made his disastrous sortie. She probably felt that children should be trained and kept in line as strictly as horses.

Murray reflected that he had never met a woman who was crazy about horses whom he had liked. They were narrow, righteous, humorless women, and usually not good-looking. Beatrice had a rosy, almost raw-looking complexion. Her hair was dull and graying and cut with no style. She wore no lipstick—an eccentricity that was a declaration of piety or contemptuous carelessness in a woman at that time. Her loosely belted mushroom-colored dress announced that she had no hopes of this dinner party and made no concessions to it.

Barbara, by way of contrast, was wearing a polished-cotton skirt of yellow and orange and copper colors, a tight black belt, a low-necked black blouse, and large, cheap hoop earrings. One of the things about Barbara that Murray did not understand and was not proud of—as opposed to the things he did not understand but was proud of—would have to be this taste she had for cheaply provocative clothes. Low necklines, cinch belts, tight toreador pants. She would go out into the streets of Walley showing off her body, which was lavish, in the style of the time—or one of the styles of the time, the style not of Audrey Hepburn but of Tina Louise—and the embarrassment Murray felt about this was complex and unmentionable. He felt that she was doing something that didn't fit in with her seriousness and aloofness, her caustic tone. She was behaving in a way that his mother might have predicted. ("I'm sure she is really a nice girl, but I'm not sure she has been very well educated," his mother had said, and even Murray understood that she was not referring to the books Barbara might have read or the marks she had got at school.) What was more troubling was that she was behaving in a way that didn't even tie in with her sexual nature, or what Murray knew of it—and he had to assume he knew everything. She was not really very passionate. Sometimes he thought that she pretended to be more passionate than she was. That was what these clothes reminded him of and why he couldn't mention them to her. There was something unsure, risky, excessive about them. He was willing to see all sorts of difficult things about Barbara—her uncharitableness, perhaps, or intransigence—but nothing that made her seem a little foolish, or sad.

There was a bouquet of lilacs in the center of the table. They got in the way of the serving dishes and dropped their messy flowers on the tablecloth. Murray became more and more irritated at the sight of them, and at last he said, "Barbara—do we really have to have those flowers on the table?" (The fed-up voice of a proper husband.) "We can't even see around them to talk."

At the moment, nobody was talking.

Barbara bent forward, shamelessly showing cleavage. She lifted the bouquet without a word, creating a shower of lilac blossoms onto the cloth and the meat platter. One of her earrings fell off and landed in the applesauce.

They should have laughed then. But nobody was able to. Barbara gave Murray a look of doom. He thought that they might as well get up now, they might as well get up from the table and abandon the unwanted food and inert conversation. They might as well go their own ways.

Victor picked the earring out of the applesauce with a spoon. He wiped it on his napkin and, bowing slightly to Barbara, laid it beside her plate. He said, "I have been trying to think who it is that is the heroine of a book that you remind me of."

Barbara clipped the earring back onto her ear. Beatrice looked past or through her husband's head at the tasteful but inexpensive wallpaper—cream medallions on an ivory ground— that Murray's mother had chosen for the gardener's cottage.

"It is Katerina Ivanovna Verkhovtsev," said Victor. "She is the fiancée—"

"I know who she is," said Barbara. "I think she's a pain."

Murray knew by the abrupt halt of her words that she had been about to say "pain in the arse."

"It's Beatrice," Murray said to Barbara as he helped her do the dishes. He had apologized about the lilacs. He said that it was Beatrice who had unnerved him, who had blighted the evening for them all. "Victor isn't himself with her," he said. "He had his light hidden under a bushel." He thought of Beatrice descending on Victor to extinguish him. Her jabbing bones. Her damp skirts.

"I could do without either one," said Barbara, and it was then that they had the exchange about conspicuous people and secret missions. But they ended up finishing the wine and laughing about the behavior of Adam and Felicity.

Victor began to come around in the evenings. Apparently the dinner party had not signalled for him any break or difficulty in

the friendship. In fact, it seemed to have brought him a greater
ease. He was able now to say something about his marriage—not
a complaint or an explanation, just something like "Beatrice
wants . . ." or, "Beatrice believes . . ."—and be sure that a good
deal would be understood.

And after a while he said more.

"Beatrice is impatient that I do not have the barn ready for
the horses, but I have to first deal with the drainage problems
and the tiles have not come. So it is not a very fine atmosphere
on the farm. But a beautiful summer. I am happy here."

Finally he said, "Beatrice has the money. You know that?
So she is obliged to call the piper. No—have I got that wrong?"

It was as Murray had suspected.

"He married her for her money and now he has to work for
it," said Barbara. "But he gets time for visiting."

"He can't work all day and all evening," Murray said. "He
doesn't come by for coffee in the daytime anymore."

This was the way they continued to talk about Victor—
Barbara sniping, Murray defending. It had become a game. Murray was relieved to see that Barbara didn't make Victor feel
unwelcome; she didn't seem displeased when he showed up in
the evenings.

He usually arrived around the time that Murray was putting
the lawnmower away or picking up some of the children's toys or
draining the wading pool or moving the sprinkler on his mother's
lawn. (His mother, as usual, was spending part of the summer far
away, in the Okanagan Valley.) Victor would try to help, bend-
ing to these tasks like a bemused and gentle robot. Then they
moved the two wooden lawn chairs to the middle of the yard and
sat down. They could hear Barbara working in the kitchen,
without turning the lights on, because, she said, they made her
hot. When she had finished, she would take a shower and come
out into the yard barefoot, barelegged, her long hair wet, smelling of lemon soap. Murray went into the house and made three
drinks, with gin and tonic and ice and limes. Usually he forgot

that Barbara didn't keep the limes in the refrigerator, and had to call out demanding to know where they were or if she had forgotten to buy any. Victor vacated his chair and stretched out on the grass, his cigarette glowing in the half-dark. They looked up and tried to see a satellite—still a rare and amazing thing to see. They could hear sprinklers, and sometimes distant shrieks, police sirens, laughter. That was the sound of television programs, coming through the open windows and screen doors along the street. Sometimes there was the slap of screen doors closing as people left those programs behind for a moment, and boisterous but uncertain voices calling into the other back yards where people sat drinking, as they did, or watching the sky. There was a sense of people's lives audible but solitary, floating free of each other under the roof of beech and maple branches in front of the houses, and in the cleared spaces behind, just as people in the same room, talking, float free on the edge of sleep. The sound of ice cubes tinkling unseen was meditative, comforting.

Sometimes the three of them played a game that Barbara had invented or adapted from something else. It was called Oranges and Apples, and she used it to keep the children occupied on car trips. It was a game of choices, going from very easy to very hard. Peanut butter or oatmeal porridge was where you might start, going on to peanut butter or applesauce, which was harder. The really hard choices could be between two things you liked very much or two things you disliked very much or between things that were for some reason almost impossible to compare. There was no way to win. The pleasure was in thinking up tormenting choices or in being tormented by them, and the end came only when somebody cried, "I give up. I can't stand it. It's too stupid. I don't want to think about it anymore!"

Would you rather eat fresh corn on the cob or homemade strawberry ice cream?

Would you sooner dive into a cool lake on a blistering hot day or enter a warm kitchen where there is fresh bread baking after you've walked through a bog in a snowstorm?

Would you prefer to make love to Mrs. Khrushchev or Mrs. Eisenhower?

Would you rather eat a piece of cold pork fat or listen to a speech at the Kiwanis luncheon?

Things were going badly at the farm. The well water was not safe to drink. The tops of the potatoes wilted from a blight. Insects of many sorts invaded the house, and the drains were still not completed. But it seemed that this was nothing compared to the human malevolence. One evening before Barbara came out to join them, Victor said to Murray, "I cannot eat any longer at the farm. I must eat all my meals at the coffee shop."

"Is it as unpleasant as all that?" said Murray.

"No, no. It is always unpleasant, but what I have discovered now is worse than the unpleasantness."

Poison. Victor said that he had found a bottle of prussic acid. He did not know how long Beatrice had had it but he did not think very long. There was no use for it on the farm. There was only the one use that he could think of.

"Surely not," said Murray. "She wouldn't do that. She isn't crazy. She isn't a poisoning sort of person."

"But you have no idea. You have no idea what sort of person she is or what she might do. You think she would not poison, she is an English lady. But England is full of murders and often it is the ladies and gentlemen and the husbands and wives. I cannot eat in her house. I wonder if I am safe even to sleep there. Last night I lay awake beside her, and in her sleep she was as cold as a snake. I got up and lay on the floor in the other room."

Murray remembered then the caretaker's apartment, empty now for years. It was on the third floor of the store building, at the back.

"Well, if you really think so," he said. "If you really want to move out . . ." And after Victor had accepted, with surprise, relief, and gratitude, Murray said, "Barbara will get it cleaned up for you."

It did not occur to him at that time that he himself or Victor might be capable of sweeping out and scrubbing some dirty rooms. It did not occur to Barbara, either. She cleaned out the apartment the next day, and provided sheets and towels and a few pots and dishes, though of course she was skeptical about the danger of poisoning. "What good would he be to her dead?"

Victor got a job immediately. He became the night watch-man at the surface installation of the salt mine. He liked working at night. He didn't have the use of a car anymore, so he walked to work at midnight and back to the apartment in the morning. If Murray was in the store before eight-thirty, he would hear Victor climbing the back stairs. How did he sleep, in the bright daylight in that little box of a room under the hot flat roof?

"I sleep beautifully," Victor said. "I cook, I eat, I sleep. I have relief. It is all of a sudden peace."

And one day Murray came home unexpectedly, in the middle of the afternoon.

Those words took shape in his mind afterward. They were so trite and sombre. *One day I came home unexpectedly . . .* Is there ever a story of a man who comes home unexpectedly and finds a delightful surprise?

He came home unexpectedly, and he found—not Victor and Barbara in bed together. Victor was not in the house at all—nobody was in the house. Victor was not in the yard. Adam was in the yard, splashing in the plastic pool. Not far away from the pool Barbara was lying on the faded quilt, stained with sun-tan oil, that they used when they went to the beach. She was wearing her strapless black bathing suit, a garment that resem-bled a corset and would not be considered at all attractive in a few years' time. It cut straight across the thighs, and pushed them together; it tightly confined the waist and stomach and hips, and uplifted and thrust out the breasts so that they appeared to be made of something at least as firm as Styrofoam. Her arms, legs, chest, and shoulders looked white in the sun, though they would show a tan when she came indoors. She was not reading, though she had a book open beside her. She was lying on her back with her arms loose at her sides. Murray was just about to call to her through the screen door, but he didn't.

Why not? He saw her lift one arm, to shield her eyes. Then she lifted her hips, she changed her position slightly. The movement might have been seen as entirely natural, casual—one of those nearly involuntary adjustments that our bodies make. What told Murray that it wasn't? Some pause or deliberateness, a self-consciousness, about that slight swelling and settling of the flesh made it clear to him—a man who knew this woman's body—that the woman wasn't alone. In her thoughts, at least, she wasn't alone.

Murray moved to the window over the sink. The yard was hidden from the back alley and the delivery platform at the back of the store by a high cedar hedge. But it was possible to see the back yard—the part of the back yard where Barbara lay—from the apartment window of the third floor. Barbara had not put up any curtains in the apartment. And Murray saw Victor sitting there, in that window. Victor had brought a chair over so that he could sit and look out at his ease. There was something odd about his face, as if he had a gas mask on.

Murray went to the bedroom and got the binoculars that he had bought recently. (He had thought of going for country walks and teaching the children to know the birds.) He moved very quietly through the house. Adam was making quite a lot of distracting noise outside.

When he looked at Victor through the binoculars, he saw a face like his own—a face partly hidden by binoculars. Victor had them, too. Victor was looking through binoculars at Barbara.

It appeared that he was naked—at least, what you could see of him was naked—sitting on a straight-backed chair at the window in his hot room. Murray could feel the heat of the room and the sweat-slicked hard seat of the chair and the man's powerful but controlled and concentrated excitement. And looking at Barbara he could feel the glow along the surface of her body, the energy all collected at the skin, as she gave herself up to this assault. She lay not quite still—there was a constant ripple passing over her, with little turns and twitches. Stirrings, shiftings. It was unbearable to watch. In the presence of her child in the middle of the day, in her own back yard, she lay on the grass inviting him. Promising—no, she was already providing—the most exquisite cooperation. It was obscene and enthralling and unbearable.

Murray could see himself—a man with binoculars watching a man with binoculars watching a woman. A scene from a movie. A comedy.

He did not know where to go. He could not go out into the yard and put a stop to this. He could not go back to the store and be aware of what was going on over his head. He left the house and got out the car, which he kept in his mother's garage, and went for a drive. Now he had another set of words to add to *One day I came home unexpectedly: I understood that my life had changed.*

But he did not understand it. He said, My life has changed, my life has been changed, but he did not understand it at all.

He drove around the back streets of Walley and over a railway crossing, out into the country. Everything looked as usual and yet like a spiteful imitation of itself. He drove with the windows down, trying to get a breeze, but he was going too slowly. He was driving at the town speed outside the town limits. A truck honked to get by him. This was in front of the brickyard. The noise of the truck's horn and the sunlight glaring off the bricks hit him all at once, banged him on the head so that he whimpered, as if he had a hangover.

Daily life continued, ringed by disaster as by a jubilant line of fire. He felt his house transparent, his life transparent—but still standing—himself a stranger, soft-footed and maliciously observant. What more would be revealed to him? At supper his daughter said, "Mommy, how come we never go to the beach this summer?" and it was hard to believe she didn't know everything.

"You do go," said Barbara. "You go with Heather's mother."

"But how come you and me and Adam don't go?"

"Adam and I like it here." Very smug and secure Barbara sounds—creamy. "I got tired of talking to the Other Mothers."

"Don't you like Heather's mother?"

"Sure."

"You don't."

"I do. I'm just lazy, Felicity. I'm unsociable."

"You don't," said Felicity with satisfaction. She left the table, and Barbara began to describe, as if for Murray's entertainment, the beach encampment set up by the Other Mothers. Their folding chairs and umbrellas, inflatable toys and mattresses, towels and changes of clothing, lotions, oils, antiseptic, Band-Aids, sun hats, lemonade, Kool-Aid, home-frozen popsicles, and healthful goodies. "Which are supposed to keep the little brutes from whining for French fries," said Barbara. "They never look at the lake unless one of their kids is in it. They talk about their kids' asthma or where they get the cheapest T-shirts."

Victor still came to visit in the evenings. They still sat in the back yard and drank gin. Now it seemed that in the games and the aimless conversations both Victor and Barbara deferred to Murray, laughed appreciatively, applauded any joke or his sighting of a falling star. He often left them alone together. He went into the kitchen to get more gin or ice; he went to check on the children, pretending that he had heard one of them cry out. He imagined then that Victor's long bare foot would slide out of its sandal and would graze, then knead, Barbara's offered calf, her outstretched thigh. Their hands would slide over whatever parts of each other they could reach. For a risky instant they might touch tongues. But when he came clattering out they were always prudently separated, talking some treacherous ordinary talk.

Victor had to leave earlier than he used to, to get to work at the salt mine. "Off to the salt mine," he would say—the same thing so many people said around here, the joke that was literally true.

Murray made love to Barbara then. He had never been so rough with her, or so free. He had a sense of despair and corruption. This is destruction, he thought. Another sentence in his head: *This is the destruction of love.* He fell asleep at once and woke up and had her again. She was full of a new compliance and passivity and she kissed him goodbye at breakfast with what seemed to him a strange, new, glistening sympathy. The sun shone every day, and in the mornings, particularly, it hurt his eyes. They were drinking more—three or four drinks now, instead of two—in the evenings, and he was putting more gin in them.

There came a time every afternoon when he couldn't stay in the store any longer, so he drove out into the country. He drove through the inland towns—Logan, Carstairs, Dalby Hill. Sometimes he drove as far as the hunting camp that had belonged to his father and now belonged to him. There he got out and walked, or sat on the steps of the neglected, boarded-up cabin. Sometimes he felt in all his trouble a terrible elation. He was being robbed. He was being freed of his life.

That summer, as in other summers, there came a Sunday when they spent the day picking blackberries along the country roads. Murray and Barbara and Adam and Felicity picked blackberries, and on the way home they bought sweet corn at a farmer's stand. Barbara made the annual supper of the first corn on the cob with the first fresh-blackberry pie. The weather had changed even as they were picking the berries, and when they bought the corn the farmer's wife was putting up the shutters on her stand and had loaded what she hadn't sold into the back of a truck. They were her last customers. The clouds were dark, and the kind of wind they hadn't felt for months was lifting the boughs of the trees and tearing off the dry leaves. A few drops of rain slapped the windshield, and by the time they reached Walley they were driving through a full-blown rainstorm. The house was so chilly that Murray turned on the furnace, and with the first wave of heat a cellar smell was driven through the house—that forgotten cave smell of roots, earth, damp concrete.

Murray went out in the rain and picked up the sprinkler, the plastic pool. He shoved the lawn chairs under the eaves.

"Is our summer over?" he said to Barbara, shaking the rain off his head.

The children watched "Walt Disney," and the boiling of the corn clouded the windows. They ate the supper. Barbara washed the dishes while Murray put the children to bed. When he shut the door on them and came out to the kitchen, he found Barbara sitting at the table in the near dark, drinking coffee. She was wearing one of last winter's sweaters.

"What about Victor?" Murray said. He turned on the lights. "Did you leave any blankets for him over in the apartment?"

"No," said Barbara.

"Then he'll be cold tonight. There's no heat on in the building."

"He can come and get some blankets if he's cold," said Barbara.

"He wouldn't come and ask," Murray said.

"Why not?"

"He just wouldn't."

Murray went to the hall closet and found two heavy blankets. He carried them into the kitchen.

"Don't you think you better take these over?" He laid them on the table, in front of her.

"Why not you?" said Barbara. "How do you even know he's there?"

Murray went to the window over the sink. "His light's on. He's there."

Barbara got up stiffly. She shuddered, as if she'd been holding herself tightly and now felt a chill.

"Is that sweater going to be enough?" said Murray. "Don't you need a coat? Aren't you going to comb your hair?"

She went into the bedroom. When she came out, she was wearing her white satin blouse and black pants. She had combed her hair and put on some new, very pale lipstick. Her mouth looked bleached-out, perverse, in her summer-tanned face.

Murray said, "No coat?"

"I won't have time to get cold."

He laid the blankets on her arms. He opened the door for her.

"It's Sunday," she said. "The doors'll be locked."

"Right," said Murray, and got the spare keys from the kitchen hook. He made sure she knew which one of them opened the side door of the building.

He watched the glimmer of her blouse until it vanished, and then he walked all through the house very quickly, taking noisy breaths. He stopped in the bedroom and picked up the clothes she had taken off. Her jeans and shirt and sweater. He held them up to his face and smelled them and thought, This is like a play. He wanted to see if she had changed her underpants. He shook out her jeans but the pants weren't there. He looked in the clothes hamper but he didn't see them. Could she have been sly enough to slip them under the children's things? What was the use of being sly now?

Her jeans had the smell jeans get when they've been worn a while without being washed—a smell not just of the body but of its labors. He could smell cleaning powder in them, and old cooking. And there was flour that she'd brushed off on them tonight, making the pastry for the pie. The smell of the shirt was of soap and sweat and perhaps of smoke. Was it smoke—was it cigarette smoke? He wasn't sure, as he sniffed again, that it was smoke at all. He thought of his mother saying that Barbara was not well educated. His mother's clothes would never smell this way, of her body and her life. She had meant that Barbara was not well-mannered, but couldn't she also have meant—*loose?* A loose woman. When he heard people say that, he'd always thought of an unbuttoned blouse, clothes slipping off the body, to indicate its appetite and availability. Now he thought that it could mean just that—loose. A woman who could get loose, who wasn't fastened down, who was not reliable, who could roll away.

She had got loose from her own family. She had left them completely. Shouldn't he have understood by that how she could leave him?

Hadn't he understood it, all the time?

He had understood that there would be surprises.

He went back to the kitchen. (*He stumbles into the kitchen.*) He poured himself half a tumbler of gin, without tonic or ice. (*He pours half a tumbler of gin.*) He thought of further humiliations. His mother would get a new lease on life. She would take over the children. He and the children would move into his mother's house. Or perhaps the children would move and he would remain here, drinking gin. Barbara and Victor might come to see him, wanting to be friends. They might establish a household and ask him over in the evenings, and he might go.

No. They would not think of him. They would banish the thought of him, they would go away.

As a child, Murray had seldom got into fights. He was diplomatic and good-humored. But eventually he had been in a fight and had been knocked to the ground of the Walley school-yard, knocked out, probably, for half a minute. He lay on his back in a daze, and saw the leaves on a bough above him turn into birds—black, then bright as the sun poked through and the wind stirred them. He was knocked into a free, breezy space where every shape was light and changeable and he himself the same. He lay there and thought, *It's happened to me.*

The flight of seventy-eight steps from the beach to the park on top of the cliffs is called the Sunset Steps. Beside these steps there is a sign on which the time of the sunset is posted for every day from the beginning of June to the end of September. "SEE THE SUN SET TWICE," the sign says, with an arrow pointing to the steps. The idea is that if you run very quickly from the bottom to the top of the steps you can see the last arc of the sun disappear a second time. Visitors think that this notion, and the custom of posting the sunset time, must be an old Walley tradition. Actually, it is a new wrinkle dreamed up by the Chamber of Commerce.

The boardwalk is new as well. The old-fashioned bandstand in the park is new. There was never a bandstand there before. All this charm and contrivance pleases visitors—Murray can hardly be against it; he is in the tourist business himself—and nowadays it pleases the townspeople as well. During that summer in the sixties, when Murray spent so much time driving around the country, it looked as if everything from an earlier time was being torn up, swept away, left to rot, disregarded. The new machinery was destroying the design of the farms, trees were cut down for wider roads, village stores and schools and houses were being abandoned. Everybody alive seemed to be yearning toward parking lots and shopping centers and suburban lawns as smooth as paint. Murray had to face up to being out of step, to having valued, as if they were final, things that were only accidental and temporary.

Out of such facing up, no doubt, came the orgy of smashing and renovating, which he was to get into a few months later.

And now it looks as if the world has come round to Murray's old way of thinking. People are restoring old houses and building new houses with old-style verandas. It is hard to find anybody who is not in favor of shade trees and general stores, pumps, barns, swings, nooks and crannies. But Murray himself can't quite recall the pleasure he took in these things, or find much shelter.

When he has walked beyond the end of the boardwalk to where the cedar trees crowd onto the beach, he sits on a boulder. First he noticed what a strange, beautiful boulder this was, with a line through it as if it had been split diagonally and the halves fitted together again not quite accurately—the pattern was jagged. He knew enough geology to understand that the line was a fault, and that the boulder must have come from the Precambrian shield that was a hundred miles away from here. It was rock formed before the last Ice Age; it was far older than the shore on which it sat. Look at the way it had been folded, as well as split—the layer on top hardened in waves like lapping cream.

He stopped being interested in the boulder and sat down on it. Now he sits looking at the lake. A line of turquoise blue at the horizon, fine as if drawn with turquoise ink, then a clear blue to the breakwater, shading into waves of green and silver breaking on the sand. La Mer Douce the French had called this lake. But of course it could change color in an hour; it could turn ugly, according to the wind and what was stirred up from the bottom.

People will sit and watch the lake as they'd never watch a field of waving grass or grain. Why is that, when the motion is the same? It must be the washing away, the wearing away, that compels them. The water all the time returning—eating, altering, the shore.

A similar thing happens to a person dying that kind of death. He has seen his father, he has seen others. A washing away, a vanishing—one fine layer after another down to the lighted bone.

He isn't looking in that direction, but he knows when Barbara comes into sight. He turns and sees her at the top of the steps. Tall Barbara, in her fall wrap of handwoven wheat-colored wool, starting down with no particular hurry or hesitation, not holding on to the rail—her usual deliberate yet indifferent air. He can't tell anything from the way she moves.

When Barbara opened the back door, her hair was wet from the rain—stringy—and her satin blouse ruinously spotted.

"What are you doing?" she said. "What are you drinking? Is that straight gin?"

Then Murray said what neither of them ever mentioned or forgot. "Didn't he want you?" he said.

Barbara came over to the table and pushed his head against the wet satin and the cruel little buttons, pushed it mercilessly between her hard breasts. "We are never going to talk about it," she said. "We never will. O.K.?" He could smell the cigarette smoke on her now, and the smell of the foreign skin. She held him till he echoed her.

"O.K."

And she held to what she'd said, even when he told her that Victor had gone away on the morning bus and had left a note addressed to both of them. She didn't ask to see or touch the note, she didn't ask what was in it.

("I am full of gratitude and now I have enough money that I think it is time for me to follow my life elsewhere. I think of going to Montreal where I will enjoy speaking French.")

At the bottom of the steps Barbara bends down and picks up something white. She and Murray walk toward each other along the boardwalk, and in a minute Murray can see what it is: a white balloon, looking somewhat weakened and puckered.

"Look at this," Barbara says as she comes up to him. She reads from a card attached to the string of the balloon. " 'Anthony Burler. Twelve years old. Joliet Elementary School. Crompton, Illinois. October 15th.' That's three days ago. Could it have flown over here in just three days?

"I'm O.K.," she says then. "It wasn't anything. It wasn't anything bad. There isn't anything to worry about."

"No," says Murray. He holds her arms, he breathes the leafy, kitchen smell of her black-and-white hair.

"Are you shaking?" she says.

He doesn't think that he is.

Easily, without guilt, in the long-married way, he cancels out the message that flashed out when he saw her at the top of the steps: *Don't disappoint me again.*

He looks at the card in her hand and says, "There's more. 'Favorite book—*The Last of the Mohicans.*' "

"Oh, that's for the teacher," Barbara says, with the familiar little snort of laughter in her voice, dismissing and promising. "That's a lie."

Pictures of the Ice

Three weeks before he died—drowned in a boating accident in a lake whose name nobody had heard him mention—Austin Cobbett stood deep in the clasp of a three-way mirror in Crawford's Men's Wear, in Logan, looking at himself in a burgundy sports shirt and a pair of cream, brown, and burgundy plaid pants. Both permanent press.

"Listen to me," Jerry Crawford said to him. "With the darker shirt and the lighter pants you can't go wrong. It's youthful."

Austin cackled. "Did you ever hear that expression 'mutton dressed as lamb'?"

"Referred to ladies," Jerry said. "Anyway, it's all changed now. There's no old men's clothes, no old ladies' clothes anymore. Style applies to everybody."

When Austin got used to what he had on, Jerry was going to talk him into a neck scarf of complementary colors and a cream pullover. Austin needed all the cover-up he could get. Since his wife died, about a year ago, and they finally got a new minister at the United Church (Austin, who was over seventy, was officially retired but had been hanging on and filling in while they haggled over hiring a new man and what they would pay him), he had lost weight, his muscles had shrunk, he was getting the potbellied caved-in shape of an old man. His neck was corded and his nose lengthened and his cheeks drooping. He was a stringy old rooster—stringy but tough, and game enough to gear up for a second marriage.

"The pants are going to have to be taken in," Jerry said. "You can give us time for that, can't you? When's the happy happy day?"

Austin was going to be married in Hawaii, where his wife, his wife-to-be, lived. He named a date a couple of weeks ahead.

Phil Stadelman from the Toronto Dominion Bank came in then and did not recognize Austin from the back, though Austin was his own former minister. He'd never seen him in clothes like that.

Phil told his AIDS joke—Jerry couldn't stop him.

Why did the Newfie put condoms on his ears?

Because he didn't want to get hearing aids.

Then Austin turned around, and instead of saying, "Well, I don't know about you fellows, but I find it hard to think of AIDS as a laughing matter," or "I wonder what kind of jokes they tell in Newfoundland about the folks from Huron County," he said, "That's rich." He laughed.

That's rich. Then he asked Phil's opinion of his clothes.

"Do you think they're going to laugh when they see me coming in Hawaii?"

Karin heard about this when she went into the doughnut place to drink a cup of coffee after finishing her afternoon stint as a crossing guard. She sat at the counter and heard the men talking at a table behind her. She swung around on the stool and said, "Listen, I could have told you, he's changed. I see him every day and I could have told you."

Karin is a tall, thin woman with a rough skin and a hoarse voice and long blond hair dark for a couple of inches at the roots. She's letting it grow out dark and it's got to where she could cut it short, but she doesn't. She used to be a lanky blond girl, shy and pretty, riding around on the back of her husband's motorcycle. She has gone a little strange—not too much or she wouldn't be a crossing guard, even with Austin Cobbett's recommendation. She interrupts conversations. She never seems to wear anything but her jeans and an old navy-blue duffel coat. She has a hard and suspicious expression and she has a public grudge against her ex-husband. She will write things on his car, with her finger: *Fake Christian. Kiss arse Phony. Brent Duprey is a snake.* Nobody knows that she wrote *Lazarus Sucks*, because she went back (she does this at night) and rubbed it off with her sleeve. Why? It seemed dangerous, something that might get her into trouble—the trouble being of a vaguely supernatural kind, not a talk with the Chief of Police—and she has nothing against Lazarus in the Bible, only against Lazarus House, which is the place Brent runs, and where he lives now.

Karin lives where she and Brent lived together for the last few months—upstairs over the hardware store, at the back, a big room with an alcove (the baby's) and a kitchen at one end. She spends a lot of her time over at Austin's, cleaning out his house, getting everything ready for his departure to Hawaii. The house he lives in, still, is the old parsonage, on Pondicherry Street. The church has built the new minister a new house, quite nice, with a patio and a double garage—ministers' wives often work now; it's a big help if they can get jobs as nurses or teachers, and in that case you need two cars. The old parsonage is a grayish-white brick house with blue-painted trim on the veranda and the gables. It needs a lot of work. Insulating, sandblasting, new paint, new window frames, new tiles in the bathroom. Walking back to her own place at night, Karin sometimes occupies her mind thinking what she'd do to that place if it was hers and she had the money.

Austin shows her a picture of Sheila Brothers, the woman he is to marry. Actually, it's a picture of the three of them—Austin, his wife, and Sheila Brothers, in front of a log building and some pine trees. A Retreat, where he—they—first met Sheila. Austin has on his minister's black shirt and turned collar; he looks shifty, with his apologetic, ministerial smile. His wife is looking away from him, but the big bow of her flowered scarf flutters against his neck. Fluffy white hair, trim figure. Chic. Sheila Brothers—Mrs. Brothers, a widow—is looking straight ahead, and she is the only one who seems really cheerful. Short fair hair combed around her face in a businesslike way, brown slacks, white sweatshirt, with the fairly large bumps of her breasts and stomach plain to see, she meets the camera head-on and doesn't seem worried about what it will make of her.

"She looks happy," Karin says.

"Well. She didn't know she was going to marry me, at the time."

He shows her a postcard picture of the town where Sheila lives. The town where he will live in Hawaii. Also a photograph of her house. The town's main street has a row of palm trees down the middle, it has low white or pinkish buildings, lampposts with brimming flower baskets, and over all a sky of deep turquoise in which the town's name—a Hawaiian name there is no hope of pronouncing or remembering—is written in flowing letters like silk ribbon. The name floating in the sky looked as possible as anything else about it. As for the house, you could hardly make it out at all—just a bit of balcony among the red and pink and gold flowering trees and bushes. But there was the beach in front of it, the sand pure as cream and the jewel-bright waves breaking. Where Austin Cobbett would walk with friendly Sheila. No wonder he needed all new clothes.

What Austin wants Karin to do is clear everything out. Even his books, his old typewriter, the pictures of his wife and children. His son lives in Denver, his daughter in Montreal. He has written to them, he has talked to them on the phone, he has asked them to claim anything they want. His son wants the dining-room furniture, which a moving-truck will pick up next week. His daughter said she didn't want anything. (Karin think she's apt to reconsider; people always want *something*.) All the furniture, books, pictures, curtains, rugs, dishes, pots, and pans are to go to the Auction Barn. Austin's car will be auctioned as well, and his power mower and the snowblower his son gave him last Christmas. These will be sold after Austin leaves for Hawaii, and the money is to go to Lazarus House. Austin started Lazarus House when he was a minister. Only he didn't call it that; he called it Turnaround House. But now they have decided—Brent Duprey has decided—it would be better to have a name that is more religious, more Christian.

At first Austin was just going to give them all these things to use in or around the House. Then he thought that it would be showing more respect to give them the money, to let them spend it as they liked, buying things they liked, instead of using his wife's dishes and sitting on his wife's chintz sofa.

"What if they take the money and buy lottery tickets with it?" Karin asks him. "Don't you think it'll be a big temptation to them?"

"You don't get anywhere in life without temptations," Austin says, with his maddening little smile. "What if they won the lottery?"

"Brent Duprey is a snake."

Brent has taken over the whole control of Lazarus House, which Austin started. It was a place for people to stay who wanted to stop drinking or some other way of life they were in; now it's a born-again sort of place, with nightlong sessions of praying and singing and groaning and confessing. That's how Brent got hold of it—by becoming more religious than Austin. Austin got Brent to stop drinking; he pulled and pulled on Brent until he pulled him right out of the life he was leading and into a new life of running this House with money from the church, the government, and so on, and he made a big mistake, Austin did, in thinking he could hold Brent there. Brent once started on the holy road went shooting on past; he got past Austin's careful quiet kind of religion in no time and cut Austin out with the people in his own church who wanted a stricter, more ferocious kind of Christianity. Austin was shifted out of Lazarus House and the church at about the same time, and Brent bossed the new minister around without difficulty. And in spite of this, or because of it, Austin wants to give Lazarus House the money.

"Who's to say whether Brent's way isn't closer to God than mine is, after all?" he says.

Karin says just about anything to anybody now. She says to Austin, "Don't make me puke."

Austin says she must be sure to keep a record of her time, so she will be paid for all this work, and also, if there is anything here that she would particularly like, to tell him, so they can discuss it.

"Within reason," he says. "If you said you'd like the car or the snowblower, I guess I'd be obliged to say no, because that would be cheating the folks over at Lazarus House. How about the vacuum cleaner?"

Is that how he sees her—as somebody who's always thinking about cleaning houses? The vacuum cleaner is practically an antique, anyway.

"I bet I know what Brent said when you told him I was going to be in charge of all this," she says. "I bet he said, 'Are you going to get a lawyer to check up on her?' He did! Didn't he?"

Instead of answering that, Austin says, "Why would I trust a lawyer any more than I trust you?"

"Is that what you said to him?"

"I'm saying it to you. You either trust or you don't trust, in my opinion. When you decide you're going to trust, you have to start where you are."

Austin rarely mentions God. Nevertheless you feel the mention of God hovering on the edge of sentences like these, and it makes you so uneasy—Karin gets a crumbly feeling along her spine—that you wish he'd say it and get it over with.

Four years ago Karin and Brent were still married, and they hadn't had the baby yet or moved to their place above the hardware store. They were living in the old slaughterhouse. That was a cheap apartment building belonging to Morris Fordyce, but it really had at one time been a slaughterhouse. In wet weather Karin could smell pig, and always she smelled another smell that she thought was blood. Brent sniffed around the walls and got down and sniffed the floor, but he couldn't smell what she was smelling. How could he smell anything but the clouds of boozy breath that rose from his own gut? Brent was a drunk then, but not a sodden drunk. He played hockey on the O. T. (over thirty, old-timers) hockey team—he was quite a bit older than Karin—and he claimed that he had never played sober. He worked for Fordyce Construction for a while, and then he worked for the town, cutting up trees. He drank on the job when he could, and after work he drank at the Fish and Game Club or at the Green Haven Motel Bar, called the Greasy Heaven. One night he got a bulldozer going, which was sitting outside the Greasy Heaven, and he drove it across town to the Fish and Game Club. Of course he was caught, and charged with impaired driving of a bulldozer, a big joke all over town. Nobody who laughed at the joke came around to pay the fine. And Brent just kept getting wilder. Another night he took down the stairs that led to their apartment. He didn't bash the steps out in a fit of temper; he removed them thoughtfully and methodically, steps and uprights one by one, backing downstairs as he did so and leaving Karin cursing at the top. First she was laughing at him—she had had a few beers herself by that time—then, when she realized he was in earnest, and she was being marooned there, she started cursing. Coward neighbors peeped out of the doors behind him.

Brent came home the next afternoon and was amazed, or

pretended to be. "What happened to the *steps?*" he yelled. He stomped around the hall, his lined, exhausted, excited face working, his blue eyes snapping, his smile innocent and conniving. "God damn that Morris! God-damn steps caved in. I'm going to sue the shit out of him. God damn *fuck!*" Karin was upstairs with nothing to eat but half a package of Rice Krispies with no milk, and a can of yellow beans. She had thought of phoning somebody to come with a ladder, but she was too mad and stubborn. If Brent wanted to starve her, she would show him. She would starve.

That time was really the beginning of the end, the change. Brent went around to see Morris Fordyce to beat him up and tell him about how he was going to have the shit sued out of him, and Morris talked to him in a reasonable, sobering way until Brent decided not to sue or beat up Morris but to commit suicide instead. Morris called Austin Cobbett then, because Austin had a reputation for knowing how to deal with people who were in a desperate way. Austin didn't talk Brent out of drinking then, or into the church, but he talked him out of suicide. Then, a couple of years later when the baby died, Austin was the only minister they knew to call. By the time he came to see them, to talk about the funeral, Brent had drunk everything in the house and gone out looking for more. Austin went after him and spent the next five days—with a brief time out for burying the baby—just staying with him on a bender. Then he spent the next week nursing him out of it, and the next month talking to him or sitting with him until Brent decided he would not drink anymore, he had been put in touch with God. Austin said that Brent meant by that that he had been put in touch with the fullness of his own life and the power of his innermost self. Brent said it was not for one minute himself; it was God.

Karin went to Austin's church with Brent for a while; she didn't mind that. She could see, though, that it wasn't going to be enough to hold Brent. She saw him bouncing up to sing the hymns, swinging his arms and clenching his fists, his whole body primed up. It was the same as he was after three or four beers when there was no way he could stop himself going for more. He was bursting. And soon enough he burst out of Austin's hold and took a good part of the church with him. A lot of people had wanted that loosening, more noise and praying and singing and not so much quiet persuading talking; they'd been wanting it for a long while.

None of it surprised her. It didn't surprise her that Brent learned to fill out papers and make the right impression and get government money; that he took over Turnaround House, which Austin had got him into, and kicked Austin out. He'd always been full of possibilities. It didn't really surprise her that he got as mad at her now for drinking one beer and smoking one cigarette as he used to do when she wanted to stop partying and go to bed at two o'clock. He said he was giving her a week to decide. No more drinking, no more smoking, Christ as her Saviour. One week. Karin said don't bother with the week. After Brent was gone, she quit smoking, she almost quit drinking, she also quit going to Austin's church. She gave up on nearly everything but a slow, smoldering grudge against Brent, which grew and grew. One day Austin stopped her on the street and she thought he was going to say some gentle, personal, condemning thing to her, for her grudge or her quitting church, but all he did was ask her to come and help him look after his wife, who was getting home from the hospital that week.

Austin is talking on the phone to his daughter in Montreal. Her name is Megan. She is around thirty, unmarried, a television producer.

"Life has a lot of surprises up its sleeve," Austin says. "You know this has nothing to do with your mother. This is a new life entirely. But I regret . . . No, no. I just mean there's more than one way to love God, and taking pleasure in the world is surely one of them. That's a revelation that's come on me rather late.

Too late to be of any use to your mother. . . . No. Guilt is a sin and a seduction. I've said that to many a poor soul that liked to wallow in it. Regret's another matter. How could you get through a long life and escape it?"

I was right, Karin is thinking; Megan does want something. But after a little more talk—Austin says that he might take up golf, don't laugh, and that Sheila belongs to a play-reading club, he expects he'll be a star at that, after all his pulpit haranguing—the conversation comes to an end. Austin comes out to the kitchen—the phone is in the front hall; this is an old-fashioned house—and looks up at Karin, who is cleaning out the high cupboards.

"Parents and children, Karin," he says, sighing, sighing, looking humorous. "Oh, what a tangled web we weave, when first we—have children. Then they always want us to be the same, they want us to be parents—it shakes them up dreadfully if we should do anything they didn't think we'd do. Dreadfully."

"I guess she'll get used to it," Karin says, without much sympathy.

"Oh, she will, she will. Poor Megan."

Then he says he's going uptown to have his hair cut. He doesn't want to leave it any longer, because he always looks and feels so foolish with a fresh haircut. His mouth turns down as he smiles—first up, then down. That downward slide is what's noticeable on him everywhere—face slipping down into neck wattles, chest emptied out and mounded into that abrupt, queer little belly. The flow has left dry channels, deep lines. Yet Austin speaks—it's his perversity to speak—as if out of a body that is light and ready and a pleasure to carry around.

In a short time the phone rings again and Karin has to climb down and answer it.

"Karin? Is that you, Karin? It's Megan!"

"Your father's just gone up to get a haircut."

"Good. Good. I'm glad. It gives me a chance to talk to you. I've been hoping I'd get a chance to talk to you."

"Oh," says Karin.

"Karin. Now, listen. I know I'm behaving just the way adult children are supposed to behave in this situation. I don't like it. I don't like that in myself. But I can't help it. I'm suspicious. I wonder what's going on. Is he all right? What do you think of it? What do you think of this woman he's going to marry?"

"All I ever saw of her is her picture," Karin says.

"I am terribly busy right now and I can't just drop everything and come home and have a real heart-to-heart with him. Anyway, he's very difficult to talk to. He makes all the right noises, he seems so open, but in reality he's very closed. He's never been at all a personal kind of person, do you know what I mean? He's never done anything before for a *personal* kind of reason. He always did things *for* somebody. He always liked to find people who *needed* things done for them, a lot. Well, you know that. Even bringing you into the house, you know, to look after Mother—it wasn't exactly for Mother's sake or his sake he did that."

Karin can picture Megan—the long, dark, smooth hair, parted in the middle and combed over her shoulders, the heavily made-up eyes and tanned skin and pale-pink lipsticked mouth, the handsomely clothed plump body. Wouldn't her voice bring such looks to mind even if you'd never seen her? Such smoothness, such rich sincerity. A fine gloss on every word and little appreciative spaces in between. She talks as if listening to herself. A little too much that way, really. Could she be drunk?

"Let's face it, Karin. Mother was a snob." (Yes, she is drunk.) "Well, she had to have something. Dragged around from one dump to another, always doing good. Doing good wasn't her thing at all. So now, *now*, he gives it all up, he's off to the easy life. In Hawaii! Isn't it bizarre?"

"Bizarre." Karin has heard that word on television and heard people, mostly teen-agers, say it, and she knows it is not the church bazaar Megan's talking about. Nevertheless that's what the word makes her think of—the church bazaars that Megan's mother used to organize, always trying to give them some style and make things different. Striped umbrellas and a sidewalk café one year, Devonshire teas and a rose arbor the next. Then she thinks of Megan's mother on the chintz-covered sofa in the living room, weak and yellow after her chemotherapy, one of those padded, perky kerchiefs around her nearly bald head. Still, she could look up at Karin with a faint, formal surprise when Karin came into the room. "Was there something you wanted, Karin?" The thing that Karin was supposed to ask her, she would ask Karin.

Bizarre. Bazaar. Snob. When Megan got in that dig, Karin should have said, at least, "I know that." All she can think to say is "Megan. This is costing you money."

"Money, Karin! We're talking about my *father*. We're talking about whether my father is sane or whether he has flipped his *wig*, Karin!"

A day later a call from Denver. Don, Austin's son, is calling to tell his father that they better forget about the dining-room furniture, the cost of shipping it is too high. Austin agrees with him. The money could be better spent, he says. What's furniture? Then Austin is called upon to explain about the Auction Barn and what Karin is doing.

"Of course, of course, no trouble," Austin says. "They'll list everything they get and what it sold for. They can easily send a copy. They've got a computer, I understand. No longer the Dark Ages up here. . . .

"Yes," Austin says. "I hoped you'd see it that way about the money. It's a project close to my heart. And you and your sister are providing well for yourselves. I'm very fortunate in my children. . . .

"The Old Age Pension and my minister's pension," he says. "Whatever more could I want? And this lady, this lady, I can tell you, Sheila—she is not short of money, if I can put it that way. . . ." He laughs rather mischievously at something his son says.

After he hangs up, he says to Karin, "Well, my son is worried about my finances and my daughter is worried about my mental state. My mental-emotional state. The male and female way of looking at things. The male and female way of expressing their anxiety. Underneath it's the same thing. The old order changeth, yielding place to new."

Don wouldn't remember everything that was in the house, anyway. How could he? He was here the day of the funeral and his wife wasn't with him; she was too pregnant to come. He wouldn't have her to rely on. Men don't remember that sort of thing well. He just asked for the list so that it would look as if he were keeping track of everything and nobody'd better try to hoodwink him. Or hoodwink his father.

There were things Karin was going to get, and nobody need know where she had got them. Nobody came up to her place. A willow-pattern plate. The blue-and-gray flowered curtains. A little, fat jug of ruby-colored glass with a silver lid. A white damask cloth, a tablecloth, that she had ironed till it shone like a frosted snowfield, and the enormous napkins that went with it. The tablecloth alone weighed as much as a child, and the napkins would flop out of wineglasses like lilies—if you had wineglasses. Just as a start, she has already taken home six silver spoons in her coat pocket. She knows enough not to disturb the silver tea service or the good dishes. But some pink glass dishes for dessert, with long stems, have taken her eye. She can see her place transformed, with these things in it. More than that, she can feel the quiet and content they would extend to her. Sitting in a room so furnished, she wouldn't need to go out. She would never need to think of Brent, and ways to torment him. A person sitting in such a room could turn and floor anybody trying to intrude.

Was there something you wanted?

On Monday of Austin's last week—he was supposed to fly to Hawaii on Saturday—the first big storm of the winter began.

The wind came in from the west, over the lake; there was driving snow all day and night. Monday and Tuesday the schools were closed, so Karin didn't have to work as a guard. But she couldn't stand staying indoors; she put on her duffel coat and wrapped her head and half her face in a wool scarf and plowed through the snow-filled streets to the parsonage.

The house is cold, the wind is coming in around the doors and windows. In the kitchen cupboard along the west wall, the dishes feel like ice. Austin is dressed but lying down on the living-room sofa, wrapped in various quilts and blankets. He is not reading or watching television or dozing, as far as she can tell—just staring. She makes him a cup of instant coffee.

"Do you think this'll stop by Saturday?" she says. She has the feeling that if he doesn't go Saturday, he just may not go at all. The whole thing could be called off, all plans could falter.

"It'll stop in due time," he says. "I'm not worried."

Karin's baby died in a snowstorm. In the afternoon, when Brent was drinking with his friend Rob and watching television, Karin said that the baby was sick and she needed money for a taxi to take him to the hospital. Brent told her to fuck off. He thought she was just trying to bother him. And partly she was— the baby had just thrown up once, and whimpered, and he didn't seem very hot. Then about suppertime, with Rob gone, Brent went to pick up the baby and play with him, forgetting that he was sick. "This baby's like a hot coal!" he yelled at Karin, and wanted to know why she hadn't got the doctor, why she hadn't taken the baby to the hospital. "You tell me why," said Karin, and they started to fight. "You said he didn't need to go," said Karin. "O.K., so he doesn't need to go." Brent called the taxi company, and the taxis weren't going out because of the storm, which up to then neither he nor Karin had noticed. He called the hospital and asked them what to do, and they said to get the fever down by wrapping the baby in wet towels. So they did that, and by midnight the storm had quieted down and the snowplows were out on the streets and they got the baby to the hospital. But he died. He probably would have died no matter what they'd done; he had meningitis. Even if he'd been a fussed-over precious little baby in a home where the father didn't get drunk and the mother and father didn't have fights, he might have died; he probably would have died, anyway.

Brent wanted it to be his fault, though. Sometimes he wanted it to be their fault. It was like sucking candy to him, that confession. Karin told him to shut up, she told him to *shut up.*

She said, "He would have died anyway."

When the storm is over, Tuesday afternoon, Karin puts on her coat and goes out and shovels the parsonage walk. The temperature seems to be dropping even lower; the sky is clear. Austin says they're going to go down to the lake to look at the ice. If there is a big storm like this fairly early in the year, the wind drives the waves up on the shore and they freeze there. Ice is everywhere, in unlikely formations. People go down and take pictures. The paper often prints the best of them. Austin wants to take some pictures, too. He says it'll be something to show people in Hawaii. So Karin shovels the car out, too, and off they go, Austin driving with great care. And nobody else is down there. It's too cold. Austin hangs on to Karin as they struggle along the boardwalk—or where the boardwalk must be, under the snow. Sheets of ice drop from the burdened branches of the willow trees to the ground, and the sun shines through them from the west; they're like walls of pearl. Ice is woven through the wire of the high fence to make it like a honeycomb. Waves have frozen as they hit the shore, making mounds and caves, a crazy landscape, out to the rim of the open water. And all the playground equipment, the children's swings and climbing bars, has been transformed by ice, hung with organ pipes or buried in what looks like half-carved statues, shapes of ice that might be people, animals, angels, monsters, left unfinished.

Karin is nervous when Austin stands alone to take pictures. He seems shaky to her—and what if he fell? He could break a leg, a hip. Old people break a hip and that's the end of them.

Even taking off his gloves to work the camera seems risky. A frozen thumb might be enough to keep him here, make him miss his plane.

Back in the car, he does have to rub and blow on his hands. He lets her drive. If something dire happened to him, would Sheila Brothers come here, take over his care, settle into the parsonage, countermand his orders?

"This is strange weather," he says. "Up in northern Ontario it's balmy, even the little lakes are open, temperatures above freezing. And here we are in the grip of the ice and the wind straight off the Great Plains."

"It'll be all the same to you when you get to Hawaii," Karin says firmly. "Northern Ontario or the Great Plains or here, you'll be glad to be out of it. Doesn't she ever call you?"

"Who?" says Austin.

"*Her.* Mrs. Brothers."

"Oh, Sheila. She calls me late at night. The time's so much earlier, in Hawaii."

The phone rings with Karin alone in the house the morning before Austin is to leave. A man's voice, uncertain and sullen-sounding.

"He isn't here right now," Karin says. Austin has gone to the bank. "I could get him to call you when he comes in."

"Well, it's long distance," the man says. "It's Shaft Lake."

"Shaft Lake," repeats Karin, feeling around on the phone shelf for a pencil.

"We were just wondering. Like we were just checking. That we got the right time that he gets in. Somebody's got to drive down and meet him. So he gets in to Thunder Bay at three o'clock, is that right?"

Karin has stopped looking for a pencil. She finally says, "I guess that's right. As far as I know. If you called back around noon, he'd be here."

"I don't know for sure I can get to a phone around noon. I'm at the hotel here but then I got to go someplace else. I'd just as soon leave him the message. Somebody's going to meet him at the airport in Thunder Bay three o'clock tomorrow. O.K.?"

"O.K.," says Karin.

"You could tell him we got him a place to live, too."

"Oh. O.K."

"It's a trailer. He said he wouldn't mind living in a trailer. See, we haven't had any minister here in a long time."

"Oh," says Karin. "O.K. Yes. I'll tell him."

As soon as she has hung up, she finds Megan's number on the list above the phone, and dials it. It rings three or four times and then Megan's voice comes on, sounding brisker than the last time Karin heard it. Brisk but teasing.

"The lady of the house regrets that she cannot take your call at the moment, but if you would leave your name, message, and phone number she will try to get back to you as soon as possible."

Karin has already started to say she is sorry, but this is important, when she is interrupted by a beep, and realizes it's one of those machines. She starts again, speaking quickly but distinctly after a deep breath.

"I just wanted to tell you. I just wanted you to know. Your father is fine. He is in good health, and mentally he is fine and everything. So you don't have to worry. He is off to Hawaii tomorrow. I was just thinking about—I was just thinking about our conversation on the phone. So I thought I'd tell you, not to worry. This is Karin speaking."

And she just gets all that said in time, when she hears Austin at the door. Before he can ask or wonder what she's doing there in the hall, she fires a series of questions at him. Did he get to the bank? Did the cold make his chest hurt? When was it the Auction Barn truck was coming? When did the people from the Board want the parsonage keys? Was he going to phone Don and Megan before he left or after he got there, or what?

Yes. No. Monday for the truck. Tuesday for the keys, but no rush—if she wasn't finished, then Wednesday would be O.K. No more phone calls. He and his children have said all they need to say to each other. Once he's there, he will write them a letter. Write each of them a letter.

"After you're married?"

Yes. Well. Maybe sooner than that.

He has laid his coat across the bannister railing. Then she sees him put out a hand to steady himself, holding on to the railing. He pretends to be fiddling around with his coat.

"You O.K.?" she says. "You want a cup of coffee?"

For a moment he doesn't say anything. His eyes swim past her. How can anybody believe that this tottery old man, whose body looks to be shrivelling day by day, is on his way to marry a comforting widow and spend his days from now on walking on a sunny beach? It isn't in him to do such a thing, ever. He means to wear himself out, quick, quick, on people as thankless as possible, thankless as Brent. Meanwhile fooling all of them into thinking he's changed his spots. Otherwise, somebody might stop him going. Slipping out from under, fooling them, enjoying it.

But he really is after something in the coat. He brings out a pint of whiskey.

"Put a little of that in a glass for me," he says. "Never mind the coffee. Just a precaution. Against weakness. From the cold."

He is sitting on the steps when she brings him the whiskey. He drinks it shakily. He wags his head back and forth, as if trying to get it clear. He stands up. "Much better," he says. "Oh, very much better. Now, about those pictures of the ice, Karin. I was wondering, could you pick them up next week? If I left you the money? They're not ready yet."

Even though he's just in from the cold, he's white. Put a candle behind his face, it'd shine through as if he were wax or thin china.

"You'll have to leave me your address," she says. "Where to send them."

"Just hang on to them till I write you. That'd be best."

*   *   *

So she has ended up with a whole roll of pictures of the ice, along with all those other things that she had her mind set on. The pictures show the sky bluer than it ever was, but the weaving in the fence, the shape of the organ pipes are not so plain to see. There needs to be a human figure, too, to show the size that things were. She should have taken the camera and captured Austin—who has vanished. He has vanished as completely as the ice, unless the body washes up in the spring. A thaw, a drowning, and they both disappear. Karin looks at these pictures of the pale, lumpy ice monstrosities, these pictures Austin took, so often that she gets the feeling that he is in them, after all. He's a blank in them, but bright.

She thinks now that he knew. Right at the last he knew that she'd caught on to him, she understood what he was up to. No matter how alone you are, and how tricky and determined, don't you need one person to know? She could be the one for him. Each of them knew what the other was up to, and didn't let on, and that was a link beyond the usual. Every time she thinks of it, she feels approved of—a most unexpected thing.

She puts one of the pictures in an envelope, and sends it to Megan. (She tore the list of addresses and phone numbers off the wall, just in case.) She sends another to Don. And another, stamped and addressed, across town, to Brent. She doesn't write anything on the pictures or enclose any note. She won't be bothering any of these people again. The fact is, it won't be long till she'll be leaving here.

She just wants to make them wonder.

Goodness and Mercy

Bugs said so long to the disappearing land, a dark-blue finger of Labrador. The ship was passing through the Strait of Belle Isle, on its third day out from Montreal.

"Now I've got to make it to the white cliffs of Dover," she said. She made a face, rounding her eyes and her small, adept mouth, her singer's mouth, as if she had to accept some nuisance. "Else it's over the side and feed the fishes."

Bugs was dying, but she had been a very slender, white-skinned woman before she started that, so there wasn't a shocking difference. Her bright-silver hair was cut in a clever fluffed-out bob by her daughter Averill. Her pallor was by no means ghastly, and the loose tops and caftans that Averill had made for her concealed the state of her arms and her upper body. Occasional expressions of fatigue and distress blended in with an old expression she had—a humorous, hardened plaintiveness. She was not looking at all bad, and her coughing was under control.

"That's a joke," she said to Averill, who was paying for the trip out of some money left to her by the father she had never seen, to remember. When they made the arrangements, they hadn't known what was going to happen—or that it was going to happen as soon as now looked likely.

"Actually, I intend to hang around making your life miserable for years to come," Bugs said. "I look better. Don't you think? Anyway, in the morning. I'm eating. I was thinking I'd start taking little walks. I walked to the rail yesterday, when you weren't here."

They had a cabin on the boat deck, with a chair for Bugs set up outside. There was a bench under the cabin window, occupied now by Averill and in the mornings by the University of Toronto professor whom Bugs called her admirer, or "that professorial jerk."

This was happening on a Norwegian passenger-carrying freighter, in the late seventies, in the month of July. All the way across the North Atlantic the weather was sunny, the sea flat and bright as glass.

Bugs' real name, of course, was June. Her real name, and her singing name, was June Rodgers. For the last year and three months she had not sung in public. For the last eight months she had not gone to the Conservatory to give lessons. She had a few students coming to the apartment on Huron Street, in the evenings and on Saturdays, so that Averill could accompany them on the piano. Averill worked at the Conservatory, in the office. She biked home for lunch every day, to see if Bugs was all right. She didn't say she was doing it for that reason. She had the excuse of her special lunch—skim milk, wheat germ, and a banana mixed up in the blender. Averill was usually trying to lose weight.

Bugs had sung at weddings, she had been the paid soloist with church choirs, she had sung in the *Messiah* and the *St. Matthew Passion* and in Gilbert and Sullivan. She had sung supporting roles in Toronto productions of operas with famous imported stars. For a while in the fifties she had shared a radio program with a popular drunken tenor, who had got them both sacked. The name June Rodgers had been well enough known all the time that Averill was growing up. It was well enough known, at least, among the people that Averill usually met. It was a surprise for Averill, more than for Bugs, to run into people now who didn't recognize it.

People on the boat hadn't recognized it. About half of the thirty or so passengers were Canadians, most of them from around Toronto, but they hadn't recognized it. "My mother sang Zerlina," Averill said during her first conversation with the professor. "In *Don Giovanni*, in 1964." She had been ten at the time and remembered the occasion as one filled with glory. Apprehension, flurry, crisis—a sore throat cured by yoga. A peasant costume with a ruffled pink-and-gold skirt over piles of petticoats. Glory.

"Honey, Zerlina is just not a household word," Bugs said to her afterward. "Also, professors are dumb. They are dumber than ordinary. I could be nice and say they know about things we don't, but as far as I'm concerned they don't know shit."

But she let the professor sit beside her and tell her things about himself every morning. She told Averill what she'd learned. He walked the deck for one hour before breakfast. At home he walked six miles a day. He had caused a certain amount of scandal at the university a few years ago by marrying his young wife (his dimwit wife, said Bugs), whose name was Leslie. He had made enemies, stirred up envy and discontent among his colleagues with his dalliance, and then by divorcing his wife and marrying this girl who was one year younger than his oldest child. From then on, certain people were out to get him, and they did. He was a biologist, but he had devised a sort of general-science course—he called it a scientific-literacy course—for students in the humanities: a lively, unalarming course that he hoped would be a modest breakthrough. He got the approval of the higher-ups, but the course was scuttled by members of his own department, who devised all kinds of cumbersome, silly requirements and prerequisites. He retired early.

"I think that was it," Bugs said. "I couldn't keep my mind on it. Also, young women can make very frustrating mates for older men. Youth can be boring. Oh, yes. With an older woman

a man can relax. The rhythms of her thoughts and memories—
yes, the rhythms of her thoughts and memories will be more in
harmony with his. What puke!"

Down the deck the young wife, Leslie, sat working on a
needlepoint cover for a dining-room chair. This was the third
cover she had done. She needed six altogether. The two women
she sat with were glad to admire her pattern—it was called Tudor
Rose—and they talked about needlepoint covers that they had
made. They described how these fitted in with the furnishings of
their houses. Leslie sat between them, somewhat protected. She
was a soft, pink-skinned, brown-haired girl whose youth was
draining away. She invited kindness, but Bugs had not been very
kind to her when she hauled the needlepoint out of her bag.

"Oh, my," said Bugs. She threw up her hands and waggled
her skinny fingers. "These hands," she said, and got the better of
a fit of coughing—"these hands have done plenty of things I am
not proud of, but I must say they have never picked up a knitting
needle or an embroidery needle or a crochet hook or even sewn
on a button if there was a safety pin handy. So I'm hardly the
person to appreciate, my dear."

Leslie's husband laughed.

Averill thought that what Bugs said was not completely
true. It was Bugs who had taught her how to sew. Bugs and
Averill both took a serious interest in clothes and were attentive
to fashion, in a playful, unintimidated way. Some of their best
hours together had been spent in cutting up material, pinning it
together, getting inspirations.

The caftans, the loose tops that Bugs wore on the boat,
were patchworks of silk and velvet and brightly patterned cotton
and crocheted lace—all from old dresses and curtains and table-
cloths that Averill had picked up at secondhand stores. These
creations were greatly admired by Jeanine, an American woman
on the boat, who was making friends zealously.

"Where did you find those gorgeous things?" said Jeanine,
and Bugs said, "Averill. Averill made them. Isn't she clever?"

"She's a genius," said Jeanine. "You're a genius, Averill."

"She should make theatre costumes," Bugs said. "I keep telling her."

"Yes, why don't you?" said Jeanine.

Averill flushed and could not think of anything to say, anything to placate Bugs and Jeanine, who were smiling at her.

Bugs said, "I'm just as glad she's not, though. I'm just as glad she's here. Averill is my treasure."

Walking the deck, away from Bugs, Jeanine asked Averill, "You mind telling me how old you are?"

Averill said twenty-three, and Jeanine sighed. She said that she was forty-two. She was married, but not accompanied by her husband. She had a long tanned face with glossy pinkish-mauve lips and shoulder-length hair, thick and smooth as an oak plank. She said that people often told her she looked as if she was from California, but actually she was from Wisconsin. She was from a small city in Wisconsin, where she had been the hostess of a radio phone-in show. Her voice was low and persuasive and full of satisfaction, even if she disclosed a problem, a grief, a shame.

She said, "Your mother is charming."

Averill said, "People either think that or they can't stand her."

"Has she been ill long?"

"She's recuperating," said Averill. "She had pneumonia last spring." This was what they had agreed to say.

Jeanine was more eager to be friends with Bugs than Bugs was to be friends with her. Nevertheless Bugs slid into her customary half-intimacy, confiding some things about the professor and disclosing the name she had thought up for him: Dr. Faustus. His wife's name was Tudor Rose. Jeanine thought these names appropriate and funny. Oh, delightful, she said.

She did not know the name that Bugs had given her. Glamour Puss.

Averill walked around the deck and listened to people talking. She thought about how sea voyages were supposed to be about getting away from it all, and how "it all" presumably meant your life, the way you lived, the person you were at home. Yet in all the conversations she overheard people were doing just the opposite. They were establishing themselves—telling about their jobs and their children and their gardens and their dining rooms. Recipes were offered, for fruitcake and compost heaps. Also ways of dealing with daughters-in-law and investments. Tales of illness, betrayal, real estate. *I said. I did. I always believe. Well, I don't know about you, but I.*

Averill, walking past with her face turned toward the sea, wondered how you got to do this. How did you learn to be so stubborn and insistent and to claim your turn?

I did it all over last fall in blue and oyster.

I'm afraid I have never been able to see the charms of opera.

That last was the professor, imagining that he could put Bugs in her place. And why did he say he was afraid?

Averill didn't get to walk alone for very long. She had her own admirer, who would stalk her and cut her off at the rail. He was an artist, a Canadian artist from Montreal, who sat across from her in the dining room. When he was asked, at the first meal, what kind of pictures he painted, he had said that his latest work was a figure nine feet high, entirely wrapped in bandages, which bore quotations from the American Declaration of Independence. How interesting, said some polite Americans, and the artist said with a tight sneer, I'm glad you think so.

"But why," said Jeanine, with her interviewer's adroit response to hostility (a special rich kindness in the voice, a more alert and interested smile), "why did you not use Canadian quotations of some sort?"

"Yes, I was wondering that, too," said Averill. Sometimes she tried to get into conversations this way, she tried to echo or expand the things that other people said. Usually it did not work well.

Canadian quotations turned out to be a sore subject with the artist. Critics had taken him to task for that very thing, accusing him of insufficient nationalism, missing the very point that he was trying to make. He ignored Jeanine, but followed Averill from the table and harangued her for what seemed like hours, developing a ferocious crush on her as he did so. Next morning he was waiting to go in to breakfast with her, and afterward he asked her if she had ever done any modelling.

"*Me?*" said Averill. "I'm way too fat."

He said he didn't mean with clothes on. If he had been another sort of artist, he said (she gathered that the other sort was the sort he despised), he would have picked her out immediately as a model. Her big golden thighs (she was wearing shorts, which she didn't put on again), her long hair like caramelized sugar, her square shoulders and unindented waist. A goddess figure, goddess coloring, goddess of the harvest. He said she had a pure and childish scowl.

Averill thought that she must remember to keep smiling.

He was a stocky, swarthy, irritable-looking man. Bugs named him Toulouse-Lautrec.

Men had fallen in love with Averill before. Twice she had promised to marry them, then had had to get out of it. She had slept with the ones she was engaged to, and with two or three others. Actually, four others. She had had one abortion. She was not frigid—she did not think so—but there was something about her participation in sex that was polite and appalled, and it was always a relief when they let go of her.

She dealt with the artist by granting him a conversation early in the day, when she felt strong and almost lighthearted. She didn't sit down with him, and during the afternoon and evening she kept him at arm's length. Part of her strategy was to take up with Jeanine. That was all right, as long as Jeanine talked about her own life and didn't move in on Averill's.

"Your mother is a gallant woman and very charming," Jeanine said. "But charming people can be very manipulative. You live with her, don't you?"

Averill said yes, and Jeanine said, "Oh, I'm sorry. I hope I'm not being too intrusive? I hope I haven't offended you?"

Averill was really only puzzled, in a familiar way. Why did people so quickly take for granted that she was stupid?

"You know, I've gotten so used to interviewing people," Jeanine said. "I'm actually quite bad at ordinary conversation. I've forgotten how to communicate in a nonprofessional situation. I'm too blunt and I'm too *interested*. I need help with that."

The whole point about coming on this trip, she said, was to get herself back to normal reality and find out who she really was when not blatting away into a microphone. And to find out who she was outside of her marriage. It was an agreement between her husband and herself, she said, that every so often they would take these little trips away from each other, they would test the boundaries of the relationship.

Averill could hear what Bugs would have to say about that. "Test the boundaries of the relationship," Bugs would say. "She means get laid aboard ship."

Jeanine said that she did not rule out a shipboard romance. That is, before she had a look at the available men she had not ruled it out. Once she got a look, she resigned herself. Who could it be? The artist was short and ugly and anti-American. That in itself wouldn't have been entirely off-putting, but he was infatuated with Averill. The professor had a wife on board— Jeanine was not going to scramble around copulating in linen closets. Also he was long-winded, had little grainy warts on his eyelids, and was taken up with Bugs. All the other men were out for one reason or another—they had wives with them, or they were too old to please her or too young for her to please them, or they were chiefly interested in each other or in members of the crew. She would have to use the time to give her skin a good overhaul and to read a book all the way through.

"Who would you pick, though," she said to Averill, "if you were picking for me?"

"What about the captain?" said Averill.

"Brilliant," Jeanine said. "A long shot, but brilliant."

She found out that the captain's age was O.K.—he was

fifty-four. He was married, but his wife was back in Bergen. He had three children, grown up or nearly. He himself was not a Norwegian but a Scot, born in Edinburgh. He had gone to sea at sixteen and had captained this freighter for ten years. Jeanine discovered all this by asking him. She told him that she was going to do an article for a magazine, on passenger-carrying freighters. (She might really do this.) He gave her a tour of the ship and included his own cabin. She thought that a good sign.

His cabin was spick-and-span. There was a photograph of a large, pleasant-looking woman wearing a thick sweater. The book he was reading was by John le Carré.

"He won't give her a tumble," Bugs said. "He's too canny for her. A canny Scot."

Averill had not thought twice about revealing Jeanine's confidences, if they were confidences. She was used to bringing home all information, all enlivening tidbits—home to the apartment on Huron Street, to the cabin on the boat deck, to Bugs. All stirred into the busy pot. Bugs herself was a marvel at egging people on—she got extravagant tangled revelations from unlikely sources. So far as Averill knew, she had not kept anything a secret.

Bugs said that Jeanine was a type she had seen before. Glitz on the surface and catastrophe underneath. A mistake to get too chummy with her, she told Averill, but she remained fairly chummy herself. She told Jeanine stories that Averill had heard before.

She told about Averill's father, whom she did not describe as a jerk or an admirer but as a cautious old bugger. Old to her way of thinking—in his forties. He was a doctor, in New York. Bugs was living there; she was a young singer trying to get her start. She went to him for a sore throat, sore throats being the bugbear of her life.

"Eye, ear, nose, and throat man," Bugs said. "How was I to know he wouldn't stop there?"

He had a family. Of course. He came to Toronto, once, to a medical conference. He saw Averill.

"She was standing up in her crib, and when she saw him she howled like a banshee. I said to him, Do you think she's got my voice? But he was not in the mood for jokes. She scared him off. Such a cautious old bugger. I think he only slipped up the once.

"I've always used bad language," Bugs said. "I like it. I liked it long before it got to be so popular. When Averill had just started to school, the teacher phoned and asked me to come in for a talk. She said she was concerned about some words that Averill was using. When Averill broke her pencil or anything, she said, Oh, shit. Or maybe, Oh, fuck. She said whatever she was used to hearing me say at home. I never warned her. I just thought she'd realize. And how could she? Poor Averill. I was a rotten mother. And that's not the worst part. Do you think I owned up to that teacher and said she got it from me? Indeed not! I behaved like a lady. Oh dear. Oh, I do appreciate you telling me. Oh dear. I'm an awful person. Averill always knew it. Didn't you, Averill?"

Averill said yes.

On the fourth day, Bugs stopped going down to the dining room for dinner.

"I notice I'm getting a bit gray around the gills by that time," she said. "I don't want to turn the professor off. He may not be so stuck on older women as he lets on."

She said she ate enough at breakfast and lunch. "Breakfast was always my best meal. And here I eat a huge breakfast."

Averill came back from dinner with rolls and fruit.

"Lovely," said Bugs. "Later."

She had to sleep propped up.

"Maybe the nurse has oxygen," Averill said. There was no doctor on the ship, but there was a nurse. Bugs did not want to see her. She did not want oxygen.

"These are not bad," she said of her coughing fits. "They are not as bad as they sound. Just little spasms. I've been figuring out—what they are punishment for. Seeing I never smoked. I thought maybe—singing in church and not believing? But no. I think—*Sound of Music*. Maria. God hates it."

Averill and Jeanine played poker in the evenings with the artist and the Norwegian first mate. Averill always went back to the boat deck a few times to check on Bugs. Bugs would be asleep or pretending to be asleep, the fruit and buns by her bed untouched. Averill pulled out of the game early. She did not go to bed immediately, though she had made a great point of being so sleepy that she could not keep her eyes open. She slipped into the cabin to retrieve the uneaten buns, then went out on deck. She sat on the bench beneath the window. The window was always wide open on the warm, still night. Averill sat there and ate the buns as quietly as she could, biting with care through the crisp, delicious crust. The sea air made her just as hungry as it was supposed to do. Or else it was having somebody in love with her—the tension. Under those circumstances she usually gained weight.

She could listen to Bugs' breathing. Little flurries and halts, ragged accelerations, some snags, snores, and achieved straight runs. She could hear Bugs half-wake, and shift and struggle and prop herself higher up in the bed. And she could watch the captain, when he came out for his walk. She didn't know if he saw her. He never indicated. He never looked her way. He looked straight ahead. He was getting his exercise, at night, when there would be the least chance of having to be sociable. Back and forth, back and forth, close to the rail. Averill stayed still—she felt like a fox in the brush. A night animal, watching him. But she didn't think he would be startled if she should move or call out. He was alert to everything on the ship, surely. He knew she was there but could ignore her, out of courtesy, or his own sense of confidence.

She thought of Jeanine's designs on him, and agreed with

Bugs that they were doomed to failure. Averill would be disappointed if they were not doomed to failure. The captain did not seem to her a needy man. He did not need to disturb you, or flatter, or provoke, or waylay you. None of that *look at me, listen to me, admire me, give me*. None of that. He had other things on his mind. The ship, the sea, the weather, the cargo, his crew, his commitments. The passengers must be an old story to him. Cargo of another sort, requiring another sort of attention. Idle or ailing, lustful or grieving, curious, impatient, mischievous, remote—he would have seen them all before. He would know things about them right away, but never more than he needed to know. He would know about Jeanine. An old story.

How did he decide when to go in? Did he time himself, did he count his steps? He was gray-haired and straight-backed, with a thickness of body around the waist and the stomach speaking not of indulgence but of a peaceable authority. Bugs had not thought up any name for him. She had called him a canny Scot, but beyond that she had taken no interest. There were no little tags about him for Bugs to get hold of, no inviting bits of showing-off, no glittery layers ready to flake away. He was a man made long ago, not making himself moment by moment and using whomever he could find in the process.

One night before the captain appeared, Averill heard singing. She heard Bugs singing. She heard Bugs wake and resettle herself and start singing.

Sometimes in the last months Bugs had sung a phrase during a lesson, she had sung under her breath, with great caution, and out of necessity, to demonstrate something. She did not sing like that now. She sang lightly, as she used to do in practice, saving her strength for the performance. But she sang truly and adequately, with unimpaired—or almost unimpaired—sweetness.

"*Vedrai carino,*" Bugs sang, just as she used to sing when setting the table or looking out the rainy window of the apartment, making a light sketch that could be richly filled in if she chose. She might have been waiting for somebody at those times, or wooing an improbable happiness, or just limbering up for a concert.

> "Vedrai carino,
> Se sei buonino,
> Che bel remedio,
> Ti voglio dar."

Averill's head had pulled up when the singing started, her body had tightened, as at a crisis. But there was no call for her; she stayed where she was. After the first moment's alarm, she felt just the same thing, the same thing she always felt, when her mother sang. The doors flew open, effortlessly, there was the lighted space beyond, a revelation of kindness and seriousness. Desirable, blessed joy, and seriousness, a play of kindness that asked nothing of you. Nothing but to accept this bright order. That altered everything, and then the moment Bugs stopped singing it was gone. Gone. It seemed that Bugs herself had taken it away. Bugs could imply that it was just a trick, nothing more. She could imply that you were a bit of a fool to take such notice of it. It was a gift that Bugs was obliged to offer, to everybody.

There. That's all. You're welcome.

Nothing special.

Bugs had that secret, which she openly displayed, then absolutely protected—from Averill, just as from everybody else.

Averill is not particularly musical, thank God.

The captain came on deck just as Bugs finished singing. He might have caught the tail end of it or been waiting decently in the shadows until it was over. He walked, and Averill watched, as usual.

Averill could sing in her head. But even in her head she never sang the songs that she associated with Bugs. None of Zerlina's songs, or the soprano parts of the oratorios, not even "Farewell to Nova Scotia" or any of the folk songs that Bugs mocked for their sappy sentiments though she sang them angelically. Averill had a hymn that she sang. She hardly knew where it came from. She couldn't have learned it from Bugs. Bugs disliked hymns, generally speaking. Averill must have picked it up at church, when she was a child, and had to go along with Bugs when Bugs was doing a solo.

It was the hymn that starts out, "The Lord's my Shepherd." Averill did not know that it came from a psalm—she had not been to church often enough to know about psalms. She did know all the words in the hymn, which she had to admit were full of strenuous egotism, and straightforward triumph, and, particularly in one verse, a childish sort of gloating:

> My table Thou hast furnished,
> In Presence of my Foes

How blithely and securely and irrationally Averill's head-voice sang these words, while she watched the captain pace in front of her, and later, when she herself walked safely down to the rail:

> Goodness and Mercy all my Life
> Shall surely follow me;
> And in God's House forevermore
> My dwelling place shall be.

Her silent singing wrapped around the story she was telling herself, which she extended further every night on the deck. (Averill often told herself stories—the activity seemed to her as unavoidable as dreaming.) Her singing was a barrier set between the world in her head and the world outside, between her body and the onslaught of the stars, the black mirror of the North Atlantic.

Bugs stopped going down to lunch. She still went to breakfast, and was lively then, and for an hour or so afterward. She said she didn't feel any worse, she was tired of listening and talking. She didn't sing again, at least not when Averill could hear her.

On the ninth night, which was the last night out, before they were to dock at Tilbury, Jeanine gave a party in her cabin. Jeanine had the largest and best cabin on the boat deck. She provided champagne, which she had brought on board for this purpose, and whiskey and wine, along with caviar, grapes, heaps of smoked salmon and steak tartare and cheese and flatbread, from the unsuspected resources of the kitchen. "I'm squandering," she said. "I'm flying high. I'll be wandering around Europe with a knapsack on my back stealing eggs out of henhouses. I don't care. I'll take all your addresses and when I'm utterly broke I'll come and stay with you. Don't laugh!"

Bugs had meant to go to the party. She had stayed in bed all day, not even going to breakfast, in order to save her strength. She got up and washed, then propped herself back against the pillows to do her makeup. She did it beautifully, eyes and all. She brushed out and teased and sprayed her hair. She put on her grand soloist's dress, which Averill had made—an almost straight-cut but ample long dress of dark-purple silk, its wide sleeves lined with more silk, of iridescent pink and silver.

"Aubergine," said Bugs. She turned to make the dress flare out at the hem. The turn made her unsteady, and she had to sit down.

"I should do my nails," she said. "I'll wait a little, though. I'm too jittery."

"I could do them," Averill said. She was pinning up her hair.

"Could you? But I don't think. I don't think I'll go. After all. I think I'd rather just stay here and rest. Tomorrow I have to be in good shape. Landing."

Averill helped her take off the dress and wash her face and put her nightgown back on. She helped her into bed.

"It's a crime about the dress," Bugs said. "Not to go. It deserves to get out. You should wear it. You wear it. Please."

Averill did not think that purple suited her, but she ended up discarding her own green dress and putting on Bugs'. She went down the hall to the party, feeling strange, defiant, and absurd. It was all right—everybody had dressed up, some to a remarkable extent. Even the men had decked themselves out somehow. The artist wore an old tuxedo jacket with his jeans, and the professor appeared in a white suit of rather floppy cut, looking like a plantation dandy. Jeanine's dress was black and skimpy, worn with seamed black stockings and big chunks of gold jewelry. Leslie was swathed in taffeta, with red and pink roses on a creamy ground. Over her curvy bum the material was bunched out into one huge rose, whose petals the professor kept patting and tweaking and arranging to best advantage. It would seem that he was newly entranced with her. She was relieved and proud, shyly blooming.

"Your mother is not coming to the party?" said the professor to Averill.

"Parties bore her," Averill said.

"I get the impression that many things bore her," the professor said. "I have noticed that with performing artists, and it is understandable. They have to concentrate so much on themselves."

"Who is this—the Statue of Liberty?" said the artist, brushing the silk of Averill's dress. "Is there a woman inside there at all?"

Averill had heard that he had been discussing her with Jeanine lately, wondering if she was possibly a lesbian, and Bugs was not her mother but her rich and jealous lover.

"Is there a woman or a hunk of concrete?" he said, molding the silk to her hip.

Averill didn't care. This was the last night that she would have to see him. And she was drinking. She liked to drink. She liked especially to drink champagne. It made her feel not excited but blurry and forgiving.

She talked to the first mate, who was engaged to a girl from the mountains and showed an agreeable lack of love interest in herself.

She talked to the cook, a handsome woman who had formerly taught English in Norwegian high schools and was now intent on a more adventurous life. Jeanine had told Averill that the cook and the artist were believed to be sleeping together, and a certain challenging, ironic edge to the cook's friendliness made Averill think that this might be true.

She talked to Leslie, who said that she had once been a harpist. She had been a young harpist playing dinner music in a hotel, and the professor had spotted her behind the ferns. She had not been a student, as people thought. It was after they became involved that the professor had her enroll in some courses, to develop her mind. She giggled over her champagne and said that it had not worked. She had resisted mind development but had given up the harp.

Jeanine spoke to Averill in a voice as low and confidential as she could make it. "How will you manage with her?" she said. "What will you do in England? How can you take her on a train? This is serious."

"Don't worry," Averill said.

"I have not been open with you," said Jeanine. "I have to go to the bathroom, but I want to tell you something when I come out."

Averill hoped that Jeanine did not intend to make more disclosures about the artist or give more advice about Bugs. She didn't. When she came out of the bathroom, she began to talk about herself. She said that she was not on a little vacation, as she had claimed. She had been turfed out. By her husband, who had left her for a sexpot moron who worked as a receptionist at the station. Being a receptionist involved doing her nails and occasionally answering the telephone. The husband considered that he and Jeanine should still be friends, and he would come to visit, helping himself to the wine and describing the pretty ways of his paramour. How she sat up in bed, naked, doing—what else?—her fingernails. He wanted Jeanine to laugh with him and commiserate with him over his ill-judged and besotted love. And she did—Jeanine did. Time and again she fell in with what he wanted and listened to his tales and watched her wine disappear. He said he loved her—Jeanine—as if she were the sister he'd never had. But now Jeanine meant to pull him out of her life by the roots. She was up and away. She meant to live.

She still had her eye on the captain, though it was the eleventh hour. He had turned down champagne and was drinking whiskey.

The cook had brought up a coffee tray for those who did not drink or who wished to sober up early. When somebody finally tried a cup, the cream proved to be on the turn—probably from sitting for a while in the warm room. Unflustered, the cook took it away, promising to bring back fresh. "It will be good on the pancakes in the morning," she said. "With brown sugar, on the pancakes."

Jeanine said that somebody had told her once that when the milk was sour you could suspect that there was a dead body on the ship.

"I thought it was a kind of superstition," Jeanine said. "But he said no, there's a reason. The ice. They have used all the ice to keep the body, so the milk goes sour. He said he had known it to happen, on a ship in the tropics."

The captain was asked, laughingly, if there was any such problem on board this ship.

He said not that he knew of, no. "And we have plenty of refrigerator space," he said.

"Anyway, you bury them at sea, don't you?" said Jeanine. "You can marry or bury at sea, can't you? Or do you really refrigerate them and send them home?"

"We do as the case dictates," said the captain.

But had it happened with him, he was asked—were there bodies kept, had there been burials at sea?

"A young chap once, one of the crew, died of appendicitis. He hadn't any family we knew of; we buried him at sea."

"That's a funny expression, when you think of it," said Leslie, who was giggling at everything. "Buried at sea."

"Another time—" said the captain. "Another time, it was a lady."

Then he told Jeanine and Averill, and a few others who were standing around, a story. (Not Leslie—her husband took her away.)

One time on this ship, the captain said, there were two sisters travelling together. This was on a different run, a few years ago, in the South Atlantic. The sisters looked twenty years apart in age, but that was only because one of them was very sick. She might not have been so much the elder—perhaps she was not the elder at all. Probably they were both in their thirties. Neither one was married. The one who was not sick was very beautiful.

"The most beautiful woman I have ever seen in my life," said the captain, speaking solemnly, as if describing a view or a building.

She was very beautiful, but she did not pay attention to anybody except her sister, who was laid up in the cabin with what was probably a heart condition. The other one used to go out at night and sit on the bench outside the window of their cabin. She might walk to the rail and back, but she never stirred far from the window. The captain supposed that she was staying within hearing distance, in case her sister needed her. (There was no medical person on board at that time.) He could see her sitting there when he went out for his late-night walk, but he pretended not to see her, because it seemed to him she didn't want to be seen, or to have to say hello.

But there was a night when he was walking past and he heard her call to him. She called so softly he barely heard her. He went over to the bench, and she said, Captain, I'm sorry, my sister has just died.

I'm sorry, my sister has just died.

She led him into the cabin, and she was absolutely right. Her sister was lying on the bed next to the door. Her eyes were half open, she had just died.

"Things were in a bit of a mess, the way they sometimes are on such occasions," the captain said. "And by the way she re-acted to that I knew she hadn't been in the cabin when it happened, she'd been outside."

Neither the captain nor the woman said a word. They set to work together to get things cleaned up, and they washed the body off and straightened it out and closed the eyes. When they were finished, the captain asked whom he should notify. No-body, the woman said. Nobody. There is nobody but the two of us, she said. Then will you have the body buried at sea, the captain asked her, and she said yes. Tomorrow, he said—tomorrow morning—and she said, Why do we have to wait, couldn't we do it now?

Of course that was a good idea, though the captain wouldn't have urged it on her himself. The less the other passengers, and even the crew, have to be aware of a death on board, the better. And it was hot weather, summer in the South Atlantic. They wrapped the body up in one of the sheets, and between them they put it out through the window, which was wide open for air. The dead sister was light—wasted. They carried her to the rail. Then the captain said that he would just go and get some rope and tie the body up in the sheet so that it wouldn't fall out when they dropped it over. Couldn't we use scarves, she said, and she ran back to the cabin and came out with an assortment of scarves and sashes, very pretty stuff. He bound the body up in the sheet with those and said that he would now go and get his book, to read the service for the dead. The woman laughed and said, What good is your book to you here? It's too dark to read. He saw that she dreaded being left alone with the body. She was right, too, about its being too dark to read. He could have got a flashlight. He didn't know whether he had even thought of that. He really did not want to leave her; he did not like the state she was in.

He asked her what he should say, then. Some prayers?

Say whatever you like, she said, and he said the Lord's

Prayer—he did not recall if she joined in—then something like, Lord Jesus Christ, in Thy name we commit this woman to the deep; have mercy on her soul. Something like that. They picked up the body and rolled it over the rail. It hardly made a splash.

She asked if that was all, and he told her yes. He would just have to fill out some papers and make up the death certificate. What did she die of, he asked. Was it a heart attack? He wondered what kind of spell he had been under not to have asked that before.

Oh, she said, I killed her.

"I knew it!" Jeanine cried. "I knew it was murder!"

The captain walked the woman back to the bench under the window of the cabin—all lit up now like Christmas—and asked her what she meant. She said she had been sitting here, where she was now, and she heard her sister call. She knew her sister was in trouble. She knew what it was—her sister needed an injection. She never moved. She tried to move—that is, she kept thinking of moving; she saw herself going into the cabin and getting out the needle, she saw herself doing that, but she wasn't moving. She strained herself to do it but she didn't. She sat like stone. She could no more move than you can move out of some danger's way in a dream. She sat and listened until she knew that her sister was dead. Then the captain came and she called to him.

The captain told her that she had not killed her sister.

Wouldn't her sister have died anyway, he said. Wouldn't she have died very soon? If not tonight, very soon? Oh, yes, she said. Probably. Not probably, the captain said. Certainly. Not probably—certainly. He would put heart attack on the death certificate, and that would be all there was to it. So now you must calm down, he said. Now you know it will be all right.

He pronounced "calm" in the Scottish way, to rhyme with "lamb."

Yes, the woman said, she knew that part of it would be all right. I'm not sorry, she said. But I think you have to remember what you have done.

"Then she went over to the rail," the captain said, "and of course I went along with her, because I couldn't be sure what she meant to do, and she sang a hymn. That was all. I guess it was her contribution to the service. She sang so you could hardly hear her, but the hymn was one I knew. I can't recall it, but I knew it perfectly well."

"Goodness and Mercy all my Life," Averill sang then, lightly but surely, so that Jeanine squeezed her around the waist and exclaimed, "Well, Champagne Sally!"

The captain showed a moment's surprise. Then he said, "I believe that may have been it." He might have been relinquishing something—a corner of his story—to Averill. "That may have been it."

Averill said, "That's the only hymn I know."

"But is that all?" Jeanine said. "There wasn't any family fortune involved, or they weren't both in love with the same man? No? I guess it wasn't TV."

The captain said no, it wasn't TV.

Averill believed that she knew the rest of it. How could she help knowing? It was her story. She knew that after the woman sang the hymn, the captain took her hand off the rail. He held her hand to his mouth and kissed it. He kissed the back of it, then the palm-to-rhyme-with-lamb. Her hand that had lately done its service to the dead.

In some versions of the story, that was all he did, that was enough. In other versions, he was not so easily satisfied. Nor was she. She went with him inside, along the corridor into the lighted cabin, and there he made love to her on the very bed that according to him they had just stripped and cleaned, sending its occupant and one of its sheets to the bottom of the ocean. They landed on that bed because they couldn't wait to get to the other bed under the window, they couldn't wait to hurtle into the lovemaking that they kept up till daybreak and that would have to last them the rest of their lives.

Sometimes they turned the light off, sometimes they didn't care.

The captain had told it as if the mother and daughter were sisters and he had transported the boat to the South Atlantic and he had left off the finale—as well as supplying various details of his own—but Averill believed that it was her story he had told. It was the story that she had been telling herself night after night on the deck, her perfectly secret story, delivered back to her. She had made it, and he had taken it and told it, safely.

Believing that such a thing could happen made her feel weightless and distinct and glowing, like a fish lit up in the water.

Bugs did not die that night. She died two weeks later, in the Royal Infirmary in Edinburgh. She had managed to get that far, on the train.

Averill was not with her when she died. She was a couple of blocks away, eating a baked potato from a takeout shop.

Bugs made one of her last coherent remarks about the Royal Infirmary. She said, "Doesn't it sound *Old World?*"

Averill, coming out to eat after having been in the hospital room all day, had been surprised to find that there was still so much light in the sky, and that so many lively, brightly dressed people were in the streets, speaking French and German, and probably lots of other languages that she couldn't recognize. Every year at this time, the captain's home town held a festival.

Averill brought Bugs' body home on a plane, to a funeral with fine music, in Toronto. She found herself sitting beside another Canadian returning from Scotland—a young man who had played in a famous amateur golf tournament and had not done as well as he had expected. Failure and loss made these two kind to each other, and they were easily charmed by the other's ignorance of the world of sport and of music. Since he lived in Toronto, it was easy for the young man to show up at the funeral.

In a short time he and Averill were married. After a while they were less kind and less charmed, and Averill began to think that she had chosen her husband chiefly because Bugs would have thought the choice preposterous. They were divorced.

But Averill met another man, a good deal older than herself, a high-school drama teacher and play director. His talent was more reliable than his good will—he had an offhand, unsettlingly flippant and ironical manner. He either charmed people or aroused their considerable dislike. He had tried to keep himself free of entanglements.

Averill's pregnancy, however, persuaded them to marry. Both of them hoped for a daughter.

Averill never saw again, or heard from, any of the people who were on the boat.

Averill accepts the captain's offering. She is absolved and fortunate. She glides like the spangled fish, inside her dark silk dress.

She and the captain bid each other good night. They touch hands ceremoniously. The skin of their hands is flickering in the touch.

Oh, What Avails

I—Deadeye Dick

They are in the dining room. The varnished floor is bare except for the rug in front of the china cabinet. There is not much furniture—a long table, some chairs, the piano, the china cabinet. On the inside of the windows, all the wooden shutters are closed. These shutters are painted a dull blue, a grayish blue. Some of the paint on them, and on the window frames, has flaked away. Some of it Joan has encouraged to flake away, using her fingernails.

This is a very hot day in Logan. The world beyond the shutters is swimming in white light; the distant trees and hills have turned transparent; dogs seek the vicinity of pumps and the puddles round the drinking fountains.

Some woman friend of their mother's is there. Is it the schoolteacher Gussie Toll, or the station agent's wife? Their mother's friends are lively women, often transient—adrift and independent in attitude if not in fact.

*   *   *

On the table, under the fan, the two women have spread out cards and are telling their fortunes. They talk and laugh in a way that Joan finds tantalizing, conspiratorial. Morris is lying on the floor, writing in a notebook. He is writing down how many copies of *New Liberty* magazine he sold that week, and who has paid and who still owes money. He is a solid-looking boy of about fifteen, jovial but reserved, wearing glasses with one dark lens.

When Morris was four years old, he was roaming around in the long grass at the foot of the yard, near the creek, and he tripped over a rake that had been left lying there, prongs up. He tripped, he fell on the prongs, his brow and eyelid were badly cut and his eyeball was grazed. As long as Joan can remember—she was a baby when it happened—he has had a scar, and been blind in one eye, and worn glasses with a smoky lens.

A tramp left the rake there. So their mother said. She told the tramp she would give him a sandwich if he raked up the leaves under the walnut trees. She gave him the rake, and the next time she looked he was gone. He got tired of raking, she guessed, or he was mad at her for asking him to work first. She forgot to go and look for the rake. She had no man to help her with anything. Within a little more than half a year, she had to sustain these three things: Joan's birth, the death of her husband in a car accident (he had been drinking, she believed, but he wasn't drunk), and Morris's falling on the rake.

She never took Morris to a Toronto doctor, a specialist, to have a better job done fixing up the scar or to get advice about the eye. She had no money. But couldn't she have borrowed some (Joan, once she was grown up, wondered this), couldn't she have gone to the Lions Club and asked them to help her, as they sometimes did help poor people in an emergency? No. No, she couldn't. She did not believe that she and her children were poor in the way that people helped by the Lions Club were poor. They lived in a large house. They were landlords, collecting rent from three small houses across the street. They still owned the lumberyard, though they were sometimes down to one employee. (Their mother liked to call herself Ma Fordyce, after a widow on a radio soap opera, Ma Perkins, who also owned a lumberyard.) They had not the leeway of people who were properly poor.

What is harder for Joan to understand is why Morris himself has never done anything. Morris has plenty of money now. And it wouldn't even be a question of money anymore. Morris pays his premiums on the government health-insurance plan, just the way everybody else does. He has what seem to Joan very right-wing notions about mollycoddling and individual responsibility and the impropriety of most taxes, but he pays. Wouldn't it make sense to him to try to get something back? A neater job on the eyelid? One of those new, realistic artificial eyes, whose magic sensitivity enables them to move in unison with the other, real eye? All that would entail is a trip to a clinic, a bit of inconvenience, some fussing and fiddling.

All it would entail is Morris's admission that he'd like a change. That it isn't shameful, to try to turn in the badge misfortune has hung on you.

Their mother and her friend are drinking rum-and-Coke. There is a laxity in the house that might surprise most people Joan and Morris go to school with. Their mother smokes, and drinks rum-and-Coke on hot summer days, and she allows Morris to smoke and to drive the car by the time he's twelve years old. (He doesn't like rum.) Their mother doesn't mention misfortune. She tells about the tramp and the rake, but Morris's eye now might as well be some special decoration. She does give them the idea of being part of something special. Not because their grandfather started the lumberyard—she laughs at that, she says he was just a woodcutter who got lucky, and she herself was nobody, she came to town as a bank clerk—and not because of their large, cold, unmanageable house, but because of something private, enclosed, in their small family. It has to do with the way they joke, and talk about people. They have private names—their mother has made up most of them—for almost everybody in town. And she knows a lot of poetry, from school or somewhere. She will fix a couple of lines on somebody, summing them up in an absurd and unforgettable way. She looks out the window and says a bit of poetry and they know who has gone by. Sometimes she comes out with it as she stirs the porridge they eat now and then for supper as well as for breakfast, because it is cheap.

Morris's jokes are puns. He is dogged and sly-faced about this, and their mother pretends to be driven crazy. Once, she told him that if he didn't stop she would empty the sugar bowl over his mashed potatoes. He didn't, and she did.

There is a smell in the Fordyce house, and it comes from the plaster and wallpaper in the rooms that have been shut off, and the dead birds in the unused chimneys, or the mice whose seed-like turds they find in the linen cupboard. The wooden doors in the archway between the dining room and living room are closed, and only the dining room is used. A cheap partition shuts off the side hall from the front hall. They don't buy coal or repair the ailing furnace. They heat the rooms they live in with two stoves, burning ends from the lumberyard. None of this is important, none of their privations and difficulties and economies are important. What is important? Jokes and luck. They are lucky to be the products of a marriage whose happiness lasted for five years and proclaimed itself at parties and dances and on wonderful escapades. Reminders are all around—gramophone records, and fragile, shapeless dresses made of such materials as apricot georgette and emerald silk moiré, and a picnic hamper with a silver flask. Such happiness was not of the quiet kind; it entailed lots of drinking, and dressing up, with friends—mostly from other places, even from Toronto—who have now faded away, many of them, too, smitten by tragedy, the sudden poverty of those years, the complications.

They hear the knocker banging on the front door, the way no caller with decent manners would bang it.

"I know, I know who that'll be," says their mother. "It'll be Mrs. Loony Buttler, what do you want to bet?" She slips out of her canvas shoes and slides the archway doors open carefully, without a creak. She tiptoes to the front window of the no longer used living room, from which she can squint through the shutters and see the front veranda. "Oh, shoot," she says. "It is."

Mrs. Buttler lives in one of the three cement-block houses across the road. She is a tenant. She has white hair, but she pushes it up under a turban made of different-colored pieces of velvet. She wears a long black coat. She has a habit of stopping children on the street and asking them things. Are you just getting home from school now—did you have to stay in? Does your mother know you chew gum? Did you throw bottle caps in my yard?

"Oh, shoot," their mother says. "There isn't anybody I'd sooner not see."

Mrs. Buttler isn't a constant visitor. She arrives irregularly, with some long rigmarole of complaint, some urgent awful news. Many lies. Then, for the next several weeks, she passes the house without a glance, with the long quick strides and forward-thrust head that take away all the dignity of her black outfit. She is preoccupied and affronted, muttering to herself.

The knocker sounds again, and their mother walks softly to the doorway into the front hall. There she stops. On one side of the big front door is a pane of colored glass with a design so intricate that it's hard to see through, and on the other, where a pane of colored glass has been broken (one night when we partied a bit too hard, their mother has said), is a sheet of wood. Their mother stands in the doorway barking. *Yap-yap-yap*, she barks, like an angry little dog shut up alone in the house. Mrs. Buttler's turbanned head presses against the glass as she tries to see in. She can't. The little dog barks louder. A frenzy of barking—angry excitement—into which their mother works the words *go away, go away, go away.* And *loony lady, loony lady, loony lady. Go away, loony lady, go away.*

Mrs. Buttler stands outside for some time in the white heat. She blocks the light through the glass.

On her next visit she says, "I never knew you had a dog."

"We don't," their mother says. "We've never had a dog. Often I think I'd like a dog. But we've never had one."

"Well, I came over here one day, and there was nobody home. Nobody came to the door, and, I could swear to it, I heard a dog barking."

"It may be a disturbance in your inner ear, Mrs. Buttler," their mother says next. "You should ask the doctor."

"I think I could turn into a dog quite easily," their mother says later. "I think my name would be Skippy."

They got a name for Mrs. Buttler. Mrs. Buncler, Mrs. Buncle, and finally Mrs. Carbuncle. It suited. Without knowing exactly what a carbuncle was, Joan understood how the name fitted, attaching itself memorably to something knobby, deadened, awk-ward, intractable in their neighbor's face and character.

Mrs. Carbuncle had a daughter, Matilda. No husband, just this daughter. When the Fordyces sat out on the side veranda after supper—their mother smoking and Morris smoking, too, like the man of the house—they might see Matilda going around the corner, on her way to the confectionery that stayed open late, or to get a book out of the library before it closed. She never had a friend with her. Who would bring a friend to a house ruled by Mrs. Carbuncle? But Matilda didn't seem lonely or shy or unhappy. She was beautifully dressed. Mrs. Carbuncle could sew—in fact, that was how she made what money she made, doing tailoring and alterations for Gillespie's Ladies' and Men's Wear. She dressed Matilda in pale colors, often with long white stockings.

"Rapunzel, Rapunzel, let down thy gold hair," their mother says softly, seeing Matilda pass by. "How can she be Mrs. Carbuncle's daughter? You tell me!"

Their mother says there is something fishy. She wouldn't be at all surprised—she wouldn't be at *all* surprised—to find out that Matilda is really some rich girl's child, or the child of some adulterous passion, whom Mrs. Carbuncle is being paid to raise. Perhaps, on the other hand, Matilda was kidnapped as a baby, and knows nothing about it. "Such things happen," their mother says.

The beauty of Matilda, which prompted this talk, was truly of the captive-princess kind. It was the beauty of storybook illustrations. Long, waving, floating light-brown hair with golden lights in it, which was called blond hair in the days before there were any but the most brazen artificial blondes. Pink-and-white skin, large, mild blue eyes. "The milk of human kindness" was an expression that came mysteriously into Joan's head when she thought of Matilda. And there was something milky about the blue of Matilda's eyes, and her skin, and her looks altogether. Something milky and cool and kind—something stupid, possibly. Don't all those storybook princesses have a tender blur, a veil of stupidity over their blond beauty, an air of unwitting sacrifice, helpless benevolence? All this appeared in Matilda at the age of twelve or thirteen. Morris's age, in Morris's room at school. But she did quite well there, so it seemed she wasn't stupid at all. She was known as a champion speller.

Joan collected every piece of information about Matilda that she could find and became familiar with every outfit that Matilda wore. She schemed to meet her, and because they lived in the same block she often did. Faint with love, Joan noted every variation in Matilda's appearance. Did her hair fall forward over her shoulders today or was it pushed back from her cheeks?

Had she put a clear polish on her fingernails? Was she wearing the pale-blue rayon blouse with the tiny edging of lace around the collar, which gave her a soft and whimsical look, or the starched white cotton shirt, which turned her into a dedicated student? Matilda owned a string of glass beads, clear pink, the sight of which, on Matilda's white neck, caused a delicate sweat to break out along the insides of Joan's arms.

At one time Joan invented other names for her. "Matilda" brought to mind dingy curtains, gray tent flaps, a slack-skinned old woman. How about Sharon? Lilliane? Elizabeth? Then, Joan didn't know how, the name Matilda became transformed. It started shining like silver. The "il" in it was silver. But not metallic. In Joan's mind the name gleamed now like a fold of satin.

The matter of greetings was intensely important, and a pulse fluttered in Joan's neck as she waited. Matilda of course must speak first. She might say "Hi," which was lighthearted, comradely, or "Hello," which was gentler and more personal. Once in a while she said "Hello, Joan," which indicated such special notice and teasing regard that it immediately filled Joan's eyes with tears and laid on her a shameful, exquisite burden of happiness.

This love dwindled, of course. Like other trials and excitements, it passed away, and Joan's interest in Matilda Buttler returned to normal. Matilda changed, too. By the time Joan was in high school, Matilda was already working. She got a job in a lawyer's office; she was a junior clerk. Now that she was making her own money, and was partway out of her mother's control—only partway, because she still lived at home—she changed her style. It seemed that she wanted to be much less of a princess and much more like everybody else. She got her hair cut short, and wore it in the trim fashion of the time. She started wearing makeup, bright-red lipstick that hardened the shape of her mouth. She dressed the way other girls did—in long, tight slit skirts, and blouses with floppy bows at the neck, and ballerina shoes. She lost her pallor and aloofness. Joan, who was planning to get a scholarship and study art and archeology at the University of Toronto, greeted this Matilda with composure. And the last shred of her worship vanished when Matilda began appearing with a boyfriend.

The boyfriend was a good-looking man about ten years older than Matilda. He had thinning dark hair and a pencil mustache and a rather unfriendly, suspicious, determined expression. He was very tall, and he bent toward Matilda, with his arm around her waist, as they walked along the streets. They walked on the streets so much because Mrs. Carbuncle had taken a huge dislike to him and would not let him inside the house. At first he didn't have a car. Later he did. He was said to be either an airplane pilot or a waiter in a posh restaurant, and it was not known where Matilda had met him. When they walked, his arm was actually below Matilda's waist—his spread fingers rested securely on her hipbone. It seemed to Joan that this bold, settled hand had something to do with his gloomy and challenging expression.

But before this, before Matilda got a job, or cut her hair, something happened that showed Joan—by then long past being in love—an aspect, or effect, of Matilda's beauty that she hadn't suspected. She saw that such beauty marked you—in Logan, anyway—as a limp might, or a speech impediment. It isolated you—more severely, perhaps, than a mild deformity, because it could be seen as a reproach. After she realized that, it wasn't so surprising to Joan, though it was still disappointing, to see that Matilda would do her best to get rid of or camouflage that beauty as soon as she could.

Mrs. Buttler, Mrs. Carbuncle, invading their kitchen as she does every so often, never removes her black coat and her multicolored velvet turban. That is to keep your hopes up, their mother says. Hopes that she's about to leave, that you're going to get free of her in under three hours. Also to cover up whatever god-awful outfit she's got on underneath. Because she's got that coat, and is willing to wear it every day of the year, Mrs. Carbuncle never has to change her dress. A smell issues from her—camphorated, stuffy.

She arrives in mid-spiel, charging ahead in her talk—about something that has happened to her, some person who has outraged her, as if you were certain to know what it was or who. As if her life were on the news and you had just failed to catch the last couple of bulletins. Joan is always eager to listen to the first half hour or so of this report, or tirade, preferably from outside the room, so that she can slip away when things start getting repetitious. If you try to slip away from where Mrs. Carbuncle can see you, she's apt to ask sarcastically where you're off to in such a hurry, or accuse you of not believing her.

Joan is doing that—listening from the dining room, while pretending to practice her piano piece for the public-school Christmas concert. Joan is in her last year at the public grade school, and Matilda is in her last year at high school. (Morris will drop out, after Christmas, to take over the lumberyard.) It's a Saturday morning in mid-December—gray sky and an iron frost. Tonight the high-school Christmas Dance, the only formal dance of the year, is to be held in the town armory.

It's the high-school principal who has got into Mrs. Carbuncle's bad books. This is an unexceptional man named Archibald Moore, who is routinely called by his students Archie Balls, or Archie Balls More, or Archie More Balls. Mrs. Carbuncle says he isn't fit for his job. She says he can be bought and everybody knows it; you'll never pass out of high school unless you slip him the money.

"But the exams are marked in Toronto," says Joan's mother, as if genuinely puzzled. For a while, she enjoys pushing things along, with mild objections and queries.

"He's in cahoots with them, too," says Mrs. Carbuncle. "Them, too." She goes on to say that if money hadn't changed hands he'd never have got out of high school himself. He's very stupid. An ignoramus. He can't solve the problems on the black-board or translate the Latin. He has to have a book with the English words all written in on top. Also, a few years ago, he made a girl pregnant.

"Oh, I never heard that!" says Joan's mother, utterly genteel.

"It was hushed up. He had to pay."

"Did it take all the profits he made on the examinations?"

"He ought to have been horsewhipped."

Joan plays the piano softly—"Jesu, Joy of Man's Desiring" is her piece, and very difficult—because she hopes to hear the name of the girl, or perhaps how the baby was disposed of. (One time, Mrs. Carbuncle described the way a certain doctor in town disposed of babies, the products of his own licentious outbursts.) But Mrs. Carbuncle is swinging around to the root of her griev-ance, and it seems to be something about the dance. Archibald Moore has not managed the dance in the right way. He should make them all draw names for partners to take. Or else he should make them all go without partners. Either one or the other. That way, Matilda could go. Matilda hasn't got a partner—no boy has asked her—and she says she won't go alone. Mrs. Carbuncle says she will. She says she will make her. The reason she will make her is that her dress cost so much. Mrs. Carbuncle enumerates. The cost of the net, the taffeta, the sequins, the boning in the midriff (it's strapless), the twenty-two-inch zipper. She made this dress herself, putting in countless hours of labor, and Matilda wore it once. She wore it last night in the high-school play on the stage in the town hall, and that's all. She says she won't wear it tonight; she won't go to the dance, because nobody has asked her. It is all the fault of Archibald Moore, the cheater, the fornicator, the ignoramus.

Joan and her mother saw Matilda last night. Morris didn't go—he doesn't want to go out with them anymore in the eve-nings. He would sooner listen to the radio or scribble figures, probably having to do with the lumberyard, in a special note-book. Matilda played the role of a mannequin a young man falls in love with. Their mother told Morris when she came home that he was smart to stay away—it was an infinitely silly play. Matilda did not speak, of course, but she did hold herself still for a long time, showing a lovely profile. The dress was wonderful—a snow cloud with silver sequins glinting on it like frost.

Mrs. Carbuncle has told Matilda that she has to go. Partner or not, she has to go. She has to get dressed in her dress and put on a coat and be out the door by nine o'clock. The door will be locked till eleven, when Mrs. Carbuncle goes to bed.

But Matilda still says she won't go. She says she will just sit in the coal shed at the back of the yard. It isn't a coal shed anymore, it's just a shed. Mrs. Carbuncle can't buy coal any more than the Fordyces can.

"She'll freeze," says Joan's mother, really concerned with the conversation for the first time.

"Serve her right," Mrs. Carbuncle says.

Joan's mother looks at the clock and says she is sorry to be rude but she has just remembered an appointment she has uptown. She has to get a tooth filled, and she has to hurry—she has to ask to be excused.

So Mrs. Carbuncle is turned out—saying that it's the first time she heard of filling teeth on a Saturday—and Joan's mother immediately phones the lumberyard to tell Morris to come home.

Now there is the first argument—the first real argument—that Joan has ever heard between Morris and their mother. Morris keeps saying no. What his mother wants him to do he won't do. He sounds as if there were no convincing him, no ordering him. He sounds not like a boy talking to his mother but like a man talking to a woman. A man who knows better than she does, and is ready for all the tricks she will use to make him give in.

"Well, I think you're very selfish," their mother says. "I think you can't think of anybody but yourself. I am very disappointed in you. How would you like to be that poor girl with her loony mother? Sitting in the *coal shed*? There are things a gen-

tleman will do, you know. Your father would have known what
to do."

Morris doesn't answer.

"It's not like proposing marriage or anything. What will it
cost you?" their mother says scornfully. "Two dollars each?"

Morris says in a low voice that it isn't that.

"Do I very often ask you to do anything you don't want to
do? Do I? I treat you like a grown man. You have all kinds of
freedom. Well, now I ask you to do something to show that you
really can act like a grownup and deserve your freedom, and what
do I hear from you?"

This goes on a while longer, and Morris resists. Joan does
not see how their mother is going to win and wonders that she
doesn't give up. She doesn't.

"You don't need to try making the excuse that you can't
dance, either, because you can, and I taught you myself. You're
an elegant dancer!"

Then, of all things, Morris must have agreed, because the
next thing Joan hears is their mother saying, "Go and put on a
clean sweater." Morris's boots sound heavily on the back stairs,
and their mother calls after him, "You'll be glad you did this!
You won't regret it!"

She opens the dining-room door and says to Joan, "I don't
hear an awful lot of piano-playing in here. Are you so good you
can give up practicing already? The last time I heard you play
that piece through, it was terrible."

Joan starts again from the beginning. But she doesn't keep
it up after Morris comes down the stairs and slams the door, and
their mother, in the kitchen, turns on the radio, opens the
cupboards, begins putting together something for lunch. Joan
gets up from the piano bench and goes quietly across the dining
room, through the door into the hall, right up to the front door.
She puts her face against the colored glass. You can't see in
through this glass, because the hall is dark, but if you get your eye
in the right place you can see out. There is more red than any
other color, so she chooses a red view—though she has managed

every color in her time—blue and gold and green; even if there's just a tiny leaf of it, she has figured a way to squint through.

The gray cement-block house across the street is turned to lavender. Morris stands at the door. The door opens, and Joan can't see who has opened it. Is it Matilda or is it Mrs. Carbuncle? The stiff, bare trees and the lilac bush by the door of that house are a dark red, like blood. Morris's good yellow sweater is a blob of golden red, a stoplight, at the door.

Far back in the house, Joan's mother is singing along with the radio. She doesn't know of any danger. Between the front door, the scene outside, and their mother singing in the kitchen, Joan feels the dimness, the chilliness, the frailty and impermanence of these high half-bare rooms—of their house. It is just a place to be judged like other places—it's nothing special. It is no protection. She feels this because it occurs to her that their mother may be mistaken. In this instance—and further, as far as her faith and suppositions reach—she may be mistaken.

It is Mrs. Carbuncle. Morris has turned away and is coming down the walk and she is coming after him. Morris walks down the two steps to the sidewalk, he walks across the street very quickly without looking around. He doesn't run, he keeps his hands in his pockets, and his pink, blood-eyed face smiles to show that nothing that is happening has taken him by surprise. Mrs. Carbuncle is wearing her loose and tattery seldom-seen housedress, her pink hair is wild as a banshee's; at the top of her steps she halts and shrieks after him, so that Joan can hear her through the door, "We're not so bad off we need some Deadeye Dick to take my daughter to a dance!"

II—Frazil Ice

Morris looks to Joan like the caretaker when she sees him out in front of the apartment building, cutting the grass. He is wearing dull-green work pants and a plaid shirt, and, of course, his glasses, with the dark lens. He looks like a man who is competent, even authoritative, but responsible to someone else. Seeing him with a gang of his own workmen (he has branched out from the lumberyard into the construction business), you'd probably take him for the foreman—a sharp-eyed, fair-minded foreman with a solid but limited ambition. Not the boss. Not the owner of the apartment building. He is round-faced and partly bald, with a recent tan and new freckles showing on the front of his scalp. Sturdy but getting round-shouldered, or is that just the way he looks when pushing the mower? Is there a look bachelors get, bachelor sons—bachelor sons who have cared for old parents, particularly mothers? A closed-in, patient look that verges on humility? She thinks that it's almost as if she were coming to visit an uncle.

This is 1972, and Joan herself looks younger than she did ten years ago. She wears her dark hair long, tucked back behind her ears; she makes up her eyes but not her mouth; she dresses in voluminous soft bright cottons or brisk little tunics that cover only a couple of inches of her thighs. She can get away with this—she hopes she can get away with it—because she is a tall, slim-waisted woman with long, well-shaped legs.

Their mother is dead. Morris has sold the house and built, or rebuilt, this and other apartment buildings. The people who bought the house are making it into a nursing home. Joan has told her husband that she wants to go home—that is, back to Logan—to help Morris get settled, but she knows, in fact, that he will be settled; with his grasp of things Morris always seemed settled. All he needs Joan to help him with is the sorting out of some boxes and a trunk, full of clothes, books, dishes, pictures, curtains, that he doesn't want or doesn't have space for and has stored temporarily in the basement of his building.

Joan has been married for years. Her husband is a journalist. They live in Ottawa. People know his name—they even know what he looks like, or what he looked like five years ago, from his picture at the top of a back-page column in a magazine. Joan is used to being identified as his wife, here and elsewhere. But in

Logan this identification carries a special pride. Most people here do not care for the journalist's wit, which they think cynical, or for his opinions, but they are pleased that a girl from this town has got herself attached to a famous, or semi-famous, person.

She has told her husband that she will be staying here for a week. It's Sunday evening when she arrives, a Sunday late in May, with Morris cutting the first grass of the year. She plans to leave on Friday, spending Saturday and Sunday in Toronto. If her husband should find out that she has not spent the entire week with Morris, she has a story ready—about having decided, when Morris no longer needed her, to visit a woman friend she has known since college. Perhaps she should tell that story anyway—it would be safer. She worries about whether she should take the friend into her confidence.

It is the first time she has ever managed anything of this sort.

The apartment building runs deep into the lot, its windows looking out on parking space or on the Baptist church. A driving shed once stood here, for the farmers to leave their horses in during the church service. It's a red brick building. No balconies. Plain, plain.

Joan hugs Morris. She smells cigarettes, gasoline, soft, worn, sweaty shirt, along with the fresh-cut grass. "Oh, Morris, you know what you should do?" she shouts over the sound of the lawnmower. "You should get an eyepatch. Then you'd look just like Moshe Dayan!"

Every morning Joan walks to the post office. She is waiting for a letter from a man in Toronto, whose name is John Brolier. She wrote to him and told him Morris's name, the name of Logan, the number of Morris's post-office box. Logan has grown, but it is still too small to have home delivery.

On Monday morning she hardly hopes for a letter. On Tuesday she does hope for one. On Wednesday she feels she should have every reasonable expectation. Each day she is dis-appointed. Each day a suspicion that she has made a fool of herself—a feeling of being isolated and unwanted—rises closer to the surface. She has taken a man at his word when he didn't mean it. He has thought again.

The post office she goes to is a new, low pinkish brick building. The old one, which used to make her think of a castle, has been torn down. The look of the town has greatly changed. Not many houses have been pulled down, but most have been improved. Aluminum siding, sandblasted brick, bright roofs, wide double-glazed windows, verandas demolished or enclosed as porches. And the wide, wild yards have disappeared—they were really double lots—and the extra lots have been sold and built on. New houses crowd in between the old houses. These are all suburban in style, long and low, or split-level. The yards are tidy and properly planned, with nests of ornamental shrubs, round and crescent-shaped flower beds. The old habit of growing flowers like vegetables, in a row beside the beans or potatoes, seems to have been forgotten. Many of the great shade trees have been cut down. They were probably getting old and dangerous. The shabby houses, the long grass, the cracked sidewalks, the deep shade, the unpaved streets full of dust or puddles—all of this, which Joan remembers, is not to be found. The town seems crowded, diminished, with so many spruced-up properties, so much deliberate arrangement. The town of her childhood—that haphazard, dreamy Logan—was just Logan going through a phase. Its leaning board fences and sun-blistered walls and flow-ering weeds were no permanent expression of what the town could be. And people like Mrs. Buttler—costumed, obsessed—seemed to be bound to that old town and not to be possible anymore.

Morris's apartment has one bedroom, which he has given to Joan. He sleeps on the living-room sofa. A two-bedroom apartment would surely have been more convenient for the times when he has visitors. But he probably doesn't intend to have visitors, very many of them, or very often. And he wouldn't want to lose out on the rent from the larger apartment. He must have considered taking one of the bachelor apartments in the basement, so that he'd be getting the rent from the one-bedroom place as well, but he must have decided that that would be going too far. It would look mingy, it would call attention. It would be a kind of self-indulgence better avoided.

The furniture in the apartment comes from the house where Morris lived with their mother, but not much of it dates from the days when Joan lived at home. Anything that looked like an antique has been sold, and replaced with fairly durable, fairly comfortable furniture that Morris has been able to buy in quantity. Joan sees some things she sent as birthday presents, Christmas presents. They don't fit in quite as well, or liven things up as much, as she had hoped they would.

A print of St. Giles Church recalls the year she and her husband spent in Britain—her own embarrassing postgraduate homesickness and transatlantic affection. And here on the glass tray on top of the coffee table, politely and prominently displayed, is a book she sent to Morris. It's a history of machinery. There are sketches of machines in it, and plans of machines, from the days before photography, from Greek and Egyptian times. Then photographs from the nineteenth century to the present day—road machines, farm machines, factory machines, sometimes shot from a distance, sometimes on the horizon, sometimes seen from close up and low down. Some photographs stress the workings of the machines, both minute and prodigious; others strive to make machines look as splendid as castles or as thrilling as monsters. "What a wonderful book for my brother!" Joan remembers saying to the friend who was with her in the bookstore. "My brother is crazy about machinery." *Crazy about machinery*—that was what she said.

Now she wonders what Morris really thought of this book.

Would he like it at all? He wouldn't actually dislike it. He might be puzzled by it, he might discount it. For it wasn't true that he was crazy about machinery. He used machinery—that was what machinery was for.

Morris takes her on drives in the long spring evenings. He takes her around town and out into the countryside, where she can see what enormous fields, what vistas of corn or beans or wheat or clover, those machines have enabled the farmers to create, what vast and parklike lawns the power mowers have brought into being. Clumps of lilacs bloom over the cellars of abandoned farmhouses. Farms have been consolidated, Morris tells her. He knows the value. Not just houses and buildings but fields and trees, woodlots and hills appear in his mind with a cash value and a history of cash value attached to them, just as every person he mentions is defined as someone who has got ahead or has not got ahead. Such a way of looking at things is not at all in favor at this time—it is thought to be unimaginative and old-fashioned and callous and destructive. Morris is not aware of this, and his talk of money rambles on with a calm enjoyment. He throws in a pun here and there. He chuckles as he tells of certain chancy transactions or extravagant debacles.

While Joan listens to Morris, and talks a little, her thoughts drift on a familiar, irresistible underground stream. She thinks about John Brolier. He is a geologist, who once worked for an oil company, and now teaches (science and drama) at what is called an alternate school. He used to be a person who was getting ahead, and now he is not getting ahead. Joan met him at a dinner party in Ottawa a couple of months ago. He was visiting friends who were also friends of hers. He was not accompanied by his wife, but he had brought two of his children. He told Joan that if she got up early enough the next morning he would take her to see something called "frazil ice" on the Ottawa River.

She thinks of his face and his voice and wonders what could compel her at this time to want this man. It does not seem to have much to do with her marriage. Her marriage seems to her commodious enough—she and her husband have twined together, developing a language, a history, a way of looking at things. They talk all the time. But they leave each other alone, too. The miseries and nastiness that surfaced during the early years have eased or diminished.

What she wants from John Brolier appears to be something that a person not heard from in her marriage, and perhaps not previously heard from in her life, might want. What is it about him? She doesn't think that he is particularly intelligent and she isn't sure that he is trustworthy. (Her husband is both intelligent and trustworthy.) He is not as good-looking as her husband, not as "attractive" a man. Yet he attracts Joan, and she already has a suspicion that he has attracted other women. Because of his intensity, a kind of severity, a deep seriousness—all focussed on sex. His interest won't be too quickly satisfied, too lightly turned aside. She feels this, feels the promise of it, though so far she is not sure of anything.

Her husband was included in the invitation to look at the frazil ice. But it was only Joan who got up and drove to the riverbank. There she met John Brolier and his two children and his hosts' two children in the freezing, pink, snowbound winter dawn. And he really did tell her about frazil ice, about how it forms over the rapids without ever quite getting a chance to freeze solid, and how when it is swept over a deep spot it mounds up immediately, magnificently. He said that this was how they had discovered where the deep holes were in the riverbed. And he said, "Look, if you can ever get away—if it's possible—will you let me know? I really want to see you. You know I do. I want to, very much."

He gave her a piece of paper that he must have had ready. A box number written on it, of a postal station in Toronto. He didn't even touch her fingers. His children were capering around, trying to get his attention. When can we go skating? Can we go to the warplanes museum? Can we go and see the Lancaster Bomber? (Joan saved this up to tell her husband, who would enjoy it, in view of John Brolier's pacifism.)

She did tell her husband, and he teased her. "I think that

jerk with the monk's haircut has taken a shine to you," he said. How could her husband believe that she could fall in love with a man who wore a fringe of thinning hair combed down over his forehead, who had rather narrow shoulders and a gap between his front teeth, five children from two wives, an inadequate income, an excitable and pedantic way of talking, and a proclaimed interest in the writings of Alan Watts? (Even when the time came when he had to believe it, he couldn't.)

When she wrote, she mentioned lunch, a drink, or coffee. She did not tell him how much time she had left open. Perhaps that was all that would happen, she thinks. She would go to see her woman friend after all. She has put herself, though cautiously, at this man's disposal. Walking to the post office, checking her looks in shopwindows, she feels herself loosed, in jeopardy. She has done this, she hardly knows why. She only knows that she cannot go back to the life she was living or to the person she was before she went out that Sunday morning to the river. Her life of shopping and housekeeping and married lovemaking and part-time work in the art-gallery bookstore, and dinner parties and holidays and ski outings at Camp Fortune—she cannot accept that as her only life, she cannot continue it without her sustaining secret. She believes that she does mean to continue it, and in order to continue it she must have this other. This other what? This investigation—to herself she still thinks of it as an investigation.

Put like that, what she was up to might sound coldhearted indeed. But how can a person be called coldhearted who walks to the post office every morning in such a fainthearted condition, who trembles and holds her breath as she turns the key in the lock, and walks back to Morris's apartment feeling so drained, bewildered, deserted? Unless this, too, is part of what she is investigating?

Of course she has to stop and talk to people about her son and daughter and her husband and her life in Ottawa. She has to recognize high-school friends and recall her childhood, and all this seems tedious and irritating to her. The houses themselves, as she walks past—their tidy yards and bright poppies and peonies in bloom—seem tedious to the point of being disgusting. The voices of people who talk to her strike her as harsh and stupid and self-satisfied. She feels as if she had been shunted off to some corner of the world where the real life and thoughts, the uproar and energy of the last few years have not penetrated at all. They have not very effectively penetrated Ottawa, either, but there, at least, people have heard rumors, they have tried imitations, they have got wind of what might be called profound, as well as trivial, changes of fashion. (Joan and her husband, in fact, make fun of some of these people—those who showily take up trends, go to encounter groups and holistic healers, and give up drink for dope.) Here even the trivial changes have hardly been heard of. Back in Ottawa next week, and feeling especially benevolent toward her husband, eager to fill up their time together with chat, Joan will say, "I'd have given thanks if somebody had even handed me an alfalfa-sprout sandwich. Really. It was that bad."

"No, I haven't room" is what Joan keeps saying as she and Morris go through the boxes. There are things here she would have thought she'd want, but she doesn't. "No. I can't think where I'd put it." No, she says, to their mother's dance dresses, the fragile silk and cobwebby georgette. They'd fall apart the first time anybody put them on, and Claire, her daughter, will never be interested in that kind of thing—she wants to be a horse trainer. No to the five wineglasses that didn't get broken, and no to the leatherette-bound copies of Lever and Lover, George Borrow, A. S. M. Hutchinson. "I have too much stuff now," she says sadly as Morris adds all this to the pile to go to the auction rooms. He shakes out the little rug that used to lie on the floor in front of the china cabinet, out of the sun, and that they were not supposed to walk on because it was valuable.

"I saw one exactly like that a couple of months ago," she says. "It was in a secondhand store, not even an antique store. I was in there looking for old comics and posters for Rob's birthday. I saw one just the same. At first I didn't even know where I'd seen it before. Then I felt quite shocked. As if there were only supposed to be one of them in the world."

"How much did they want for it?" says Morris.

"I don't know. It was in better condition."

She doesn't understand yet that she doesn't want to take anything back to Ottawa because she herself won't be staying in the house there for much longer. The time of accumulation, of acquiring and arranging, of padding up the corners of her life, has come to an end. (It will return years later, and she will wish she had saved at least the wineglasses.) In Ottawa, in September, her husband will ask her if she still wants to buy wicker furniture for the sunroom, and if she would like to go to the wicker store, where they're having a sale on summer stock. A thrill of distaste will go through her then—at the very thought of looking for chairs and tables, paying for them, arranging them in the room—and she will finally know what is the matter.

On Friday morning there is a letter in the box with Joan's name typed on it. She doesn't look at the postmark; she tears the envelope open gratefully, runs her eyes over it greedily, reads without understanding. It seems to be a chain letter. A parody of a chain letter, a joke. If she breaks the chain, it says, DIRE CALAMITY will befall her. Her fingernails will rot and her teeth will grow moss. Warts as big as cauliflowers will sprout on her chin, and her friends will avoid her. What can this be, thinks Joan. A code in which John Brolier has seen fit to write to her? Then it occurs to her to look at the postmark, and she does, and she sees that the letter comes from Ottawa. It comes from her son, obviously. Rob loves this sort of joke. His father would have typed the envelope for him.

She thinks of her child's delight when he sealed up the envelope and her own state of mind when she tore it open.

Treachery and confusion.

Late that afternoon, she and Morris open the trunk, which they have left till the last. She takes out a suit of evening clothes—a man's evening clothes, still in a plastic sheath, as if they had not been worn since being cleaned. "This must be Father's," she says. "Look, Father's old evening clothes."

"No, that's mine," says Morris. He takes the suit from her, shakes down the plastic, stands holding it out in front of him over both arms. "That's my old soup-and-fish—it ought to be hanging up in the closet."

"What did you get it for?" Joan says. "A wedding?" Some of Morris's workmen lead lives much more showy and ceremonious than his, and they invite him to elaborate weddings.

"That, and some things I have to go to with Matilda," Morris says. "Dinner dances, big dress-up kinds of things."

"With Matilda?" says Joan. "Matilda *Buttler?*"

"That's right. She doesn't use her married name." Morris seems to be answering a slightly different question, not the one Joan meant to ask. "Strictly speaking, I guess she doesn't have a married name."

Joan hears again the story she just now remembers having heard before—or read before, in their mother's long, lively letters. Matilda Buttler ran off to marry her boyfriend. The expression "ran off" is their mother's, and Morris seems to use it with unconscious emphasis, a son's respect—it's as if the only way he can properly talk about this, or have the right to talk about it, were in his mother's language. Matilda ran off and married that man with the mustache, and it turned out that her mother's suspicions, her extravagant accusations had for once some grounds. The boyfriend turned out to be a bigamist. He had a wife in England, which was where he came from. After he had been with Matilda three or four years—fortunately, there were no children—the other wife, the real wife, tracked him down. The marriage to Matilda was annulled; Matilda came back to Logan, came back to live with her mother, and got a job in the courthouse.

"How could she?" says Joan. "Of all the stupid things to do."

"Well. She was young," says Morris, with a trace of stubbornness or discomfort in his voice.

"I don't mean *that*. I mean coming back."

"Well, she had her mother," Morris says, apparently without irony. "I guess she didn't have anybody else."

Looming above Joan, with his dark-lensed eye, and the suit laid like a body over his arms, he looks gloomy and troubled. His face and neck are unevenly flushed, mottled. His chin trembles slightly and he bites down on his lower lip. Does he know how his looks give him away? When he starts to talk again, it's in a reasonable, explanatory tone. He says that he guesses it didn't much matter to Matilda where she lived. In a way, according to her, her life was over. And that was where he, Morris, came into the picture. Because every once in a while Matilda had to go to functions. Political banquets. Retirement banquets. Functions. It was a part of her job, and it would be awkward if she didn't go. But it was also awkward for her to go alone—she needed an escort. And she couldn't go with a man who might get ideas, not understanding how things stood. Not understanding that Matilda's life, or a certain part of Matilda's life, was over. She needed somebody who understood the whole business and didn't need explanations. "Which is me," says Morris.

"Why does she think that way?" says Joan. "She's not so old. I bet she's still good-looking. It wasn't her fault. Is she still in love with him?"

"I don't think it's my place to ask her any questions."

"Oh, Morris!" Joan says, in a fond dismissive voice that surprises her, it sounds so much like her mother's. "I bet she is. In love with him still."

Morris goes off to hang his evening clothes in a closet in the apartment, where they can wait for his next summons to be Matilda's escort.

In bed that night, lying awake, looking out at the street light shining through the fresh leaves on the square, squat tower of the Baptist church, Joan has something to think about besides her own plight. (She thinks of that, too, of course.) She thinks of Morris and Matilda dancing. She sees them in Holiday Inn ballrooms, on golf-club dance floors, wherever it is that the functions are held. In their unfashionable formal clothes, Matilda's hair in a perfect sprayed bouffant, Morris's face glistening with the sweat of courteous effort. But it probably isn't an effort; they probably dance very well together. They are so terribly, perfectly balanced, each with stubbornly preserved and wholeheartedly accepted flaws. Flaws they could quite easily disregard or repair. But they would never do that. Morris in love with Matilda—in that stern, unfulfilled, lifelong way—and she in love with her bigamist, stubbornly obsessed with her own mistake and disgrace. They dance in Joan's mind's eye—sedate and absurd, romantic. Who but Morris after all, with his head full of mortgages and contracts, could turn out to be such a romantic?

She envies him. She envies them.

She has been in the habit of putting herself to sleep with a memory of John Brolier's voice—his hasty, lowered voice when he said, "I want to, very much." Or she pictured his face; it was a medieval face, she thought—long and pale and bony, with the smile she dismissed as tactical, the sober, glowing, not dismissible dark eyes. Her imagining won't work tonight; it won't open the gates for her into foggy, tender territory. She isn't able to place herself anywhere but here, on the hard single bed in Morris's apartment—in her real and apparent life. And nothing that works for Morris and Matilda is going to work for her. Not self-denial, the exaltation of balked desires, no kind of high-flown helplessness. She is not to be so satisfied.

She knows that, and she knows what she will have to do. She casts her mind ahead—inadmissibly, shamefully, she casts her mind ahead, fumbling for the shape of the next lover.

That won't be necessary.

What Joan has forgotten altogether is that mail comes to small-town post offices on Saturday. Saturday isn't a mailless day here. Morris has gone to see what's in his box; he hands her the letter. The letter sets up a time and place. It is very brief, and signed only with John Brolier's initials. This is wise, of course. Such brevity, such caution, is not altogether pleasing to Joan, but in her relief, her transformation, she doesn't dwell on it.

She tells Morris the story she meant to tell him had the letter come earlier. She has been summoned by her college friend, who got word that she was here. While she washes her hair and packs her things, Morris takes her car to the cut-rate gas bar north of town and fills up the tank.

Waving goodbye to Morris, she doesn't see any suspicion on his face. But perhaps a little disappointment. He has two days less to be with someone now, two days more to be alone. He wouldn't admit to such a feeling. Maybe she imagines it. She imagines it because she has a feeling that she's waving to her husband and her children as well, to everybody who knows her, except the man she's going to meet. All so easily, flawlessly deceived. And she feels compunction, certainly. She is smitten by their innocence; she recognizes an irreparable tear in her life. This is genuine—her grief and guilt at this moment are genuine, and they'll never altogether vanish. But they won't get in her way, either. She is more than glad; she feels that she has no choice but to be going.

III—Rose Matilda

Ruth Ann Leatherby is going with Joan and Morris to the cemetery. Joan is a little surprised about this, but Morris and Ruth Ann seem to take it for granted. Ruth Ann is Morris's book-keeper. Joan has known of her for years, and may even have met her before. Ruth Ann is the sort of pleasant-looking, middle-sized, middle-aged woman whose looks you don't remember. She lives now in one of the bachelor apartments in the basement of Morris's building. She is married, but her husband hasn't been around for a long time. She is a Catholic, so has not thought about getting a divorce. There is some tragedy in her background—a house fire, a child?—but it has been thoroughly absorbed and is not mentioned.

It is Ruth Ann who got the hyacinth bulbs to plant on their parents' graves. She had heard Morris say it would be nice to have something growing there, and when she saw the bulbs on sale at the supermarket she bought some. A wife-woman, thinks Joan, observing her. Wife-women are attentive yet self-possessed, they are dedicated but cool. What is it that they are dedicated to?

Joan lives in Toronto now. She has been divorced for twelve years. She has a job managing a bookstore that specializes in art books. It's a pleasant job, though it doesn't pay much; she has been lucky. She is also lucky (she knows that people say she is lucky, for a woman of her age) in having a lover, a friend-lover—Geoffrey. They don't live together; they see each other on weekends and two or three times during the week. Geoffrey is an actor. He is talented, cheerful, adaptable, poor. One weekend a month he spends in Montreal with a woman he used to live with and their child. On these weekends, Joan goes to see her children, who are grown up and have forgiven her. Her son, too, is an actor—in fact, that's how she met Geoffrey. Her daughter is a journalist, like her father. And what is there to forgive? Many parents got divorced, most of them shipwrecked by affairs, at about the same time. It seems that all sorts of marriages begun in the fifties without misgivings, or without misgivings that anybody could know about, blew up in the early seventies, with a lot of spectacular—and, it seems now, unnecessary, extravagant—complications. Joan thinks of her own history of love with no regret but some amazement. It's as if she had once gone in for skydiving.

And sometimes she comes to see Morris. Sometimes she gets Morris to talk about the very things that used to seem incomprehensible and boring and sad to her. The peculiar structure of earnings and pensions and mortgages and loans and investments and legacies that Morris sees underlying every human life—that interests her. It's still more or less incomprehensible to her, but its existence no longer seems to be a sorry delusion. It reassures her in some way. She's curious about how people believe in it.

This lucky woman, Joan, with her job and her lover and her striking looks—more remarked upon now than ever before in her life (she is as thin as she was at fourteen and has a wing, a foxtail, of silver white in her very short hair)—is aware of a new danger, a threat that she could not have imagined when she was younger. She couldn't have imagined it even if somebody described it to her. And it's hard to describe. The threat is of a change, but it's not the sort of change one has been warned about. It's just this—that suddenly, without warning, Joan is apt to think: *Rubble.* Rubble. You can look down a street, and you can see the shadows, the light, the brick walls, the truck parked under a tree, the dog lying on the sidewalk, the dark summer awning, or the grayed snowdrift—you can see all these things in their temporary separateness, all connected underneath in such a troubling, satisfying, necessary, indescribable way. Or you can see rubble. Passing states, a useless variety of passing states. Rubble.

Joan wants to keep this idea of rubble at bay. She pays attention now to all the ways in which people seem to do that. Acting is an excellent way—she has learned that from being with Geoffrey. Though there are gaps in acting. In Morris's sort of life or way of looking at things, there seems to be less chance of gaps.

As they drive through the streets, she notices that many of the old houses are reëmerging; doors and porches that were sensible modern alterations fifteen or twenty years ago are giving way to traditional verandas and fanlights. A good thing, surely. Ruth Ann points out this feature and that, and Joan approves but thinks there is something here that is strained, meticulous.

Morris stops the car at an intersection. An old woman

crosses the street in the middle of the block ahead of them. She strides across the street diagonally, not looking to see if there's anything coming. A determined, oblivious, even contemptuous stride, in some way familiar. The old woman is not in any danger; there is not another car on the street, and nobody else walking, just a couple of young girls on bicycles. The old woman is not so old, really. Joan is constantly revising her impressions these days of whether people are old or not so old. This woman has white hair down to her shoulders and is wearing a loose shirt and gray slacks. Hardly enough for the day, which is bright but cold.

"There goes Matilda," says Ruth Ann. The way that she says "Matilda"—without a surname, in a tolerant, amused, and distant tone—announces that Matilda is a character.

"Matilda!" says Joan, turning toward Morris. "Is that Matilda? What ever happened to her?"

It's Ruth Ann who answers, from the back seat. "She just started getting weird. When was it? A couple of years ago? She started dressing sloppy, and she thought people were taking things off her desk at work, and you'd say something perfectly decent to her and she'd be rude back. It could have been in her makeup."

"Her *makeup?*" says Joan.

"Heredity," Morris says, and they laugh.

"That's what I meant," says Ruth Ann. "Her mother was across the street in the nursing home for years before she died— she was completely out of it. And even before she went in there, you'd see her lurking around the yard—she looked like Halloween. Anyway, Matilda got a little pension when they let her go at the courthouse. She just walks around. Sometimes she talks to you as friendly as anything, other times not a word. And she never fixes up. She used to look so nice."

Joan shouldn't be so surprised, so taken aback. People change. They disappear, and they don't all die to do it. Some die—John Brolier has died. When Joan heard that, several months after the fact, she felt a pang, but not so sharp a pang as when she once heard a woman say at a party, "Oh, John Brolier, yes. Wasn't he the one who was always trying to seduce you by dragging you out to look at some natural marvel? God, it was uncomfortable!"

"She owns her house," Morris says. "I sold it to her about five years ago. And she's got that bit of pension. If she can hold on till she's sixty-five, she'll be O.K."

Morris digs up the earth in front of the headstone; Joan and Ruth Ann plant the bulbs. The earth is cold, but there hasn't been a frost. Long bars of sunlight fall between the clipped cedar trees and the rustling poplars, which still hold many gold leaves, on the rich green grass.

"Listen to that," says Joan, looking up at the leaves. "It's like water."

"People like it," says Morris. "Very pop'lar sound."

Joan and Ruth Ann groan together, and Joan says, "I didn't know you still did that, Morris."

Ruth Ann says, "He never stops."

They wash their hands at an outdoor tap and read a few names on the stones.

"Rose Matilda," Morris says.

For a moment Joan thinks that's another name he's read; then she realizes he's still thinking of Matilda Buttler.

"That poem Mother used to say about her," he says. "Rose Matilda."

"Rapunzel," Joan says. "That was what Mother used to call her. 'Rapunzel, Rapunzel, let down thy gold hair.' "

"I know she used to say that. She said 'Rose Matilda,' too. It was the start of a poem."

"It sounds like a lotion," Ruth Ann says. "Isn't that a skin lotion? Rose Emulsion?"

" 'Oh, what avails,' " says Morris firmly. "That was the start of it. 'Oh, what avails.' "

"Of course, I don't know hardly any poems," says Ruth

Ann, versatile and unabashed. She says to Joan, "Does it ring a bell with you?"

She has really pretty eyes, Joan thinks—brown eyes that can look soft and shrewd at once.

"It does," says Joan. "But I can't think what comes next."

Morris has cheated them all a little bit, these three women. Joan, Ruth Ann, Matilda. Morris isn't habitually dishonest— he's not foolish that way—but he will cut a corner now and then. He cheated Joan a long time ago, when the house was sold. She got about a thousand dollars less out of that than she should have. He thought she would make it up in the things she chose to take back to her house in Ottawa. Then she didn't choose anything. Later on, when she and her husband had parted, and she was on her own, Morris considered sending her a check, with an explanation that there had been a mistake. But she got a job, she didn't seem short of money. She has very little idea of what to do with money anyway—how to make it work. He let the idea drop.

The way he cheated Ruth Ann was more complicated, and had to do with persuading her to declare herself a part-time employee of his when she wasn't. This got him out of paying certain benefits to her. He wouldn't be surprised if she had figured all that out, and had made a few little adjustments of her own. That was what she would do—never say anything, never argue, but quietly get her own back. And as long as she just got her own back—he'd soon notice if it was any more—he wouldn't say anything, either. She and he both believe that if people don't look out for themselves what they lose is their own fault. He means to take care of Ruth Ann eventually anyway.

If Joan found out what he had done, she probably wouldn't say anything, either. The interesting part, to her, would not be the money. She has some instinct lacking in that regard. The interesting part would be: why? She'd worry that around and get her curious pleasure out of it. This fact about her brother would lodge in her mind like a hard crystal—a strange, small, light-refracting object, a bit of alien treasure.

He didn't cheat Matilda when he sold her the house. She got that at a very good price. But he told her that the hot-water heater he had put in a year or so before was new, and of course it wasn't. He never bought new appliances or new materials when he was fixing up the places he owned. And three years ago last June, at a dinner dance in the Valhalla Inn, Matilda said to him, "My hot-water heater gave out. I had to replace it."

They were not dancing at the time. They were sitting at a round table, with some other people, under a canopy of floating balloons. They were drinking whiskey.

"It shouldn't have done that," Morris said.

"Not after you'd put it in new," said Matilda, smiling. "You know what I think?"

He kept looking at her, waiting.

"I think we should have another dance before we have anything more to drink!"

They danced. They had always danced easily together, and often with some special flourish. But this time Morris felt that Matilda's body was heavier and stiffer than it had been—her responses were tardy, then overdone. It was odd that her body should seem unwilling when she was smiling and talking to him with such animation, and moving her head and shoulders with every sign of flirtatious charm. This, too, was new—not at all what he was used to from her. Year after year she had danced with him with a dreamy pliancy and a serious face, hardly talking at all. Then, after she had had a few drinks, she would speak to him about her secret concerns. Her concern. Which was always the same. It was Ron, the Englishman. She hoped to hear from him. She stayed here, she had come back here, so that he would know where to find her. She hoped, she doubted, that he would divorce his wife. He had promised, but she had no faith in him. She heard from him eventually. He said he was on the move, he would write again. And he did. He said that he was going to look her up. The letters were posted in Canada, from different, distant cities. Then she didn't hear. She wondered if he was alive; she thought of detective agencies. She said she didn't speak of this to anybody but Morris. Her love was her affliction, which nobody else was permitted to see.

Morris never offered advice; he never laid a comforting hand on her except as was proper, in dancing. He knew exactly how he must absorb what she said. He didn't pity her, either. He had respect for all the choices she had made.

It was true that the tone had changed before the night at the Valhalla Inn. It had taken on a tartness, a sarcastic edge, which pained him and didn't suit her. But this was the night he felt it all broken—their long complicity, the settled harmony of their dancing. They were like some other middle-aged couple, pretending to move lightly and with pleasure, anxious not to let the moment sag. She didn't mention Ron, and Morris, of course, did not ask. A thought started forming in his mind that she had seen him finally. She had seen Ron or heard that he was dead. Seen him, more likely.

"I know how you could pay me back for that heater," she teased him. "You could put in a lawn for me! When has that lawn of mine ever been seeded? It looks terrible; it's riddled with creeping Charlie. I wouldn't mind having a decent lawn. I'm thinking of fixing up the house. I'd like to put burgundy shutters on it to counter the effect of all that gray. I'd like a big window in the side. I'm sick of looking out at the nursing home. Oh, Morris, do you know they've cut down your walnut trees! They've levelled out the yard, they've fenced off the creek!"

She was wearing a long, rustling peacock-blue dress. Blue stones in silver disks hung from her ears. Her hair was stiff and pale, like spun taffy. There were dents in the flesh of her upper arms; her breath smelled of whiskey. Her perfume and her makeup and her smile all spoke to him of falsehood, determination, and misery. She had lost interest in her affliction. She had lost her nerve to continue as she was. And in her simple, dazzling folly, she had lost his love.

"If you come around next week with some grass seed and show me how to do it, I'll give you a drink," she said. "I'll even make you supper. It embarrasses me to think that all these years you've never sat down at my table."

"You'd have to plow it all up and start fresh."

"Plow it all up, then! Why don't you come Wednesday? Or is that your evening with Ruth Ann Leatherby?"

She was drunk. Her head dropped against his shoulder, and he felt the hard lump of her earring pressing through his jacket and shirt into his flesh.

The next week, he sent one of his workmen to plow up and seed Matilda's lawn, for nothing. The man didn't stay long. According to him, Matilda came out and yelled at him to get off her property, what did he think he was doing there, she could take care of her own yard. You better scram, she said to him.

"Scram." That was a word Morris could remember his own mother using. And Matilda's mother had used it, too, in her old days of vigor and ill will. Mrs. Buttler, Mrs. Carbuncle. *Scram out of here.* Deadeye Dick.

He did not see Matilda for some time after that. He didn't run into her. If some business had to be done at the courthouse, he sent Ruth Ann. He got word of changes that were happening, and they were not in the direction of burgundy shutters or house renovation.

"Oh, what avails the sceptred race!" says Joan suddenly when they are driving back to the apartment. And as soon as they get there she goes to the bookcase—it's the same old glass-fronted bookcase. Morris didn't sell that, though it's almost too high for this living room. She finds their mother's *Anthology of English Verse.*

"First lines," she says, going to the back of the book.

"Sit down and be comfortable, why don't you?" says Ruth Ann, coming in with the late-afternoon drinks. Morris gets whiskey-and-water, Joan and Ruth Ann white-rum-and-soda. A liking for this drink has become a joke, a hopeful bond, between the two women, who understand that they are going to need something.

Joan sits and drinks, pleased. She runs her finger down the page. "Oh what, oh what—" she murmurs.

"Oh, what the form divine!" says Morris, with a great sigh of retrieval and satisfaction.

They were taught specialness, Joan thinks, without particular regret. The tag of poetry, the first sip of alcohol, the late light of an October afternoon may be what's making her feel peaceful, indulgent. They were taught a delicate, special regard for themselves, which made them go out and grab what they wanted, whether love or money. But that's not altogether true, is it? Morris has been quite disciplined about love, and abstemious. So has she been about money—in money matters she has remained clumsy, virginal.

There's a problem, though, a hitch in her unexpected pleasure. She can't find the line. "It's not in here," she says. "How can it not be in here? Everything Mother knew was in here." She takes another, businesslike drink and stares at the page. Then she says, "I know! I know!" And in a few moments she has it; she is reading to them, in a voice full of playful emotion:

> "Ah, what avails the sceptred race,
> Ah, what the form divine!
> What every virtue, every grace,
> Rose Aylmer—Rose Matilda—all
> were thine!"

Morris has taken off his glasses. He'll do that now in front of Joan. Maybe he started doing it sooner in front of Ruth Ann. He rubs at the scar as if it were itchy. His eye is dark, veined with gray. It isn't hard to look at. Under its wrapping of scar tissue it's as harmless as a prune or a stone.

"So that's it," Morris says. "So I wasn't wrong."

Differently

Georgia once took a creative-writing course, and what the instructor told her was: Too many things. Too many things going on at the same time; also too many people. Think, he told her. What is the important thing? What do you want us to pay attention to? Think.

Eventually she wrote a story that was about her grandfather killing chickens, and the instructor seemed to be pleased with it. Georgia herself thought that it was a fake. She made a long list of all the things that had been left out and handed it in as an appendix to the story. The instructor said that she expected too much, of herself and of the process, and that she was wearing him out.

The course was not a total loss, because Georgia and the instructor ended up living together. They still live together, in Ontario, on a farm. They sell raspberries, and run a small publishing business. When Georgia can get the money together, she goes to Vancouver to visit her sons. This fall Saturday she has taken the ferry across to Victoria, where she used to live. She did this on an impulse that she doesn't really trust, and by midafternoon, when she walks up the driveway of the splendid stone house where she used to visit Maya, she has already been taken over some fairly shaky ground.

When she phoned Raymond, she wasn't sure that he would ask her to the house. She wasn't sure that she even wanted to go there. She had no notion of how welcome she would be. But Raymond opens the door before she can touch the bell, and he hugs her around the shoulders and kisses her twice (surely he didn't use to do this?) and introduces his wife, Anne. He says he has told her what great friends they were, Georgia and Ben and he and Maya. Great friends.

Maya is dead. Georgia and Ben are long divorced.

They go to sit in what Maya used to call, with a certain flat cheerfulness, "the family room."

(One evening Raymond had said to Ben and Georgia that it looked as if Maya wasn't going to be able to have any children. "We try our best," he said. "We use pillows and everything. But no luck."

"Listen, old man, you don't do it with pillows," Ben said boisterously. They were all a little drunk. "I thought you were the expert on all the apparatus, but I can see that you and I are going to have to have a little talk."

Raymond was an obstetrician and gynecologist.

By that time Georgia knew all about the abortion in Seattle, which had been set up by Maya's lover, Harvey. Harvey was also a doctor, a surgeon. The bleak apartment in the run-down building, the bad-tempered old woman who was knitting a sweater, the doctor arriving in his shirtsleeves, carrying a brown-paper bag that Maya hysterically believed must contain the tools of his trade. In fact, it contained his lunch—an egg-and-onion sandwich. Maya had the smell of that in her face all the time he and Mme. Defarge were working her over.

Maya and Georgia smiled at each other primly while their husbands continued their playful conversation.)

Raymond's curly brown hair has turned into a silvery fluff, and his face is lined. But nothing dreadful has happened to him—no pouches or jowls or alcoholic flush or sardonic droop of defeat. He is still thin, and straight, and sharp-shouldered, still fresh-smelling, spotless, appropriately, expensively dressed. He'll make a brittle, elegant old man, with an obliging boy's smile. There's that sort of shine on both of them, Maya once said glumly. She was speaking of Raymond and Ben. Maybe we should soak them in vinegar, she said.

The room has changed more than Raymond has. An ivory leather sofa has replaced Maya's tapestry-covered couch, and of course all the old opium-den clutter, Maya's cushions and pampas grass and the gorgeous multicolored elephant with the tiny sewn-on mirrors—that's all gone. The room is beige and ivory, smooth and comfortable as the new blond wife, who sits on the arm of Raymond's chair and maneuvers his arm around her, placing his hand on her thigh. She wears slick-looking white pants and a cream-on-white appliquéd sweater, with gold jewelry. Raymond gives her a couple of hearty and defiant pats.

"Are you going someplace?" he says. "Possibly shopping?"

"Righto," says the wife. "Old times." She smiles at Georgia. "It's O.K.," she says. "I really do have to go shopping."

When she has gone, Raymond pours drinks for Georgia and himself. "Anne is a worrywart about the booze," he says. "She won't put salt on the table. She threw out all the curtains in the house to get rid of the smell of Maya's cigarettes. I know what you may be thinking: Friend Raymond has got hold of a luscious blonde. But this is actually a very serious girl, and a very steady girl. I had her in my office, you know, quite a while before Maya died. I mean, I had her *working* in my office. I don't mean that the way it sounds! She isn't as young as she looks, either. She's thirty-six."

Georgia had thought forty. She is tired of the visit already, but she has to tell about herself. No, she is not married. Yes, she works. She and the friend she lives with have a farm and a publishing business. Touch and go, not much money. Interesting. A male friend, yes.

"I've lost all track of Ben somehow," Raymond says. "The last I heard, he was living on a boat."

"He and his wife sail around the West Coast every summer," Georgia says. "In the winter they go to Hawaii. The Navy lets you retire early."

"Marvellous," says Raymond.

Seeing Raymond has made Georgia think that she has no idea what Ben looks like now. Has he gone white-haired, has he thickened around the middle? Both of these things have happened to her—she has turned into a chunky woman with a healthy olive skin, a crest of white hair, wearing loose and rather splashy clothes. When she thinks of Ben, she sees him still as a handsome Navy officer, with a perfect Navy look—keen and serious and self-effacing. The look of someone who longed, bravely, to be given orders. Her sons must have pictures of him around—they both see him, they spend holidays on his boat. Perhaps they put the pictures away when she comes to visit. Perhaps they think of protecting these images of him from one who did him hurt.

On the way to Maya's house—Raymond's house—Georgia walked past another house, which she could easily have avoided. A house in Oak Bay, which in fact she had to go out of her way to see.

It was still the house that she and Ben had read about in the real-estate columns of the Victoria *Colonist*. Roomy bungalow under picturesque oak trees. Arbutus, dogwood, window seats, fireplace, diamond-paned windows, character. Georgia stood outside the gate and felt a most predictable pain. Here Ben had cut the grass, here the children had made their paths and hideaways in the bushes, and laid out a graveyard for the birds and snakes killed by the black cat, Domino. She could recall the inside of the house perfectly—the oak floors she and Ben had laboriously sanded, the walls they had painted, the room where she had lain in drugged misery after having her wisdom teeth out. Ben had read aloud to her, from *Dubliners*. She couldn't

remember the title of the story. It was about a timid poetic sort
of young man, with a mean pretty wife. Poor bugger, said Ben
when he'd finished it.

Ben liked fiction, which was surprising in a man who also
liked sports, and had been popular at school.

She ought to have stayed away from this neighborhood.
Everywhere she walked here, under the chestnut trees with their
flat gold leaves, and the red-limbed arbutus, and the tall Garry
oaks, which suggested fairy stories, European forests, woodcut-
ters, witches—everywhere her footsteps reproached her, saying
what-for, what-for, what-for. This reproach was just what she had
expected—it was what she courted—and there was something
cheap about doing such a thing. Something cheap and useless.
She knew it. But *what-for, what-for, what-for, wrong-and-waste,
wrong-and-waste* went her silly, censorious feet.

Raymond wants Georgia to look at the garden, which he
says was made for Maya during the last months of her life. Maya
designed it; then she lay on the tapestry couch (setting fire to it
twice, Raymond says, by dozing off with a cigarette lit), and she
was able to see it all take shape.

Georgia sees a pond, a stone-rimmed pond with an island in
the middle. The head of a wicked-looking stone beast—a moun-
tain goat?—rears up on the island, spouting water. Around the
pond a jungle of Shasta daisies, pink and purple cosmos, dwarf
pines and cypresses, some other miniature tree with glossy red
leaves. On the island, now that she looks more closely, are mossy
stone walls—the ruins of a tiny tower.

"She hired a young chap to do the work," Raymond says.
"She lay there and watched him. It took all summer. She just lay
all day and watched him making her garden. Then he'd come in
and they'd have tea, and talk about it. You know, Maya didn't
just design that garden. She imagined it. She'd tell him what
she'd been imagining about it, and he'd take off from there. I
mean, this to them was not just a garden. The pond was a lake
in this country they had some name for, and all around the lake

were forests and territories where different tribes and factions lived. Do you get the picture?"

"Yes," says Georgia.

"Maya had a dazzling imagination. She could have written fantasy or science fiction. Whatever. She was a creative person, without any doubt about it. But you could not get her to seriously use her creativity. That goat was one of the gods of that country, and the island was like a sacred place with a former temple on it. You can see the ruins. They had the religion all worked out. Oh, and the literature, the poems and the legends and the history—everything. They had a song that the queen would sing. Of course it was supposed to be a translation, from that language. They had some of that figured out, too. There had been a queen that was shut up in that ruin. That temple. I forget why. She was getting sacrificed, probably. Getting her heart torn out or some gruesome thing. It was all complicated and melodramatic. But think of the effort that went into it. The creativity. The young chap was an artist by profession. I believe he thought of himself as an artist. I don't know how she got hold of him, actually. She knew people. He supported himself doing this kind of thing, I imagine. He did a good job. He laid the pipes, everything. He showed up every day. Every day he came in when he was finished and had tea and talked to her. Well, in my opinion, they didn't have just tea. To my knowledge, not just tea. He would bring a little substance, they would have a little smoke. I told Maya she should write it all down.

"But you know, the instant he was finished, off he went. Off he went. I don't know. Maybe he got another job. It didn't seem to me that it was my place to ask. But I did think that even if he had got a job he could have come back and visited her now and then. Or if he'd gone off on a trip somewhere he could have written letters. I thought he could have. I expected that much of him. It wouldn't have been any skin off his back. Not as I see it. It would have been nice of him to make her think that it hadn't been just a case of—of hired friendship, you know, all along."

Raymond is smiling. He cannot repress, or perhaps is not aware of, this smile.

"For that was the conclusion she must have come to," he says. "After all that nice time and imagining together and egging each other on. She must have been disappointed. She must have been. Even at that stage, such a thing would matter a lot to her. You and I know it, Georgia. It would have mattered. He could have treated her a little more kindly. It wouldn't have had to be for very long."

Maya died a year ago, in the fall, but Georgia did not hear about it until Christmas. She got the news in Hilda's Christmas letter. Hilda, who used to be married to Harvey, is now married to another doctor, in a town in the interior of British Columbia. A few years ago she and Georgia, both visitors, met by chance on a Vancouver street, and they have written occasional letters since.

"Of course you knew Maya so much better than I did," Hilda wrote. "But I've been surprised how often I've thought about her. I've been thinking of all of us, really, how we were, fifteen or so years ago, and I think we were just as vulnerable in some ways as the kids with their acid trips and so on, that were supposed to be marked for life. Weren't we marked—all of us smashing up our marriages and going out looking for adventure? Of course, Maya didn't smash up her marriage, she of all people stayed where she was, so I suppose it doesn't make much sense what I'm saying. But Maya seemed the most vulnerable person of all to me, so gifted and brittle. I remember I could hardly bear to look at that vein in her temple where she parted her hair."

What an odd letter for Hilda to write, thought Georgia. She remembered Hilda's expensive pastel plaid shirtdresses, her neat, short, fair hair, her good manners. Did Hilda really think she had smashed up her marriage and gone out looking for adventure under the influence of dope and rock music and revolutionary costumes? Georgia's impression was that Hilda had left Harvey, once she found out what he was up to—or some of what he was up to—and gone to the town in the interior where she sensibly took up her old profession of nursing and in due time married another, presumably more trustworthy doctor. Maya and Georgia had never thought of Hilda as a woman like themselves. And Hilda and Maya had not been close—they had particular reason not to be. But Hilda had kept track; she knew of Maya's death, she wrote these generous words. Without Hilda, Georgia would not have known. She would still have been thinking that someday she might write to Maya, there might come a time when their friendship could be mended.

The first time that Ben and Georgia went to Maya's house, Harvey and Hilda were there. Maya was having a dinner party for just the six of them. Georgia and Ben had recently moved to Victoria, and Ben had phoned Raymond, who had been a friend of his at school. Ben had never met Maya, but he told Georgia that he had heard that she was very clever, and weird. People said that she was weird. But she was rich—an heiress—so she could get away with it.

Georgia groaned at the news that Maya was rich, and she groaned again at the sight of the house—the great stone-block house with its terraced lawns and clipped bushes and circular drive.

Georgia and Ben came from the same small town in Ontario, and had the same sort of families. It was a fluke that Ben had been sent to a good private school—the money had come from a great-aunt. Even in her teens, when she was proud of being Ben's girl and prouder than she liked to let on about being asked to the dances at that school, Georgia had a low opinion of the girls she met there. She thought rich girls were spoiled and brainless. She called them twits. She thought of herself as a girl—and then a woman—who didn't much like other girls and women. She called the other Navy wives "the Navy *ladies.*" Ben was sometimes entertained by her opinions of people and at other times asked if it was really necessary to be so critical.

He had an inkling, he said, that she was going to like Maya. This didn't predispose Georgia in Maya's favor. But Ben turned out to be right. He was very happy then, to have come up with somebody like Maya as an offering to Georgia, to have found a couple with whom he and Georgia could willingly link up as friends. "It'll be good for us to have some non-Navy friends," he was to say. "Some wife for you to knock around with who isn't so conventional. You can't say Maya's conventional."

Georgia couldn't. The house was more or less what she had expected—soon she learned that Maya called it "your friendly neighborhood fortress"—but Maya was a surprise. She opened the door herself, barefoot, wearing a long shapeless robe of coarse brown cloth that looked like burlap. Her hair was long and straight, parted high at one temple. It was almost the same dull-brown color as the robe. She did not wear lipstick, and her skin was rough and pale, with marks like faint bird tracks in the hollows of her cheeks. This lack of color, this roughness of texture about her seemed a splendid assertion of quality. How indifferent she looked, how arrogant and indifferent, with her bare feet, her unpainted toenails, her queer robe. The only thing that she had done to her face was to paint her eyebrows blue—to pluck out all the hairs of her eyebrows, in fact, and paint the skin blue. Not an arched line—just a little daub of blue over each eye, like a swollen vein.

Georgia, whose dark hair was teased, whose eyes were painted in the style of the time, whose breasts were stylishly preferred, found all this disconcerting, and wonderful.

Harvey was the other person there whose looks Georgia found impressive. He was a short man with heavy shoulders, a slight potbelly, puffy blue eyes, and a pugnacious expression. He came from Lancashire. His gray hair was thin on top but worn long at the sides—combed over his ears in a way that made him look more like an artist than a surgeon. "He doesn't even look to me exactly clean enough to be a surgeon," Georgia said to Ben afterward. "Wouldn't you think he'd be something like a sculptor? With gritty fingernails? I expect he treats women badly." She was recalling how he had looked at her breasts. "Not like Raymond," she said. "Raymond worships Maya. And he is extremely clean."

(Raymond has the kind of looks everybody's mother is crazy about, Maya was to say to Georgia, with slashing accuracy, a few weeks after this.)

The food that Maya served was no better than you would expect at a family dinner, and the heavy silver forks were slightly tarnished. But Raymond poured good wine that he would have liked to talk about. He did not manage to interrupt Harvey, who told scandalous and indiscreet hospital stories, and was blandly outrageous about necrophilia and masturbation. Later, in the living room, the coffee was made and served with some ceremony. Raymond got everybody's attention as he ground the beans in a Turkish cylinder. He talked about the importance of the aromatic oils. Harvey, halted in mid-anecdote, watched with an unkindly smirk, Hilda with patient polite attention. It was Maya who gave her husband radiant encouragement, hung about him like an acolyte, meekly and gracefully assisting. She served the coffee in beautiful little Turkish cups, which she and Raymond had bought in a shop in San Francisco, along with the coffee grinder. She listened demurely to Raymond talking about the shop, as if she recalled other holiday pleasures.

Harvey and Hilda were the first to leave. Maya hung on Raymond's shoulder, saying goodbye. But she detached herself once they were gone, her slithery grace and wifely demeanor discarded. She stretched out casually and awkwardly on the sofa and said, "Now, don't you go yet. Nobody gets half a chance to talk while Harvey is around—you have to talk after."

And Georgia saw how it was. She saw that Maya was hoping not to be left alone with the husband whom she had aroused—for whatever purposes—by her showy attentions. She saw that Maya was mournful and filled with a familiar dread at the end of her dinner party. Raymond was happy. He sat down on the end of the sofa, lifting Maya's reluctant feet to do so. He rubbed one of her feet between his hands.

"What a savage," Raymond said. "This is a woman who won't wear shoes."

"Brandy!" said Maya, springing up. "I knew there was something else you did at dinner parties. You drink brandy!"

"He loves her but she doesn't love him," said Georgia to Ben, just after she had remarked on Raymond's worshipping Maya and being very clean. But Ben, perhaps not listening carefully, thought she was talking about Harvey and Hilda.

"No, no, no. There I think it's the other way round. It's hard to tell with English people. Maya was putting on an act for them. I have an idea about why."

"You have an idea about everything," said Ben.

Georgia and Maya became friends on two levels. On the first level, they were friends as wives; on the second as themselves. On the first level, they had dinner at each other's houses. They listened to their husbands talk about their school days. The jokes and fights, the conspiracies and disasters, the bullies and the victims. Terrifying or pitiable schoolfellows and teachers, treats and humiliations. Maya asked if they were sure they hadn't read all that in a book. "It sounds just like a story," she said. "A boys' story about school."

They said that their experiences were what the books were all about. When they had talked enough about school, they talked about movies, politics, public personalities, places they had travelled to or wanted to travel to. Maya and Georgia could join in then. Ben and Raymond did not believe in leaving women out of the conversation. They believed that women were every bit as intelligent as men.

On the second level, Georgia and Maya talked in each other's kitchens, over coffee. Or they had lunch downtown. There were two places, and only two, where Maya liked to have lunch. One was the Moghul's Court—a seedy, grandiose bar in a large, grim railway hotel. The Moghul's Court had curtains of moth-eaten pumpkin-colored velvet, and desiccated ferns, and waiters who wore turbans. Maya always dressed up to go there, in droopy, silky dresses and not very clean white gloves and amazing hats that she found in secondhand stores. She pretended to be a widow who had served with her husband in various outposts of the Empire. She spoke in fluty tones to the sullen young waiters, asking them, "Could you be so good as to . . ." and then telling them they had been terribly, terribly kind.

She and Georgia worked out the history of the Empire widow, and Georgia was added to the story as a grumpy, secretly Socialistic hired companion named Miss Amy Jukes. The widow's name was Mrs. Allegra Forbes-Bellyea. Her husband had been Nigel Forbes-Bellyea. Sometimes Sir Nigel. Most of one rainy afternoon in the Moghul's Court was spent in devising the horrors of the Forbes-Bellyea honeymoon, in a damp hotel in Wales.

The other place that Maya liked was a hippie restaurant on Blanshard Street, where you sat on dirty plush cushions tied to the tops of stumps and ate brown rice with slimy vegetables and drank cloudy cider. (At the Moghul's Court, Maya and Georgia drank only gin.) When they lunched at the hippie restaurant, they wore long, cheap, pretty Indian cotton dresses and pretended to be refugees from a commune, where they had both been the attendants or concubines of a folksinger named Bill Bones. They made up several songs for Bill Bones, all mild and tender blue-eyed songs that contrasted appallingly with his greedy and licentious ways. Bill Bones had very curious personal habits.

When they weren't playing these games, they talked in a headlong fashion about their lives, childhoods, problems, husbands.

"That was a horrible place," Maya said. "That school."

Georgia agreed.

"They were poor boys at a rich kids' school," Maya said. "So they had to try hard. They had to be a credit to their families."

Georgia would not have thought Ben's family poor, but she knew that there were different ways of looking at such things.

Maya said that whenever they had people in for dinner or the evening, Raymond would pick out beforehand all the records he thought suitable and put them in a suitable order. "I think sometime he'll hand out conversational topics at the door," Maya said.

Georgia revealed that Ben wrote a letter every week to the great-aunt who had sent him to school.

"Is it a nice letter?" said Maya.

"Yes. Oh, yes. It's very nice."

They looked at each other bleakly, and laughed. Then they announced—they admitted—what weighed on them. It was the innocence of these husbands—the hearty, decent, firm, contented innocence. That is a wearying and finally discouraging thing. It makes intimacy a chore.

"But do you feel badly," Georgia said, "talking like this?"

"Of course," said Maya, grinning and showing her large perfect teeth—the product of expensive dental work from the days before she had charge of her own looks. "I have another reason to feel badly," she said. "But I don't know whether I do. I do and I don't."

"I know," said Georgia, who up until that moment hadn't known, for sure.

"You're very smart," Maya said. "Or I'm very obvious. What do you think of him?"

"A lot of trouble," Georgia said judiciously. She was pleased with that answer, which didn't show how flattered she felt by the disclosure, or how heady she found this conversation.

"You aren't just a-whistlin' 'Dixie,'" Maya said, and she told the story about the abortion. "I am going to break up with him," she said. "Any day now."

But she kept on seeing Harvey. She would relate, at lunch, some very disillusioning facts about him, then announce that she had to go, she was meeting him at a motel out on the Gorge Road, or at the cabin he had on Prospect Lake.

"Must scrub," she said.

She had left Raymond once. Not for Harvey. She had run away with, or to, a musician. A pianist—Nordic and sleepy-looking but bad-tempered—from her society-lady, symphony-benefit days. She travelled with him for five weeks, and he deserted her in a hotel in Cincinnati. She then developed frightful chest pains, appropriate to a breaking heart. What she really had was a gallbladder attack. Raymond was sent for, and he came and got her out of the hospital. They had a little holiday in Mexico before they came home.

"That was it, for me," Maya said. "That was your true and desperate love. Nevermore."

What then, was Harvey?

"Exercise," said Maya.

Georgia got a part-time job in a bookstore, working several evenings a week. Ben went away on his yearly cruise. The summer turned out to be unusually hot and sunny for the West Coast. Georgia combed her hair out and stopped using most of her makeup and bought a couple of short halter dresses. Sitting on her stool at the front of the store, showing her bare brown shoulders and sturdy brown legs, she looked like a college girl—clever but full of energy and bold opinions. The people who came into the store liked the look of a girl—a woman—like Georgia. They liked to talk to her. Most of them came in alone. They were not exactly lonely people, but they were lonely for somebody to talk to about books. Georgia plugged in the kettle behind the desk and made mugs of raspberry tea. Some favored customers brought in their own mugs. Maya came to visit and lurked about in the background, amused and envious.

"You know what you've got?" she said to Georgia. "You've

got a salon! Oh, I'd like to have a job like that! I'd even like an ordinary job in an ordinary store, where you fold things up and find things for people and make change and say thank you very much, and colder out today, will it rain?"

"You could get a job like that," said Georgia.

"No, I couldn't. I don't have the discipline. I was too badly brought up. I can't even keep house without Mrs. Hanna and Mrs. Cheng and Sadie."

It was true. Maya had a lot of servants, for a modern woman, though they came at different times and did separate things and were nothing like an old-fashioned household staff. Even the food at her dinner parties, which seemed to show her own indifferent touch, had been prepared by someone else.

Usually, Maya was busy in the evenings. Georgia was just as glad, because she didn't really want Maya coming into the store, asking for crazy titles that she had made up, making Georgia's employment there a kind of joke. Georgia took the store seriously. She had a serious, secret liking for it that she could not explain. It was a long, narrow store with an old-fashioned funnelled entryway between two angled display windows. From her stool behind the desk Georgia was able to see the reflections in one window reflected in the other. This street was not one of those decked out to receive tourists. It was a wide east-west street filled in the early evening with a faintly yellow light, a light reflected off pale stucco buildings that were not very high, plain storefronts, nearly empty sidewalks. Georgia found this plainness liberating after the winding shady streets, the flowery yards and vine-framed windows of Oak Bay. Here the books could come into their own, as they never could in a more artful and enticing suburban bookshop. Straight long rows of paperbacks. (Most of the Penguins then still had their orange-and-white or blue-and-white covers, with no designs or pictures, just the unadorned, unexplained titles.) The store was a straight avenue of bounty, of plausible promises. Certain books that Georgia had never read, and probably never would read, were important to her, because of the stateliness or mystery of their titles. *In Praise of Folly. The Roots of Coincidence. The Flowering of New England. Ideas and Integrities.*

Sometimes she got up and put the books in stricter order. The fiction was shelved alphabetically, by author, which was sensible but not very interesting. The history books, however, and the philosophy and psychology and other science books were arranged according to certain intricate and delightful rules—having to do with chronology and content—that Georgia grasped immediately and even elaborated on. She did not need to read much of a book to know about it. She got a sense of it easily, almost at once, as if by smell.

At times the store was empty, and she felt an abundant calm. It was not even the books that mattered then. She sat on the stool and watched the street—patient, expectant, by herself, in a finely balanced and suspended state.

She saw Miles' reflection—his helmeted ghost parking his motorcycle at the curb—before she saw him. She believed that she had noted his valiant profile, his pallor, his dusty red hair (he took off his helmet and shook out his hair before coming into the store), and his quick, slouching, insolent, invading way of moving, even in the glass.

It was no surprise that he soon began to talk to her, as others did. He told her that he was a diver. He looked for wrecks, and lost airplanes, and dead bodies. He had been hired by a rich couple in Victoria who were planning a treasure-hunting cruise, getting it together at the moment. Their names, the destination were all secrets. Treasure-hunting was a lunatic business. He had done it before. His home was in Seattle, where he had a wife and a little daughter.

Everything he told her could easily have been a lie.

He showed her pictures in books—photographs and drawings, of mollusks, jellyfish, the Portuguese man-of-war, sargasso weed, the Caribbean flying fish, the girdle of Venus. He pointed out which pictures were accurate, which were fakes. Then he went away and paid no more attention to her, even slipping out of the store while she was busy with a customer. Not a hint of a goodbye. But he came in another evening, and told her about a drowned man wedged into the cabin of a boat, looking out the watery window in an interested way. By attention and avoidance, impersonal conversations in close proximity, by his oblivious prowling, and unsmiling, lengthy, gray-eyed looks, he soon had Georgia in a disturbed and not disagreeable state. He stayed away two nights in a row, then came in and asked her, abruptly, if she would like a ride home on his motorcycle.

Georgia said yes. She had never ridden on a motorcycle in her life. Her car was in the parking lot; she knew what was bound to happen.

She told him where she lived. "Just a few blocks up from the beach," she said.

"We'll go to the beach, then. We'll go and sit on the logs."

That was what they did. They sat for a while on the logs. Then, though the beach was not quite dark or completely deserted, they made love in the imperfect shelter of some broom-bushes. Georgia walked home, a strengthened and lightened woman, not in the least in love, favored by the universe.

"My car wouldn't start," she told the baby-sitter, a grandmother from down the street. "I walked all the way home. It was lovely, walking. Lovely. I enjoyed it so much."

Her hair was wild, her lips were swollen, her clothes were full of sand.

Her life filled up with such lies. Her car would be parked beside outlying beaches, on the logging roads so conveniently close to the city, on the wandering back roads of the Saanich Peninsula. The map of the city that she had held in her mind up till now, with its routes to shops and work and friends' houses, was overlaid with another map, of circuitous routes followed in fear (not shame) and excitement, of flimsy shelters, temporary hiding places, where she and Miles made love, often within hearing distance of passing traffic or a hiking party or a family picnic. And Georgia herself, watching her children on the roundabout, or feeling the excellent shape of a lemon in her hand at the supermarket, contained another woman, who only a few hours before had been whimpering and tussling on the ferns, on the sand, on the bare ground, or, during a rainstorm, in her own car—who had been driven hard and gloriously out of her mind and drifted loose and gathered her wits and made her way home again. Was this a common story? Georgia cast an eye over the other women at the supermarket. She looked for signs—of dreaminess or flaunting, a sense of dramain a woman's way of dressing, a special rhythm in her movements.

How many, she asked Maya.

"God knows," said Maya. "Do a survey."

Trouble began, perhaps, as soon as they said that they loved each other. Why did they do that—defining, inflating, obscuring whatever it was they did feel? It seemed to be demanded, that was all—just the way changes, variations, elaborations in the lovemaking itself might be demanded. It was a way of going further. So they said it, and that night Georgia couldn't sleep. She did not regret what had been said or think that it was a lie, though she knew that it was absurd. She thought of the way Miles sought to have her look into his eyes during lovemaking— something Ben expressly did not do—and she thought of how his eyes, at first bright and challenging, became cloudy and calm and sombre. That way she trusted him—it was the only way. She thought of being launched out on a gray, deep, baleful, magnificent sea. Love.

"I didn't know this was going to happen," she said in Maya's kitchen the next day, drinking her coffee. The day was warm, but she had put on a sweater to huddle in. She felt shaken, and submissive.

"No. And you don't know," said Maya rather sharply. "Did he say it, too? Did he say he loved you, too?"

Yes, said Georgia, yes, of course.

"Look out, then. Look out for next time. Next time is always pretty tricky when they've said that."

And so it was. Next time a rift opened. At first they simply tested it, to see if it was there. It was almost like a new diversion to them. But it widened, it widened. Before any words were said to confirm that it was there, Georgia felt it widen, she coldly felt it widen, though she was desperate for it to close. Did he feel the same thing? She didn't know. He, too, seemed cold—pale, deliberate, glittering with some new malicious intent.

They were sitting recklessly, late at night, in Georgia's car among the other lovers at Clover Point.

"Everybody here in these cars doing the same thing we're doing," Miles had said. "Doesn't that idea turn you on?"

He had said that at the very moment in their ritual when they had been moved, last time, to speak brokenly and solemnly of love.

"You ever think of that?" he said. "I mean, we could start with Ben and Laura. You ever imagine how it would be with you and me and Ben and Laura?"

Laura was his wife, at home in Seattle. He had not spoken of her before, except to tell Georgia her name. He had spoken of Ben, in a way that Georgia didn't like but passed over.

"What does Ben think you do for fun," he'd said, "while he is off cruising the ocean blue?"

"Do you and Ben usually have a big time when he gets back?"

"Does Ben like that outfit as much as I do?"

He spoke as if he and Ben were friends in some way, or at least partners, co-proprietors.

"You and me and Ben and Laura," he said, in a tone that seemed to Georgia insistently and artificially lecherous, sly, derisive. "Spread the joy around."

He tried to fondle her, pretending not to notice how offended she was, how bitterly stricken. He described the generous exchanges that would take place among the four of them abed. He asked whether she was getting excited. She said no, disgusted. Ah, you are but you won't give in to it, he said. His voice, his caresses grew more bullying. What is so special about you, he asked softly, despisingly, with a hard squeeze at her breasts. Georgia, why do you think you're such a queen?

"You are being cruel and you know you're being cruel," said Georgia, pulling at his hands. "Why are you being like this?"

"Honey, I'm not being cruel," said Miles, in a slippery mock-tender voice. "I'm being horny. I'm horny again is all." He began to pull Georgia around, to arrange her for his use. She told him to get out of the car.

"Squeamish," he said, in that same artificially and hatefully tender voice, as if he were licking fanatically at something loathsome. "You're a squeamish little slut."

Georgia told him that she would lean on the horn if he didn't stop. She would lean on the horn if he didn't get out of the car. She would yell for somebody to call the police. She did lean against the horn as they struggled. He pushed her away, with a whimpering curse such as she'd heard from him at other times, when it meant something different. He got out.

She could not believe that such ill will had erupted, that things had so stunningly turned around. When she thought of this afterward—a good long time afterward—she thought that perhaps he had acted for conscience's sake, to mark her off from Laura. Or to blot out what he had said to her last time. To humiliate her because he was frightened. Perhaps. Or perhaps all this seemed to him simply a further, and genuinely interesting, development in lovemaking.

She would have liked to talk it over with Maya. But the possibility of talking anything over with Maya had disappeared. Their friendship had come suddenly to an end.

The night after the incident at Clover Point, Georgia was sitting on the living-room floor playing a bedtime card game with her sons. The phone rang, and she was sure that it was Miles. She had been thinking all day that he would call, he would have to call to explain himself, to beg her pardon, to say that he had been testing her, in a way, or had been temporarily deranged by circumstances that she knew nothing about. She would not forgive him immediately. But she would not hang up.

It was Maya.

"Guess what weird thing happened," Maya said. "Miles phoned me. Your Miles. It's O.K., Raymond isn't here. How did he even know my name?"

"I don't know," said Georgia.

She had told him it, of course. She had offered wild Maya up for his entertainment, or to point out what a novice at this game she herself was—a relatively chaste prize.

"He says he wants to come and talk to me," Maya said. "What do you think? What's the matter with him? Did you have a fight? . . . Yes? Oh, well, he probably wants me to persuade you to make up. I must say he picked the right night. Raymond's at the hospital. He's got this balky woman in labor; he may have to stay and do a section on her. I'll phone and tell you how it goes. Shall I?"

After a couple of hours, with the children long asleep, Georgia began to expect Maya's call. She watched the television news, to take her mind off expecting it. She picked up the phone to make sure there was a dial tone. She turned off the television after the news, then turned it on again. She started to watch a movie; she watched it through three commercial breaks without going to the kitchen to look at the clock.

At half past midnight she went out and got into her car and drove to Maya's house. She had no idea what she would do there. And she did not do much of anything. She drove around the circular drive with the lights off. The house was dark. She could see that the garage was open and Raymond's car was not there. The motorcycle was nowhere in sight.

She had left her children alone, the doors unlocked. Nothing happened to them. They didn't wake up and discover her defection. No burglar, or prowler, or murderer surprised her on her return. That was a piece of luck that she did not even appreciate. She had gone out leaving the door open and the lights on, and when she came back she hardly recognized her folly, though she closed the door and turned out some lights and lay down on the living-room sofa. She didn't sleep. She lay still, as if the smallest movement would sharpen her suffering, until she saw the day getting light and heard the birds waking. Her limbs were stiff. She got up and went to the phone and listened again for the dial tone. She walked stiffly to the kitchen and put on the kettle and said to herself the words *a paralysis of grief.*

A paralysis of grief. What was she thinking of? That was what she would feel, how she might describe the way she would feel, if one of her children had died. Grief is for serious matters, important losses. She knew that. She would not have bartered away an hour of her children's lives to have had the phone ring at ten o'clock last night, to have heard Maya say, "Georgia, he's desperate. He's sorry; he loves you very much."

No. But it seemed that such a phone call would have given her a happiness that no look or word from her children could give her. Than anything could give her, ever again.

She phoned Maya before nine o'clock. As she was dialling, she thought that there were still some possibilities to pray for. Maya's phone had been temporarily out of order. Maya had been ill last night. Raymond had been in a car accident on his way home from the hospital.

All these possibilities vanished at the first sound of Maya's voice, which was sleepy (pretending to be sleepy?) and silky with deceit. "Georgia? Is that Georgia? Oh, I thought it was going to be Raymond. He had to stay over at the hospital in case this poor wretched woman needed a C-section. He was going to call me—"

"You told me that last night," said Georgia.

"He was going to call me— Oh, Georgia, I was supposed to call you! Now I remember. Yes. I was supposed to call you, but I thought it was probably too late. I thought the phone might wake up the children. I thought, Oh better just leave it till morning!"

"How late was it?"

"Not awfully. I just thought."

"What happened?"

"What do you mean, what happened?" Maya laughed, like a lady in a silly play. "Georgia, are you in a state?"

"What happened?"

"Oh, Georgia," said Maya, groaning magnanimously but showing an edge of nerves. "Georgia, I'm sorry. It was nothing. It was just nothing. I've been rotten, but I didn't mean to be. I offered him a beer. Isn't that what you do when somebody rides up to your house on a motorcycle? You offer him a beer. But then he came on very lordly and said he only drank Scotch. And he said he'd only drink Scotch if I would drink with him. I thought he was pretty high-handed. Pretty high-handed pose. But I really was doing this for you, Georgia—I was wanting to find out what was on his mind. So I told him to put the motorcycle behind the garage, and I took him to sit in the back garden. That was so if I heard Raymond's car I could chase him out the back way and he could walk the motorcycle down the lane. I am not about to unload anything *new* onto Raymond at this point. I mean even something innocent, which this started out to be."

Georgia, with her teeth chattering, hung up the phone. She never spoke to Maya again. Maya appeared at her door, of course, a little while later, and Georgia had to let her in, because the children were playing in the yard. Maya sat down contritely at the kitchen table and asked if she could smoke. Georgia did not answer. Maya said she would smoke anyway and she hoped it was all right. Georgia pretended that Maya wasn't there. While Maya smoked, Georgia cleaned the stove, dismantling the elements and putting them back together again. She wiped the counters and polished the taps and straightened out the cutlery drawer. She mopped the floor around Maya's feet. She worked briskly, thoroughly, and never quite looked at Maya. At first she was not sure whether she could keep this up. But it got easier. The more earnest Maya became—the further she slipped from sensible remonstrance, half-amused confession, into true and fearful regret—the more fixed Georgia was in her resolve, the more grimly satisfied in her heart. She took care, however, not to appear grim. She moved about lightly. She was almost humming.

She took a knife to scrape out the grease from between the counter tiles by the stove. She had let things get into a bad way.

Maya smoked one cigarette after another, stubbing them out in a saucer that she fetched for herself from the cupboard. She said, "Georgia, this is so stupid. I can tell you, he's not worth it. It was nothing. All it was was Scotch and opportunity."

She said, "I am really sorry. Truly sorry. I know you don't believe me. How can I say it so you will?"

And, "Georgia, listen. You are humiliating me. Fine. Fine. Maybe I deserve it. I do deserve it. But after you've humiliated me enough we'll go back to being friends and we'll laugh about this. When we're old ladies, I swear we'll laugh. We won't be able to remember his name. We'll call him the motorcycle sheikh. We will."

Then, "Georgia, what do you want me to do? Do you want me to throw myself on the floor? I'm about ready to. I'm trying to keep myself from snivelling, and I can't. I'm snivelling, Georgia. O.K.?"

She had begun to cry. Georgia put on her rubber gloves and started to clean the oven.

"You win," said Maya. "I'll pick up my cigarettes and go home."

She phoned a few times. Georgia hung up on her. Miles phoned, and Georgia hung up on him, too. She thought he sounded cautious but smug. He phoned again and his voice trembled, as if he were striving just for candor and humility, bare love. Georgia hung up at once. She felt violated, shaken.

Maya wrote a letter, which said, in part, "I suppose you know that Miles is going back to Seattle and whatever home fires he keeps burning there. It seems the treasure thing had fallen through. But you must have known he was bound to go sometime and you'd have felt rotten then, so now you've got the rotten feeling over with. So isn't that O.K.? I don't say this to excuse myself. I know I was weak and putrid. But can't we put it behind us now?"

She went on to say that she and Raymond were going on a long-planned holiday to Greece and Turkey, and that she hoped very much that she would get a note from Georgia before she left. But if she didn't get any word she would try to understand what Georgia was telling her, and she would not make a nuisance of herself by writing again.

She kept her word. She didn't write again. She sent, from Turkey, a pretty piece of striped cloth large enough for a tablecloth. Georgia folded it up and put it away. She left it for Ben to find after she moved out, several months later.

"I'm happy," Raymond tells Georgia. "I'm very happy, and the reason is that I'm content to be an ordinary sort of person with an ordinary calm life. I am not looking for any big revelation or any big drama or any messiah of the opposite sex. I don't go around figuring out how to make things more interesting. I can say to you quite frankly I think Maya made a mistake. I don't mean she wasn't very gifted and intelligent and creative and so on, but she was looking for something—maybe she was looking for something that just is not there. And she tended to despise a lot that she had. It's true. She didn't want the privileges she had. We'd travel, for example, and she wouldn't want to stay in a comfortable hotel. No. She had to go on some trek that involved riding on poor, miserable donkeys and drinking sour milk for breakfast. I suppose I sound very square. Well, I suppose I am. I am square. You know, she had such beautiful silver. Magnificent silver. It was passed down through her family. And she couldn't be bothered to polish it or get the cleaning woman to polish it. She wrapped it all up in plastic and hid it away. She hid it away—you'd think it was a disgrace. How do you think she envisaged herself? As some kind of hippie, maybe? Some kind of free spirit? She didn't even realize it was her money that kept her afloat. I'll tell you, some of the free spirits I've seen pass in and out of this house wouldn't have been long around her without it.

"I did all I could," said Raymond. "I didn't scoot off and leave her, like her Prince of Fantasy Land."

Georgia got a vengeful pleasure out of breaking with Maya. She was pleased with the controlled manner in which she did it. The deaf ear. She was surprised to find herself capable of such control, such thoroughgoing punishment. She punished Maya. She punished Miles, through Maya, as much as she could. What she had to do, and she knew it, was to scrape herself raw, to root out all addiction to the gifts of those two pale prodigies. Miles and Maya. Both of them slippery, shimmery—liars, seducers, finaglers. But you would have thought that after such scourging she'd have scuttled back into her marriage and locked its doors, and appreciated what she had there as never before.

That was not what happened. She broke with Ben. Within a year, she was gone. Her way of breaking was strenuous and unkind. She told him about Miles, though she spared her own pride by leaving out the part about Miles and Maya. She took no care—she had hardly any wish—to avoid unkindness. On the night when she waited for Maya to call, some bitter, yeasty spirit entered into her. She saw herself as a person surrounded by, living by, sham. Because she had been so readily unfaithful, her marriage was a sham. Because she had gone so far out of it, so quickly, it was a sham. She dreaded, now, a life like Maya's. She dreaded just as much a life like her own before this happened. She could not but destroy. Such cold energy was building in her she had to blow her own house down.

She had entered with Ben, when they were both so young, a world of ceremony, of safety, of gestures, concealment. Fond appearances. More than appearances. Fond contrivance. (She

thought when she left that she would have no use for contrivance anymore.) She had been happy there, from time to time.
She had been sullen, restless, bewildered, and happy. But she
said most vehemently, Never, never. I was never happy, she
said.

People always say that.

People make momentous shifts, but not the changes they
imagine.

Just the same, Georgia knows that her remorse about the way she
changed her life is dishonest. It is real and dishonest. Listening
to Raymond, she knows that whatever she did she would have to
do again. She would have to do it again, supposing that she had
to be the person she was.

Raymond does not want to let Georgia go. He does not
want to part with her. He offers to drive her downtown. When
she has gone, he won't be able to talk about Maya. Very likely
Anne has told him that she does not want to hear any more on
the subject of Maya.

"Thank you for coming," he says on the doorstep. "Are you
sure about the ride? Are you sure you can't stay to dinner?"

Georgia reminds him again about the bus, the last ferry. She
says no, no, she really wants to walk. It's only a couple of miles.
The late afternoon so lovely, Victoria so lovely. I had forgotten,
she says.

Raymond says once more, "Thank you for coming."

"Thank you for the drinks," Georgia says. "Thank you, too.
I guess we never believe we are going to die."

"Now, now," says Raymond.

"No. I mean we never behave—we never behave as if we
believed we were going to die."

Raymond smiles more and more and puts a hand on her
shoulder. "How should we behave?" he says.

"Differently," says Georgia. She puts a foolish stress on the word, meaning that her answer is so lame that she can offer it only as a joke.

Raymond hugs her, then involves her in a long chilly kiss. He fastens onto her with an appetite that is grievous but unconvincing. A parody of passion, whose intention neither one of them, surely, will try to figure out.

She doesn't think about that as she walks back to town through the yellow-leafed streets with their autumn smells and silences. Past Clover Point, the cliffs crowned with broombushes, the mountains across the water. The mountains of the Olympic Peninsula, assembled like a blatant backdrop, a cutout of rainbow tissue paper. She doesn't think about Raymond, or Miles, or Maya, or even Ben.

She thinks about sitting in the store in the evenings. The light in the street, the complicated reflections in the windows. The accidental clarity.

Wigtime

When her mother was dying in the Walley Hospital, Anita came home to take care of her—though nursing was not what she did anymore. She was stopped one day in the corridor by a short, broad-shouldered, broad-hipped woman with clipped grayish-brown hair.

"I heard you were here, Anita," this woman said, with a laugh that seemed both aggressive and embarrassed. "Don't look so dumfounded!"

It was Margot, whom Anita had not seen for more than thirty years.

"I want you to come out to the house," Margot said. "Give yourself a break. Come out soon."

Anita took a day off and went to see her. Margot and her husband had built a new house overlooking the harbor, on a spot where there used to be nothing but scrubby bushes and children's secret paths. It was built of gray brick and was long and low. But high enough at that, Anita suggested—high enough to put some noses out of joint across the street, in the handsome hundred-year-old houses with their prize view.

"Bugger them," said Margot. "They took up a petition against us. They went to the Committee."

But Margot's husband already had the Committee sewed up.

Margot's husband had done well. Anita had already heard that. He owned a fleet of buses that took children to school and senior citizens to see the blossoms in Niagara and the fall leaves in Haliburton. Sometimes they carried singles clubs and other holidayers on more adventurous trips—to Nashville or Las Vegas.

Margot showed her around. The kitchen was done in almond—Anita made a mistake, calling it cream—with teal-green and butter-yellow trim. Margot said that all that natural-wood look was passé. They did not enter the living room, with its rose carpet, striped silk chairs, and yards and yards of swooping pale-green figured curtains. They admired it from the doorway—all exquisite, shadowy, inviolate. The master bedroom and its bath were done in white and gold and poppy red. There was a Jacuzzi and a sauna.

"I might have liked something not so bright myself," said Margot. "But you can't ask a man to sleep in pastels."

Anita asked her if she ever thought about getting a job.

Margot flung back her head and snorted with laughter. "Are you kidding? Anyway, I do have a job. Wait till you see the big lunks I have to feed. Plus this place doesn't exactly run itself on magic horsepower."

She took a pitcher of sangria out of the refrigerator and put it on a tray, with two matching glasses. "You like this stuff? Good. We'll sit and drink out on the deck."

Margot was wearing green flowered shorts and a matching top. Her legs were thick and marked with swollen veins, the flesh of her upper arms was dented, her skin was brown, mole-spotted, leathery from lots of sun. "How come you're still thin?" she asked with amusement. She flipped Anita's hair. "How come you're not gray? Any help from the drugstore? You look pretty." She said this without envy, as if speaking to somebody younger than herself, still untried and unseasoned.

It looked as if all her care, all her vanity, went into the house.

Margot and Anita both grew up on farms in Ashfield Township. Anita lived in a drafty shell of a brick house that hadn't had any new wallpaper or linoleum for twenty years, but there was a stove in the parlor that could be lit, and she sat in there in peace and comfort to do her homework. Margot often did her homework sitting up in the bed she had to share with two little sisters. Anita seldom went to Margot's house, because of the crowdedness and confusion, and the terrible temper of Margot's father. Once, she had gone there when they were getting ducks ready for market. Feathers floated everywhere. There were feathers in the milk jug and a horrible smell of feathers burning on the stove. Blood was puddled on the oilclothed table and dripping to the floor.

Margot seldom went to Anita's house, because without exactly saying so Anita's mother disapproved of the friendship. When Anita's mother looked at Margot, she seemed to be totting things up—the blood and feathers, the stovepipe sticking through the kitchen roof, Margot's father yelling that he'd tan somebody's arse.

But they met every morning, struggling head down against the snow that blew off Lake Huron, or walking as fast as they could through a predawn world of white fields, icy swamps, pink sky, and fading stars and murderous cold. Away beyond the ice on the lake they could see a ribbon of open water, ink-blue or robin's-egg, depending upon the light. Pressed against their chests were notebooks, textbooks, homework. They wore the skirts, blouses, and sweaters that had been acquired with difficulty (in Margot's case there had been subterfuge and blows) and were kept decent with great effort. They bore the stamp of Walley High School, where they were bound, and they greeted each other with relief. They had got up in the dark in cold rooms with frost-whitened windows and pulled underwear on under their nightclothes, while stove lids banged in the kitchen, dampers were shut, younger brothers and sisters scurried to dress themselves downstairs. Margot and her mother took turns going out to the barn to milk cows and fork down hay. The father drove them all hard, and Margot said they'd think he was sick if he didn't hit somebody before breakfast. Anita could count herself lucky, having brothers to do the barn work and a father who did not usually hit anybody. But she still felt, these mornings, as if she'd come up through deep dark water.

"Think of the coffee," they told each other, battling on toward the store on the highway, a ramshackle haven. Strong tea, steeped black in the country way, was the drink in both their houses.

Teresa Gault unlocked the store before eight o'clock, to let them in. Pressed against the door, they saw the fluorescent lights come on, blue spurts darting from the ends of the tubes, wavering, almost losing heart, then blazing white. Teresa came smiling like a hostess, edging around the cash register, holding a cherry-red quilted satin dressing gown tight at the throat, as if that could protect her from the freezing air when she opened the door. Her eyebrows were black wings made with a pencil, and she used another pencil—a red one—to outline her mouth. The bow in the upper lip looked as if it had been cut with scissors.

What a relief, what a joy, then, to get inside, into the light, to smell the oil heater and set their books on the counter and take their hands out of their mittens and rub the pain from their fingers. Then they bent over and rubbed their legs—the bare inch or so that was numb and in danger of freezing. They did not wear stockings, because it wasn't the style. They wore ankle socks inside their boots (their saddle shoes were left at school). Their skirts were long—this was the winter of 1948–49—but there was still a crucial bit of leg left unprotected. Some country girls wore stockings under their socks. Some even wore ski pants pulled up bulkily under their skirts. Margot and Anita would never do that. They would risk freezing rather than risk getting themselves laughed at for such countrified contrivances.

Teresa brought them cups of coffee, hot black coffee, very sweet and strong. She marvelled at their courage. She touched a finger to their cheeks or their hands and gave a little shriek and a shudder. "Like ice! Like ice!" To her it was amazing that anybody would go out in the Canadian winter, let alone walk a mile in it. What they did every day to get to school made them heroic and strange in her eyes, and a bit grotesque.

This seemed to be particularly so because they were girls. She wanted to know if such exposure interfered with their periods. "Will it not freeze the eggs?" was what she actually said. Margot and Anita figured this out and made a point, thereafter, of warning each other not to get their eggs frozen. Teresa was not vulgar—she was just foreign. Reuel had met and married her overseas, in Alsace-Lorraine, and after he went home she followed on the boat with all the other war brides. It was Reuel who ran the school bus, this year when Margot and Anita were seventeen and in grade twelve. Its run started here at the store and gas station that the Gaults had bought on the Kincardine highway, within sight of the lake.

Teresa told about her two miscarriages. The first one took place in Walley, before they moved out here and before they owned a car. Reuel scooped her up in his arms and carried her to the hospital. (The thought of being scooped up in Reuel's arms caused such a pleasant commotion in Anita's body that in order to experience it she was almost ready to put up with the agony that Teresa said she had undergone.) The second time happened here in the store. Reuel, working in the garage, could not hear her weak cries as she lay on the floor in her blood. A customer came in and found her. Thank God, said Teresa, for Reuel's sake even more than her own. Reuel would not have forgiven himself. Her eyelids fluttered, her eyes did a devout downward swoop, when she referred to Reuel and their intimate life together.

While Teresa talked, Reuel would be passing in and out of

the store. He went out and got the engine running, then left the bus to warm up and went back into the living quarters, without acknowledging any of them, or even answering Teresa, who interrupted herself to ask if he had forgotten his cigarettes, or did he want more coffee, or perhaps he should have warmer gloves. He stomped the snow from his boots in a way that was more an announcement of his presence than a sign of any concern for floors. His tall, striding body brought a fan of cold air behind it, and the tail of his open parka usually managed to knock something down—Jell-O boxes or tins of corn, arranged in a fancy way by Teresa. He didn't turn around to look.

Teresa gave her age as twenty-eight—the same age as Reuel's. Everybody believed she was older—up to ten years older. Margot and Anita examined her close up and decided that she looked burned. Something about her skin, particularly at the hairline and around the mouth and eyes, made you think of a pie left too long in the oven, so that it was not charred but dark brown around the edges. Her hair was thin, as if affected by the same drought or fever, and it was too black—they were certain it was dyed. She was short, and small-boned, with tiny wrists and feet, but her body seemed puffed out below the waist, as if it had never recovered from those brief, dire pregnancies. Her smell was like something sweet cooking—spicy jam.

She would ask anything, just as she would tell anything. She asked Margot and Anita if they were going out with boys yet.

"Oh, why not? Does your fathers not let you? I was attracting to boys by the time I was fourteen, but my father would not let me. They come and whistle under my window, he chases them away. You should pluck your eyebrows. You both. That would make you look nicer. Boys like a girl when she makes herself all nice. That is something I never forget. When I was on the boat coming across the Atlantic Ocean with all the other wives, I spend all my time preparing myself for my husband. Some of those wives, they just sat and played cards. Not me! I was washing my hair and putting on a beautiful oil to soften my skin, and I rubbed and rubbed with a stone to get the rough spots off my feet. I forget what you call them—the rough spots on the feet's skin? And polish my nails and pluck my eyebrows and do myself all up like a prize! For my husband to meet me in Halifax. While all those others do is sit and play cards and gossiping, gossiping with each other."

They had heard a different story about Teresa's second miscarriage. They had heard that it happened because Reuel told her he was sick of her and wanted her to go back to Europe, and in her despair she had thrown herself against a table and dislodged the baby.

At side roads and at farm gates Reuel stopped to pick up students who were waiting, stomping their feet to keep warm or scuffling in the snowbanks. Margot and Anita were the only girls of their age riding the bus that year. Most of the others were boys in grades nine and ten. They could have been hard to handle, but Reuel quelled them even as they came up the steps.

"Cut it out. Hurry up. On board if you're coming on board."

And if there was any start of a fracas on the bus, any hooting or grabbing or punching, or even any moving from seat to seat or too much laughing and loud talk, Reuel would call out, "Smarten up if you don't want to walk! Yes, you there—I mean you!" Once, he had put a boy out for smoking, miles from Walley. Reuel himself smoked all the time. He had the lid of a mayonnaise jar sitting on the dashboard for an ashtray. Nobody challenged him, ever, about anything he did. His temper was well known. It was thought to go naturally with his red hair.

People said he had red hair, but Margot and Anita remarked that only his mustache and the hair right above his ears was red. The rest of it, the hair receding from the temples but thick and wavy elsewhere, especially in the back, which was the part they most often got to see—the rest was a tawny color like the pelt of a fox they had seen one morning crossing the white road. And the hair of his heavy eyebrows, the hair along his arms and on the backs of his hands, was still more faded, though it glinted in any light. How had his mustache kept its fire? They spoke of this. They discussed in detail, coolly, everything about him. Was he good-looking or was he not? He had a redhead's flushed and spotty skin, a high, shining forehead, light-colored eyes that seemed ferocious but indifferent. Not good-looking, they decided. Queer-looking, actually.

But when Anita was anywhere near him she had a feeling of controlled desperation along the surface of her skin. It was something like the far-off beginning of a sneeze. This feeling was at its worst when she had to get off the bus and he was standing beside the step. The tension flitted from her front to her back as she went past him. She never spoke of this to Margot, whose contempt for men seemed to her firmer than her own. Margot's mother dreaded Margot's father's lovemaking as much as the children dreaded his cuffs and kicks, and had once slept all night in the granary, with the door bolted, to avoid it. Margot called lovemaking "carrying on." She spoke disparagingly of Teresa's "carrying on" with Reuel. But it had occurred to Anita that this very scorn of Margot's, her sullenness and disdain, might be a thing that men could find attractive. Margot might be attractive in a way that she herself was not. It had nothing to do with prettiness. Anita thought that she was prettier, though it was plain that Teresa wouldn't give high marks to either of them. It had to do with a bold lassitude that Margot showed sometimes in movement, with the serious breadth of her hips and the already womanly curve of her stomach, and a look that would come over her large brown eyes—a look both defiant and helpless, not matching up with anything Anita had ever heard her say.

By the time they reached Walley, the day had started. Not a star to be seen anymore, nor a hint of pink in the sky. The town, with its buildings, streets, and interposing routines, was set up like a barricade against the stormy or frozen-still world they'd woken up in. Of course their houses were barricades, too, and so was the store, but those were nothing compared to town. A block inside town, it was as if the countryside didn't exist. The great drifts of snow on the roads and the wind tearing and howling through the trees—that didn't exist. In town, you had to behave as if you'd always been in town. Town students, now thronging the streets around the high school, led lives of privilege and ease. They got up at eight o'clock in houses with heated bedrooms and bathrooms. (This was not always the case, but Margot and Anita believed it was.) They were apt not to know your name. They expected you to know theirs, and you did.

The high school was like a fortress, with its narrow windows and decorative ramparts of dark-red brick, its long flight of steps and daunting doors, and the Latin words cut in stone: *Scientia Atque Probitas*. When they got inside those doors, at about a quarter to nine, they had come all the way from home, and home and all stages of the journey seemed improbable. The effects of the coffee had worn off. Nervous yawns overtook them, under the harsh lights of the assembly hall. Ranged ahead were the demands of the day: Latin, English, geometry, chemistry, history, French, geography, physical training. Bells rang at ten to the hour, briefly releasing them. Upstairs, downstairs, clutching books and ink bottles, they made their anxious way, under the hanging lights and the pictures of royalty and dead educators. The wainscoting, varnished every summer, had the same merciless gleam as the principal's glasses. Humiliation was imminent. Their stomachs ached and threatened to growl as the morning wore on. They feared sweat under their arms and blood on their skirts. They shivered going into English or geometry classes, not because they did badly in those classes (the fact was that they did quite well in almost everything) but because of the danger of being asked to get up and read something, say a poem off by heart or write the solution to a problem on the blackboard in front of the class. *In front of the class*—those were dreadful words to them.

Then, three times a week, came physical training—a special problem for Margot, who had not been able to get the money out of her father to buy a gym suit. She had to say that she had left her suit at home, or borrow one from some girl who was being excused. But once she did get a suit on she was able to loosen up and run around the gym, enjoying herself, yelling for the basketball to be thrown to her, while Anita went into such rigors of self-consciousness that she allowed the ball to hit her on the head.

Better moments intervened. At noon hour they walked downtown and looked in the windows of a beautiful carpeted store that sold only wedding and evening clothes. Anita planned a springtime wedding, with bridesmaids in pink-and-green silk and overskirts of white organza. Margot's wedding was to take place in the fall, with the bridesmaids wearing apricot velvet. In Woolworth's they looked at lipsticks and earrings. They dashed into the drugstore and sprayed themselves with sample cologne. If they had any money to buy some necessity for their mothers, they spent some of the change on cherry Cokes or sponge toffee. They could never be deeply unhappy, because they believed that something remarkable was bound to happen to them. They could become heroines; love and power of some sort were surely waiting.

Teresa welcomed them, when they got back, with coffee, or hot chocolate with cream. She dug into a package of store cookies and gave them Fig Newtons or marshmallow puffs dusted with colored coconut. She took a look at their books and asked what homework they had. Whatever they mentioned, she, too, had studied. In every class, she had been a star.

"English—perfect marks in my English! But I never knew then that I would fall in love and come to Canada. Canada! I think it is only polar bears living in Canada!"

Reuel wouldn't have come in. He'd be fooling around with

the bus or with something in the garage. His mood was usually fairly good as they got on the bus. "All aboard that's coming aboard!" he would call. "Fasten your seat belts! Adjust your oxygen masks! Say your prayers! We're takin' to the highway!" Then he'd sing to himself, just under the racket of the bus, as they got clear of town. Nearer home his mood of the morning took over, with its aloofness and unspecific contempt. He might say, "Here you are, ladies—end of a perfect day," as they got off. Or he might say nothing. But indoors Teresa was full of chat. Those school days she talked about led into wartime adventures: a German soldier hiding in the garden, to whom she had taken a little cabbage soup; then the first Americans she saw—black Americans—arriving on tanks and creating a foolish and wonderful impression that the tanks and the men were all somehow joined together. Then her little wartime wedding dress being made out of her mother's lace tablecloth. Pink roses pinned in her hair. Unfortunately, the dress had been torn up for rags to use in the garage. How could Reuel know?

Sometimes Teresa was deep in conversation with a customer. No treats or hot drinks then—all they got was a flutter of her hand, as if she were being borne past in a ceremonial carriage. They heard bits of the same stories. The German soldier, the black Americans, another German blown to pieces, his leg, in its boot, ending up at the church door, where it remained, everybody walking by to look at it. The brides on the boat. Teresa's amazement at the length of time it took to get from Halifax to here on the train. The miscarriages.

They heard her say that Reuel was afraid for her to have another baby.

"So now he always uses protections."

There were people who said they never went into that store anymore, because you never knew what you'd have to listen to, or when you'd get out.

In all but the worst weather Margot and Anita lingered at the spot where they had to separate. They spun the day out a little longer, talking. Any subject would do. Did the geography teacher look better with or without his mustache? Did Teresa and Reuel still actually carry on, as Teresa implied? They talked so easily and endlessly that it seemed they talked about everything. But there were things they held back.

Anita held back two ambitions of hers, which she did not reveal to anybody. One of them—to be an archeologist—was too odd, and the other—to be a fashion model—was too conceited. Margot told her ambition, which was to be a nurse. You didn't need any money to get into it—not like university—and once you graduated you could go anywhere and get a job. New York City, Hawaii—you could get as far away as you liked.

The thing that Margot kept back, Anita thought, was how it must really be at home, with her father. According to her, it was all like some movie comedy. Her father beside himself, a hapless comedian, racing around in vain pursuit (of fleet, mocking Margot) and rattling locked doors (the granary) and shouting monstrous threats and waving over his head whatever weapon he could get hold of—a chair or a hatchet or a stick of firewood. He tripped over his own feet and got mixed up in his own accusations. And no matter what he did, Margot laughed. She laughed, she despised him, she forestalled him. Never, never did she shed a tear or cry out in terror. Not like her mother. So she said.

After Anita graduated as a nurse, she went to work in the Yukon. There she met and married a doctor. This should have been the end of her story, and a good end, too, as things were reckoned in Walley. But she got a divorce, she moved on. She worked again and saved money and went to the University of British Columbia, where she studied anthropology. When she came home to look after her mother, she had just completed her Ph.D. She did not have any children.

"So what will you do, now you're through?" said Margot.

People who approved of the course Anita had taken in life

usually told her so. Often an older woman would say, "Good for you!" or, "I wish I'd had the nerve to do that, when I was still young enough for it to make any difference." Approval came sometimes from unlikely quarters. It was not to be found everywhere, of course. Anita's mother did not feel it, and that was why, for many years, Anita had not come home. Even in her present sunken, hallucinatory state, her mother had recognized her, and gathered her strength to mutter, "Down the drain."

Anita bent closer.

"*Life,*" her mother said. "Down the *drain.*"

But another time, after Anita had dressed her sores, she said, "So glad. So glad to have—a *daughter.*"

Margot didn't seem to approve or disapprove. She seemed puzzled, in an indolent way. Anita began talking to her about some things she might do, but they kept being interrupted. Margot's sons had come in, bringing friends. The sons were tall, with hair of varying redness. Two of them were in high school and one was home from college. There was one even older, who was married and living in the West. Margot was a grandmother. Her sons carried on shouted conversations with her about the whereabouts of their clothes, and what supplies of food, beer, and soft drinks there were in the house, also which cars would be going where at what times. Then they all went out to swim in the pool beside the house, and Margot called, "Don't anybody dare go in that pool that's got suntan lotion on!"

One of the sons called back, "Nobody's *got* it on," with a great show of weariness and patience.

"Well, somebody had it on yesterday, and they went in the pool, all right," replied Margot. "So I guess it was just somebody that snuck up from the beach, eh?"

Her daughter Debbie arrived home from dancing class and showed them the costume she was going to wear when her dancing school put on a program at the shopping mall. She was to impersonate a dragonfly. She was ten years old, brown-haired, and stocky, like Margot.

"Pretty hefty dragonfly," said Margot, lolling back in the deck chair. Her daughter did not arouse in her the warring energy that her sons did. Debbie tried for a sip of the sangria, and Margot batted her away.

"Go get yourself a drink out of the fridge," she said. "Listen. This is our visit. O.K.? Why don't you go phone up Rosalie?"

Debbie left, trailing an automatic complaint. "I wish it wasn't *pink* lemonade. Why do you always make *pink* lemonade?"

Margot got up and shut the sliding doors to the kitchen. "Peace," she said. "Drink up. After a while I'll get us some sandwiches."

Spring in that part of Ontario comes in a rush. The ice breaks up into grinding, jostling chunks on the rivers and along the lake-shore; it slides underwater in the pond and turns the water green. The snow melts and the creeks flood, and in no time comes a day when you open your coat and stuff your scarf and mittens in your pockets. There is still snow in the woods when the blackflies are out and the spring wheat showing.

Teresa didn't like spring any better than winter. The lake was too big and the fields too wide and the traffic went by too fast on the highway. Now that the mornings had turned balmy, Margot and Anita didn't need the store's shelter. They were tired of Teresa. Anita read in a magazine that coffee discolored your skin. They talked about whether miscarriages could cause chemical changes in your brain. They stood outside the store, wondering whether they should go in, just to be polite. Teresa came to the door and waved at them, peekaboo. They waved back with a little flap of their hands the way Reuel waved back every morning—just lifting a hand from the steering wheel at the last moment before he turned onto the highway.

Reuel was singing in the bus one afternoon when he had dropped off all the other passengers. "He knew the world was round-o," he sang. "And uh-uhm could be found-o."

He was singing a word in the second line so softly they couldn't catch it. He was doing it on purpose, teasing. Then he sang it again, loud and clear so that there was no mistake.

> "He knew the world was round-o,
> And tail-o could be found-o."

They didn't look at each other or say anything till they were walking down the highway. Then Margot said, "Big fat nerve he's got, singing that song in front of us. Big fat *nerve*," she said, spitting the word out like the worm in an apple.

But only the next day, shortly before the bus reached the end of its run, Margot started humming. She invited Anita to join, poking her in the side and rolling her eyes. They hummed the tune of Reuel's song; then they started working words into the humming, muffling one word, then clearly singing the next, until they finally got their courage up and sang the whole two lines, bland and sweet as "Jesus Loves Me."

> "He knew the world was round-o,
> And tail-o could be found-o."

Reuel did not say a word. He didn't look at them. He got off the bus ahead of them and didn't wait by the door. Yet less than an hour before, in the school driveway, he had been most genial. One of the other drivers looked at Margot and Anita and said, "Nice load you got there," and Reuel said, "Eyes front, Buster," moving so that the other driver could not watch them stepping onto the bus.

Next morning before he pulled away from the store, he delivered a lecture. "I hope I'm going to have a couple of ladies on my bus today and not like yesterday. A girl saying certain things is not like a man saying them. Same thing as a woman getting drunk. A girl gets drunk or talks dirty, first thing you know she's in trouble. Give that some thought."

Anita wondered if they had been stupid. Had they gone too far? They had displeased Reuel and perhaps disgusted him, made him sick of the sight of them, just as he was sick of Teresa. She was ashamed and regretful and at the same time she thought Reuel wasn't fair. She made a face at Margot to indicate this, turning down the corners of her mouth. But Margot took no notice. She was tapping her fingertips together, looking demurely and cynically at the back of Reuel's head.

Anita woke up in the night with an amazing pain. She thought at first she'd been wakened by some calamity, such as a tree falling on the house or flames shooting up through the floor-boards. This was shortly before the end of the school year. She had felt sick the evening before, but everybody in the family was complaining of feeling sick, and blaming it on the smell of paint and turpentine. Anita's mother was painting the linoleum, as she did every year at this time.

Anita had cried out with pain before she was fully awake, so that everybody was roused. Her father did not think it proper to phone the doctor before daybreak, but her mother phoned him anyway. The doctor said to bring Anita in to Walley, to the hospital. There he operated on her and removed a burst appendix, which in a few hours might have killed her. She was very sick for several days after the operation, and had to stay nearly three weeks in the hospital. Until the last few days, she could not have any visitors but her mother.

This was a drama for the family. Anita's father did not have the money to pay for the operation and the stay in the hospital—he was going to have to sell a stand of hard-maple trees. Her mother took the credit, rightly, for saving Anita's life, and as long as she lived she would mention this, often adding that she had gone against her husband's orders. (It was really only against his advice.) In a flurry of independence and self-esteem she began to drive the car, a thing she had not done for years. She visited Anita every afternoon and brought news from home. She had finished painting the linoleum, in a design of white and yellow done with a sponge on a dark-green ground. It gave the impression of a distant meadow sprinkled with tiny flowers. The milk inspector had complimented her on it, when he stayed for dinner. A late calf had been born across the creek and nobody could figure out how the cow had got there. The honeysuckle was in bloom in the hedge, and she brought a bouquet and commandeered a vase from the nurses. Anita had never seen her sociability turned on like this before for anybody in the family.

Anita was happy, in spite of weakness and lingering pain. Such a fuss had been made to prevent her dying. Even the sale of the maple trees pleased her, made her feel unique and treasured. People were kind and asked nothing of her, and she took up that kindness and extended it to everything around her. She forgave everyone she could think of—the principal with his glittery glasses, the smelly boys on the bus, unfair Reuel and chattering Teresa and rich girls with lamb's-wool sweaters and her own family and Margot's father, who must suffer in his rampages. She didn't tire all day of looking at the thin yellowish curtains at the window and the limb and trunk of a tree visible to her. It was an ash tree, with strict-looking corduroy lines of bark and thin petal leaves that were losing their fragility and sharp spring green, toughening and darkening as they took on summer maturity. Everything made or growing in the world seemed to her to deserve congratulations.

She thought later that this mood of hers might have come from the pills they gave her for the pain. But perhaps not entirely.

She had been put in a single room because she was so sick. (Her father had told her mother to ask how much extra this was costing, but her mother didn't think they would be charged, since they hadn't asked for it.) The nurses brought her magazines, which she looked at but could not read, being too dazzled and comfortably distracted. She couldn't tell whether time passed quickly or slowly, and she didn't care. Sometimes she dreamed or imagined that Reuel visited her. He showed a sombre tenderness, a muted passion. He loved but relinquished her, caressing her hair.

A couple of days before she was due to go home, her mother came in shiny-faced from the heat of summer, which was now upon them, and from some other disruption. She stood at the end of Anita's bed and said, "I always knew you thought it wasn't fair of me."

By this time Anita had felt a few holes punched in her happiness. She had been visited by her brothers, who banged against the bed, and her father, who seemed surprised that she expected to kiss him, and by her aunt, who said that after an operation like this a person always got fat. Now her mother's face, her mother's voice came pushing at her like a fist through gauze.

Her mother was talking about Margot. Anita knew that immediately by a twitch of her mouth.

"You always thought I wasn't fair to your friend Margot. I was never fussy about that girl and you thought I wasn't fair. I know you did. So now it turns out. It turns out I wasn't so wrong after all. I could see it in her from an early age. I could see what you couldn't. That she had a sneaky streak and she was oversexed."

Her mother delivered each sentence separately, in a reckless loud voice. Anita did not look at her eyes. She looked at the little brown mole beneath one nostril. It seemed increasingly loathsome.

Her mother calmed down a little, and said that Reuel had taken Margot to Kincardine on the school bus at the end of the day's run on the very last day of school. Of course they had been alone in the bus at the beginning and the end of the run, ever since Anita got sick. All they did in Kincardine, they said, was eat French-fried potatoes. What nerve! Using a school bus for their jaunts and misbehaving. They drove back that evening, but Margot did not go home. She had not gone home yet. Her father had come to the store and beat on the gas pumps and broken them, scattering glass as far as the highway. He phoned the police about Margot, and Reuel phoned them about the pumps. The police were friends of Reuel's, and now Margot's father was bound over to keep the peace. Margot stayed on at the store, supposedly to escape a beating.

"That's all it is, then," Anita said. "Stupid God-damned gossip."

But no. But no. And don't swear at me, young lady.

Her mother said that she had kept Anita in ignorance. All this had happened and she had said nothing. She had given Margot the benefit of the doubt. But now there was no doubt. The news was that Teresa had tried to poison herself. She had recovered. The store was closed. Teresa was still living there, but Reuel had taken Margot with him and they were living here, in Walley. In a back room somewhere, in the house of friends of his. They were living together. Reuel was going out to work at the garage every day, so you could say that he was living with them both. Would he be allowed to drive the school bus in future? Not likely. Everybody was saying Margot must be pregnant. Javex, was what Teresa took.

"And Margot never confided in you," Anita's mother said. "She never sent you a note or one thing all the time you've been in here. Supposed to be your friend."

Anita had a feeling that her mother was angry at her not only because she'd been friends with Margot, a girl who had disgraced herself, but for another reason as well. She had the feeling that her mother was seeing the same thing that she herself could see—Anita unfit, passed over, disregarded, not just by Margot but by life. Didn't her mother feel an angry disappointment that Anita was not the one chosen, the one enfolded by drama and turned into a woman and swept out on such a surge of life? She would never admit that. And Anita could not admit that she felt a great failure. She was a child, a know-nothing, betrayed by Margot, who had turned out to know a lot. She said sulkily, "I'm tired talking." She pretended to fall asleep, so that her mother would have to leave.

Then she lay awake. She lay awake all night. The nurse who came in the next morning said, "Well, don't you look like the last show on earth! Is that incision bothering you? Should I see if I can get you back on the pills?"

"I hate it here," Anita said.

"Do you? Well, you only have one more day till you can go home."

"I don't mean the hospital," Anita said. "I mean *here*. I want to go and live somewhere else."

The nurse did not seem to be surprised. "You got your grade twelve?" she said. "O.K. You can go in training. Be a nurse. All it costs is to buy your stuff. Because they can work you for nothing while you're training. Then you can go and get a job anyplace. You can go all over the world."

That was what Margot had said. And now Anita was the one who would become a nurse, not Margot. She made up her mind that day. But she felt that it was second best. She would rather have been chosen. She would rather have been pinned down by a man and his desire and the destiny that he arranged for her. She would rather have been the subject of scandal.

"Do you want to know?" said Margot. "Do you want to know really how I got this house? I mean, I didn't go after it till we could afford it. But you know with men—something else can always come first? I put in my time living in dumps. We lived one place, there was just that stuff, you know that under-carpeting stuff, on the floor? That brown hairy stuff looks like the skin off some beast? Just look at it and you can feel things crawling on you. I was sick all the time anyway. I was pregnant with Joe. This was in behind the Toyota place, only it wasn't the Toyota then. Reuel knew the landlord. Of course. We got it cheap."

But there came a day, Margot said. There came a day about

five years ago. Debbie wasn't going to school yet. It was in June. Reuel was going away for the weekend, on a fishing trip up to northern Ontario. Up to the French River, in northern Ontario. Margot had got a phone call that she didn't tell anybody about.

"Is that Mrs. Gault?"

Margot said yes.

"Is it Mrs. Reuel Gault?"

Yes, said Margot, and the voice—it was a woman's or maybe a young girl's voice, muffled and giggling—asked her if she wanted to know where her husband might be found next weekend.

"You tell me," said Margot.

"Why don't you check out the Georgian Pines?"

"Fine," said Margot. "Where is that?"

"Oh, it's a campground," the voice said. "It's a real nice place. Don't you know it? It's up on Wasaga Beach. You just check it out."

That was about a hundred miles to drive. Margot made arrangements for Sunday. She had to get a sitter for Debbie. She couldn't get her regular sitter, Lana, because Lana was going to Toronto on a weekend jaunt with members of the high-school band. She was able to get a friend of Lana's who wasn't in the band. She was just as glad that it turned out that way, because it was Lana's mother, Dorothy Slote, that she was afraid she might find with Reuel. Dorothy Slote did Reuel's bookkeeping. She was divorced, and so well known in Walley for her numerous affairs that high-school boys would call to her from their cars, on the street, "Dorothy Slot, she's hot to trot!" Sometimes she was referred to as Dorothy Slut. Margot felt sorry for Lana—that was why she had started hiring her to take care of Debbie. Lana was not going to be as good-looking as her mother, and she was shy and not too bright. Margot always got her a little present at Christmastime.

On Saturday afternoon Margot drove to Kincardine. She was gone only a couple of hours, so she let Joe and his girlfriend take Debbie to the beach. In Kincardine she rented another car—a van, as it happened, an old blue crock pot of a thing like what the hippies drove. She also bought a few cheap clothes and a rather expensive, real-looking wig. She left them in the van, parked in a lot behind a supermarket. On Sunday morning she drove her car that far, parked it in the lot, got into the van, and changed her clothes and donned the wig, as well as some extra makeup. Then she continued driving north.

The wig was a nice light-brown color, ruffled up on top and long and straight in the back. The clothes were tight pink denim pants and a pink-and-white striped top. Margot was thinner then, though not *thin*. Also, buffalo sandals, dangly earrings, big pink sunglasses. The works.

"I didn't miss a trick," said Margot. "I did my eyes up kind of Cleopatra-ish. I don't believe my own kids could've recognized me. The mistake I made was those pants—they were too tight and too hot. Them and the wig just about killed me. Because it was a blazing hot day. And I was kind of awkward at parking the van, because I'd never driven one before. Otherwise, no problems."

She drove up Highway 21, the Bluewater, with the window down to get a breeze off the lake, and her long hair blowing and the van radio tuned to a rock station, just to get her in the mood. In the mood for what? She had no idea. She smoked one cigarette after another, trying to steady her nerves. Men driving along kept honking at her. Of course the highway was busy, of course Wasaga Beach was jammed, a bright, hot Sunday like this, in June. Around the beach the traffic was just crawling, and the smell of French fries and noon-hour barbecues pressed down like a blanket. It took her a while just to find the campground, but she did, and paid her day fee, and drove in. Round and round the parking lot she drove, trying to spot Reuel's car. She didn't see it. Then it occurred to her that the lot would be just for day visitors. She found a parking place.

Now she had to reconnoitre the entire grounds, on foot.

She walked first all through the campground part. Trailer hook-ups, tents, people sitting out beside the trailers and tents drinking beer and playing cards and barbecuing lunch—more or less just what they would have been doing at home. There was a central playground, with swings and slides kept busy, and kids throwing Frisbees, and babies in the sandbox. A refreshment stand, where Margot got a Coke. She was too nervous to eat anything. It was strange to her to be in a family place yet not part of any family.

Nobody whistled or made remarks to her. There were lots of long-haired girls around showing off more than she did. And you had to admit that what they had was in better condition to be shown.

She walked the sandy paths under the pines, away from the trailers. She came to a part of the grounds that looked like an old resort, probably there long before anybody ever thought of trailer hookups. The shade of the big pines was a relief to her. The ground underneath was brown with their needles—hard dirt had turned to a soft and furry dust. There were double cabins and single cabins, painted dark green. Picnic tables beside them. Stone fireplaces. Tubs of flowers in bloom. It was nice.

There were cars parked by some of the cabins, but Reuel's wasn't there. She didn't see anybody around—maybe the people who stayed in cabins were the sort who went down to the beach. Across the road was a place with a bench and a drinking fountain and a trash can. She sat down on the bench to rest.

And out he came. Reuel. He came out of the cabin right across from where she was sitting. Right in front of her nose. He was wearing his bathing trunks and he had a couple of towels slung over his shoulders. He walked in a lazy, slouching way. A roll of white fat sloped over the waistband of his trunks. "Straighten up, at least!" Margot wanted to yell at him. Was he slouching like that because he felt sneaky and ashamed? Or just worn out with happy exercise? Or had he been slouching for a long time and she hadn't noticed? His big strong body turning into something like custard.

He reached into the car parked beside the cabin, and she knew he was reaching for his cigarettes. She knew, because at the same moment she was fumbling in her bag for hers. If this was a movie, she thought—if this was only a movie, he'd come springing across the road with a light, keen to assist the stray pretty girl. Never recognizing her, while the audience held its breath. Then recognition dawning, and horror—incredulity and horror. While she, the wife, sat there cool and satisfied, drawing deep on her cigarette. But none of this happened, of course none of it happened; he didn't even look across the road. She sat sweating in her denim pants, and her hands shook so that she had to put her cigarette away.

The car wasn't his. What kind of car did Dorothy Slut drive?

Maybe he was with somebody else, somebody totally unknown to Margot, a stranger. Some stranger who figured she knew him as well as his wife.

No. No. Not unknown. Not a stranger. Not in the least a stranger. The door of the cabin opened again, and there was Lana Slote. Lana, who was supposed to be in Toronto with the band. Couldn't baby-sit Debbie. Lana, whom Margot had always felt sorry for and been kind to because she thought the girl was slightly lonesome, or unlucky. Because she thought it showed, that Lana was brought up mostly by old grandparents. Lana seemed old-fashioned, prematurely serious without being clever, and not very healthy, as if she were allowed to live on soft drinks and sugared cereal and whatever mush of canned corn and fried potatoes and macaroni-and-cheese loaf those old people dished up for supper. She got bad colds with asthmatic complications, her complexion was dull and pale. But she did have a chunky, appealing little figure, well developed front and back, and chipmunk cheeks when she smiled, and silky, flat, naturally blond hair. She was so meek that even Debbie could boss her around, and the boys thought she was a joke.

Lana was wearing a bathing suit that her grandmother might have chosen for her. A shirred top over her bunchy little breasts and a flowered skirt. Her legs were stumpy, untanned. She stood there on the step as if she was afraid to come out—afraid to appear in a bathing suit or afraid to appear at all. Reuel had to go over and give her a loving little spank to get her moving. With numerous lingering pats he arranged one of the towels around her shoulders. He touched his cheek to her flat blond head, then rubbed his nose in her hair, no doubt to inhale its baby fragrance. Margot watched it all.

They walked away, down the road to the beach, respectably keeping their distance. Father and child.

Margot observed now that the car was a rented one. From a place in Walkerton. How funny, she thought, if it had been rented in Kincardine, at the same place where she rented the van. She wanted to put a note under the windshield wiper, but she didn't have anything to write on. She had a pen but no paper. But on the grass beside the trash can she spied a Kentucky Fried Chicken bag. Hardly a grease spot on it. She tore it into pieces, and on the pieces she wrote—or printed, actually, in capital letters—these messages:

YOU BETTER WATCH YOURSELF,
YOU COULD END UP IN JAIL.

·

THE VICE SQUAD WILL GET YOU IF
YOU DON'T WATCH OUT.

·

PERVERTS NEVER PROSPER.

·

LIKE MOTHER LIKE DAUGHTER.

·

BETTER THROW THAT ONE BACK IN
THE FRENCH RIVER, IT'S NOT FULL GROWN.

·

SHAME.

·

SHAME.

She wrote another that said "BIG FAT SLOB WITH YOUR BABY-FACED MORON," but she tore that up—she didn't like the tone of it. Hysterical. She stuck the notes where she was sure they would be found—under the windshield wiper, in the crack of the door, weighed down by stones on the picnic table. Then she hurried away with her heart racing. She drove so badly, at first, that she almost killed a dog before she got out of the parking lot. She did not trust herself on the highway, so she drove on back roads, gravel roads, and kept reminding herself to keep her speed down. She wanted to go fast. She wanted to take off. She felt right on the edge of blowing up, blowing to smithereens. Was it good or was it terrible, the way she felt? She couldn't say. She felt that she had been cut loose, nothing mattered to her, she was as light as a blade of grass.

But she ended up in Kincardine. She changed her clothes and took off the wig and rubbed the makeup off her eyes. She put the clothes and the wig in the supermarket trash bin—not without thinking what a pity—and she turned in the van. She wanted to go into the hotel bar and have a drink, but she was afraid of what it might do to her driving. And she was afraid of what she might do if any man saw her drinking alone and came up with the least remark to her. Even if he just said, "Hot day," she might yelp at him, she might try to claw his face off.

Home. The children. Pay the sitter. A friend of Lana's. Could she be the one who had phoned? Get takeout for supper. Pizza—not Kentucky Fried, which she would never be able to think of again without being reminded. Then she sat up late, waiting. She had some drinks. Certain notions kept banging about in her head. Lawyer. Divorce. Punishment. These notions hit her like gongs, then died away without giving her any idea about how to proceed. What should she do first, what should she do next, how should her life go on? The children all had appointments of one kind or another, the boys had summer jobs, Debbie was about to have a minor operation on her ear. She couldn't take them away; she'd have to do it all herself, right in the middle of everybody's gossip—which she'd had enough of once before. Also, she and Reuel were invited to a big anniversary party next weekend; she had to get the present. A man was coming to look at the drains.

Reuel was so late getting home that she began to be afraid he'd had an accident. He'd had to go around by Orangeville, to deliver Lana to the home of her aunt. He'd pretended to be a high-school teacher transporting a member of the band. (The real teacher had been told, meanwhile, that Lana's aunt was sick and Lana was in Orangeville looking after her.) Reuel's stomach was upset, naturally, after those notes. He sat at the kitchen table chewing tablets and drinking milk. Margot made coffee, to sober herself for the fray.

Reuel said it was all innocent. An outing for the girl. Like Margot, he'd felt sorry for her. Innocent.

Margot laughed at that. She laughed, telling about it.

"I said to him, 'Innocent! I know your innocent! Who do you think you're talking to,' I said, 'Teresa?' And he said, 'Who?' No, really. Just for a minute he looked blank, before he remembered. He said, 'Who?' "

Margot thought then, What punishment? Who for? She thought, he'll probably marry that girl and there'll be babies for sure and pretty soon not enough money to go around.

Before they went to bed at some awful hour in the morning, she had the promise of her house.

"Because there comes a time with men, they really don't want the hassle. They'd rather weasel out. I bargained him down to the wire, and I got pretty near everything I wanted. If he got balky about something later on, all I'd have to say was 'Wigtime!' I'd told him the whole thing—the wig and the van and where I sat and everything. I'd say that in front of the kids or anybody, and none of them would know what I was talking about. But he'd know! Reuel would know. *Wigtime!* I still say it once in a while, whenever I think it's appropriate."

She fished a slice of orange out of her glass and sucked, then chewed on it. "I put a little something else in this besides the wine," she said. "I put a little vodka, too. Notice?"

She stretched her arms and legs out in the sun.

"Whenever I think it's—appropriate."

Anita thought that Margot might have given up on vanity but she probably hadn't given up on sex. Margot might be able to contemplate sex without fine-looking bodies or kindly sentiments. A healthy battering.

And what about Reuel—what had he given up on? Whatever he did, it wouldn't be till he was ready. That was what all Margot's hard bargaining would really be coming up against—whether Reuel was ready or not. That was something he'd never feel obliged to tell her. So a woman like Margot can still be fooled—this was what Anita thought, with a momentary pleasure, a completely comfortable treachery—by a man like Reuel.

"Now you," said Margot, with an ample satisfaction. "I told you something. Time for you to tell me. Tell me how you decided to leave your husband."

Anita told her what had happened in a restaurant in British Columbia. Anita and her husband, on a holiday, went into a roadside restaurant, and Anita saw there a man who reminded her of a man she had been in love with—no, perhaps she had better say infatuated with—years and years ago. The man in the restaurant had a pale-skinned, heavy face, with a scornful and evasive expression, which could have been a dull copy of the face of the man she loved, and his long-legged body could have been a copy of that man's body if it had been struck by lethargy. Anita could hardly tear herself away when it came time to leave the restaurant. She understood that expression—she felt that she was tearing herself away, she got loose in strips and tatters. All the way up the Island Highway, between the dark enclosing rows of tall fir and spruce trees, and on the ferry to Prince Rupert, she felt an absurd pain of separation. She decided that if she could feel such a pain, if she could feel more for a phantom than she could ever feel in her marriage, she had better go.

So she told Margot. It was more difficult than that, of course, and it was not so clear.

"Then did you go and find that other man?" said Margot.

"No. It was one-sided. I couldn't."

"Somebody else, then?"

"And somebody else, and somebody else," said Anita, smiling. The other night when she had been sitting beside her mother's bed, waiting to give her mother an injection, she had thought about men, putting names one upon another as if to pass the time, just as you'd name great rivers of the world, or capital cities, or the children of Queen Victoria. She felt regret about some of them but no repentance. Warmth, in fact, spread from the tidy buildup. An accumulating satisfaction.

"Well, that's one way," said Margot staunchly. "But it seems weird to me. It does. I mean—I can't see the use of it, if you don't marry them." She paused. "Do you know what I do, sometimes?" She got up quickly and went to the sliding doors. She listened, then opened the door and stuck her head inside. She came back and sat down.

"Just checking to see Debbie's not getting an earful," she said. "Boys, you can tell any horrific personal stuff in front of them and you might as well be speaking Hindu, for all they ever listen. But girls listen. Debbie listens. . . .

"I'll tell you what I do," she said. "I go out and see Teresa."

"Is she still there?" said Anita with great surprise. "Is Teresa still out at the store?"

"What store?" said Margot. "Oh, no! No, no. The store's gone. The gas station's gone. Torn down years ago. Teresa's in the County Home. They have this what they call the Psychiatric Wing out there now. The weird thing is, she worked out there for years and years, just handing round trays and tidying up and doing this and that for them. Then she started having funny spells herself. So now she's sometimes sort of working there and she's sometimes just *there*, if you see what I mean. When she goes off, she's never any trouble. She's just pretty mixed up. Talk-talk-talk-talk-talk. The way she always did, only more so. All she has any idea of doing is talk-talk-talk, and fix herself up. If you come and see her, she always wants you to bring her some bath oil or perfume or makeup. Last time I went out, I took her some of that highlight stuff for her hair. I thought that was taking a chance, it was kind of complicated for her to use. But she read the directions, she made out fine. She didn't make a mess. What I mean by mixed up is, she figures she's on the boat. The boat with the war brides. Bringing them all out to Canada."

"War brides," Anita said. She saw them crowned with white feathers, fierce and unsullied. She was thinking of war bonnets.

She didn't need to see him, for years she hadn't the least wish to see him. A man undermines your life for an uncontrollable time, and then one day there's nothing, just a hollow where he was, it's unaccountable.

"You know what just flashed on my mind this minute?" said Margot. "Just how the store used to look in the morning. And us coming in half froze."

Then she said in a flattened, disbelieving voice, "She used to come and beat on the door. Out there. Out there, when Reuel was with me in the room. It was awful. I don't know. I don't know—do you think it was love?"

From up here on the deck the two long arms of the breakwater look like floating matchsticks. The towers and pyramids and conveyor belts of the salt mine look like large solid toys. The lake is glinting like foil. Everything seems bright and distinct and harmless. Spellbound.

"We're all on the boat," says Margot. "She thinks we're all on the boat. But she's the one Reuel's going to meet in Halifax, lucky her."

Margot and Anita have got this far. They are not ready yet to stop talking. They are fairly happy.

A Note on the Type

The text of this book has been set in Goudy Old Style, one of the more than a hundred typefaces designed by Frederic William Goudy (1865–1947). Although Goudy began his career as a bookkeeper, he was so inspired by the appearance of several newly published books from the Kelmscott Press that he devoted the remainder of his life to typography, in an attempt to bring to the printers of the United States a better understanding of the movement led by William Morris.

Produced in 1914, Goudy Old Style reflects the absorption of a generation of designers with things "ancient." Its smooth, even color, combined with its generous curves and ample cut, marks it as one of Goudy's finest achievements.

Composed by American–Stratford Graphic Services, Inc.,
Brattleboro, Vermont

Printed and bound by The Haddon Craftsmen, Inc.,
Scranton, Pennsylvania

Designed by Valarie J. Astor